Mike Lunnon-Wood was born in A
and New Zealand. He worked in the N
moving to West Sussex. His writing wa
research he conducted, spending time v
in support of each book. Mike Lunno
survived by his son, Piers.

CH00548169

BY THE SAME AUTHOR

The British Military Quartet:

Let Not the Deep
King's Shilling
Long Reach
Congo Blue (originally published as Heraklion Blue)

Other fiction titles:

Dark Rose
Angel Seven
Somewhere Out there

THE PROTECTOR

Mike Lunnon-Wood

SILVERTAIL BOOKS • *London*

This edition published by Silvertail Books in 2020
www.silvertailbooks.com
Copyright © Mike Lunnon-Wood 2020
1
The right of Mike Lunnon-Wood to be identified as the author
of this work has been asserted in accordance
with the Copyright, Design and Patents Act 1988
A catalogue record of this book is available from the British Library
978-1-913727-03-1

PROLOGUE

1984

The charred remains of the house's wooden frame stood, stark and smoking, as the young fireman played his hose back and forth in the first rays of the morning. In the dawn shadows, a gaggle of boys in dressing gowns watched quietly, and beyond them the group of teachers and staff who had come running when the watchman raised the alarm.

The ambulance had already been gone for more than an hour, but the shocked silence hung in the early light. For most of the watchers it had been their first view of death: the pathetic charred bundle that was eased with gloved hands into the green zip-up bag. The watchman had seen the fire from the other end of the school – the flames licking out from the spare room's window and catching the lower branches of the fir tree that had stood and shaded the house for forty years. From there, the fire had raced up through the branches, crackling and roaring. Those staff and prefects not keeping the boys in their dormitories, away from the danger, ran to help, but were forced to stand impotently back by the heat and smoke.

Later that morning, as the boys walked towards the dining hall for breakfast, they could see the grey police car still down at Mr Morton's house, and for those who had been huddled at their dormitory windows, the topic was rich and exciting. One boy suggested that they would have to identify the body by dental records. Another guffawed at his friend's stupidity, saying that they already knew who it was: Mr Morton. the Languages Master from the senior school. They walked quietly for a moment, each remembering the shambling old man, seemingly as old as the hills, who walked the cloistered main quadrangle in an old tweed jacket, discussing history with his twelfth year students. For those seniors he had taught there were no jokes or macabre speculative statements. They had recognised something rare in the man and, for most of them, his classes were an intellectual journey.

He had arrived in the area the previous year and agreed, after some consideration, to take the senior German students as a replacement for the sick department head. He had then begun teaching a pilot course in Russian and finally stood in teaching his first love, history. For the those lucky enough to sit before him, he managed to give the normally dry topic a fresh modern perspective. Sometimes, as a direct answer to a question, he would talk briefly of his years at Corpus Christi Cambridge. For him, the schoolboys were a refreshing change of pace, eminently suitable for a retired academic. They had none of the idle, slightly indolent ease of the Cambridge students and absorbed knowledge like computers with a discipline that delighted him. They called him Teddy, a name they thought original – but, in fact, he had been called that in 1943 when he had first gone up as a very junior Don.

What the students, staff and the policeman at the grey car didn't know was that, in 1944, he was also called that by three men who were ostensibly employed by the Army, but seemed to spend a lot of time in Whitehall sorting out the bickering between two divisions of Military Intelligence. Teddy Morton had an eye for bright young people and, over the next thirty years, recruited many for MI6. In time, he was added to the full payroll and used when events demanded a fresh mind on an old problem, a mind unsullied by politics, departmental strife or personal vested interests.

CHAPTER ONE

In spite of the new wallpaper and pictures, the room still had a neglected air, its high ceiling showing the damp, and the threadbare carpet, the paths of feet long ago. The original furniture had been replaced by modern Swedish pine that someone had put together from a kit – as alien in the old house as the man who sat in one of the chairs. A nail protruded from a spot where a stag's head once hung and there were stories about the young men who would throw their hats from the hall as they slid down the wide oak banisters, trying to land their hats between the antlers squarely atop the deer's head. That was long ago. Nowadays, the huge old house just had two full time occupants, both staff. The official comings and goings were rarer now and the stand-up gas heater, with its orange and red plastic coal, sitting sadly in the hearth symbolised the economies of the times.

Yuri Simonov calmly puffed on his cigarette and occasionally fingered the razor nick on his chin with studied indifference. He liked the English cigarettes supplied to him and, as he smoked, he watched as Mrs Hogan changed the tapes on the recorder. He was a medium grade defector who had been in the United Kingdom for seven weeks now, all of it except the first two days here at the house in Sussex. All KGB were given the medium grade and, when an individual crossed over, they were debriefed where possible by the same team of people. Mary Hogan was a doctor who routinely worked for MI6 but sometimes found her skills hired out to Special Branch and MI5. Yuri Simonov was, however, a 6 catch – and, with the computer that selected code names currently on confectionery, he had been labelled "FRUIT GUM" and driven down to the wringer in Midhurst.

The house was a two-storey Georgian Mansion set discreetly off the road. In its time, it had seen many people with thick European accents repeat their stories over and over to endlessly patient listeners.

Simonov scratched at the nick again, his lank grey hair resting on the worn collar of his shirt. His watery brown eyes peered from a roundish florid face. He was, Mrs Hogan thought, two stone overweight.

"When can I go shopping?" he asked abruptly. "I want to go to Spencers and Marks."

"Other way round, Yuri," Mrs Hogan replied patiently.

"What?

"Other way round," she repeated, still facing the tape machine. "It's Marks and Spencer, and you can't go there until we're finished and Mr Bellamy says you can."

David Bellamy was in charge of the de-brief team and, at that moment, was in the town shopping to alleviate the monotony of the diet. The cook had spent twenty years cooking in a boarding school and Bellamy said everything tasted steamed.

"He doesn't like me," Simonov muttered.

"Of course he likes you," she said placatingly, then turned back to the table. "Now then, where were we, mmm?"

She knew very well where they were but adopted the almost maternal manner because that seemed to work the best with this particular individual.

"Ah yes, we were going over the early 80s again..."

"We have gone over this all before!" he exclaimed, waving the cigarette theatrically.

"Let's do it again, shall we? Just make sure we haven't forgotten anything?" She paused and smiled at him before continuing, "1982 Yuri, February. You moved across to the Fourth Directorate for six weeks..."

And so, Yuri Simonov began to talk.

Occasionally, Mrs Hogan interrupted him with open questions, leading him astray with red herrings to see if he would return to track again, constantly checking his story. Her tactics moved with the mood – sometimes cajoling, other times sympathetic, sometimes bullying and, at other moments, playing on the vanity that most defectors displayed. They had been aware for some time that a structural change

2

within the KGB had begun moving specialists between directorates. Yuri Simonov was an analyst, a political scientist who specialised in extremism and terrorist groups. As such, he had nothing that MI6 wanted, but he had moved about the separate directorates enough that he could fill many holes in the files. He could put names to pictures, cover policy issues and possibly even isolate the latest concerns of the Komitet Gestabetvich Bedresknay.

So far, the seven weeks of his interrogation had been a waste of time. He had offered nothing substantial – barely, Bellamy considered, covering his room and board.

It was after lunch that day, pate and cheeses and a strictly rationed can of John Smiths Yorkshire Bitter, that things began to change.

"Then I moved back to First at the Sverdlov office." He belched softly, smiling with embarrassment. "Back on routine material. PLO, Hezbollah. They never let me develop anything fully – always change to this, change to that, Mujahedin one week, Serbs the next, never anything interesting like the Knives group. One of your people was on that in '82 as well. Mismanaged, I was. Totally mismanaged!"

He seemed to be enjoying the word.

"Yes, I'm sure," Mrs Hogan said, leaning forward imperceptibly in her seat. "What was that about one of our people? Knives, was it?"

"Yes, interesting group! Long Knives."

"Long Knives... as in Reichstag?"

"Yes," he said quickly.

"What about them?" she replied, goading him. "It's ancient history."

"History repeats itself," he replied smugly, reaching for the cigarettes. "Your Churchill said that."

"What about them then? Who are they and what are they?"

"Ask your man who was on it," he replied.

Gotcha-you-little-shit, she thought, trying not to seem too interested.

"Who was that?" she asked in the same tone of voice, praying that the tape machine was working properly.

"Don't you know?" he snapped back. He was suddenly fidgeting now, in obvious discomfort.

"No and neither do you," she fired back.

"Yes I do!"

"How could you know that?"

"I do!"

"BULLSHIT!" she snarled. "How would you know? What are you? The big shot spy master?"

He leant forward angrily, the challenge thrown down. "I do... I do, I do!" Childishly now. "There's someone in your..." He stopped suddenly, sitting back and going visibly pale before her eyes. "My God they will kill us. I am a dead man."

Oh goody, she thought, *the gossip has gone down and dirty. This is what I'm paid for, this is what I'm good at.*

She pressed the button on the chair leg beside her left knee. Seven weeks.

"Yuri, who told you we had someone on this Reichstag group?"

"Not Reichstag," he replied almost automatically. "Long Knives."

"Who told you? Come on Yuri, we can go shopping later if you like..."

Next door, David Bellamy leapt for the spare headphones, his eyes glancing at the secondary logging recorder as its spools turned slowly, recording the conversation next door.

That evening, as Yuri sat morosely sipping his second can of John Smiths, his evening meal uneaten on the table, a courier drove the day's tapes up to London where David Bellamy – in his capacity as head of the wringer team – had telephoned the Milburn office of no less a personage than the Deputy Director General of MI6, Sir Martin Callows.

Callows was not only DDG. He was the last in a long string of knee jerk reactions that began in Downing Street and, steam-rollering over the Minister, ended up at the feet of the Director General of the service Sir Gordon Tansey-Williams. Milburn – or more correctly, Department E – had long been a thorn in the side of Whitehall.

Moved into a building of that name in the late'60s, the move was that of a street fighter slipping a white glove over the fist that wore the brass knuckles hoping the latest bruised victim would forget it was there. Theirs was the nasty end of the business, to be kept firmly away from the Embassy parties and military attachés, away from the legitimate Foreign Office types.

They handlcd thc dirty work, the jobs no-one else would do, either because they were inherently dangerous, or likely to fail, or both. They provided couriers and bag-men, protection for their parent MI6 people, resourceful people to fulfil tasks given up as lost – and, when things got really bad, they provided what was called the 'forward pack', a team that consisted of a controller, an operator – and a group of the little-known 'Acton Fairies'.

They had none of the prolonged satisfaction of the Department D people who ran their networks of agents, or 'friends'. They just came in when the wheels had come off an operation and someone was in real trouble, or when Whitehall wanted people on whom they could turn their fire.

The Acton Fairies were the striking arm of the service. When MI6 began recruiting operatives in earnest in 1939 they gave the training of unarmed combat, marksmanship and the black arts in general to the most feared man the Royal Marines had ever produced. Sergeant Norman Tidwell was famous for his slanderous accusations of the sexual preferences of his pupils and in time, rightly or wrongly, the name became part of the service law. The Acton Fairies were still trained in Acton but, since then, the black arts had become blacker, the exponents less careful about covering their tracks – and, in 1981, three of them had badly botched the kidnapping of an Argentinean within yards of Gatwick Airport. Two bystanders had died and, because both were third world immigrants only minutes into the land of milk and honey. the Left's reaction was swift and virulent.

It was this indiscretion that had directly led to Callows' appointment Sir Martin's job was to control Milburn. Those that knew about these things didn't argue that the department had its place in the scheme of things but a low profile was of the utmost importance, or those who didn't know would be demanding its demise.

Milburn was run by career Six men who were seconded to the department for anything up to three years. There was one man who had been there five and it was generally acknowledged that he wouldn't be going back into the MI6 mainstream. He had made a mistake – and mistakes, where lives were concerned, are not forgotten. It was he who took the tapes and transcripts from the driver of the battered Citroen and carried them up the steep dark stairs past the silent ex-Fairy porters to Sir Martin's office.

Sir Martin himself was a large crag-faced man with a thick mane of grey hair, hooded eyes and a voice like gravel. He had rarely raised it, speaking only in moderate tones punctuated by harsh barks of dry laughter. He was tipped to be the next Director General and was, everyone agreed, a real bastard. Since his arrival at Milburn he had taken the department in his huge fist and shaken it until it began making the right kinds of noises.

There would be no more bungled jobs and embarrassed Governments.

Callow took the large brown envelope from the man and, without raising his head, said, "Get Burmeister up here," into his intercom.

Finally, he pulled the papers clear and began reading, his leonine eyes creasing as they scanned the transcript.

Thirty seconds later, John Burmeister knocked and entered through a second door. He was one of the career men on attachment from D, the intelligence gathering section, and looked the part in a Saville Row suit of dark blue wool. He was wearing a Royal Artillery tie he wasn't entitled to, but he was one of those men who didn't give a damn. Dropping into one of the easy chairs that Sir Martin was indicating, he crossed one leg over the other, looking like a city banker with his iron grey hair and his air of confident wealth.

Sir Martin gave a porcine grunt and thrust the transcript across.

"Read this. Yuri Simonov's temper tantrum is laced with something that smells."

Burmeister took the typed pages and began to slowly read, knowing better than to hurry and miss anything.

Fifteen minutes later, he spoke.

"My God, she's saying..."

"She's telling us we have a mole," Sir Martin finished.

"Christ, where are we looking?"

"In Six certainly," Sir Martin replied. "Here at Milburn possibly. Who knows." Then he leaned inward and uttered two words with unutterable force. "Find him!"

"Sir Martin," Burmeister appealed, "I'm not George Smiley..."

"By the time this is over, you will wish you were. Get on with it. I will get you a sniffer dog across from C, but I'm not having Five or Special Branch nosing round my bailiwick. Not yet... I don't want him flushed until we're ready. Understood?"

"Yes, Sir Martin." Burmeister stood. "I'll want to go down and talk to Simonov myself, of course."

"No, leave it to the shrink. That woman has found his key. She's bloody good, John. She judges at Crufts, you know. Dogs and defectors! Ha!" He barked his laugh and then his eyelids dropped menacingly. "Find him for me, John. Use the sniffer, give him access to everything, create a reason for it that will cover his work, and give him whatever support he needs. I will hang this bastard at the gallows!"

Burmeister knew he would do just that.

Forty minutes later, Sir Martin joined Sir Gordon Tansey-Williams at his club, the latter already clutching his habitual drink, a fiery Cape Brandy, in his fist.

"Thought I would find you here," Callows began.

"Well Martin, what have your yobbos been up to?" Tansey-Williams replied jovially. He had had a good day.

"I wish it were that simple," Callows muttered, beckoning a waiter. "Let's take a walk." He nodded towards the billiard room, usually deserted at this time of the day, and together they headed in that direction. "We have a little problem..."

"What sort of problem?"

"Moscow Centre. They have someone inside Six."

That was all it took. Thirty seconds later – Callows' drink untouched

– they were on their way back to Tansey-Williams' offices, the Director General's day now ruined, and within twenty minutes they were back within Century House, the electronically swept sterile environment of the Secret Intelligence Service

Soon, Callows' brief was over and Tansey-Williams leant back in his leather chair.

"Firstly, how much credence do you place on this Simonov?"

"I am inclined to believe it. It slipped out. It wasn't meant to."

"Not telling us what he thinks we want to hear, eh?"

"Certainly not, and it's not fibs either." He used the current jargon for the normally ultra subtle dis-information so favoured by Moscow centre.

"You seem very sure of that," Tansey-Williams said. "Why?"

Callows shrugged uncharacteristically. "Gut feel."

Tansey-Williams walked to the window and looked out over the light traffic, negotiating the drizzle dampened streets. He had a real respect for Callows' gut feelings, a respect developed over the last sixteen years.

"Done then. Clamp this right down," he said. "I want it rated as top priority. What have you initiated?"

"I've given it to John Burmeister, but he'll need help. A sniffer. I'd like it to remain a Milburn task for the present. If the mole is in here, it will be easier to keep quiet."

"Did you ever meet Henry Arnold?"

Callows shook his head, his eyes interested.

"Retired a year ago. Ex Department 'C'. Pragmatic, clever. Probably the best sniffer we ever had."

"Never even heard his name," Callows said. "I had someone else in mind..."

"I'll get him recalled and attached to Milburn. Young he is not, but a mind like a steel trap. Exactly what you are looking for."

The following morning, Arnold agreed to return to work, ostensibly to begin compiling the official history of the service during its 1939-45 birth pangs. Century House, short of space for the tiresome request, sent him over to Milburn where, somewhat surprisingly, they seemed to have an office free. Armed with a clearance to enter all filing areas, he began shuffling the corridors, perpetually pushing his spectacles back up his long nose and humming to himself. It was during the afternoon of the first day that he asked to see the references to 'Long Knives', reasoning that whoever had accessed the file had either directly or indirectly triggered the contact with Moscow Centre.

The normal staff at the Midhurst wringer had been supplemented overnight by an Acton Fairy. Another was due that evening. Mrs Hogan occasionally caught a glimpse of him as he walked a seemingly irregular patrol through the grounds of the house. She looked back to Simonov. All of the previous morning's confident bluster was gone – and now his answers were dragged out painfully.

"Yuri, we know you aren't cleared for access to information like that. Your material comes in from the Directorates. That I accept. But in that material you certainly would not learn of the existence of a KGB operative inside our little gang, would you?"

"I was mistaken," he said softly.

"No you weren't, Yuri. You believed it and you still do." She stopped to let that statement sink in for a moment before continuing. "Who are you protecting? Someone let it slip, didn't they? Someone told you. A friend?"

He said nothing, his watery eyes staring at the wall behind her head. Very occasionally a spark of real strength surfaced but now it seemed smothered in fear. *I'm losing this,* she thought. *Ease off with the pressure and let's try something a little more basic.*

"Well, let's have a cup of tea, shall we? We have been working hard, you know. Perhaps its time for a little relaxation."

He looked up at her.

"Shopping?" he asked.

"Not today, Yuri. The man outside wouldn't like that. Perhaps tomorrow." She paused. "But there are things you can do here."

She stood and walked to look out the window.

"You are a man. A man in your prime," she said flatteringly. "In Moscow you must have had you pick of the girls. Perhaps we can organise some company for you?"

He looked up at her quickly, a slightly shocked look on his face.

"No not me, Yuri," she chuckled, "but we have some nice girls, speak Russian, make borsch, talk about troika rides in the snow... would you like that?"

He looked away again.

Well, well, she thought, *let's try the other.*

"Of course, if you'd like to chat with someone who has been there recently, someone sympathetic, one of our young chaps only got in last week."

He looked up quickly, his eyes now displaying interest.

Gotcha! she thought triumphantly.

"He would be very sympathetic, Yuri. Would you like that?"

"Well, maybe," he mumbled. "Would he be..."

"Very sympathetic, Yuri. I think you know what I mean. He's only twenty four, blonde and very athletic. He's very nice. But we would have to talk first, Yuri..."

"It's difficult," he began. "I don't..."

"It was your lover, wasn't it, Yuri? The friend. He told you."

"He didn't love me," Yuri said bitterly. "He's run off with someone else. He just used me. Used to make me do things after he had been with others."

She walked over and sat down next to him on the couch. "Men are buggers, aren't they?" she agreed, the pun going right over his head. "They just have no feelings."

Yuri Simonov began to talk.

The central files had been computerised for some years but the service still maintained vast storage areas for the items that could never be stored on disc. Faded news clippings, photographs and letters that could never be electronically enhanced sufficiently joined the tons of case files that needed a mainframe just to index the information.

Arnold sat with the operator, who accessed his terminal and found nine references to 'Long Knives': seven of them to the original group in pre-war Germany, with reference notes to the hard copy vault; one to the notes of an investigation handed over by MI5, dealing with neo-Nazis in Clapham; and one file that had been purged.

"What does this mean?" he asked the operator.

"Oh, normally it means the data has been dumped... but that can't be right. We don't purge anything here. Must be a glitch. "

"A what?"

"A glitch. A fault in the software."

"I'd like you to unglitch it," Arnold said, his eyes narrowing, the smell of the quarry becoming strong.

"I'll have to get an engineer," she replied, "but even then a purge is sometimes just that."

"Tell me," he said, "who can get at this machine. To purge." He pronounced the last word with distaste.

At 6.17 that evening, a courier left with the day's tapes and transcripts and Mrs Hogan – feeling tired but good – began her drive home to Guildford. The cook had prepared steak and kidney pie and, just before 8pm, Yuri sat at another kit-set pine table in the oversized dining room, with the handyman and one of the Acton Fairies for company.

The handyman was a retired soldier – good with roses, paintbrushes and a screwdriver, but his conversation was limited. The bodyguard was eating quickly, shovelling the food into his mouth and enviously eyeing the glass of beer at Yuri's place. Finally finished, he pushed his seat back and wordlessly went to relieve his partner.

Yuri ate silently, smiling occasionally at the handyman and wishing that his company for the evening would arrive. He didn't so much want to jump into bed with someone as he wanted someone to talk to. Mrs Hogan suggested it was the real reason he had finally left Russia – the secrets, the hidden smiles, the furtive embraces. Here in the west, she had said, one could be gay and proud of it. He liked that word and smiled to himself as if it was all a bit of a joke. Then he lifted another fork of Mrs Bennet's pie to his lips.

The two figures crossed the wall at the alarm system's weakest point. Directional microphones set into the shrubbery at intervals backed up the pressure wires that surrounded the large garden, but where they silently dropped to the ground the mics had been removed after constant interference from the electricity substation on the road's edge.

The leading man, garbed in black, pointed out the line of the wire in the darkness and together they moved forward towards the house. Time was short.

The bodyguard patrolling the grounds almost walked into them as he skirted the greenhouse. as he jerked his weapon up toward the moving shadow and dived down into the only available cover, he never saw the second figure, just felt the milliseconds of unbelievable pain as the nine-inch blade drove into his spinal column at the base of his skull.

The other bodyguard was eating opposite Yuri at the table when the two men burst through the door. He rose spinning, snatching the gun off the table in one fluid motion, kicking the table over his charge as the first of the nine millimetre parabellum rounds hit him in the chest, throwing him backwards through the air like a rag doll.

The same gunman turned his weapon on the Russian and fired a measured burst from three feet. The second man fired a scything burst that knocked the handyman backwards into the kitchen, then ran through to finish the job. There he also found Mrs Bennet, who died trying not to drop the fruit salad, a look of abject disappointment on her face as the crystal bowl shattered, splattering sticky peach juice all over her spotless floor.

The car carrying Yuri's company arrived forty minutes later. He was a male prostitute who had been used by MI6 on several occasions and was well compensated for his tasks, most of which he thoroughly enjoyed. His driver felt uneasy at the gates when his efforts on the horn were ignored.

"Wait here," he said, "and don't fuckin' move." With that he climbed the gates, calling all the time to lessen the chance of being mistaken for an intruder.

Minutes later, he was back. Without a word, he turned the car around and drove into town looking for a call box, his hands shaking on the wheel.

The Duty Officer at Milburn took the call in the ops room and waved a hand at the two staffers present for a bit of quiet.

"Say again," he said, "nice clear line but I didn't catch that," reminding the caller that the line wasn't secured.

"I was bringing a fella down to Midhurst... Know who I am?" he said exasperated.

"Yes, go ahead."

"He won't be needed. What's needed is a cleaning team from the office"

The Duty Officer, new to the post, wasn't up on the latest Milburn jargon.

"A cleaning team? What on earth..."

"Fucksakes! We've been hit. They're all fuckin' dead. Get onto Mr Black or Mr Burmeister. Get 'em down here now and get the local nick advised to keep clear."

"Oh Jesus..."

He dropped the phone and took the stairs three at a time hoping that Burmeister was still in the building.

Burmeister arrived back at Milburn just before midnight in the company of Adrian Black, the officer in charge of counter espionage. Black was a stocky man, the son of a Yorkshire miner, who had been recruited from the Metropolitan Police Special Branch by MI5 and later transferred to MI6 after a personality clash with the head of their Counter Espionage Section. He spoke appalling German, hated computers – and was, Callows thought, the best counter intelligence officer he'd even seen, a man with the real ability to break down the component parts of a problem into their simplest form and deal with each without ever losing sight of the whole.

In his office, Sir Martin stood in front of a small heater that blew warm air.

"Well?" he snapped. "What the hell happened?"

"Two men, over the wall. Took out the first man outside, entered, killed FRUIT GUM and the remainder of the staff and left immediately. No-one seems to have heard a bloody thing. Spent casings were nine mill. The lab people have what forensic evidence we could muster."

"Summary?" Sir Martin asked abruptly.

"They were after FRUIT GUM. That seems certain. The rest were incidental. Very professional. Very slick."

"Very unlike the KGB," Black added.

Burmeister said nothing.

"Say again?'

"Too messy," Black went on. "We've seen their assassinations over the years. Poisons, advanced untraceable chemicals, maybe a well-placed bullet if absolutely necessary. This butcher's shop? No way."

"I disagree," Burmeister said quickly. "This would be just like them, a break in pattern..."

"All the risk for some middle-aged poofter analyst? Not the Centre we know and love. Not unless he knew something he shouldn't have and..."

"What makes you think that?" Burmeister snapped.

"...the hit was set up very quickly," Black concluded. "No time to import a specialist."

Sir Martin often used the fact that the two men disliked each other – and that both were fiercely ambitious – to his advantage, but given the brief he had issued to Burmeister the night before, he felt bound to support him.

"I think we should assume KGB until proven otherwise. Adrian, you had better get together with 5 and SB. Brief 'em. Let 'em know there's been a murder."

"With due respect, Sir Martin, this isn't your normal high street murder. This was a team put together for something quite specific. The man we had in that safe house. It's my patch. I want in on the story. I want to know what I am up against here."

Callows considered it for a moment. Then, with a sinking finality, he said, "I'm sorry, Adrian. You know I can't do that."

The media did get hold of the story. A Midhurst policeman, having to justify his long shift, related the occurrence to his wife who used the story to excuse his non-appearance at a dinner party. Within an hour, a large National Daily short of lead stories had begun piecing together the bits – and, at 4am the following morning, the D Notice Committee immediately authorised the Director General's request and a notice was slapped on the issue.

Special Branch and Security Service specialists were swarming all over the safe house, Tansey-Williams having reluctantly handed the matter over to them. Operations within the Realm, he grudgingly had to agree, were their responsibility.

He did, however, decline to make available the transcript tapes or advise the MI5 case officer of the details of Yuri Simonov's de-brief.

CHAPTER TWO

His shoulder ached. It was always bad in the damp. He stretched the arm high over his head to ease it, then leant back to the icon on the scarred wooden table. With the small scalpel in his right hand, he scraped the grime from the painting's surface. His hands were what people noticed first, those and his eyes, and the powerful aura he exuded.

The hands were large, with powerful cords of muscle built by the constant rhythmic squeezing of a piece of India rubber that was never out of reach. Some people smoked, some drank. Titus Quayle did both and squeezed bits of rubber.

The psychiatrists had found it interesting, a legacy of the two years in the dark filth of the Libyan prison. They likened the bond between the man and inanimate object to a child with his security blanket. But they were wrong. If they had looked into his flinty blue eyes they would have known that. He was forty-six years old but the time in the prison made him look older. Almost two years later, his skin was still scarred and his once rich black hair was laced with grey at the temples. He kept it cropped short and, as he bent over the icon, listening to the rain on the tin roof, he occasionally ran a hand across the aching shoulder.

He stopped, leant the postcard size painting against an earthenware jug and sat back to study it, his right hand taking the piece of rubber from the bench and squeezing it.

Born in Malaya in 1941, he was the only child of a quiet wraith-like librarian's daughter who had uncharacteristically run off and married the seventh son of the Earl of Dagenham, Charles Moncrief Montague Quayle. Realising that, as the seventh son, he was unlikely to benefit from his father's estate, Quayle had given the entire family the traditional two fingered salute at the dinner table one night and the next day booked passage to Singapore, collecting the librarian's daughter en route to Tilbury docks. He was convinced that, beneath the quiet nature and ill-fitting staid dresses, there lurked a ripe body and an adventurous spirit – and by Christmas 1938 they were managing a rubber plantation in Malaya's Cameron Highlands. Emily Quayle would often walk the rows of trees with her husband, supervising the tappers. And when their son was born, she felt she could not be happier. Charles Quayle had always hated his proliferation of Christian names and his wish had been that his son should have one name and a short one at that. And so, reared on the tales of Scott's Antarctic Expedition and the courage of Captain Oates, he had called his son Titus. For Emily, the existence was idyllic.

But it wasn't to last long.

When war came to Malaya, Charles Quayle dispatched his wife and new son down to fortress Singapore, bravely took his gun and stupidly stood in the way of the entire Imperial Japanese Army – leaving his widow and child to spend the next few years in Changi prison. After the war, Emily met and later married another Englishman, an engineer who came and went from their lives as projects and the drink permitted, and with some relief she accepted the new Earl's correspondence offer to educate young Titus in England.

The quiet tough little chap arrived at Southampton with his mother in 1948 and was immediately enrolled in a preparatory school allied to Eton. From there on, the years flashed by, the boy showing a real aptitude for languages and history – and, in 1959, he entered Corpus Christi College at Cambridge.

He was now alone, his mother having died several years before when a Yemeni had thrown a hand grenade into the car she was driving through Aden. His stepfather, drunk beside her after a night in the mess, had survived after the removal of a leg but in his guilt had never spoken to Titus again.

His tutor at Cambridge was Edward Morton, a German and Russian Languages specialist. The kindly quick-witted Don soon became more than just mentor to the young man, the pair of them sitting up late at night discussing theology, politics, history, playing chess or poring over the tutor's small collection of Russian icons.

The art form became Quayle's escape from the modern world and he found, in his first fumbling attempts at restoration, a real pleasure. Twenty-five years after leaving Cambridge, he could still not walk past a damaged or neglected piece without buying it to restore. There was a large cardboard box of damaged and grimy items awaiting his touch beneath the bookshelves in the main room.

By now, the rain had stopped. Stretching, he walked from the kitchen towards the long stone veranda and the single hardback bright blue chair given to him by the owner of a cafe in the village. The furnishings in the villa were sparse, and yet splendid. An old sagging double bed in one room, a camp stretcher in the other, and an old chintz lounge suite in the main living room were all that he had ever bought. Upended wooden beer crates served as small tables and an old rosewood door he had found in Thailand rested incongruously on four building blocks as a coffee table in front of the sofa. The rest of the place was filled with books and whatever odd items he had collected over the years. There was an antique gramophone with a brass horn and, on two walls, fine silk Qom carpets had been haphazardly hung, with other Tabriz and Isfahans scattered on the stone floors.

The walls were all white and an old wood bladed fan swished slowly from the high cool ceiling in the main room. The psychiatrists had told him to live with others, become part of a community, so he did exactly the opposite and found the old villa perched on a hillside across from the tiny village on the island of Serifos. From the front he could see the sparkling waters of the Aegean, and sitting at the kitchen table he could watch the path that wound its way down into the narrow gorge and up from the village. Visitors were infrequent but, some evenings, he would walk down and drink harsh red wine with the cafe owner, a sometimes morose, sometimes gregarious, individual called Nico. Then, the evening over, he would walk the dark path up the hillside to the silent house to await sleep, the nightmares and the demons it brought, and would later wake with his heart pounding, a silent scream on his lips sometimes two or three times before the dawn.

Sitting on the blue chair, he thought about the message the boy had bought over from the village that morning and watched as the distant ferry ploughed her way towards the harbour below.

A woman had phoned and was coming to stay. She sounded nice. Would she stay long, the boy's mother wanted to know, because if she would, she could bring up flowers and clean sheets and some cheese and tomatoes. He slipped the boy some drachmas and said to help her with her case when she arrived in the village, then went back to work on the small gold icon.

It would be Holly Morton. He had first seen her when she was a gangly sixteen year old and he was in his last year at Cambridge. She had since married and they had lost touch until her father's funeral. Then her husband had been killed in a pile-up on the M25 and, four months later she had phoned, just to say hello. Even then, he could hear the tension in her voice – and his offer of a place to lick her wounds had been accepted.

It was right that he should help. Holly was the daughter of his friend and mentor and the nearest thing he had to family. The Service had once been family. Teddy Morton and MI6. For him the two were inseparable because the Don had recruited him. It wasn't just the languages ability. It was the silent strength of the loner and buckets of pure nerve that interested the faceless men in London.

It began with a student prank, common enough in Cambridge. A young man and his girlfriend inebriated enough for the dare attempted to climb the outside wall of the Kings College Chapel. Three quarters of the way up the girl looked down and, suddenly sober, froze against the hard cold stone. Her boyfriend couldn't budge her and she began to cry, her grip weakening by the second. Quayle, returning to his College, pushed through the gaggle of watching students and began to climb the wall below her, talking all the time, encouraging her to hold on.

Pushing the boyfriend aside, he moved his body outside hers and coaxed her into moving downwards, his bulk reassuring against her back. At one point, she lost her grip and, for several seconds, the watching group below held their breath as Quayle took her entire weight on his knees, his hands gripping the gaps in the stones with almost obscene strength, before she scrabbled another hold. From below, a camera flash lit the wall and, a minute later, they dropped the last eight feet to the ground.

By breakfast, the word was out. The Cambridge evening paper had the pictures – and Quayle was certain that, if they published them, then the girl on the wall would be sent down. The College could only ignore so much; pictures in the paper demanded action. That lunch time, Quayle donned a borrowed suit and, armed with a couple of other props, walked into the offices of the newspaper, charmed his way past the receptionist and within minutes was in the photo section. After finding both the print and the negatives, he stuffed both into his briefcase and walked out, handing the receptionist a salesman's calling card with a flourish. Not once had he been challenged.

The story was told with some relish by those few in the know – and, in the Masters' rooms, an Australian tutor shook his head, saying, "That boy has more nerve than a bull ant," and chuckling delightedly.

Edward Morton smiled and agreed. He decided there and then to talk to the people at Century.

He watched her walk up the path, the boy chattering to her, the suitcase balanced on his head. She had lost weight since he had seen her last and her hair was scraped back in a loose bun. Brown hair, blue eyes, and a sprinkle of freckles made her look younger than she was. When she arrived at the steps, her smile was forced to cover her shocked expression.

"Hello Titus," she said brightly. "Well, I'm here."

"So you are," he smiled back, taking her case from the boy.

He showed her through to the bedroom and gestured at the curtainless window uncomfortably.

"I borrowed the chest of drawers. I'm sorry the mirror's cracked."

"Never mind, this will be very comfy."

"I'll put the kettle on."

"That would be nice," she said, the smile now genuine.

Later, her bag unpacked, she walked out to the veranda where he sat on the steps, alongside a tea tray of mismatched cups and saucers and an old dented teapot.

In the sunlight, he looked worse, the broad deep criss-crossed scars across his back that she knew could only have come from floggings. Across his shoulder a more jagged scar rose in a discoloured ridge, and through the short hair she could see other smaller scars across the back of his head.

She lowered herself beside him, took the cup from his hand, and saw the small purple circular scar above its powerful cords of tendon.

She looked up into his eyes. "My God Ti, what did they do to you?"

He looked at his hand, as if noticing the old wound for the first time, and clenched the fist.

"My own fault. You father always said I was an obstinate bugger."

He smiled then, but his ice blue eyes were hard and flecked.

"I saw pictures once at Guys." She raised her hand to her mouth as the realisation dawned. "Crucifixion marks. Oh my God, they crucified you... and your back?"

"Means I wear a shirt down into the cafe. Stops the tourists gawking. Drink your tea."

They sat in an awkward silence for a minute before she lowered the cup and spoke. "Hugh phoned before I left. Hugh Cockburn."

"I'm surprised you came then," he replied softly.

"Why?"

"I am dangerous. Didn't he tell you? Prolonged psychological trauma."

"Poppycock!" she snorted. Quayle laughed, softly thinking how like her father she was. "Anyway, he sends his regards," she finished.

They had been recruited the same year, Hugh from Oxford, and had met at the Foreign Office induction meeting. The front was maintained until they'd completed the battery and language tests and, on the third morning, the pair had been told to pack a bag. The first phase of their training was in a converted school in Lincolnshire where they were thrown in with a handful of actively serving intelligence officers from the army, three people from MI5 and an Australian identified only by his code name of 'Douglas'. There they learnt the rudiments of fieldcraft, the networking, recruiting, cyphers and cut-outs, and endured the all important know-your-enemy lectures. where a middle-aged matronly type with a caustic tongue hammered in the latest details on the KGB, GRU and their satellite counterparts, the counter intelligence people from 5 being pitted against the others for the practical sessions. Each of the nine course subjects would be expanded on in detail on later courses at other facilities.

Within days, the trainers had isolated the particular abilities of the students. Hugh Cockburn had begun to score very highly on the logistical planning and management sessions, with Quayle the opposite, very direct and preferring to think through a problem and then solve it alone. Six months later, as Quayle left for the combat school at Acton, Hugh was sent on to the languages facility to brush up his French. Their paths had crossed frequently over the years and they had remained friends – with Hugh actually working as Quayle's controller on two occasions while under the cover of Cultural Attaché in Bucharest. Quayle's skills had driven him underground from the start and he became one of only four British truly covert operatives on the MI6 full-time payroll. They were used all over the world wherever necessary, to support the local Station Chief on high risk tasks.

"How is Hugh?" Quayle asked.

"He's fine. Thinks you got the shitty end of the deal."

"Did he say that?" Quayle was surprised. It would have been most unlike Hugh to breach security by even discussing personnel he associated with.

"No, but I could tell. All this bloody cloak and dagger nonsense. Daddy was the same. All the mysterious trips down to London to see chaps in some boring club. Foreign Office my eye!"

Quayle said nothing.

"Go on," she said, "deny it!"

"Deny what?" he grinned.

"You're bloody impossible, the lot of you!"

"Drink your tea" he said patiently.

She smiled and looked at him. "Its nice to see you again, Ti..."

During the first few days they took lots of walks through the hills, eating in small tavernas whenever they were hungry. It was Holly, having badgered him out of the house, who did most of the talking. People who came across the odd looking couple found it difficult to label them, the pretty English woman and her big silent companion. He had a way of making men uneasy in his presence, his motives and intentions unknown. The effect was softened by the woman, who sometimes threw her head back and laughed, touching his arm like a comfortable old friend, and at other times sat locked in her own thoughts.

As the days went by, they dropped into an easy routine. Quayle worked on his icons at the big kitchen table which they had moved onto the veranda, a pair of incongruous bi-focal spectacles on his nose, while Holly sat on a big cushion against the white stucco wall, devouring his library or sometimes preparing scones in clouds of flour dust. Meals were simple affairs of feta cheese salads with fresh sardines, or bread from the village with spiced meats and bottles of cold beer.

The nights were when things were different, each with their private pain in the dark lonely hours, Holly in the old saggy bed, and Quayle with his nightmares across the other side of the house on the camp stretcher.

It was the first night that Holly understood Hugh's veiled warning about Quayle, when she heard him moaning and crying out in his sleep. She had walked through to his room and, in the moonlight, had seen him bunched up, teeth grinding, the wounds in his subconscious open and weeping.

Suddenly he jerked awake, his eyes wide and unseeing. Then he saw her in the doorway and smiled hesitantly, obviously embarrassed at being seen. But it was Holly who felt the intruder. Half of her wanted to go and hold him like you would a child who had bad dreams, and half of her was frightened by it all. For her Titus Quayle wasn't just a man. He was a hero figure from her childhood, the strongest man she had ever known, and what in God's name had happened that could drive something so strong into a sweating moaning huddle the moment his conscious relaxed?

Some nights, when it was very bad, he got up and smoked on the veranda – because awake he could handle it. If she too was awake, she could smell the smoke, and sometimes she got up and they played chess.

It was in the second week, when the wind shrieked and rain lashed through the cracks under the doors, that she gathered up her blankets and crept through to his room, dragging the mattress after her. She had never liked storms and. as she lay awake in her loneliness, a jagged pitchfork of lightning flashed across the room. Quayle lowered his left hand down, his fingers running through her hair. In the dark and thunder it was what she needed. Feeling that, not even the storm could touch her she slept.

The mattress stayed on the floor beside Quayle's stretcher and, one night, soon after – when his demons came and he lay rigidly tense and sweating – she climbed up onto the cot and soothed him, holding his head against her breasts. He could hear her heart beat through the thin t-shirt. The next day, she moved the mattress back to the bed that night she slept spooned against his back.

Nothing was said by either about the arrangement and, on the third night they slept together, Titus slept through without waking for the first time in over two years.

Some days he borrowed Nico's brother's boat, a brightly painted traditional twenty-two footer, and they sailed around to one of the remote bays. Holly dozed in the sun on the foredeck and Quayle – now Hemingway-esque, with a new stubble beard – sat hard in the stern, the sheets and tiller in his hands as he coaxed the old boat to windward, sometimes muttering sweet things to her, sometimes calling her all the nasty names a man can call a boat.

Once the anchor was down, he would free dive to the bottom stretching his lungs, always counting to sixty before slowly surfacing.

Today he didn't dive, but swam ashore with powerful measured strokes, and she watched him jog up the hillside to a white building, its trellised patio covered in bright blooms of bougainvillaea. Ten minutes later he returned with a bag in his teeth and, pulling himself over the side of the boat, held it up grinning.

"Ice. One needs ice with Ouzo!" And, with that, he produced a small bottle of Ouzo from his wet pocket.

It was that week that Holly asked a relative of Nico's who was about to visit Athens a favour and, when he returned, she presented Quayle with a set of fine sable hair brushes. It was the first spontaneous present that anyone had ever given him and he accepted them awkwardly, not knowing what to say. The next day he used them for the fine gilt work on a Seventeenth Century Romanian piece. He reciprocated with a feisty little black tom kitten, who stood with his tiny paws set, and hissed at everything until she scooped him up. Sitting in the palm of her hand, pressed up against her cheek, he found her acceptable, and from that moment on forgot the hiss and began playfully biting her hair.

People in the village began to notice other changes. Bright potted plants now sat on the windowsills, curtains hung in the bedroom window, and Quayle seemed to smile more when shopping in the store. He would also take time with the people, perhaps take an Ouzo and a plate of sardines, and he showed the children a trick with a coin that he seemed to pluck from their ears. There was a rumour that he was a doctor struck off for drinking because, when the body of a tourist was washed up on the beach, he seemed to know how long it had been in the water just by looking at it, and why else would he live on the Island unless he was struck off? The women of the village, who loved to gossip, liked the change. Some Sundays, Holly walked down to the village and attended church, not understanding the service but worshipping nevertheless. The women of the village liked that and smiled at her. It was not good for a man to be alone, but they did agree that living together was unseemly and with luck they would marry soon. It was only really talk – for the island had long been smothered in tourists in the summer, and modern values mixed happily with the Greek Orthodox beliefs.

The eccentricity of the image was strengthened when Nico had one of his periodic problems paying the bank back their loan.

The restaurant was doing well – but Nico favoured his luck with the cards too often and, being a great lover, he was therefore proverbially an unlucky gambler. This surely was the reason, he morosely told Quayle.

"Bullshit Nico, you just don't cheat as well as they do. How much are you in for?"

"I must have three hundred thousand drachmas at the bank on Friday," he replied, "or it is gone... poof!" He waved his hand in the air dramatically.

The next day, a boy arrived with six hundred thousand in an envelope –and Nico, knowing who it was from, duly wrote out a share transfer on a paper serviette for half of the raucous noisy sixty seat taverna until the debt was repaid. Signing with a dramatic flourish, he thanked all the Saints profusely and sent the boy back up the hill. The next day, the Englishman was not only a struck-off doctor, but a rich one, with another story that he was a famous respected smuggler. That night, there was much smashing of plates and emotional singing – but Quayle and Holly remained in the villa on the hill.

"He will be terribly disappointed," she said.

"So let him. I just lent him some money. He's going on like I donated a kidney."

"He loves you like a brother," she admonished – and Quayle smiled briefly, turning up the lamp wick. They were sitting on the veranda and, down below, the coloured strings of lights along the waterfront twinkled in the warm breeze.

"How long will you stay here?" she asked. "I mean, it's wonderful and peaceful and warm, but..."

"... but not enough going on for a person like me?" he finished ruefully.

"Yes."

"I don't know. I like it still. I own this place, so if I go I will always come back sometime. Nico would keep an eye on it. I know a man in

Italy. His name is Marc. He deals in paintings. He wants me to go into business with him. I find them and he sells 'em. The trouble is the very good ones are in Russia, and the Russians take a dim view of their national treasures being hawked on the open market. That means being a bit clever about it, and Marc isn't the clever type." He smiled again in the soft light. "He's the type who gets caught. Just like Nico."

"Then you best ignore it?"

"No," he said softly. "Can't do that."

"Why not, Ti? I'm sure the Russian police would advise it."

"Because he would get caught and I wouldn't and because he is my friend."

There seemed to be no arguing with that so she went inside, took a another bottle of wine from the fridge, and came back carrying it and the kitten together.

"When?" she asked, too casually, screwing the corkscrew down.

"Maybe next year. Just one trip would be best. In through Kiev and make the buys. Set up a conduit to get the pieces out. Shouldn't be a problem..."

And then the sweat broke out on his forehead. Someone had said that about the Libya job. Just pop in and pick up the plans for the chemical factory. Easy as falling off a log. But they were there at the buy, black uniformed police everywhere. They had known he was coming.

There was no trial, no phone call, no contact. Just the blindfolded bone-jarring ride in the back of the truck and the boot in his back and the dirt and blood in his mouth and Jebel Muhkta Prison.

Holly saw the look in his eyes and moved quickly to break the spell.

"Here," she said placing the little black street fighter on his lap, "I will pour the wine," and she watched with satisfaction as his big scarred hand moved gently over the cat's back.

That night they made love for the first time, Holly lying beneath his bulk, feeling his strength, loving him back fiercely as the warm wind blew through the window. Afterwards she lay in the crook of his arm, her head on his chest, and listened to him breathe, frightened of losing him because she loved him.

27

*

KGB General Nikolai Borshin climbed from the car and told his driver to wait. Holding his pass up to the guards with his good left hand, he walked through the massive wooden gates with a mixture of trepidation and delight. He wasn't sure what he expected of the grounds, but it wasn't only the huge firs and old pines that rutted the path. He took a deep breath and inhaled the scent of summer trees, the rich sap and pine needles taking him back to memories of his boyhood. He had always liked things in their natural state. The basic wholesome things.

As he stepped over a fallen branch, he saw the house through the trees. It was a traditional Russian building, low-eaved and with split log walls, the chinks long ago filled with the moss that grew across the timbers like a green velvet mantle. Bright blooms sprang from painted wooden tubs in the warm summer sunlight and only the small forest of communications aerials in the background gave any hint that this was the twentieth century.

As he walked, he straightened his blouse and squared away his cap. Head of the Fourth Directorate KGB he may be, but this was the dacha of the Chairman of the Supreme Soviet himself.

Soon he was ushered into the cool entrance hall by a woman servant, a withered old woman who, the stories said, had been found standing on a rubble strewn roadside on a bitterly cold Leningrad morning, the Nazis only six miles away, trying to sell a pair of shoes to buy potatoes for the children at the orphanage. But no-one wanted shoes and there were no potatoes anyway – and people thought she was crazy because she saw things in the future and avoided her. Things were looking bad until a tank came along. Up in its turret was a young man, a boy almost, who saw something in her eyes, something different, something he recognised. He called to the driver to stop and jumped down, behind him the huge metal monster's engines still rumbling. Moments later, he called up and told them to throw food down, holding out a burlap bag of bread and beets and a dead chicken for the woman to take.

"Take it and feed your little ones," he had said.

"Thank you, oh thank you!" the woman said. "How did you know?"

"I remember you" he laughed. "I was there for a while."

He had an aura even then, a strength, a will that other men saw and followed.

She looked at him, her dark pebble-like eyes growing sharp with the visions, and then spoke, "You will survive this. Your destiny is greatness."

The boy – whose name was Peytor Gorbov – smiled and jumped back up on the tank, waving as it roared away. Half a century later he was still feeding the woman's orphans – but now they were kittens in his kitchen and he was General Secretary of the Supreme Soviet.

Borshin took a seat on the hard monk's bench in the hall, hiding his gloved useless hand under one crossed leg. Alone now, he listened to the sounds of the house. In another room, a clock was chiming. Somewhere, someone polishing silverware; he supposed it would be real silver here, but with the stories about basics it might just be camping utensils. He smiled at the thought and was still smiling when Peytor Gorbov walked into the hall. The smile was there, the same expansive smile he offered to Presidents and Prime Ministers, and the hand was out to shake.

He stood briefly to attention and then took the hand, nodding formally.

"I am honoured, Comrade General Secretary." It was said stiffly, for the man was uncomfortable here at the Dacha. Other meetings had been in the more familiar Kremlin.

"Nonsense," Gorbov said charmingly. "You honour no-one but God. How's your daughter?"

Borshin was taken aback a second and it showed. He was a devout Christian in the home of atheism and he had not known that Gorbov knew that. His daughter was the other immense joy in his life. She was an actress, opinionated, outspoken and constantly in trouble with the militia at the University. Even though Borshin scolded her, he was secretly proud of the fire in her blood. Gorbov smiled.

"Come, come Nikolai, you love her to bits, but she drives you crazy, yes? Mine is the same."

"You are right." Borshin smiled and Gorbov did the same.

"Come through." Gorbov led the way into what was a study, the walls lined with books. Three chairs sat at the table, and Gorbov pulled two out. "Sit down."

Borshin sat, his cap on his lap.

"So how goes the Fourth?"

"It goes well Comrade Gorbov. It is still full of brown noses and politicians, but I'm getting there."

Gorbov laughed. Seven years before, he had spotted the lean purity in Nikolai Borshin – who had been wasted in a dying section of the Second Directorate. He was youthful, strong, astonishingly talented, incorruptible and completely apolitical, despising those who curried favour and sought out influence.

Gorbov had plucked him from that obscurity and given him the plum job of Head of the Fourth Directorate, riding roughshod over the then head of the KGB, alienating other more senior men and rocking the old boy network. Gorbov didn't want his own man in the job; he wanted no-one's man in the job. He wanted a man who was untouchable, with deep convictions in something other than just the Rodina – the party – but who would die for it if asked.

As he spoke, Gorbov studied the man for the hundredth time. He never got used to the dramatic appeal, the lean hawk-like good looks only enhanced by the eye patch – which, with the short iron grey hair, gave him a swashbuckling air. But there was always something a photograph never caught, and in Nikolai Borshin it was the rebel, the non-political 'stuff-the-Party and just get it done' attitude that had stopped so many good men.

"Have you got a man, someone on the outside you can trust implicitly?" Gorbov asked.

"You better tell me what you have in mind," Borshin answered.

"I have a source in your department," he began. Borshin nodded. He expected nothing else. "Long Knives has raised its head again."

"I know," Borshin said.

"Are we still..."

"At a dead end? Yes, I'm afraid we are – but something has broken in England, as you know. I think we should put a... that was what you wanted?"

"Yes, Nikolai. That is what I want. Take a good man. The best you have. He must be in position to capitalise on anything that breaks open there."

Borshin nodded. He had pre-empted the decision by almost two months with a man on the ground in the United Kingdom, but he thought – in the light of the new interest – he would now change the individual.

The current operative was a fifty two year old Polish émigré, a man whose forte was silent observation and piecing together the bits, who reported through to the KGB man at the Embassy. He would need a new man, a man who could do both that and have the experience and confidence to react on his own initiative – because there would be no embassy orders now. He would be on his own. He thought quickly about the killings at the safe house. They may think that was us. The new man must be able to deal with that.

"He is to report directly to you," Gorbov said.

Borshin was thinking fast. He must be able to take care of himself. He needs to have been through the mill a few times. He needs to be loyal to me and to the Rodina above all. He needs to be like me. Compulsive, a man who doesn't give up. A real bastard when it counts.

"I will find the right man," he replied.

That night he worked late, methodically going through the files. There was a constant stream of perfectly cloned talent coming out of the training schools, but he went to the other end of the spectrum. He began with older men who had commendations on their files – but for some reason had been passed over for the sort of promotion one would expect for that generation. He knew what he was looking for but, unable to explain it in words, he had his secretary bring him the files in batches.

He had sent his assistant, a bright young captain, home, preferring to allow Svetlana to help. She was a graduate of the academy. Tall, blonde and lithe, she wore her hair up in a bun and was the only person in the Directorate who would look him in the eye and disagree, and he loved her for it. His wife had been dead sixteen years now and he had tired of the KGB house girls very quickly. Virtually celibate until he had met Svetlana, he disliked the thought that a girl would go to bed with him simply because he was powerful and could provide influence. She arrived one day from the typing pool downstairs to use the typewriter in his outer office, his own secretary away. He had walked back to his office having forgotten something, dressed to go home, overcoat on over his uniform, and found her there and raised an eyebrow. She had raised one back, then turned away and kept working.

"He's gone," she said.

He smiled to himself. "Oh," he said, looking into the tiny kitchenette alongside her desk. "I hear the old bugger has real French brandy up here."

She looked up frostily.

"If he has it's because he's earned it!"

He liked that. This girl had steel in her bones.

"Oh. Fond of him, are you?"

"Never met him. I'm just using his girl's typewriter. Now leave me alone to finish this."

"Dinner?" he asked.

"With you?"

"Yes. With me."

"I might – but I won't go to bed with you... and give me more than an hour's notice when you ask properly, won't you?" She looked up from the keyboard smiling, but the message there. I'm not some department tart.

Let's see how much steel you really have, he thought.

"I am not without influence, and bed won't be too bad now, will it?"

"Go to hell," she said fiercely.

He threw back his head and laughed, delighted with the find.

He leant across the desk and took the phone, dialling an internal number to the head of Administration.

"Borshin here! There is a girl in my office name of..." He looked at her. She had gone pale and stood straight to attention behind the desk. "Well?" he asked.

"Svetlana Taber, Comrade General. I'm sorry about..."

He waved a hand at her and spoke back into the phone.

"...Taber. Svetlana. I want her transferred to my office first thing tomorrow. No – as my secretary. I know she is only new." He smiled, then "Get rid of the other one. Move her to a senior position somewhere... No, no, no problem. She just doesn't have any balls." He hung up and looked at her across the desk, still standing to attention. "And you do. I like that."

He turned and walked out, his greatcoat flapping round his knees.

Now, three years later, they worked together as a closely welded team, her understanding of his style and moods absolute. She was also fiercely loyal – which he appreciated beyond anything else.

She entered the room with another batch of files and placed them at his side.

"You are tired," she said.

"I'm OK." He did not look up.

"What are you looking for, Nikolai? Let me help."

"No."

"Oh don't be so bloody pigheaded!" she retorted.

He laughed softly and ran a hand across his eye patch. Twenty years on and sometimes it still hurt. "I need a man. A very experienced man. Stubborn, good at his job, a loner, because he will be alone most of the time. Smart, canny, a hunter who thinks like his quarry. A man who gets things done without worrying about having his back patted."

"A man like you," she said.

He smiled. She understood.

"Yes."

She pulled up a chair and, sitting opposite, took a batch of files and began to read.

Two days later, she was sifting through department circulars that had arrived on her desk overnight, a collection of requests, memos, notifications and transfer orders for Borshin's signature. She was authorised to deal with all of it, but she took one item from the stack, read it twice carefully and put it to one side for him to look at. It was a pink disciplinary sheet, stapled to a non-requested transfer order. Later that morning, she requested the man's file from personnel and took it through to Borshin.

"I have one you may want to look at."

He looked up from his desk. Its surface was covered in the buff coloured folders. He nodded, leant back and lifted his coffee to his lips.

"He is younger than you had envisaged, but it's all here. Major Alexi Lenoid Kirov, born 1950. Joined late from the Army. Distinguished at the Academy, languages, English and German. Just scraped out of a committee hearing in '81 by his boss... He, ah, told a second assistant attaché what to do."

Borshin chuckled out loud and she read on, "That was in Budapest, did a tour without problems in Bonn, another in Amsterdam."

"Who was his boss?"

"A Major Sokolov."

"Initial?"

"S.K."

Borshin nodded. He knew him.

"He is on his way back now. There has been an incident in Mexico City."

Mexico City, once a prime source of intelligence, was now just a backwater. "What's he doing in that shithole?"

"He doesn't seem to have many friends in the department."

"What was the incident?" Borshin asked.

"He assaulted the Head of Rezidentura."

Borshin stood and walked to his window. Attacking a senior officer was bad, but attacking the senior KGB man in a foreign location was a very serious offence.

"Otherwise?" he asked, still looking out of the window.

34

"Exemplary. Two commendations for his work, positive acclaim from the people in Bonn."

"Pull the rest of the file. I want to know what happened in Mexico City. When is he due back here?"

"Monday. This is the file, General. All of it."

"Nothing further on the Mexico thing?"

"No."

"Someone is covering something up here." He didn't say it but she knew who he was talking about. The old boy network. "Waive normal debrief and relocation as yet. I want to meet this Major Alexi Kirov... Who did he have a go at in Mexico?"

She passed him a slip of paper with a name on it.

Kirov walked through the airport, tired and grainy-eyed. It had been a long flight via Cairo and he had not slept for three days. He was noticeable amongst the people at the baggage reclaim area because he was one of the few who were not tourists, and in spite of his western clothing and haircut, his bored demeanour made him stand out. A man of even height, with sandy blonde hair and nondescript green eyes, he hadn't shaved recently and his stubble had a reddish tinge that was softened a little by the light suntan. Collecting his bags cheerlessly, he walked through to the customs men at their barrier, not happy at all with the prospect of being back in Russia for his disciplinary enquiry. He wasn't so much concerned with the prospect of reprimand, demotion and possible suspension as he was bored with the whole affair. He just wanted it over.

He took a taxi, illegally offering hard currency to travel alone, and sat silent in the back during the drive into the city and his apartment. His sister had said she would get some milk and bread and vodka in, put some soup in the fridge, clean up the place a bit. He looked out the window at the grey colourless people and the grey colourless streets. Moscow. He hated the place. He was from Kiev.

Throwing his bags on the floor, he walked through to the tiny kitchen to turn the heating on. It might have been summer but the nights were still chilly, and the one good thing about a KGB apartment building was that they didn't scrimp on the heating.

There on the sink was a bottle of vodka. Should be in the bloody fridge, he thought, picking it up and taking a glass from the cupboard. Blowing the dust clear, he walked though to the small sitting room and sprawled in a chair. Welcome home Alexi, he said to himself, and miserably tilted the bottle to his lips.

Half an hour later, he got up, stripped his clothing off and stood under a sad little trickle of water that should have been a shower. He had just begun to soap up his hair when he thought he heard a knock at the door. He paused, shrugged to himself and kept on going. When he was finished, he walked through to the sitting room, a towel round his waist – and there, sitting in one of his two chairs, was a man, lean and hard with greying hair and an eye patch. He was wearing well-cut Italian slacks and an English blazer over a silk shirt.

"Who the fuck are you?" he asked.

The man stood and looked around the apartment, the drab walls brightened only by a fading calendar and a picture of a lake in the spring. Standard issue.

"I used to live in a place like this," he said. He turned and fixed his one good eye on Kirov. "Nikolai Borshin."

Kirov looked at him. The man oozed confidence.

"The Nikolai Borshin?" he asked with a raised eyebrow, holding the towel in case it dropped.

"Your boss, if that's what you mean."

Kirov gave a sad sort of a smile.

"I knew I was in the shit, but I wasn't expecting this."

"You could show more respect, Major Kirov. It might help your case."

"Comrade General. With respect –" He came to attention; then, feeling slightly foolish in a towel, continued, "– I'm sick of kissing arses. If you want to throw me out then throw me out. I joined up to do a job. I worked hard and I produced results but I have sucked on the crap long enough. I have been returned home in disgrace to appear before a disciplinary hearing for a act that I wilfully committed, and I would

36

commit again. I knocked that bastard's teeth out – and if anybody here gave a damn about the reasons then I wouldn't be here. So, with respect Comrade General, I have a right to be pissed off!"

"Why did you do it?"

"Is this my hearing?" Kirov asked. "Because if it is..."

"Answer me!"

"The Head of Rezidentura in Mexico leant on the cleaning women. Jobs are hard to come by. One was a good looker. That was bad enough – but, when I found him forcing himself on her thirteen year old daughter, that was enough. Rape is rape. He laughed and said they couldn't touch him. But I could. Now he's talking through a wired jaw. I'm not sorry I did it. I would do it again."

"Is that the truth?" Borshin asked.

"It is. But since when has that mattered? He is a party member."

"It matters to me," Borshin said, his voice soft with menace.

Kirov looked him direct in the eye. "I heard that about you."

Borshin smiled and, to Kirov's astonishment, moved across to the picture on the wall, lifting it carefully away exposed a small microphone. He had half expected it, but not that the General commanding the Fourth Directorate should warn him of it.

"Get dressed," he said, "and come with me."

Kirov was moved to a brand new apartment just of the Oktober Prospekt. The building was small and its other tenants were very senior public officials, most of whom he was told he would never see. When he climbed into bed that night, he wondered – having come home for a reprimand and now in splendour – just what he was getting into.

Two days later, Nikolai Borshin came by the apartment. He was accompanied by Svetlana who had an armful of files. Kirov was pleased to see him. The waiting had been difficult and the walls of the apartment seemed to be closing in on him.

"Your story checks out. Your... friend has been recalled and has seen his last overseas posting. He will be spend the rest of his career screening visas in some airport."

Kirov was relieved and it showed in his face as he came to attention. "Good. Thank you, Comrade General. What now? Do I get another posting?"

"That depends," Borshin replied. The two days had been used in a flurry of vetting, all of Kirov's known acquaintances and personal history checked and rechecked while they looked for any possible prior association with the task he was to be offered.

"On what, General Borshin?"

"On you. I have a job that needs a man. Reports to me direct. Very little if any Embassy or local network support at first. I requires two things. Loyalty to me and loyalty to the Rodina."

"If I say no?"

"A posting will be made available from the waiting list."

Kirov knew he could wait months for a new job abroad, and even then it could be to a hellhole like Guatemala City or Lusaka.

"What's the job?" he asked with a sigh and Borshin smiled widely.

CHAPTER THREE

Milburn

Henry Arnold had now spent almost three months sniffing for Yuri Simonov's mole. The job was made doubly difficult because no-one knew what real information had been passed over. The only lead was the cryptic reference to Long Knives, and that had turned up cold. Each time he tried to move his thinking onto a new tangent, his instincts pulled him back to the corrupted data bank – but every request for information from the data processing people simply left him more confused. Finally, one of them admitted that a bug was a bug and, sometimes, one just had to learn from the experience, what with the interface and the access and format omega in this configuration. He had had enough. He raised an eyebrow and left the room, resolved to find someone that could speak English about computers. All his requests for the man who had designed the system were meeting the usual problems. The team involved were now scattered over various defence projects, high priority you understand. Eventually he made the request of Sir Martin Callows himself who hurumphed, barked a laugh and picked up the phone, promising to help.

Arnold returned to his labours in the vast registry at Century and, three days later, a gangly individual in corduroy trousers and a T-shirt arrived at the registry asking for him.

"I'm Jeff," he said. "You have a hassle with the system?"

Arnold pushed his glasses up his nose. He had seen people like this before. His daughter nearly married one.

"Sort of. You designed it?"

"Yeah. One of a happy bunch. What's the problem? I'm due back at Holy Loch tonight."

"You will be going back when we are finished," Arnold said firmly, "not before."

"Whoa, relax granddad! For you, the defence of the Realm and the free world can wait."

Arnold stood. He had had enough of this. "Listen, young man. I was defending the realm before you were born. That is precisely what we are doing here, so curb your tongue! Now then, I have spent months listening to a bunch of computer freaks make excuses for their own incompetence. I have a simple question and I keep getting technical replies that are not answers but gibberish. Listen carefully."

He outlined the problem clearly and succinctly and, to his credit, the engineer listened silently before saying, "Let's have a look then," rather like a doctor.

Three minutes later, he leant back in the chair.

"Are you security" he asked Arnold.

"Yes, in a manner of speaking."

"Good. Then we don't have to call them."

"What are you saying" Arnold asked.

"We have been got at... no doubt about it."

"I thought you might say that."

"OK. Let's get your problem sorted out, then we can look at the system security."

Arnold was surprised at the casual tone. "I thought these things were supposedly impregnable?"

"Not to a whizz kid. I was at university with a dozen people who could hack into this system in a couple of days, but that isn't the problem here. Someone has gotten to it all right, but from the inside. Someone who is cleared for entry has purged your file. To do that, they had to present a series of passwords in sequence. It's not the system at fault so much as the operator. You have a bogey in here somewhere."

"Can you determine if any other files have been purged in the same manner?"

"No I can't, but one of the software writers on the team might. We all have our areas of expertise. Let me make a couple of calls and I'll see who's available..." He raised a hand. "Don't tell me! The defence of the realm! You will make them available."

"Correct," Arnold replied dryly.

"Right, well, the girl you want is Wendy Khan. She's down at Cheltenham at the moment. She is only a kid, but the brightest in the business. Don't shout at her or she'll go to IBM or someone for a million a year. OK?"

"Give her a call," Arnold said, "and I will be all sweetness and light."

She arrived the next evening, an exotic mix of coffee coloured skin, bright blue eyes, sari and a Chester accent.

Arnold took her in one long, admiring glance.

"My mother was Scottish and my father Kashmiri," she explained with an open smile.

"Ah yes, I see."

"Jeff said you were a crusty old bugger," she offered frankly, "and I wasn't to take any nonsense from you."

"I see…" he repeated, uncomfortably.

"But I can see you're really a sweetie. So what's the problem with the system?"

He began to explain and she listened.

"I think best over a glass of wine. Let me do that and, tomorrow, we shall try and rescue your input…"

It was nearly six and he nodded his agreement. Outside, the evening was damp with drizzle – and, as he walked along towards Euston Station through the sodden bustle of commuters, he tried to place his task in perspective. His son was in advertising and he had watched, fascinated, one night as he had gone through what he had called the proposition. It simply meant writing down exactly what you understood the offer to mean, then removing any nuances that were superfluous to get an exact definition. From there you could shape what you wanted to say, and to whom, without confusing the issue. It seemed a simple enough task, but watching he had learnt a new respect for the discipline. It drew clear thinking out and cast aside anything fuzzy or ill-defined.

He found himself a quiet spot in a pub and sat down to think through his proposition, nursing a small scotch and nibbling at some crisps left by the last people at the table.

We think we have a mole. Why do we think that? We think that because a KGB chappie let it slip. Was he qualified to speak on the issue? After all he was only a low level staffer... Low level yes, but he was a homosexual being rogered by someone who was closer to the action. So far so good. Even considering the post Philby-Blunt paranoia, only mild cause for concern, more a call for verification of the story. But when we start looking something is triggered, something larger, because our chap ends up dead along with four other people. Alarm bells ringing at the station house, bloody big bells because not even the KGB will sanction a kill like that. We don't kill innocents if we can possibly help it, and we don't kill operatives unless absolutely necessary, and the Kilos are the same. Yet we have four dead. Then I start to look for the mole, the reason for it all – and I find the computer data tampered with, and the only reference point gone. Synopsis is a low level Kilo blurts something that gets himself and four others chopped. The two are not synonymous.

He sat back and sipped the scotch. He rationed himself these days since his wife was dead. There were two reasons he rationalised. One was he became very maudlin when he was drunk – and the other was that his daughter gave him hell for it. She still lived at home, a solidly competent theatre sister at Great Ormond Street Children's Hospital, an avid theatregoer and currently seeing a bearded lecturer at the Polytechnic. They would be married soon and he was steeling himself for her departure from the house. He would miss her terribly, that he knew, so in deference to that he never drank more than one scotch, not these days. There had been a time when he could nudge a whole bottle, but he was younger then.

Suddenly he smiled to himself. Synonymous? No wonder they're not synonymous. He congratulated himself with the last mouthful and still smiling made his way to the station.

He sat and looked at her as she spoke, almost mesmerised by her azure blue eyes.

"This system is capable of much more than the operators ever demand of it. Now then, we can't re-capture what has been purged, but we can recall some segments that were cross referenced."

"What will that give us?" Arnold asked.

"Depends on what you're looking for. Probably some dates, maybe a name or two... But there is one facility we can use. When we designed the software, we had a check package. That was so we could actually follow up early entries and ensure they were loaded and accessible from each of the working programmes."

He smiled and she stopped.

"What?"

"Nothing. I was just thinking how nice it is to find someone who speaks English about computers."

Wendy gave him a look. "We aim to please.." Then she went on, "So, using the check package, we can access the operator security programme."

"Which will what?"

"Well, it will give you the access code of everyone who has been in for any file. In this case, it will tell you who the last persons were into your dumped area."

"Won't that have been dumped as well?"

"Absolutely not. I designed this. This was one of the extras I built in, a three stage security package. Every designer does it, little enhancements that you don't offer to the user because they would just confuse the working issues. Now, with this, the person who got at the file would have known about stages one and two. Stage three was an extra that none of the operators ever knew about. It's a pig to get at, however. I'll need about an hour..."

"And you can give me the name of the persons last into that file?"

"Yes..."

His eyes narrowed. The smell of the quarry was closer now.

"Do it," he said, "I'll be next door."

Feeling good, he got up walked purposely though to the main registry, his thoughts of the night before clear in his mind.

Later that afternoon, armed with possible names, Henry Arnold advised John Burmeister that he was ready to involve the Security Service (MI5) Counter Intelligence – and, at 9am the following morning, a team of three MI5 investigators squeezed themselves into Arnold's cubby-hole office at Milburn. The phone lines ran hot between the services, the Foreign Office and Special Branch – who wanted to add a member to the team to ensure procedures were followed and the evidence for the courts was both conclusive and irrefutable. Technically it was now MI5's case, but Callows applied pressure to allow Arnold to stay in to the kill, both for the inter-service kudos and to be sure that the job was done properly.

The prime suspect was a thirty-two year old woman who had been employed in Century main registry for six years. Her name was Meredith Jane Mortimer and she was still resident, Special Branch had established, in Datchet near Windsor. Suspect number two was the Head of Registry, but virtually discounted because his access code was used in programme checks. A team of MI5 watchers was put on Meredith Mortimer while Arnold and the investigators went to work to establish a case.

"Look, all I'm saying is this. We should have been in on this from the bloody start." The speaker was a big florid man, his red nose bulbous and moving imperceptibly as he spoke.

Arnold looked at him like he looked at dog mess on his shoes. "Just count yourself lucky you're in at all," he replied, a six man to the end.

"Look, we have systems. We need a case that will stand up in court with some lefty lawyer trying to rip it apart..."

One of the younger five chaps stood up, offering his hands in a conciliatory manner.

"Gentlemen, gentlemen, we have a spy to catch. Can I suggest we leave the bickering to our Lords and masters, and get on with the job?"

The watchers numbered thirty-six in total, six teams of six members each. The first team were, or at least appeared to be, a mother with baby, granny doing the shopping, telephone repair man, punk rocker, tow truck driver – and the leader a completely non-descript looking West Indian woman out with her man. They would follow and watch every move made by the suspect until further notice, recording all the details, photographing every meeting and painstakingly identifying every person the suspect met, spoke to or even brushed past. Every waking minute she would be shadowed.

Bit by bit, the routine fell into place. On workday mornings she walked to the Station, usually buying a paper at the tobacconist on the way and catching the 7:52 into Waterloo Station. From there she took the underground and walked the rest of the way to Century House, arriving normally at about 8:50. She lunched in the building in the canteen and headed home, trying for the 18:02 – and, once in Datchet, walked straight home. Her mother usually had dinner on, the watchers being able to identify the food on the plates, and the pair watched television till about ten.

The fifth evening, the suspect went straight to a play, throwing the watchers into momentary dismay when she by-passed the Station heading for the West End, and an extra team was brought in in case her rendezvous was in the theatre.

Saturday morning was her shopping day, and two of the team followed her around Sainsbury's, watching her load frozen kippers and tinned new potatoes into her trolley.

It was the second Saturday that she seemed to break her habitual routine. Today she left the house wearing makeup and took a taxi into Windsor. The watchers followed her into a wine bar, where she greeted and sat down with a man.

Out on the street, a woman walking her dog bent her head forward, listening carefully to the fast chat in her secreted ear-piece receiver, crossed to a parked van and quickly climbed into the back. "Camera quick," she said, passing the small confused dog to the man bent over the radio set.

He scooped up a maroon coloured handbag.

"In the bas. They have fixed it with the lens out of the crack in the end now. Viewfinder's up and the power winder is a noisy bastard – so be careful."

"Shit! I thought that was fixed!" she snapped. It had been a long day.

Three minutes later she wandered into the wine bar, placing the bag on the bar under her arm. Waiting for the noise from the kitchen to roll out with the opening of the swing doors, she began photographing the couple at the table. Inside ten minutes she had thirty-six shots exposed, paid for her drink, looked angrily at her watch like a stranded date and stalked out onto the street.

No-one on the team could identify the man she was with, so the film was rushed into MI5's lab for immediate developing, and a couple of counter intelligence people brought in to study the pictures and try and identify the stranger.

Meanwhile, the watchers stayed on the couple.

"So who the bloody hell is he?" Callows barked.

"Five are running ID checks now, Sir Martin," Adrian Black answered.

"Bloody Five. They want everything done to death. Run the bugger in to Scotland Yard," he mumbled angrily.

He paced the room like a polar bear, back and forth, his leonine head swinging as he moved.

At that moment, Henry Arnold was admitted from the anteroom.

"Ha! Arnold. You're here!"

"Yes, Sir Martin," he answered, "I came as soon as I got the call. Are we on then?"

"Looks like it. The treacherous bitch is sipping plonk in some wine bar in Windsor with an as yet unidentified man..."

Callows' fury was something to behold, and Black – ever appreciative of real drama – knew instinctively that Arnold was about to fan the flames.

"It's too soon," Arnold said disappointedly.

"What?" Callows snapped

"It's too soon. These things take months to unravel. If we have caught a Soviet agent within two weeks of watching, then she is no Mata Hari. Either that or we've just had the damnedest luck."

"Luck! Luck! You bloody cretin! Six years that conniving lying black-hearted bitch has been in Central Registry. Six bloody years, dammit!"

"Well," Arnold offered, "it could have been ten or twenty, and she could have been on an active desk rather than just filing dead material."

"Thank God for small mercies, I suppose."

The telephone rang and Black scooped it from the desk with one fluid move. He listened for ten seconds, before replacing the handset, a small smile playing his lips.

"Film quality not good. Bad light. Lousy file shots, but we have a make... Yet to be confirmed, but we have a make. The man is Peytor Minsky a.k.a Sergi Karmova. He is down as Second Cultural Attaché under the Minsky name. I know him. We've never really understood his role, but there's no doubt about it. He is hard core KGB and we have just cracked into his network."

"I'll hang the bitch!" Callows roared. Behind him, Arnold nodded to himself, thinking: that's fine, but the two issues are still not synonymous. Delighted with the success so far, he said a silent prayer for the watchers and Special Branch who would now have to make the case. But even now he could not help feeling that it was all too simple.

"Sir Martin, I feel I should warn you that, now Five has him pegged as a Kilo fisherman, they may want to leave things and see who else he has on the hook."

"Over my dead body," Callows stated flatly, his voice betraying his acceptance that it may well be the case, and his anger dying as fast at it had flared. He looked at Arnold. "Well done Henry, fine job of work."

Arnold looked up. "Sorry?"

"I said well done," Callows repeated.

"Thank you, sir, but it's not over yet... "

"What are you saying, man?"

"I'm not sure, Sir Martin. Not yet. Can I stay on it a while?"

"What's your angle?" Black asked. He had a profound respect for Arnold's thought process.

"Why did she dump the file? It doesn't make sense. It was like holding up her hand and saying 'I'm spying...'"

"I've never understood women," Callows muttered. "No. Go back to pruning roses or whatever you were doing..."

Arnold smiled. In his spare time he edited sections of the Encyclopaedia Britannica. "Can I just hang around a bit? See it finished?"

"If you must."

Later that night, the two Directors General agreed to postpone the arrest of Meredith Mortimer to allow the watchers more time to see if a second meeting would take place, and a second group of watchers was placed on the Soviet Diplomat. The fact that he had remained unknown as a KGB staffer for so long made him a real professional, and the chances he had done the tag evasion course were very high, so this was the most experienced team assembled in years. Not that he would dream of trying to lose any watchers he found; he would simply take note of them and be aware that this was not the routine watching of all Soviet diplomats, rather something special just for him. He would then drop all his illegal activities to protect his network and could lie dormant for months – or worse, hand over the function to another case officer. With six hundred Soviets accredited at their Embassy in London, identifying the new controller with MI5's limited resources would be almost impossible.

The task to crack Sergi Karmova's network fell to MI5's head of 'D' – their Counter Intelligence Section – and he quickly gave the Soviet the code name of BIG-EARS to link in the NODDY already flagged on Meredith Jane Mortimer's file. Hopefully BIG-EARS would lead Five to the others in the network which became TOYTOWN.

Resources were shifted across to 'D' and new faces were brought in. The head of 'D' considered asking for Adrian Blacks' return to Five, but knew it would be like drawing teeth from Sir Martin Callows and left it alone.

By the end of the third day, the Soviet's file was three inches thick.

There were now over seventy high resolution photos of the man and the watchers were all armed with a set of full frontal portrait, profile view and a batch of walking and talking shots. His flat in the rezendencia had been isolated and it confirmed his status. It was one of the larger three bedroom arrangements in the west wing, the floor plans thoughtfully provided by a window installation contractor who had done a double glazing job the year before and miraculously managed to plant several bugs for King and Country.

The first formal Inter Service de-brief on the TOYTOWN network was held on the ninth day of the stepped-up surveillance. MI5 bought four people along to sit in with Adrian Black, Sir Martin Callows – and, of course, Henry Arnold from MI6, who had somehow managed to stay on. The meeting was held on neutral ground in a high security area of the Foreign Office annex, a dreary prefabricated structure with dirty windows and cracked linoleum floors.

Colin Meynard-Smith, head of MI5 'D' Section, opened the meeting with a recap and the first decent profile of BIG-EARS.

"That's him," he said, flicking a colour slide up on the tatty screen at the far end. "Major Sergi Karmova. Directorate IV KGB. A fully fledged grade one Moscow Centre bovva boy."

Callows sipped noisily at a cup of tea and made a grunting noise like a wild boar. The Five people shifted uncomfortably. This was a breach of protocol. If they had known the Deputy Director General of MI6 was attending then they would have brought their own. They felt outgunned and outmanned. Black grinned at the illicit pleasure of watching his ex-comrades squirm and looked up at the face on the screen. The Russian was extremely good looking in a matinee idol fashion, with dark eyes, dark hair and a boyish grin.

Meynard-Smith went on. "He's been at the London Embassy for five years. A long posting – which is what made us think he may have been clean. Chronologically, that means he would have recruited NODDY sometime that year because her access into your missing file took place after that, along with Christ knows what else..."

Callows snorted into his cup again, but Meynard-Smith continued valiantly, "We reckon it was a honey trap in reverse. Little cutie Sergi and NODDY." With that, he changed the slide and Meredith Mortimer appeared life-size on the screen. She was a homely looking woman with large shapeless legs and mousy brown hair, clutching a tired looking handbag. "Let's just say she is a rather ordinary looking woman. A man like Sergi Karmova, wine, promises of a loving future in a rose covered cottage or a Black Sea dacha or whatever, it would not take much."

"Are they on the job?" Adrian Black asked.

"What?"

"Is he shafting her man?" Callows barked

"Yes, they went to a hotel that night. Checked in as a Mrs Thomas," Meynard-Smith answered succinctly.

Black sat back, trying to imagine the pair in bed: sweaty sheets, grunts and moans and whispered endearments, elephantine thighs wrapped round the slims hips of the matinee man.

"I reckon he earned whatever he got then," he said.

One of the Five people looked up. She was an attractive woman in her late twenties, with a Hermes scarf through her hair and a pair of sunglasses pushed up on her head. She had been studying the contents of her cup as if something alive might crawl out. "That was sexist and uncalled for," she said primly.

"Bollocks!" Callows roared, a huge grin across his face. "I agree with him. Bloody Russian deserves a medal for humping this thing." His head swung back to Meynard-Smith. "Carry on. So who else is he working then?"

This was the nitty gritty. Was he working any other agents? The KGB paymasters may have considered Meredith Mortimer worthy enough for a dedicated controller. If so, they could arrest her now.

"We haven't been able to establish that yet. It's way too soon."

Callows expected nothing else. He knew how exhaustive the work would be. Every time BIG-EARS stopped to scratch his nose, the team would be looking for a possible recipient of the potential signal. Every time he stopped to eat or buy a paper or have a drink, they would be watching for a signal or a drop-box or a dead letter pick-up location.

Just because he'd been caught red-handed with one of his cell didn't mean he was that open with all – and, as Meynard-Smith had pointed out, he couldn't work the honey trap with dead letter letters and cutouts.

"How long do you want to give it?"

"About six months to be sure," Meynard-Smith answered. "He would have to contact even his most distant agents in six months."

"Try one," Callows answered.

"Impossible!"

"One. No discussion. I have a traitor in my department. Bad enough that we may have to swallow the fact that she's been passing material from registry for four years, without it going on for any longer than absolutely necessary." His voice had a deep timbre now. He spoke quickly and eloquently, as he did when deadly earnest. Those who knew him knew that this was the time when you simply shut up and listened. "Now, you and I know that, if he doesn't make a mistake in a month, then he may not for six or a year or two years. So let's give it a month. If nothing breaks, you people arrest her – or I will do it myself under Clause Seventeen of the Official Secrets Act Amendment."

"Sir Martin…" Meynard-Smith began.

"Don't worry about your D-D G. I will phone him as soon as this meeting is over. But you must leave here understanding that you have one month only to nail BIG-EARS with anything extra. Then we look at the other alternatives, but either way Meredith Mortimer is done for."

"If we move too fast, we may have a job proving it in court…"

"I think not. If this is really a honey trap, you'll be going to court with an admission and a full confession, and tears on the pillow and the-bastard-promised-to-marry-me."

"And if not? If we're wrong and the vetting didn't work and we have a communist here?"

"She's no communist," Callows said with surprising compassion. "She's a lonely spinster helping the only man who ever looked at her twice. That's why honey traps work and that's why they will always work."

With the meeting seemingly over, they all stood, and the woman in the Hermes scarf studying Sir Martin Callows with a new respect.

"When we pick her up, I would like to talk to her," Arnold said. It had been the first time he had spoken.

Meynard-Smith was collecting his slides from the carousel. "Sorry Henry, that's SB's bailiwick."

"Who do I talk to there?"

"Chief Inspector Conners. He's all right, buy him a scotch or something." He didn't look up from his little slide box, so Arnold wrote the man's name down and walked out to get a ride back to Milburn with Adrian Black.

Three weeks later, the watchers had to admit that they were unlikely to nail the Soviet in the given month. If he had other agents in his network then he made no mistakes – and he hadn't seen Meredith Mortimer again. The MI5 Deputy Director General had made token protests about Sir Martin Callows' ultimatum but, in the end, he had to agree he had a point.

It was with three days to run that Special Branch reluctantly agreed to make the arrest. Henry Arnold joined the arresting officers and the rummage team that would take the Datchet house apart. Now, he sat in the front seat of a large four door saloon, the dusk settling over the river while, behind him, two officers argued the merits of Wolverhampton's football team. The man at his side was listening to the awkward scratchy chat on the radio.

None of them had seen the man watching from the riverbank where he sat with a fishing rod and thermos of something hot.

In the car, Arnold leant forward to wind down the window; the cigarette smoke wafting over from the back seat was making him cough.

"You all right?" someone in the back asked.

"Yes, fine," he answered. "Just the smoke."

"Won't be long now. She's never much later than this."

As if that were the cue, the radio hissed and the driver leant forward to turn up the volume.

"Right, that's it," he said, ", she's coming..."

Arnold tensed in the seat. This was it.

Someone tapped on the window and, winding it down, he looked out at a hard looking young man in a leather jacket.

"The boss says, if you want in with the first lads, then you better join us..."

Arnold nodded and climbed from the car, stretching as he did so. Then he walked back the forty feet to the second car, where three men were climbing from the darkened interior. One had a sledge hammer in his hands and another put a pistol in his pocket.

A big man in a tired looking overcoat began to speak.

"Right. We ring the bell. Sergeant, you in first. If she tries anything silly, stop her. She may have a shooter, you never know – but just make your point, don't go doing a Wyatt Earp all right?"

The man with the pistol nodded, almost bored. He must have done a few of these, Arnold thought.

"Now, watch out for 'er old mum. We don't know if she's in on the muck so treat 'er nice while she treats us nice. Who's got the warrant?"

"Me, DI," someone said.

"Let's go then." He turned to look at Arnold. "Just stay behind the lads till we know who's home."

"Isn't this a little dramatic for a spinster and her mother?" Arnold asked.

"Myra Hindly was a spinster," he said – and, seeing Arnold wasn't following, he carried on, "Look, I've had a granny pour hot oil down the stairs on me. I've had a mother with a baby in one hand and a machete in the other, and a nice little old dear in Clapham fire a sawn-off at me when I nicked her son. Men are predictable. Women? They are bloody dangerous. Believe me."

"Yes, I'm sorry," Arnold said and, feeling stupid, he followed the small group up the street to the house.

The Sergeant watched the man to his left discreetly place the sledge hammer against the wall, then pressed the bell which rang shrilly through the glass door.

Through the frosted glass they could see a figure make its way slowly up the hall and, with complete trust, opened it wide, revealing a lined cheerful face beneath a coppery woolly hat.

"Yes?"

"Are you Mrs Mortimer?" the Sergeant asked loudly, leaning forward in case she was deaf.

"Yes," she replied. "Who are you?"

"I'm from the Police Station. Mind if we come in for a chat?"

"Ooh. Yes that should be all right. I'll make some tea, shall I?" she said swinging open the door.

The Sergeant moved past her in a fluid motion, his right hand still in his pocket, the other officer going for the kitchen, the Detective Inspector straight into the living room. The last man moved up the stairs quickly, leaving Arnold awkwardly in the hall.

Meredith Mortimer stood before the cold fireplace, solid and still as stone, the blood draining from her face as the realisation set in.

"Miss Meredith Jane Mortimer?" the Detective Inspector asked.

She just nodded once, swallowing silently.

"I think you know why we are here."

She nodded again.

The old woman bustled importantly in, smiling at one and all.

"I'll just put the kettle on, shall I?"

Arnold could see the shock settling on the daughter's face, and was relieved when the Sergeant stepped forward, gently taking the old woman's arm.

"That would be nice. Let me help you. Kitchen out this way, is it darling?" And he lead her out of the room.

The Detective Inspector waited until they were clear before taking his coat off.

"Miss Mortimer, I am Detective Inspector Romney. Special Branch. I have a warrant for your arrest." He let that sink in for a moment before continuing, "Now, we can do this the easy nice way, or we can do it the sad way. The easy nice way is if you co-operate and make a statement, and help your people sort out the mess you've made. Then we can talk

54

a light sentence. The sad way is: you leave here in handcuffs, your mother in tears, spend four months in remand prison and then go to trial at the Old Bailey, and with what we have on you, you will go down for a long one in some horrible place. The sentence for high treason, in case you've forgotten, is twenty five years without remission." He paused. "So what's it to be, Miss Mortimer?"

She began to cry big silent tears down her powdery dry cheeks.

"It was just old stuff," she eventually mumbled through her sobs. Arnold found it all rather pitiful.

Her debrief was given over to Mrs Hogan, the interrogator who had provided the first clue from the 'FRUITGUM' case. Meredith Mortimer had signed an interim confession the night of her arrest and the job was now to establish her motive, technique and the scope of her treason. It had been agreed already that there would be no attempt to turn her into a double agent by feeding false information back through her. Her work in registry dealt only with past issues and the Soviets would smell a rat immediately if she were upgraded into a current operational position, supplying hot data.

They sat in a dreary drab green room in the high security remand area of the Royal Military Police facility outside Aldershot.

"It's over Meredith," Mrs Hogan said gently. "He will be going home in disgrace with all the publicity we can manage. He will never be allowed out of Russia again because every Intelligence Service in the world will have him flagged. He had a less subtle warning last night from a couple of the Fairies."

Across the old chipped table, Meredith sat in a tearful silence, broken only by the odd pathetic sob or sniff.

"Was he paying you? Was it for money? Thirty pieces of silver perhaps? Or do we have a dyed in the wool communist here?"

Meredith looked up hurt. "No," she said righteously.

"Or perhaps you just believe in freedom of access then?" she asked sarcastically.

"No! Why are you being so awful?"

"Because you betrayed your country! My country! You handed over classified information to an agent of a foreign power, to the bloody USSR! What did you bloody expect, you fool?"

Meredith began crying again.

"Oh, for God's sake, stop crying! Why? Why did you do it? What on earth possessed you? You aren't a communist. You say he didn't pay you."

"You don't understand. I knew you wouldn't. None of you would. I love him. That's why! I love him, and you have sent him away, so damn the lot of you..."

"You have done that quite well already without us. Come on, Meredith. You're no fool. You must have suspected something when you met him." Mrs Hogan's tone had become almost big sisterly. "Men that handsome don't chase girls like you and I. A sexy foreign accent like that? You've done the security courses. It must have been like a flashing light..."

The fight was gone now and she replied almost mechanically. "I meant to tell Mr Black. That's SOP, but I thought I would just wait and see what happened, then we started... you know. I'd never done it before. He was the first, and then I just knew I couldn't not see him again. It was only every six weeks or so."

"A fling is one thing. Treason is another," Mrs Hogan said dryly.

Meredith looked up with an expression that said 'were you born yesterday?'

"Without one there would not be the other," she replied in a voice that was laced with bitterness.

"When did you start seeing him?"

"March 16th. It was a Sunday. I was in the park at Great Windsor. He asked me for directions." She smiled wistfully and blew her nose.

"What year?"

"Two years ago. 1987."

Three days later, Henry Arnold received a call from the Special Branch officer at Aldershot with Mrs Hogan. The Chief Inspector had agreed that he could have half an hour that evening. After that, the plaintiff would be transferred to a woman's remand prison and be unavailable until her trial.

"That's me away then," he said cheerfully to Callows' secretary. They had developed a cheerful banter in the office with Arnold's comings and goings.

"Where? Home to the moggy and the paper?"

"Aldershot Redcaps." He winked at her. "To have a chat with Mata Hari Mortimer. All in life is never what it seems."

An hour and a half later, he showed his pass to the gate guards, entered the establishment and was shown into the high security remand area.

The woman's lawyer was present, sitting self-importantly at a table in the interview room, Mortimer in a shapeless pink cardigan beside him.

"I have only agreed to this because I have been assured it will bear well on my client's case," he said in a strained Birmingham accent.

"I wouldn't know," Arnold replied pleasantly, "but I don't need long."

"You may commence your half hour now," he replied, tight lipped.

Arnold, his patience pushed, answered abruptly, "Don't push it sonny. She is up for high treason, not some traffic offence. I am the man who caught her and I will take all the time I like! Now, why don't you take a walk? You can listen on the intercom next door."

"Rest assured, I will," he said, standing.

After he had left, Arnold shook his head in wonder looking at Meredith Mortimer. "There are better lawyers than that around, you know."

"He's from legal aid," she answered. "Anyway, he's been very nice to me."

He shrugged and sat down, his coat over his lap, and crossed one long bony leg over the other. "I just have the one question, Miss Mortimer."

She nodded at him to continue.

"Why did you purge things from the system?"

"Purge?" she asked

"Yes."

"I didn't," she said flatly.

"You sure?" Arnold pursued.

"Yes," she replied, "I'm not that stupid."

"You didn't purge the Long Knives file from the system?"

"No!"

"You didn't. You are sure of that?"

"I made a few mistakes – but, as I said, I didn't purge anything..."

Arnold's eyelids lowered and he gave a tight lipped smile, as if it were exactly the answer he was expecting. They talked for a few minutes about the file and then Arnold left.

The following evening, as he walked the last few yards down Blackheath Road toward his home, a light blue Cortina with two men inside climbed the pavement at speed and knocked him down. It then shrieked to a halt and, wheels smoking, reversed back over his broken body. Three witnesses saw the incident, one walking his dog, another a woman from her front room window. The third was the same man who had been sitting on the riverbank when Arnold and the Special Branch officers had arrested Meredith Mortimer. He remained in the shadows up the street, not talking to the police and careful not to be seen. Twenty minutes later, blue police lights illuminated the area as officers put up bright yellow tapes and a mobile incident control room arrived. Someone had already found his wallet, and inside the M.o.D. pass with its characteristic but tiny red dot in the upper left corner, which identified him as someone cleared for high security. As a result of this, Special Branch were informed. Half an hour later, Sir Martin Callows was phoned at home to be told of Henry Arnold's murder.

At precisely that moment, Meredith Mortimer was stabbed to death by an unknown assailant inside the remand centre. The accuracy of the angle of entry led a Scotland Yard pathologist, called from his dinner table for the post mortem, to remark that it was either a very lucky assailant or an expert. The blows had both penetrated the heart and death had been virtually instantaneous.

Callows said nothing, listening with intent to the debrief from Adrian Black. It was midnight and John Burmeister, as usual immaculately turned out, sat in the second chair at Callows' desk. They were awaiting the arrival of the Director General.

Black finished reading from his notebook and closed it with a final tired flick of his wrist.

"What the hell is going on?" Callows thought aloud. "First Simonov and the people in the house, then Arnold – and, at the same moment, the Mortimer woman..."

"The Soviets," Burmeister offered, "cleaning up the loose ends perhaps."

"Only in a paperback," Black said, "but they are related. Simonov gave us the clue. Our sniffer and his target got killed because they were becoming dangerous. It's not the Soviets. They were working on the same thing. That's what Simonov said..."

He paused to let it sink in while he thought about his next step. "So the next question is, what happened yesterday that meant Henry Arnold had to go, and go quickly? Once again no time for anything subtle. This was almost a warning killing. Noisy. Dramatic..."

Callows caught his drift immediately. "You're saying that Arnold's investigation turned up something yesterday, and who ever killed him knew it."

"Yes," Black said, "something like that."

"My God. That means they are all over us!"

Callows leant forward and spoke into the intercom. His ever present secretary had arrived back in the office along with Black and he called her in.

"Henry Arnold. Did he stop in to see me or anyone last night?" he asked as she entered his office, notebook and pencil in hand.

"He tried, Sir Martin, but you had gone. So had Mr Burmeister and Mr Black."

"Dammit!" he muttered.

"He tried me today as well," Black said, "but I was over at Century or something..."

Callows looked back at his secretary. "How did he seem to you, worried, anxious?"

"Definitely not. Almost pleased with himself. May I speak?" she asked respectfully.

"Certainly!"

"Well, I have been thinking. I saw him last night before he went down to Aldershot. He said something like 'all is never what it seems' with reference to Miss Mortimer. It seemed he had found something he wanted to pursue."

"He had said as much to me some weeks ago," Callows said. "Said he wanted to stay on it." He looked at Black. "Get onto the duty officer. I want his files. Everything, the FRUITGUM tapes, Arnold's work and the interview notes from Aldershot. All these killings over some honey trap files girl? Doesn't make sense!"

iThe following morning, as Sir Martin stepped into his office, there to greet him was Adrian Black, for once the usual smile missing.

"Well?" Callows asked.

"We seem to have misplaced Arnold's stuff," he said.

"What?"

"Arnold's notes and the FRUITGUM material. No longer in the files. The lot. Gone." He paused while Callows dropped his case on his desk, his mind racing at what the statement meant." I've been up all night on it. Arnold's comment to your secretary: 'all is not what it seems...' Mortimer was just a bonus. There's something else afoot here. Milburn security has been breached. Someone in this building, someone with access all down the line, has walked off with all Arnold's work."

"Who else has been advised of this?" Callows asked.

"No-one, Sir," Black answered, "but I've called in two others. One was Mrs Hogan, and the other is Mortimer's lawyer. He was in the next room when Arnold spoke to her. He remembers the question Arnold put. One question only. He asked her why she dumped the Long Knives File. She answered that she didn't. She was emphatic about it. Mrs Hogan confirms the name as the same that triggered the initial search."

"So we've been so paranoid about a mole we missed the real issue," Callows said.

"That's the way I read it, Sir."

"Right. Get Burmeister in and let's see where we go from here."

It was in the next day's interviews, when Adrian Black was talking to the Assistant Head of Registry, that the break came.

Mrs Holloway was a career Six administrator who had been working in Main Registry at Century House for seventeen years and her lead came almost as an aside.

"Of course, Henry was all through the old files by that time. He had two girls pulling hard copies for him."

"Did he find what he was looking for?" Black asked.

"No, not directly. The file he was after was on the computer system, but we came across a reference. It's almost impossible to completely erase the existence of material when you have multiple cross referencing taking place."

"Sorry. Explain?"

"When a long search is on, and material is slowly coming together, we store it in hard copy form. Only once sections are complete do we load it onto the system and dump the hard copies. All those entries are entered and referenced."

"And he found something?"

"No, I did – although at the time I wasn't sure what it was. I told him some days later that I recognised the signature of the depositor. The individual compiling the file."

"Who was that?"

"Teddy Morton." She paused and smiled at the memory. "You won't remember him. You were still with Five when he retired. He's dead now I believe."

"Did the name mean anything to Henry Arnold?"

"Oh yes. The pair were thick as thieves over the years. Teddy was about ten years older than Henry, an academic part-timer who came on the full time payroll in the mid-Sixties, while still retaining his chair at

Cambridge. Henry was chuffed with the discovery. If Teddy Morton had been the man pulling the Long Knives thread then that was significant."

"In what way?" Black asked.

"Teddy Morton was brilliant. In his day, he was the clearest thinker in this murky little pond of ours. If he had been on Long Knives for any time at all then there was skullduggery in the plot. He never wasted his time. Yes, Henry Arnold and Teddy were well respected. The other in that trio during the cold war years, was of course, Gabriella Kreski. "

"Now that name rings a bell…"

"Should do. She must be in her eighties now. She ran the Gdansk net. You'll have covered her work at Lincoln when you trained. She was WILLOW."

Black nodded as he remembered the case studies. She had lectured once, a softly spoken woman with grey hair – and that had been fifteen years ago.

"But Long Knives is long after she retired, surely?"

"Yes, but she knew Teddy Morton better than anyone. He was her protégé after she came in. She channelled his thinking. Taught him to think like a spy. Him a Cambridge man, it should have come naturally." That was a direct dig at his MI5 background and the Burgess Philby Maclean group of five, all recruited from Cambridge. He smiled and thanked her and, the next day, he drove down to Brighton to pay Gabriella Kreski a visit.

"Put Mahler on, if you will," she asked, settling slowly into a lumpy looking armchair with a sigh.

He did so, carefully handling the old recording and watching Gabriella Kreski in the mirror as the old stiff arm jerked across the turntable and lower itself onto the record.

Her face was deeply lined, pale and dry, but her brown eyes were bright and alert beneath a tight cap of almost white hair. According to records she was now eighty nine years old, but beneath the frail exterior she was as tough as old leather.

"So you want to know about Teddy, yes?"

"Yes," he said.

"Why?"

"I need to know how he was, how he thought…"

"That's no answer," she said crisply.

"You are still covered by the official secrets act?" he asked.

She nodded.

"Edward Morton was working on a file before he retired to Australia. That file has since been removed. Apparently, every trace if its existence has gone. I need to know what it was, what it involved. Then maybe I can determine why it has been removed and who did it."

"You are Counter Intelligence?" she asked.

"Yes, and I need help now. Mrs Holloway in Registry said that you and Teddy and Henry Arnold were a formidable team in the'60s."

"Ah yes. That old busybody!" she exclaimed, remembering. "And Henry. What an old woman he is! How is he?"

"He's dead, Miss Kreski," Black answered. "There are others dead too. That's why I'm here."

She took it all in in a second, her expression never changing.

"That is reason enough. Put the kettle on, young man, and I shall tell you the tale of my Teddy, my clever Teddy Morton."

She spoke for two hours, much of it history and much of it shambling anecdotes, but all of it building a picture for Black.

"So you rated him well?"

"Better!" she said sternly. "He was formidable!"

"And the file? Where do I go from here?"

"Now, you may be lucky and you may see the master's work yet. He never did anything important without backups. My first lesson to him and one he never forgot. This file was never closed by the sound of it, so somewhere he would have a copy, somewhere he could get at it when he felt the urge to think. You know, he never lost a game of chess. Never one. I used to sit with him and we would play. He did crosswords incessantly. I never saw him admit defeat ever. No. If this file was open, then he hadn't finished with it."

"But he was retired..."

"Teddy? No! Just having a break. He could no more walk away from a thing like this than walk away from a chess game or a damaged icon. He painted like he thought, like he played chess. With clarity and precision and a perseverance that was frightening."

It was now dark outside and, looking around, he asked if there was anything he could do for her before he left.

"There is one thing."

"Name it."

"I have a rather vulgar but very English passion that is hard for me – well, with my arthritis and the fish and chip shop all down those long stairs..."

He smiled and, twenty minutes later, he was unwrapping her dinner over the sink.

It was when he handed her the plate and the tomato sauce bottle that she looked up at him.

"Is this the Square file you are concerned about?"

"The what?" he asked quickly

"Something Square?" She waved a fork, cursing her memory lapse.

"No," he answered disappointedly. "Long Knives."

"Probably the same thing," she said with a flick of her ancient wrist.

"You know of it?"

She studied him for a moment, her fork poised over a piece of fish. "He was here before he went to Australia. We played chess. We talked. He thought he had the pieces of something. Something big. In America. In West Germany. And maybe, he thought, even here. It might be he was right. But it was all very vague." She shrugged as best she could with old tired shoulders. "Be careful, young man. I am old it doesn't matter for me anymore. But you be careful. This Square, if this is your Long Knives... be careful."

When he had gone, she sat and thought about it and wondered if she had helped or confused him.

CHAPTER FOUR

With Gabriella Kreski's warning fresh in his mind – and the deaths of seven people a horrific reality – Adrian Black decided to ignore normal investigation recording procedures and clamp the lid down tight. He would run a file, but he would hold it. There would be access for no other. He would report confidentially to Sir Martin Callows, and ask the D D-G to limit involvement to essential staff only. With luck, that would be John Burmeister, William Warren, the head of 'A', the Soviet desk at Century House and possibly the Director General.

When he arrived back in London, he went straight into his office, threw his coat on the hard chair in the corner and began reading the personnel file of Edward Morton, looking for a link. In his long experience with people he knew that very few men truly lived alone. Everyone had someone, or something they trusted. Edward Morton had one and he must now find it. He debated briefly going back to Gabriella Kreski's with a search warrant but dismissed the idea almost immediately. If she had a copy of the file then he would never find it. The woman had almost invented most of the accepted hiding places that the trade used and, besides, he didn't want to alienate her.

The file was thick with cross references to vetted acquaintances and people at Cambridge – and he began with those, but only after circling the reference to a daughter in red. By midnight he had made a list of people he wanted to talk to, most of whom were either in Cambridge or nearby. Even those who had retired still seemed to be unable to throw off the gown sufficiently to move away.

He picked up the phone and dialled the internal extension of the deputy head of section 'D', the real reason for Milburn, the Acton Fairies. The man was still at his desk and Black gathered up his coat and walked down the stairs to his office.

Jonno Smith was a street smart ex-field operative who had risen up the ranks slowly and was finally given the section's day to day management by Callows after being run over by a Renault while on a job in Spain. He was one of the few Fairies whose snap judgements were impeccable – and now, with a twisted spine, he had to make them from a desk.

"Hello," he said cheerfully, "come to audit my expenses or is this social?"

"Social... sort of," Black answered.

The grinning ex-fairy pulled open his bottom drawer and hauled out a bottle of Scotch. Black nodded.

"Need a man Jonno," he said taking the proffered chipped glass, "but it must be a back door job. No-one to know."

"Breaking rules?" Jonno answered. "Sorry sport. See the boss..."

"No," Black said, "it's legit, but I want it kept quiet. Not up on the deployment board. No chat."

Jonno raised an eyebrow. "You'll sign the chit?"

"Yeah."

"Good enough. What's the job?"

"Minder. Could be very boring, but if it happens I want the best you have. No qualms, no questions. I don't want some gung-ho little prat. Give me a man who's been round the traps a few times. A bloke who can keep his mouth shut and do the invisible shield bit."

"Pity. I have lots of gung-ho prats. Invisible shield?"

"Yeah."

"Strenuous stuff?"

Black shook his head and sipped his drink. It burnt like fire in his throat.

"Mr Pope," Jonno said.

"Christ, he must be sixty!" Black shot back.

"Best close protection man I've ever seen. He's been around and he knows the business. He looks like apensioner and he moves like a ferret." He stood and walked awkwardly to the filing cabinet against the wall. After pulling a buff folder clear, he passed it to Black. "Most of his jobs go of without a hitch, and when there is a hitch the hitch ends up in a morgue. The last time was that Israeli diplomat. Remember in the foyer of the Guild Hall? That was Mr Pope. No-one saw a thing, not even the cameras. Well, Pope did. Took out the Hezbollah guy from across the room. Two rounds, one between the eyes and the other under the jaw as his head flicked back from the first round..." He paused. "Anyway, he is all we have available."

"The Israeli was five years ago," Black argued scanning the files contents.

"He's retiring next month. Nice quiet job for the last time."

"Oh fucking magic Jonno," Black moaned.

"Do you want someone or not?"

"Yes... yes I do. I also want to draw a firearm. For me."

"Oh dear!" Jonno laughed. "You have been making friends haven't you?"

He briefed Jonno as best he could on the body and the job and finally handed over a piece of paper with the address in Greece. Nowhere on the paper did it mention the name of the friend she was staying with, and in fact Adrian Black didn't know. He also said that Pope was to report to him and him alone.

The next morning Black briefed Sir Martin Callows and, as Black left with a travel bag heading for Cambridge, the D D-G called John Burmeister into his office, and briefly covered the gist of Black's report. "I have had enough of this one John," he concluded. "I have lost good men. When we find whoever is responsible, don't bother with Five or Special Branch. Get a couple of those psychopaths downstairs to take care of it. I don't want to know the details. Understood?"

Burmeister smiled bleakly and nodded just once.

Pope stepped off the ferry gangway awkwardly, an old black raincoat over his left arm, his suitcase in his left hand, a trilby hat firmly on his head. Only someone looking for it would have noticed that his right hand was free. He looked like a retired policeman, or perhaps a retired non-commissioned army officer, with a short grey bristly moustache that ran to exactly the edge of his lip either side. He wore steel rimmed spectacles and beneath the round lenses his brown eyes were flat and hard. Although pressed, his charcoal grey suit was shiny with age at the knees and elbows and his black shoes were polished to a high gloss.

Here on the small wharf he stood out like a sore thumb and he knew it. He would have to get some other kit if it looked like being a long job.

No-one in the service had ever called him anything but Mr Pope. He was the kind of man who was mocked, in his absence, with a certain amount of fear by his younger colleagues, but given a goodly amount of respect by most when actually present. He lived with his sister in a small terrace house in north London and took the Underground to work and read the Daily Mail. In his spare time he worked on a complex network of miniature railway lines that ran through the converted attic, that on Sunday mornings would carry the perfect replica model trains he loved. He knew that the Americans would have taken one look at the attic layout and called him a control freak, but it wasn't control. It was the detail, the miniature perfection of it all. His sister constantly referred to them as toys and he would fix his flat eyes on her for a second and she would remember they were models.

To the people at Milburn he was just Mr Pope, an old fashioned operative from a time when to be an Acton Fairy was to be respected, a tired old war-horse in a technological age where ethics were dying.

Walking down the waterfront amongst the jostling happy tourists, he turned suddenly up an alley and disappeared from sight.

*

Later that afternoon, as Quayle was reading on the veranda and Holly was washing her hair inside, he looked down the path to see a figure walking steadily up towards the house. It was not one of the locals. He closed the book and sat watching. It was only as the figure got nearer that his eyes narrowed with recognition. *Mr Pope*, he thought. *You are not welcome here, none of you are. Not any more.* He stepped up the edge of the low wall and, as Pope took the last steps up the steep pathway, he too with some surprise recognised the other.

"Mr Quayle, isn't it?" he said.

"What do you want?"

Pope wasn't sure what to say for a moment. There had been no brief to expect an ex-service man. No-one had said that Titus Quayle was involved. If he was here, then no-one needed a body guard.

"I am looking for Mrs Clements, nee Morton," he said formally.

"What for?" Quayle asked softly, his suspicion rising.

Pope knew then that Quayle knew nothing of any threat.

"Is this your place, Mr Quayle?"

Quayle nodded.

"So Mrs Clements is your house guest here?"

"That's correct."

"Perhaps we better have a chat, Mr Quayle. There have been one or two problems in London and I have been sent out to guard her."

"What kind of problems?"

"Not my department," Pope answered stiffly, "but my brief is to make sure that Mrs Clements is covered until further notice."

"She has reverted to Morton," Quayle said absently, his mind racing. *Jesus, what is going on? The service putting a bodyguard on Holly?*

"How are your instructions coming in?" Quayle asked.

Pope said nothing, which didn't surprise him. He was now an outsider, and so hadn't really expected an answer.

"So be it," he said, "on your way. When you decide to advise me of the nature of the threat to my guest then I might allow you close enough to do your job. Until then, bugger off!"

Pope shrugged. It was a fairly normal reaction. People didn't like being guarded and normally didn't see themselves as threatened. He would wait until his first call scheduled for the next day and advise his controller in London of who his body was staying with.

At that moment, Holly stepped smiling onto the veranda, rubbing her hair with a big yellow towel. Pope looked at her carefully, as if logging her features in his memory. She seemed happy enough: no tension, no fear. There was no way she was being held here against her will here, that he could see. She was as safe here as she was with anyone. He remembered Titus Quayle well.

Nodding formally to her, he tipped his hat. "Good Morning, Mr Quayle. Miss Morton." And, with that, he began to walk back down the hill, his hat and suit incongruous on the rocky steep slope.

"Who was that?" Holly asked brightly.

"Never mind," Quayle said, "just a man I used to know." But, as he spoke, his eyes scanned the hill, not seeing its beauty or its majestic fall to the gorge like she did, but seeing the shadows and the caves and outcrops and the places a man could hide, like he had done every day since arriving.

That evening, he talked Holly out of eating in the village and they ate indoors, Quayle making light of the unusual situation by putting a candle on the table and producing a bottle of old Cognac from a dusty box. The atmosphere was tense and he barely drank and Holly noticed that. She also noticed when he rose with the dawn, walked silently to the living room window and looked out across the landscape with a pair of binoculars.

"What's going on, Ti?" she asked softly. She knew it was no ordinary morning, because it had been no ordinary night. He had lain awake most of it – not with the nightmares, just awake and alert. Now he was tense and preoccupied.

"Nothing," he replied.

"Don't patronise me..."

He turned and looked her squarely in the eye. "I wouldn't ever do that," he said.

"Well, what is going on? Eating up here? Indoors? Awake all night. Now you watching outside with field glasses?"

He didn't say anything, just looked at her.

"I'm not a bloody idiot, Ti! It was that man yesterday, wasn't it?"

He nodded. "He was here looking for you"

She was angry now. "Well, why didn't you tell me?"

"Because I know him," he answered softly.

"What sort of answer is that?" she snapped. Then, with her face blanching, she realised exactly where Quayle knew him from. "Oh God, he's one of..."

70

"Yes he is."

"What does he want with me?"

"He wouldn't say. His name is Pope. He's a close protection specialist. What you would call a bodyguard." Even as he said the word, he knew that he was much more than that. They only put Pope on people who had a bloody good chance of getting killed because someone was after them. "He is rather good at it."

"A bodyguard. For me? What on earth for?"

"I told him to stay away until he's prepared to tell us. He'll have to get authority to do that from London."

"Someone has probably made a mistake," she said with forced cheerfulness.

"Yes, possibly," he agreed, smiling. But his eyes weren't in on the smile. He had seen Mr Pope up on the hill above the house. He must have been there all night.

It was that afternoon, after they had made love, Quayle lying on the bed with the sheets tangled and damp and scrunched up beneath him, that he knew that he loved her. He was watching Holly wash with water from the big china jug, bars of sunlight filtering through the shutters and striping the shiny glow of sweat on her back, her heavy breasts rising when she lifted the hair off her neck to allow the cool breeze to move over her skin. And he knew, in that moment, that, if anything happened to her, it would be because he was already dead and her God wasn't in heaven after all.

Adrian Black had spoken with three of his list of people when he began walking back to his car in the NCP. The interviews were long and he had only managed four the day before, but at least he was steadily eliminating names from the list. He had checked for a tail several times that day – and, finding no-one, had stopped taking precautions. So it was Adrian Black's misfortune that, as he returned to his car that evening, he didn't notice that he was being followed, not by one man, but by two.

Black took the stairs down into the car park two at a time and so was looking straight down at the steps when he was attacked. A figure loomed up from behind a car, Black getting no more than a fleeting peripheral glimpse, and with lightning reactions his own arm flashed up defensively. But it was too late. The container the man had been carrying crashed into him, and in an instant, there was a searing caustic burning in his face. He tried not to scream as he went down, clawing at the pain as the second lunging splash of concentrated sulphuric acid hit him in the face and neck.

It was the students who saved him. Three graduates collecting their car ran to the screams and one, holding a doctorate in chemistry, had seen lab accidents happen and immediately recognised the smell. Together they dragged him bodily to the toilets, one pouring his tin of lemonade over the terrible still burning facial skin as they ran. There they held him over the toilet, pushing his face down and splashing water up over his face and neck, one shouting to blink quickly, and the third then running for a phone.

No-one noticed that another sandy haired man had appeared at the scene within minutes, and stood with his long coat trailing over his shoulder, watching with some sadness.

That evening, while a ophthalmic surgeon gently lifted the dressings off the terribly disfigured face, Cambridgeshire Police took an anonymous call. The attack, it said, had been a warning for the fascist to mind his own business.

Later that night, a man dressed as a porter silently made his way towards Black's room. Smiling, he held up a staff ID card to the policeman guarding the door and walked in. Seeing he was alone, he looked down upon the heavily sedated figure in the bed. What kind of people are these, he thought, who will blind and maim a man for his diligence? In Afghanistan they would do this and worse – but it was their land and they were savages. He then took a crumpled single stem flower from his pocket and placed it, and a small object wrapped in tissue, beside the bandaged head.

"Be brave, Englishman," he said softly – and, as KGB Major Alexi

Kirov turned and walked towards the door, Black's arm painfully inched upwards until his stiffly bandaged hand could grasp the item and hold it tight, wondering what it was and where the voice had come from.

At Milburn, someone going over Black's desk came across the Morton file and the ringed reference to a daughter.

"Bring her in for starters," Burmeister snapped.

The Head of the Fairies, tagged as Oberon in the 60s by an erudite wit, looked at the deployment board and allocated three men, one from Athens Station, and two from Rome to collect Holly Morton.

His deputy, Jonno Smith, had been waiting for the right moment to discreetly advise his boss that there was a single controller deployment not on the board, and instead of telling him verbally had left a time stamped message in the handover file before going on a week's leave. With all the activity the screen hadn't been read at the handover time, and now the reference had been dumped onto the history file.

"What if she's reluctant?" Oberon asked, needing to know the scope of his task, ever conscious of Sir Martin Callows three floors up.

"Just bloody get her here in one piece! She knows something! Anyone gets in the way..."

"Controller?"

"Me. Have them contact me once they arrive... Let's get this sorted out."

The man nodded. That was, after all, what the Fairies were good at.

With all the fuss and drama, no-one really noticed the long distance call for Adrian Black, and the caller – who didn't leave his name – was told he was off Station.

If Mr Pope was the old-fashioned kind of operative, then the three men who had just arrived on Serifos were the new breed.

The leader was a sallow man in his early thirties, who constantly pushed his lank black hair back up from his face as he spoke into the phone. He was from Athens Station and spoke enough Greek to get by outside the tourist areas. The other two were younger and, unlike him, were wearing jeans, training shoes and open-necked shirts with zip-up windbreakers, lounging round a table covered in dirty glasses. The jackets, unnecessary in the warmth, were to conceal the fact they were all armed.

He finished speaking to Burmeister and walked off, the other two rising and following.

Quayle recognised them with some distaste a good seventy yards from the house. Fairies. His eyes narrowed briefly with the thought. He flicked a look up the hill to where he had seen Pope the day before, putting his cup down on the tray. He didn't recognise any of them – although one seemed familiar as they approached. These were not close protection specialists. Nothing so grand. They were just muscle. Hard men. A rugby team, in the trade jargon. He didn't like the feel of things. They weren't here for niceties.

"Go inside," he said to Holly, draining his tea and again lowering the cup onto the table, this time upside down.

"Why?" she asked, looking up.

He nodded down the path.

"Where?" Her face went pale as she strained to seem normal, trying not to look at the three men now only thirty yards away.

"The loo," he said, before thinking again. "No, go right out the back. Get in the rocks. Wait for me to come and get you."

As she stepped past him into the cool shadowed interior, he walked toward the veranda edge, the empty cup back in his hand held as if full.

"That's far enough!" he called.

But they kept coming, the man in the sports jacket flanked by the other two. He looked at Quayle, recognition flashing through his eyes. The brief hadn't said to expect an ex-service man.

"I need to talk to Mrs Clements," he said. "Get her out here."

He was relieved, in a way, that subterfuge was now unnecessary, but at the same time concerned about the man opposite him. He had seen Quayle once or twice a few years before and certainly heard the stories over tea in the canteen.

74

Quayle looked at him as if he was something that had been scraped off the bottom of a shoe. "What for?" he asked, his voice low with menace.

"She's coming back to London with us. They want her."

"I don't think so," he replied. "She has nothing they want. She is a civilian."

"Hand her over, Quayle."

As he said it, one of the younger men moved round to his right side. "Quayle?" he said, giving a cocky laugh. "This is the Quayle? Looks like Dads Army to me!"

"Shaddup!" the leader said, adding softly, "Stay away from his hands..."

"Na, he's a section eight." He looked at Quayle, tapping his finger against his head, "Gaga, aren't you Dad? Shell-shocked!"

"Button it!" the leader snapped, then looked back at Quayle. "Hand her over..."

The third man had moved up on the left and the leader flicked a look sideways at him. Quayle was quick; he used the distraction to edge forward a pace. He was waiting for the trigger word. Something out of place, something pre-arranged that would mean action. He needed to be close, very close.

"I said no, Weaselface. Now, why don't you take your snotty little yobbos and go back to Milburn and tell 'em I said no?" As he spoke, he moved forward another half pace. *Get personal,* he thought. *Get them angry. Hot blood is stupid blood...*

"Who you calling snotty?"

"Hand her over, Quayle, or we'll take her," the leader said, stepping ahead of his hot tempered associate, a step nearer Quayle.

The man suddenly seemed to realise that he was close, much too close, and he smiled quickly. "Can't we discuss thi.."

The word. That was the word. Quayle recognised it as fast as the other two. As the man reached under his coat, Quayle smashed the tea cup into his face with his right hand, gouging at the eye while his left shot out and grabbed the moving hand of the man on the right, snapping two of his fingers with a vicious downward flick of his own wrist before it could reach the gun.

In his peripheral vision, he could see movement to his right. He pushed both injured men sideways towards the other and turned, lightning fast, to get first cover behind the table as the third man side-stepped his falling partners and pulled his gun clear. The other two were not out of the fight yet, but the last man had been faster than he looked.

As he landed, rolling towards the door behind the falling table, the man fired twice, the muzzle blast deafening at eight feet, the bullets knocking chips of whitewashed concrete out of the wall and hitting him in the face as he scrabbled through the door. Then, suddenly, there were more shots, snapped off very fast, muffled by something.

Quayle dodged around the door jam, his mind racing. *Jesus!* He hadn't expected either of the others back into it so fast. He slipped through into the bedroom and cleared the window in one graceless motion, then dropped into the rocky side garden, his fingers seeking and finding a large stone the size of an orange. Holding it tightly, he ducked back against the wall of the house, then began to move towards the front. One would come this way. Take the guns away from them. He didn't like guns, but when you needed one there was nothing quite like it. On his own, he would have kept moving into the rocks, but Holly was already there. He needed to keep them here. He took a breath and moved forward. It was quiet, very quiet. In short, shuffling, silent steps, he reached the veranda wall. Above he could hear nothing, but something was moving further along.

"Mr Quayle. Please show yourself. It's finished."

He recognised that voice. It was Pope.

"Where are you?" he called. That's why the shots had seemed muffled, he thought. They'd been fired from a distance. If Pope had opened fire then there were dead men there.

"Spare room, end of the veranda. I am standing now. If you have a firearm, don't shoot…"

Quayle dropped and ran the twelve yards to the far end of the wall, still holding the stone in his hand.

"Hold your gun up where I can see it!" he said, edging backwards to look upward.

There above him was Pope: grimy, dusty, unshaven still in his city suit. The only thing clean was the gun, black, oiled and lethal in his hand.

"They're Milburn," said Quayle. "What the fuck is going on?"

Pope said nothing, but his eyes flickered up at Quayle, unable to mask his surprise. Then looked back down at the three bodies. Each had taken a bullet in the centre of the chest and each had a second round either high in the neck or lower face.

"They pulled guns," Pope said. "That's enough for me. I didn't know who they were."

That seemed honest enough for Quayle. Pope was now a friendly. They could think about the other connotations later.

"I'll carry 'em away. You hose down the concrete. Then we better move..."

Pope nodded imperceptibly. As Quayle dragged the limp forms towards the garden's edge, he took the green hose pipe and did as he was asked, the cool water turning pink and frothy, laced with bits of bone and tissue, as it ran round the wall's edge.

Holly poked her head round the door as Quayle dragged the last corpse away by its feet. It was the man in the blazer and, below the terrible jagged wound inflicted by the smashed teacup, half his face had been torn away by Pope's wadcutter bullet.

She threw a hand to her mouth and looked like she was about to vomit.

"Wait inside," Quayle snapped.

For him death was nothing new. He had seen many bodies in his lifetime and had been forced into personally contributing to the tally on five occasions. The Cambodian incident was the worst. He had killed a twelve year old girl. Trapped sixteen miles out of Phnom Pen by advancing Khmer Rouge, he had been caught and, for once, his silver tongue was unable to get him clear. The man he'd been trying to escort to safety had started crying as the interrogation began, and he knew the situation was getting terminal. His charge was a Cambodian academic, prime target for the hysteria. Century wanted him out.

He had waited until there were only two guards and the girl in the room and came off the floor fast, his hands incapacitating the two guards simultaneously with fingers jabbed at pressure points. They were both armed and speed was critical. As they hit the floor, he turned to the girl, willing her not to point the gun she carried – but she was drunk on her own power, innocence as purely corrupted as only the very young can be. He jerked the gun clear from her hands as the first round went of, the muzzle blast scorching his elbow, and slammed his fist into her face in a millisecond of pure fear. Her head snapped back, her nose spewing a fountain of bright blood, and hit the wall with such force that her skull cracked and she fell dead to the floor. After that, Quayle had not hesitated. He'd simply grabbed the academic and pushed him through the window, out into the dark rubble strewn yard. It was four days until they got to the French Embassy. They saw many dead and maimed along the way.

Five minutes later, Quayle walked back into the living room. Holly sat on the floor on a magnificent silk Heraki rug, her legs crossed, her face shocked and pale.

"I told you to wait in the rocks," he said.

"I thought you'd been shot," she said, "so I came down to see if you were OK."

"What? So they could shoot you to?" He bent and took her face in his hands. "This is not over, my girl. Whatever it is, it's only just started. Now, if I tell you to do something, you do it. Your life may depend on it. OK?"

She nodded.

"Right. Go and pack a bag. Quickly now. We have to go. More will come."

"Why Titus? What have we done? " She trailed off in a little girl's voice.

"I don't know," he answered honestly.

She stood and walked slowly through to the bedroom.

Plato the cat was left with Nico – who had the key to the house and would go up in the morning to patch and whitewash the bullet chips in the wall. He and his son would move the bodies down to the water and dump them, and Quayle knew he had no need to worry. These were the islands, where people looked after one another – and, by 7pm that evening, the three of them were on a ferry heading for Hydra, Mr Pope never more than three or four feet from Holly, his right hand in the pocket of his coat, inches from his gun.

Up on the foredeck it was virtually deserted, the only sound the throb of the engines and the bow wave tumbling forever outward. Tired day trippers and tourists dozed in chairs or drank in the small smoky bar well aft. Holly sat on one of the wooden benches a few feet away and Quayle stepped up to Pope at the rail.

"Right," Quayle said softly. "You pitch up claiming to be guarding Holly, and won't say why. A couple of days later, three heavies turn up, get nasty and you do the rescue bit. Only it turns out they're Acton Fairies. You're in trouble, Mr Pope. Now, why do they want Holly and what the hell is going on?"

"I don't know much," he said stiffly.

"Just tell me what you do know."

"I've been unable to contact my control. Getting panic signals from Milburn. I made a couple of calls yesterday. Someone got to Mr Black. He's my control on this one."

"Who?"

"Mr Black. Adrian."

Quayle had come across the man.

"He's Five, isn't he?"

"Was. He transferred a couple of years ago. He was hit. Not dead, but in a bad way. Something's going on. A safe house was hit a few months ago, then Mr Arnold and some woman who had been selling stuff to the other side…"

"Henry Arnold?"

"Yes. Know him?"

Quayle nodded in the darkness.

"Then Mr Black takes over, and it's hush hush. Single controller job, not on the board. My instructions were to guard Miss Morton from any threat. He said that. Any threat."

"I don't think he meant to shoot..."

"They drew firearms," he said stolidly. "She is my body, and they drew firearms. He said any threat."

"It's a genuine enough error. I think you should contact London and go back in. Get this sorted out. Whatever is going on, Holly knows nothing about it."

"I'll stay put until Mr Black is up and around. Then he can clear me."

"And what if he dies?"

"Then I am in a bit of bother," Pope answered. "Because something wasn't right."

"What do you mean?"

"Well, I've had a lot of briefings over the years, but nothing like that one. Report to him and him alone. No-one else. I think Mr Black was onto something. Something big and, whatever it is, it's close. Very close."

"What makes you think that?" Quayle said softly. The hair on the back of his neck had risen.

"Because he was scared, Mr Quayle. He was scared and watching his own back."

Quayle turned and looked over the rail in silence, his eyes fixed on a shimmer of moonlight that lay silver across the oily black Aegean.

"So, Mr Quayle. Now you know as much as I do. I am staying on the job, like it or not. It is easier for me up close and, if you value her life, you will let me do that."

"You may work if you wish, Mr Pope," Quayle said, turning. In the moonlight, his face had taken on a new expression, hard and full of anger. "But you may wish you had gone back to London. Understand this. I am not going to let them take her in without a bloody good reason and some solid guarantees. That means that things could get nasty. Now, you're either guarding Holly or you're working for Milburn. You better give that some thought, because it looks like they may be two different things from here on in. If you're guarding Holly, I'll let you work close with one proviso: you contact no-one but Adrian Black."

"What are you going to do?" Pope asked.

"Let them get a smell of the fox. See what they do."

"That's all?" Pope asked with a raised eyebrow.

"For now."

"I have your word?"

Quayle nodded in the dark. Then it was Pope's turn to stare out at the dark sea. He tried to imagine what it would be like bent over the railway line every day, nothing to look forward to but a walk up to the tobacconist for a paper, and his sister's incessant complaints about the bus service and why didn't he want to come to the bingo. After a lifetime of living on his nerves and his reflexes, a lifetime of discipline and craftsmanship and the eye of the hunter, he knew he could not go back, not yet. To go back would mean to die grey and withered in the attic. He looked round at Holly, sitting with her knees up to her chest on the bench, her hair blowing in the wind. She had said very little since the incident on Serifos, but he knew Quayle was right. She was a civilian and a frightened one at that. It was simple. Her life was in danger and he was a close protection specialist. So be it.

He turned back to Quayle, pulled his hat down firmly on his head, and pushed his rimless spectacles up with his forefinger.

"Agreed," he said

The acting deputy department head of the Fairies at Milburn sat back and read the contact log with some concern, his bushy eyebrows creasing. He didn't like the 'no contact' tag against the three men on the Serifos job. The leader wasn't too bad, but the younger two had a lot to learn, so it wasn't the most experienced team he had seen fielded. Even reporting direct as they were to John Burmeister, the drills demanded they called in on a regular schedule. The schedule was sacred, and the second fall-back contact could and would take priority in Embassy coded transmissions back to GCHQ at Cheltenham.

The three had been due to report in at 6pm that evening, but so far there had been nothing. The second contact would be scheduled for exactly twelve hours later. He didn't like the hot seat. This was the second time he'd stood in while Jonno Smith went on leave, and the last time had been a real bastard because the wheels had come off the Helsinki job, and Oberon had come in at three in the morning and more men had gone into the field and, by the Monday afternoon, there were two dead Russians in a snow drift near the airport. Dead kilos meant everyone watching their backs in case the KGB retaliated, even though the dead men on this occasion were rogue. Selling secrets and then double crossing the buyer was always risky.

He looked up at the clock. Nine hours until the next deadline.

He moved the status on the board from green to amber alert.

Three floors up, John Burmeister had noticed that his team hadn't called in since midday – but, with other things on his plate, he hadn't given it much thought. The Greek telephone service was infamous and, without being within easy distance of the embassy, other communications were difficult. Besides, it was a routine task and, if anything, Oberon had overdone the manpower allocation with three men. He saw no reason to be concerned and pushed on with other active files, all generated by Adrian Black's list of Teddy Morton's associates and friends.

Within seconds of the team missing the second fall-back contact, the acting deputy department head took a deep breath, calmed himself, and phoned Oberon at home. By 6.40pm, after a quick call to Burmeister and a more lengthy conversation with the Station Chief in Athens, Oberon moved the team from an amber status to a 'red two': Situation Unknown but deemed Critical. The only other stage left was a 'red one': Personnel Dead or Interned, Mission Failed.

At this time, the mainstream Service at Century house became involved, because whatever had happened to the three Acton Fairies could be part of a larger effort or have wider implications, and that notification was in the overnight report on the desk of the Director General, Sir Gordon Tansey-Williams. It was the talk of the building that morning – after all, as one administrator pointed out with morbid glee, the Service hadn't lost three men on one job since 1957 and they were killed when a car crashed in Germany.

For the service, with its strictly defined areas of responsibility, the situation was now becoming confused. The job was still technically under the control of the Counter Espionage department head, but he was still in hospital and it was uncertain when, if ever, he would be out to resume his responsibilities. He had a small, very talented department – but no one individual was capable of assuming control. Burmeister, as the only other fully briefed senior man, had filled the breach temporarily – but now, with a red two code on the board, there was every chance that Milburn would lose the matter to Century.

Sir Martin Callows eased his bulk from his seat and walked ponderously to the fireplace. The whole scenario was ugly. Seven dead and one maimed for life – and now a possible three additional bodies on the tally. All his people and, so far, for nothing. Still no real smell of the quarry. All he had was Black's feel for it. Black had said he thought Henry Arnold was correct in his belief that Meredith Mortimer was an aside to the main issue. Yes she was a spy, yes she had been pillow talking with the Soviet, but that was all. She was simply the method by which Moscow Centre knew that the Service was onto something erased and hidden, something concealed with great care and valuable enough to kill for. *Something called Long Knives by the Kilos, and known about by our dead investigator whose main registry files have gone.* Callows had asked the question of the Head of the Soviet desk at Century the night before, but had been given short shift. The man was not risking his network to simply try and establish the contents of the Soviet's Long Knives file.

"What's in it?" he asked.

"Dunno. That's why we want in."

"Sorry."

"I could order you."

He knew that would be tough. They had known each other for over ten years.

"And I could refuse. Then we would both go before Tansey-Williams. Look Martin, that network is too well placed to risk it for something that might turn out to be a clever Kilo move to get us to blow a network looking for the answers... Besides, we're getting good material out now. I would not like to redirect that effort. Sorry chum."

Burmeister entered through the side door, interrupting his thoughts.

He needn't have bothered; Callows knew by his expression that there had been no word from his team.

A new case officer was assigned to attempt to fill in the rather slender file on Holly Clement nee Morton, and on his five person team was a razor sharp investigator who masqueraded as a gregarious young black girl with the unlikely name of Chloe Bowie.

She took one look at the file and headed straight for Guys Hospital. Two hours later, she had the name of Holly Clements friends and workmates and began working down the list. Sarah Moody was number three on the list and swung the door back with force, her red hair mussed and tangled.

"I'm on nights," she snapped angrily.

"I'm sorry, but it's important. My name is Chloe Bowie. May I come in?"

Why? I want to go back to bed!"

Chloe turned on the smile. "Please?" she asked, holding up her ID. "I won't take to much of your time."

"Oh, for God's sake! Yes, alright! If it's not you, it's the bloody gas board, or some dickbrain with a questionnaire. I suppose you want coffee?"

Holding her dressing gown closed with one hand and pushing her hair up out of her eyes with the other, she lead the way into the apartment. There wasn't much room in the tiny kitchen so Chloe stood solidly in the doorway while Sarah bashed cups about and noisily filled the kettle.

"I need to know about your friend Holly. Where she might be, where she might go if she were in trouble..."

Sarah turned and glared. "Is she?"

"We think she might be, yes."

"And who is 'we' precisely?" she asked arms, folded defensively across her substantial breasts. Behind her, the kettle began to make grumbling noises.

"Foreign Office." Chloe held up her ID again. "Look, all we have is a box number in Greece. We need to know where she is."

Sarah lifted the kettle and began to pour water into the cups. The silence was too long for the investigator.

"Are you mates?" Chloe asked.

"Why?

"Look, let's cut the Omerta bit. You aren't the bloody Mafia. We need her back here. We need to talk to her. But she might also be in some danger, real danger. Now, are you going to waste any more of my time or what?" Chloe stood to her full height of five feet five and glared.

"She phoned before she left. From here. Some Taverna on an island. Left a message for the people she was going to stay with. It's here somewhere."

"What is?"

"The name."

She began fishing round on top of the fridge, amongst old notes and messages and things in a basket.

"A boyfriend?"

"No, nothing like that. Family friend more like it. Remembered it because it was the same name as some American politician or something. In the news at the time."

"What? Bush?"

"No."

"George?"

"No," Sarah muttered

"Not Reagan?"

"No," she said, sifting through the bits of brown paper and jotted scraps, waving a hand. "The guy who didn't go to Vietnam. Holls said *he* wasn't like that."

"Like what?" Chloe asked

"Gutless. Here it is!" She held aloft a small square of pink paper, then dropped her eyes to read it. "Dan Quayle! See, this guy's name is Ti Quayle, care of the Taverna something, looks like Aegean."

Chloe took the note. "Aegean. Taverna Aegean. Quayle." The name rang a bell.

"I want you to promise me something," Sarah said

"What?"

"Holly's had a tough time of it recently. Her dad died couple of years ago. She doted on him, then her husband was killed in an accident. She's a real sweetie. I'm only helping you because you say she might be in danger. She doesn't need any more shit in her life right now..."

"I will bear that in mind," Cloe said honestly, thinking 'she's in it up to her eyeballs.'

*

It was midmorning in Athens, the streets crowded and noisy and the taxi drivers as dishonest as ever. Quayle paid up like a tourist, a little over the odds, not wanting to be remembered for either speaking a little Greek or knowing the correct price. He had taken Holly and Pope to a small hotel where they weren't to choosy about passports. The problem remained, however, that they looked memorable. Pope, despite dusting off his suit, looked grimy and tired, his eyes grainy with fatigue, with no luggage at all. They took two rooms, small and hot with peeling paint, but at least the windows opened and there were two beds in each.

"I'll be about three hours. Get some breakfast and some sleep if you can," Quayle said to Pope. He turned to Holly and was about to speak when, suddenly, she broke in.

"I know. Do what he says," she said.

"Mr Quayle," Pope began. "I need ammunition."

Quayle raised an eyebrow.

"I used six. I have fourteen left. Six of those are Teflon. No good for practice. I will need to do that soon."

86

"Teflon?"

"For body armour," he replied.

Quayle shook his head sadly before replying, "What do you want?"

"Nine mil' wad cutters if you can. Otherwise standard hard nose and a hacksaw blade. American are best, or Belgian. Nice shiny new ones please, and not Spanish. I'll reload them myself."

"I'll do my best," Quayle replied.

"Take care," Holly said quietly. The talk of bullets had brought her back to earth.

He nodded and smiled – and, taking a cheap seaman's cap from his bag, he pushed it into his pocket and left the room.

After he was gone, Pope pushed a chair under the door knob and climbed onto the nearest bed, his gun out and in his hand, his body shielding the other bed.

"Rest," he said. "We'll get some food sent up later."

"Here?" she asked, indicating the second bed. "I wanted a bath and though I might use the other..."

Pope shook his head. "Use this bath in here. Then that bed. No lights on and stay away from the window."

His tone of voice said the matter wasn't up for discussion, so Holly went into the cramped old fashioned bathroom, turned on the tap and stood watching the lukewarm brown water trickle down onto the stained enamel.

Quayle found the warehouse, much where he expected it to be, behind the chandler's shop in Piraeus. He was pleased, because the description he'd been given six years ago by a man now dead matched perfectly the man standing in front of him: Greek, fat and unshaven, his jowls wobbling under his porcine little eyes. His open-necked shirt had sweat stains under the arms and, as Quayle leant over the desk, he could smell his odour.

"Constantine?"

The Greek looked up and saw a big man in a scruffy jacket and a sailor's cap, squeezing something in his hand. The accent was French, guttural and harsh, the sound of the Marseilles docks. He looked at the hand and noticed the ugly purple scar.

"Who are you?" he asked, leaning back importantly on his seat. Behind him, a younger man leant indolently on a packing case, his hair brushed back in a parody of James Dean.

"That is not important. I need blank passports. I am told that you are a man who can help when one has such a need."

"Oh, who told you that?"

"A man," Quayle answered cagily.

Constantine pondered the risks for a moment – but his greed got the better of him. "I might know someone who could help you. But these things cost money. You have money?"

"How much?"

"Hundred thousand drachma each."

"Merde! I will give you that for six."

"If you are short of money, used are cheaper. I have a friend who can make a few changes, take a photo…"

"*Non*. New ones."

"Six for four hundred thousand. Used," said Constantine. "I don't have that many new ones. My last offer. Take it or leave it."

Quayle instinctively knew he was telling the truth.

"I will pay that if you can deliver now. European passports!"

Constantine raised an eyebrow. Behind him, the sharp looking youth eased onto his feet.

"Take a seat," he said, standing ponderously and wiping the sweat from his face. "I will get your merchandise." A few minutes later, he was back with a brown paper bag. "The money," he said.

"Let me see," Quayle answered.

Constantine held open the bag and took out the contents out. Quayle was relieved to see four British and two EEC passports.

Constantine shrugged. That was when Quayle knew it was only just starting. This had been all to easy. The old sell it, then get it back up the street trick. *Stuff it,* he thought. *Lets get it over with.*

Throwing Constantine a handful of notes, he scooped up the passports and jammed them into the bag.

"Constantine. I am going to leave now. If your little pretty boy follows me or tries it on, I will break his fingers. Then I will come back and break yours." He smiled charmingly, the hard tense French sailor gone, and a more worldly and considerably more threatening character emerging.

"Who are you?"

"Never mind. But I owe you one. You sold out a friend of mine once. I don't forget that kind of thing."

With the bag in his left hand, he leant forward, took the Greek's hand in his right and began to apply pressure. The cords of muscle in his hands and arms rose up in hard ridges.

Constantine gave a girlish shriek and, as the smooth hard man leapt across the floor to his boss's aid, Quayle let go the fat hand, dropped low and caught the foot flying for his groin, pulling it up and twisting. As the man flailed to fight back, Quayle heard his face hit the hard floor with a satisfying thud and put the boot in twice, hard, into his kidneys.

Still holding the bag, Quayle looked at Constantine. "Get the message?"

The Greek nodded quickly, his jowls wobbling.

Quayle walked quickly from the warehouse and, once in the alley, reversed the jacket he was wearing and pulled the plastic brim off the cap. Now he was wearing a beret and the dark blue sailor's jacket was a muddy fawn. Hailing a taxi, he told the driver to drop him at Parliament Square. There he would disappear into the thousands of tourists and make his way to the bank where he kept his Athens funds. Like most intelligence men who had spent time in the field, he had appropriated funds over the years – the slush payments, the bribe money – and secreted it in accounts dotted around the world. One never knew when one would need it. He took twenty thousand pounds and another two passports from the safe deposit box and, ten minutes later, was in a call box phoning a contact from long ago. The man told him that he would have the ammunition and be in the café opposite the hotel in two hours. Quayle then crossed the street into a large store and, now in just shirt sleeves, began buying a few things for the team:

shaving gear, clothing, toiletries, several hats of different sizes, sun glasses and two or three overnight bags to hold it all. His last stop was the Olympic Airlines office where he bought three tickets on the afternoon flight to Milan.

When he arrived back at the hotel, he was in a creamy silk shirt and sporting a Panama hat. They had to move today. The Greeks would be hesitant and slow to action any request to check passports at the airport, but if someone had put two and two together already then they may have also put a Interpol alert on the request, and to this the Greeks would have to listen. While he had two spares in other names, Pope and Holly were using their own passports to get clear of Greece. Holly was delighted to see him and promptly ordered him some breakfast. Half an hour later, he briefed them while splitting up the purchases and drying his hair still wet from the shower.

"OK, from here we go down to the café, collect the bullets and head straight to the airport. Milano."

He had chosen Milan because, from there, they could drive to Venice where he knew a forger and could get the passports done. It was also an excellent jumping off point into Europe, with the Brenner Pass into Austria only a few hours away.

"What are you going to do with your gun?" he asked Pope.

The bodyguard was now looking much more respectable, bathed, shaved and in clean clothing. He had even trimmed the thin grey pencil moustache. His eyes had lost the grainy look and were back to their familiar selves.

"What do you mean?"

"At the airport."

"I'll try my Diplomatic Warrant."

Quayle nodded in agreement. It was worth the try. The warrant normally quoted a flight number and an airline, but on occasions and in some airports they barely looked at them. A warrant issued by Her Majesty's Government was distinctive and almost unforgeable. Besides, they would have logged Pope on his way in and would be expecting him out. A small detail like a ticketing mistake would be understandable.

"Don't forget to buy Ouzo at the airport," he said to Holly.

"Why?"

"Every tourist takes some home. You are a tourist. Mr Pope and I will check in separately. We will all be travelling as individuals. We'll never be more than ten feet from you, but you must pretend you don't know either of us. Let's go."

Chloe Bowie sat straight-backed in front of the Case Officer, having taken an instant dislike to the man. He was not only sexist but a chauvinist with it.

"What have you got?" he asked, without looking up from his work.

"Holly Clement went to stay with people in Greece..."

"I know that," he interrupted.

"I have a name," Chloe said stiffly. "The name of the person she went so stay with."

"I should hope so," he said. "Look, you said you had something important?"

"The name... it rings a bell. Quayle."

It was only now that the case officer looked up. "What did you say?"

"Quayle. That was the name."

"Initial?"

"T, sir. Possibly Timothy or Thomas or..."

"Titus! Titus bloody Quayle. Ring a bell. It bloody should do, girl. He's ex-service. Retired a couple of years ago. Booted out on a section eight." He laughed then, short and hard. "Good girl! Now, get your bum upstairs and get your report written. This will set the cat amongst 'em. Three Fairies on red two and who should turn up? Titus Quayle," he wondered, "what have you done?"

He laughed again – but now it had a nervous, jagged edge, and as Chloe walked away she felt pleased. She had never met this Quayle man, but if he could drive the normally taciturn case officer to nervous chatter with just the mention of his name he was her kind of guy.

CHAPTER FIVE

Burmeister was angry.

As he paced his office, his secretary waved the visitor in without announcement. He was the senior psychiatrist used by the service, a distinguished man in his field. Dr Phelps specialised in nervous disorders brought about by extreme or prolonged stress, and he had treated several chronically ill Secret Intelligence Service people over the years.

Burmeister came straight to the point, standing over his desk, his suit coat buttoned formally. "I have problem with a diagnosis you made. Doctor Phelps."

"Presumably you are talking about Titus Quayle."

"I am," Burmeister snapped.

Phelps had been expecting the conversation to be about Quayle but had not expected Burmeister's hostility.

"There are no hard and fast rules in psychiatry, Mr Burmeister. My assessment of the patient was after two years interment in a prison which reputedly people never leave. He was systematically beaten, he was crucified, he was alternately starved of both water and food. He was the subject of sleep deprivation and physical torture. Furthermore, nobody lifted a finger to help him. He was ignored by the service and his country when he needed their help most and had to finally effect his own escape. My best judgement was that he would never again be fit for duty. There is only so much the human body or mind can take and, in this instance, the limit was reached." Phelps held up the file.

"Doctor Phelps, I have three men missing. I believe Titus Quayle is involved. Now your report suggests that the man's nerve is shot. It suggests that he would avoid involvement. It suggests he would end up a recluse, shunning the world and its problems, angry, bitter, beaten?"

"Yes, that is a view to take. I would say you have a strong chance that is how it would be two years on. Superficially, he would appear normal. Angry yes, bitter, yes... but beaten? No."

"I have reason to believe he is involved with the disappearance of my men."

"I doubt it," said the doctor. "He felt deserted, betrayed, forgotten. He felt he was expedient..."

"All operatives know that they are on their own sometimes!"

"Not for two years in a prison like that, they don't. Titus Quayle has every reason to hate the lot of you. But, in spite of that, I consider his involvement in these incidents unlikely. He was a romantic, a loyalist – essentially a patriot. These are very deep convictions and, while he may harbour resentment for the way he was treated, he is still essentially a decent man. I re-read the file before coming over, not that I needed to. I remember him well. He quoted Keats and Shelley. He has done some unpleasant things in the name of his country and has protected himself to some extent with a shield of cynicism – but, as I said, it's unlikely he would get involved again. Too many wounds that go to deep. He wouldn't want them reopened."

Burmeister thought about that for a second. "Could he have got it together?"

"What are you asking? Could time have healed?"

"Yes."

"No," said Phelps, with conviction. "Not time. Not in two years, anyway. It would take something else. A belief. A new cause – something essentially decent, something pure in spirit perhaps. One of the chaps who dropped the atom bomb on Nagasaki spent years working in an orphanage. He finally came to grips with it."

"What else?" Burmeister asked.

"It's a matter of will. It's a matter of wanting to. The human mind is a complex thing. I know as much about it as any man alive. Humans can stave off death by sheer willpower, or they can lie down and die. It all depends on what he has to live for or fight for. If, perhaps, he has loved ones..."

Burmeister thought suddenly about Morton's daughter. In the file photo she was attractive. He remembered tousled hair and a freckled smile.

"What about a woman?" he asked. "Could a woman drive him back?"

Phelps pursed his lips and thought for a second, inspecting his fingers before answering. "No-one can drive him back, but love is a powerful force. If he found something inherently decent, something he loved, something that needed him, or that he himself needed. It might draw him out. It just might."

"And what might happen if someone tried to take that... thing?" Burmeister struggled with the last word.

"If it was a woman who helped him, and you tried to harm her or take her, you would find him back alright. He would have rediscovered decency and loyalty and you would be attacking it. For how long one couldn't say, but he would be back – and back with a vengeance."

"Capable of what?"

"Almost anything. Even as a patient he struck me as enormously capable and well trained." Phelps stood. "Now it's my turn, Mr Burmeister. Hear me now! Leave him alone. He did his bit and, if he's making some recovery, then we should all be thankful – because the way he was treated was an absolute disgrace. You are concerned about the fate of your men. That I can understand. If Titus Quayle has met a woman, and she has drawn him back, and if your men threatened her, then you have every reason to be concerned for their safety. They may have gotten precisely what they asked for."

"What are you saying?"

"That he should be left alone."

"You sound like you're on his side!" Burmeister snapped.

"I am on his side, you idiot," Phelps retorted. "He is my patient!"

With little ceremony, Burmeister showed him the door and walked back to his desk. He had never liked Titus Quayle, even from the beginning – and since the Berlin incident it had been worse. He hated being shown up by anyone and Berlin was still on his file. He remembered the frightened Romanian girl from their mission and her babbled story and emotional request to see Quayle. He was in Prague at the time, so he told her to go. She had begged for a safe place to hide and he had her slung onto the street by security, irritated by her ridiculous sobbing. She had been snatched from the Embassy doors by her countrymen and Quayle had lost a friend. When he returned, he confronted Burmeister over the issue and Burmeister made a flippant remark. Quayle's punch snapped off Burmeister's front teeth and knocked him clear across his secretary's desk. Now, years later, the wound remained as strong as it had been that day.

Quayle produced a French driving licence and walked up to the Hertz desk at Milan Airport, smiling widely at the pretty girl behind the counter. Away to his left he could see Holly, an overnight bag over her shoulder, Ouzo bottle in hand. Some way behind her, Pope meandered, seemingly aimlessly, looking every inch the retired civil service type of tourist.

Quayle used French for the car arrangements. The Panama hat and silk shirt gave him a dashing flamboyant look that the Hertz girl obviously liked, because she pushed her address and phone number across at him with the forms that needed signatures.

"I will be home this evening," she said in faultless French.

"What a shame Cheri, I will be in Verona. A business matter. But another time maybe?"

"Tres bien," she smiled. "Call before you come. I will be... available. It's a silver BMW, three rows back in the rental park."

He smiled, tipped his hat and walked away with the keys. Ten minutes later, he collected Holly and Pope in the large car park. In the meantime, he had crumpled the hat and thrown it into a rubbish skip and had slipped on a pair of conservative Germanic spectacles and a lightweight pullover. Holly almost didn't recognise him.

The drive to Venice was made in near silence as Holly slept in the back seat and Pope dozed next to Quayle. His gun was in a brown paper bag on his lap and, as they had left the airport, he had reloaded the Teflon rounds into the magazine, then fussed over the new packet of bullets they had collected in Athens, shaking individual rounds and checking the seals on the casings He had had no trouble walking it through security at Athens airport – and Quayle, following him through, cynically thought it was no wonder they had hijackings there.

Soon he stopped the car at a motor way service area and bought sandwiches from a machine, coffee and a packet of sweets. Back on the road, the tyres humming on the wet surface, Holly sat up in the back, sleepily pushed the hair from her eyes and sipped at the hot bitter drink like it was nectar.

"God that's wonderful," she muttered. "Where are we?" Outside the window, beyond the crash barriers, were wet vineyards and small patchwork fields.

"About forty minutes to Venice," Quayle answered.

"Then what?" she asked, reaching for a packaged sandwich.

"Sleep for me," he answered. "Then, tomorrow, I go see a man about a dog. Get some documents done."

"Passports?" she asked.

"Mmmm."

"Isn't that a bit risky?" She leant forward over the seat between the two men. "Don't they have computers these days? You know, say when one has been stolen?"

"We'll only use these ones once or twice. We are in Europe remember. EEC Passports. Half the time you could walk through with just the cover. Just hold the things up, look miserable like every other bastard and walk on by."

"And the other half?" she asked.

"That's why we'll get good ones. If they're looking for us, then it gets more difficult. Then they need to be good. The man I'm going to see will trade these for the real thing. He can provide to order."

"What? He prints some?" she asked incredulously.

"No. He steals." He watched her face in the mirror, and laughed softly at her expression. "From people who won't miss them for a while. Happens all the time..."

Pope sat forward, yawned, and took a sandwich from the dashboard.

"I need to practice," he said unwrapping it. He had not entered the passport discussion. He had complete faith in Quayle's ability to manage the logistics of travel and accommodation. He had his own job and, to do it, he needed to exercise his skills every two days for fifteen minutes. Skeet shooting was good for the eye, a game of squash would do between times, but he now needed a range session. Fast reflex precision shooting needed gun time.

"What do you need?"

As Pope told him, Holly sat back and watched the rain on the windows, suddenly remembering the dead man on the veranda, the shattered lolling jaw, and felt the sickening fear again.

At seven that evening, with a man paid to drive the car to Verona on his way, Quayle paid off the water taxi man and they checked into the Gabrielli Hotel, entering through the back garden's canal gate.

Quayle waited, letting Holly check in with Pope as her father in the next room. He gave her half an hour and then walked round to the front through the deserted laundry area, asking if his wife and father-in-law had arrived yet.

He was shown up to the room by a portly middle-aged man and, twenty minutes later, lay in a hot bath. Stage one was over. They were clear of Greece. A few days lying low, some new papers, and they would move on, throwing the scent of the fox to the wind.

*

It was a girl on chartered yacht who saw the body. It was floating face down in the water, bobbing on the small waves. At first she thought it was rubbish bag that someone had thrown over the side – and, being conservation minded, she was about to suggest that they pulled it aboard. Then the skipper saw it. The boat was a sixty footer and, under Greek law, required a local man in command. He had been making a living at sea for fifteen years and had seen bodies before and recognised it immediately. Dropping the main, he started the engine and swung the boat back round; then, in front of his silent charter party, he hooked

97

a rope around one leg and, using the mizzen boom and a winch, hoisted the body onto the afterdeck. He had just come up from below with a blanket to cover it when one of the young men saw the second body tangled in seaweed floating nearby. The skipper had never seen a gunshot wound, but it was obviously not the fishes feeding that had left a wound like that – and accidental drownings don't have ropes around their feet – so they headed back into Serifos and the authorities.

*

Sir Martin Callows stood granite-like in the bay window of his office, his leonine head hanging down and brooding as Burmeister ran through his report.

"Get him, John. He knows something now. He was close enough to Morton and now the daughter."

"Knows something? He could be everything. He knows our systems. He's linked to the daughter. Black had her name circled. Now the team hasn't reported in, and they were going to his house..."

"Did you know that?" Callows asked.

Burmeister had been waiting for it. "No Sir, I didn't."

"Slack, John. Bloody slack. I don't pay you what I do for sloppy work. Understand!?"

"Yes."

The telephone rang, its muted buzz dying as Callows' secretary answered it. She popped her head round the door and smiled. "It's for Mr Burmeister. Urgent."

Callows nodded and Burmeister snatched the grey phone up. Thirty seconds alter, he replaced it and looked at Callows.

"Red one confirmed," he said. "Two in the sea of Serifos. Pulled out by a charter boat. Athens Station Chief has just done a positive ID. Third still missing. He sent a man up to Quayle's place. Fresh paint job on the porch, bullet holes underneath. Hair and bone fragments in the garden by the wall."

"I want him!" Callows seethed. "Concoct some suitable story. Get everyone in on it. The French, the Italians, the Germans, Interpol, Five, everyone! He's snapped. He's gone rogue. We don't need this one getting away on us. Understand?"

"I do."

Callows had lifted his head, his eyes red and angry. "Take Oberon aside. Have a chat. Metro this one. Get a few freelancers onto it. Slip the leash and let them run..."

Sixteen years before, there had been a Bader Meinhof man who had gone on a rampage, killing not only in the West Germany, but in France and Holland as well. In a six week period nineteen deaths were attributed to his actions. His name was Andre Weber and he was eventually shot to death by Surete officers on the Metro in Paris, who then melted into the crowd. No attempt was made to arrest him. He was simply executed by the first intelligence service to get to him. He had crossed the line and would never be allowed a trial. Since then, seven people had been executed in a joint inter-intelligence service action after one country's service had flagged the need. Even the KGB had co-operated on one occasion, when an ex-French agent had had a nervous breakdown and begun killing red-haired women. He had skills the police couldn't match. The intelligence community had a responsibility to clear up after itself. The technique required the man to be pushed underground by publicity and civil police. There he would need to use old contacts, old routes and known methods. There, in that other darker world, he could be trapped like a rat.

Burmeister nodded.

Quayle stood in the doorway, larger than life. In the room, the woman shrieked with delight and waddled to him, her mammoth arms encircling his waist like elephant trunks, lifting and hugging him all at once.

"Put me down Florentina," he said, still laughing.

She dropped him and stood, solid as a building, her tiny hands on immense water tank hips.

"So where have you been?" she bellowed. "Three years or more! Keep doing that and I will never marry you!" She wobbled with laughter before remembering her manners. "Coffee. I will make coffee. You will want Papa. He is coming, but until then sit and take coffee and talk with me."

She beckoned with one huge sweep of her arm and he followed her into the kitchen.

"How is he?" Quayle asked.

"Good enough for his age. His heart –" she made a very Italian waggling hand gesture, "– but the shop does well."

The shop was a small dusty gallery behind St Marks, where Eduardo Rocca sold minor modern masters, etchings, sculptures and the odd very good forgery. Venice had long been the home of many of Europe's best forgers and, in the tradition set by his father, Eduardo would move two or three a month, mostly to American and British buyers. As forgeries went they were outstanding. Several had passed through the famous auction houses in recent years, gaining the valuable transfer records and receipts that were accepted as authentications by most.

He had asked Quayle to paint for him on several occasions and, although Quayle had refused, he had valued and appraised several fine Russian pieces over the years, catching Eduardo out on three.

When Eduardo finally arrived home, a bright smile creased his old lined face at the sight of Quayle. "So you are back," he said in English. "Welcome, welcome!"

"I am, Eduardo. Thank you."

"You have come to paint for me? Eh?"

"I am but an amateur compared with the masters you have!" Quayle said gallantly.

"Ha!" Eduardo said raising his hands to the ceiling. "Flattery no less! Florentina, bring a bottle of wine. A good one." And, as the big girl waddled off to find one, Eduardo led Quayle onto the tiny balcony over the canal, bright with potted geraniums and painted sills. On the street below, a noisy restaurant served meals to tourists.

Eduardo took Quayle's hands, lifting them to the light.

"Someone didn't like what you were doing," he said bitterly. "Can you still work?"

Quayle nodded.

"And you didn't come here for idle gossip or sympathy," he said softly.

"I need to see the boatman," Quayle said.

Eduardo raised an eyebrow. The boatman was a forger but of a different kind. He supplied share transfer papers, passports, birth certificates, licences and the like. He was the best in Southern Europe and preferred to alter the original wherever possible. These days he was a hard man to find. He used cut-outs and rarely saw a client in person after a set of documents he provided landed a Mafia Cappo in a prison in New Jersey. He knew that the Americans had switched to computers that summer, but the Mafia had supplied the originals. He was not to know they were red hot. The end result had been a contract on his head and, being a natural coward, he went underground in the city of the canals, as far from the hot Mafia drylands of the south as possible.

"That is always difficult, Titus."

"I know. But I need a job done. Must be him, he is still the best."

"Leave it with me."

"No," said Quayle. "I don't want you involved. This one is likely to get nasty. I'm at the Gabrielli. Room Seventeen. Have him contact me. I will meet him anywhere he likes."

Eduardo shook his head. "No good. He won't see anyone but those he knows. You will have to use me. Tell me what you need so I can tell him."

Quayle thought about it for a second. He wanted to avoid using the old man at any cost, but he needed the papers badly. "Passports. Good ones. EEC. Two each for these photos." He held out a small packet. "Then I want him to re-work these. They'll only be good for one try each, but it will all help."

"I will try him tonight," Eduardo said.

"After that, you stay out of it," Quayle replied. "Tell him to use a drop to get them back to me." He handed over another envelope. "This should cover the work."

"Come to the shop tomorrow."

For a moment, Quayle was silent. Then he dared to venture, "Another couple of favours Eduardo..."

"Name them," the old man said proudly. He had always liked Quayle.

"Your nephew still in the gun club? I need to get a friend of mine on a range for half an hour. Some time quiet, if you know what I mean. I also need a couple of things..." He handed over a small list.

Eduardo looked and raised an eyebrow. "Should be all right. He is the membership secretary. He owes me money and he owes me silence. He is sleeping with a sixteen year old girl in the church choir. His wife would be very unimpressed. The youth of today," he sighed sadly. "I'll line up something for tomorrow night."

"Thanks Eduardo. I appreciate your help."

"Poof! It is nothing. Come tomorrow, see a fine etching I have. You will love the workmanship. It's a Durer!"

"I'll bet it is," Quayle smiled, taking a glass from Florentina who had re-entered the room with a tray in her hands.

The following morning, Quayle took Holly to meet Eduardo at the shop, the old man fussing around her like a delighted prospective father-in-law. Taking her by the hand, he stood before a large Renaissance period piece.

"You like?"

"It's wonderful," she said. "It must be hundreds of years old!"

He leant forward conspiratorially. "Three months old, six hours in the oven and some liberal treatment of dust and oil through an airbrush gun. Presto!"

Holly laughed delightedly, then stood back while Quayle and Pope made arrangements for the range session and talked other business. Quayle was pleased. The boatman had accepted the job. In three days, the papers would be ready – not bad, Quayle thought. But the old man wasn't finished.

"Titus, a word please," Eduardo said softly.

Quayle followed him back into the office where Eduardo lifted a newspaper from the desk.

"Bottom left," he said, handing it over.

Quayle quickly scanned down the page and the headline leapt at him. The bodies had been found, a gruesome find for a charter party of tourists. The story said that a madman was on the loose, and a continent wide manhunt in progress.

And there, in the centre of it all, was Quayle himself: an old photo, one taken after he had escaped from the prison. He had been thin and exhausted and he stared into the camera with sunken, hunted eyes.

"They are onto you, my friend," Eduardo said.

Quayle just grunted. He read it again, looking for mention of Holly or of Pope – but there was nothing. Now there was no doubt in his mind: this was a set up, designed to flush him out.

He looked up into the mirror on the back of the office door. In their efforts to create drama with the old photo, they had missed the opportunity to get a real likeness. No-one would put his face and the photo together.

He kept the paper and they left immediately, Pope following a few feet behind Quayle and Holly. Once back at the hotel, Quayle showed Pope the paper. The man took it carefully, placing his glasses on his nose before lifting the page. He read it twice and then handed it back, neatly folding his spectacles and putting them back in their case before speaking.

"They want you out running. You have something they want."

"Holly?"

"Not just Miss Morton. Not any more. They would have emblazoned her picture over every paper in Europe, which they may do yet. No," Pope said, "it's something else. I think they link you with the problems in London."

Quayle looked him in the eye. "And what do you think, Mr Pope?"

Pope looked back, his eyes hard and saurian. He put one hand up and stroked the thin pencil moustache. "It's possible," he answered finally.

Quayle wasn't bothered with the look. He leant forward, close to the gunman. "I could have killed you a dozen times already."

"I know that. It's not your way. That is why I think it unlikely that you are part of London's problem."

"We have a deal, Mr Pope," Quayle said menacingly. "Be sure you remember that."

He was already at the door before Pope spoke again.

"I could have killed you too, you know."

"You could have tried," Quayle said. Then, surprisingly, he smiled – and for the first time in his life Pope felt a web of fear.

That night, he sat with Holly and explained the new situation.

"Do you think Pope is right?" she asked.

"He could be. That's a bit of the service I never saw."

"Why is he still with us? It can't just be Adrian Black's orders? God, that's almost 'mine is not to question why' stuff!"

"Actually, that's the way it works at Milburn. But there is more. He's not ready to pack it in yet. He's one of the old school. A close protection specialist. A gunman. A killer, if you like."

She shuddered, remembering the bodies.

"Don't knock it," he said. "He is a consummate professional, honourable in his own way. You're an innocent and the old school don't involve innocents. I would say that he isn't ready to hang up his gun just yet and this job is staving off that day, but he also believes in what he's doing."

"Is he good?" Holly asked.

"In his day he was rated in the top three in Europe... Scares the shit out of me," he added.

The following evening, a messenger left a package at the desk just as they were about to order food up to the room. The porter walked it up to them, nodding solemnly to Holly as Quayle tipped him. In the thick envelope were the passports and the items he had asked for. As Quayle looked the documents over, he knew why the boatman was reputed to be the best forger in Europe. The documents were perfect, right down to actual entry stamps into places like Turkey, Morocco and Kenya.

They had finished eating, had read for a while and were in bed when the phone rang. Only Eduardo had the number.

"Oui."

From the mouthpiece came a moan of pain. It wasn't a human sound, more that of an animal in agony, a deep primordial groan of pain and terror.

"Eduardo!" Quayle shouted, his finger tearing at the sheets, swinging his legs over the bed.

A voice buzzed down the line: Florentina, hysterical.

"Titus, they are killing papa…"

In the background, he heard Eduardo shout, "NO… don't come Titus, don't come!" Then the voice ceased and Quayle heard the blow in the background.

Slamming the phone down, he jumped to his feet. Moments later, Pope came through the adjoining door, rolling on the floor with his gun up, looking for a target.

Quayle was pulling trousers on. "Look after Holly. Get packed. The bill is paid. After that call, they know we are here. I'll meet you at the vaporeta stop by St Marks." He pulled a shirt over his head, and sat to pull shoes on.

"What's happened?" Holly asked.

"They got at Eduardo and Florentina. They may still be there…"

"It's a trap," Pope said instantly.

"I know," Quayle said. Then he repeated: "The vaporeta stop. One hour from now."

"Please don't go, Titus." Holly grabbed his arm, her eyes wide in fear. "Please."

"I have to. They're friends and it's my fault." He stood and grabbed the small bag that Eduardo had sent.

"Oh my God, please be careful," Holly said. She was starting to cry.

Quayle looked at Pope and nodded. There was nothing to say.

Fifteen minutes later, he stood below the adjoining house and, taking a handhold, he began to climb the ornate baroque walls, moving balcony to balcony. Once on the roof he crossed silently and stood at the edge over the canal, looking down at the restaurant opposite. Eight feet below him was the tiny balcony. He listened for a second or two, but heard nothing. Then, taking the bag from his pocket, he slipped a garrote into his pocket and the fighting knife over his knuckles. The blade was five inches long, razor sharp – and around the handle, like the hand guard on an old sword, ran a heavy set of steel knuckles. The base was weighted with a heavy pommel that could crack bones on the back swing. Used by someone who knew what they were doing, the knife was a formidable weapon and could be used in almost absolute silence.

He lowered himself head first, his hands in the guttering, and looked into the room. It was dark. Someone was still there.

He could see a seated figure facing the door and he waited, looking for movement. It was a full minute before he saw the next movement. There it was: another figure standing in the darkness of the kitchen doorway. The trap.

Pulling himself back up, he moved down the rooftop until he thought he was above the bathroom window, then lowered himself over headfirst, his legs counterbalancing on the rooftop. The window was ajar, and he eased it open fully, trying not to look at the dark water thirty feet below, and hoping none of the tourists looked up to admire the pretty flowers on the balcony or the night sky. As he lowered himself down, he felt the sill take his weight, then dropped through the window in absolute silence. Once inside her paused briefly to allow his night vision to adjust, then moved to the door and paused again to begin his breathing matra. He had fought once in Japan, fought a fifth dan aikido sensai who had beat the hell out of him because he had forgotten to get his breathing and his mental state right before the bout. The reality was that he would still have taken a beating because then he was only a second dan, light years away in experience and skill, but it would not have been so fast or so painful.

He had never forgotten the lesson.

Taking a towel from the rack over the bath – very carefully in case something squeaked – he moved back to the door. Directly opposite should be the man in the chair facing three quarters right towards the door. Immediately on his right should be the kitchen and the second man. He was standing, thought Quayle; he would be fastest.

Closing his left hand over the door handle, he took a final breath, swung it back and threw the towel into the face of the man in the chair. In the same motion he swung his right hand back and up, the heavy pommel slamming into the face of the man waiting in the kitchen door. The blow hit him below the nose on the upper lip, shattering the nose and driving a splinter of bone into his brain.

Quayle dropped and rolled forward. As he came up, the other man scrabbled from the chair, trying to get the towel off his face and a gun up all at once. Quayle hit him in the groin with the steel knuckles, grabbing the gun hand and twisting until he felt the bone break. The man gasped in pain and fell to his knees, one hand to his groin, the other hanging uselessly at his stomach.

Quayle hit him again, this time high in the neck and, as he fell unconscious, the big Englishman darted around the small flat, checking room by room for a third threat. In the small bedroom, he found Eduardo and Florentina. The girl held her father's battered and bleeding head to her breast and cried in fear as the door burst open.

"It's OK. It's OK. It's me."

Florentina looked up, great silent tears rolling down her cheeks. "They have killed him. They have killed my father."

Quayle put his hand down and felt for a pulse in Eduardo's neck. "No, he is alive. Call for the doctor."

Florentina rose like a released balloon, thanking God and the angels. After she was gone, Quayle lent forward. "Don't die on me, Eduardo. You are a tough old bastard. Don't give in…" In his arms he felt the man stir and give a small groan. "Just lie still. The ambulance is coming. Florentina is fine."

Gently laying the bleeding head back, he moved into the small living room.

Florentina was talking in rapid emotional Italian into the telephone, but Quayle moved past her and lent over the unconscious man, jabbing two fingers into a pressure point.

The man came to with a startled gasp and lay there with large frightened eyes looking up at Quayle.

"Your friend is dead. I will ask you some questions. Answer them or you will die too. Comprende?"

The man nodded. Quayle felt some disgust. This was a freelance thug. No honour, no pride, no courage except for beating up an old man.

"How did you find them?"

"The forger," the man hissed through his pain..

"The boatman?" Quayle asked.

"Si."

"Where is he now?"

The man didn't answer.

"Speak!"

"Is morte..."

"Dead? You killed him?"

"No. Pierre."

"Who the fuck is Pierre?"

The man nodded his head back into the kitchen where the body lay.

"Who sent you?" Quayle asked, leaning forward.

"Geneve. The man from Geneve." And then, almost as if he knew he was a dead man for speaking too much already, he snatched at his pocket with his good hand. Quayle stopped it going any further. "They will kill me. They will kill me now."

"Which man from Geneva?"

"Just a man. French. He had money."

"What else?"

The man said nothing.

"Speak, you fucker, or I WILL KILL YOU NOW!"

"He was old and he had a ring... he had a square ring..."

Quayle could hear the sound of the ambulance boat, somewhere out on the water. He stood and, picking up the man, carried him bodily into the bathroom, where he dropped him into the bath. He then bound and gagged him, walked through to the kitchen, dragged the body of the second man in and threw it on top of him. He spoke quickly with the still sobbing girl and got a phone number from her.

He waited until the ambulance men had left, Florentina holding Eduardo's hand, and then called the number. It was the supplier of most of Eduardo's fakes, a man with connections. Quayle had met him before. He could organise to get rid of the body and decide what to do with the other. Now he had to move. If freelancers were in then Milburn might be close behind, and now Geneva was involved.

Pope and Holly waited in the shadows of a newsstand. As Quayle walked up, skirting a pool of light from a restaurant, Pope called out softly, Holly mouthing a silent prayer of thanks.

They stood in virtual silence until Quayle managed to flag a passing water taxi. He had hidden his relief well. If Pope was going to try and take Holly in, it would have been then, while he was busy with Eduardo.

"Now we get a car," he said.

After they had left the water taxi behind, he broke into and hot-wired a late model Fiat, and a few minutes later they were back on the autostrada heading for Milan.

Pope waited until Holly was dozing off in the back before he nonchalantly asked how it had gone.

"Freelancers," Quayle answered with distaste. "Eduardo will be OK."

"How did they get onto us?"

Quayle noticed the 'us'. He was feeling fuzzy, the after effect of the adrenaline surge now having left his blood stream. "They were watching the boatman. The forger. They killed him. That means we must assume they have the passport details."

"Doesn't sound like London," Pope replied with venom. "At least they do their own dirty work."

"Geneva."

"Pardon?"

"Geneva. This instruction came from there."

They drove in silence for a short while before Pope spoke again.

"Mr Quayle, have you ever heard of 'Metro'?"

Quayle looked across in the soft dashboard light. The occasional reflections in Pope's glasses gave him a sinister appearance. He knew he wasn't talking about trains.

"Carry on."

"Chap called Weber in the early '60s. Bader Meinhof. Got out of hand and we chopped him. Not only the service, but the Germans, the Dutch, the Frogs got him on the Metro in Paris. It was agreed amongst the players. Weber had to go. Police couldn't catch him. A trial would have meant hostages, the usual thing. Well, he was just the first. There were others. I worked on two of them. The players taking care of their own dirty laundry if you like. Even the Kilos helped on one. Every time freelancers have been involved. Adds pressure, makes whoever is the lucky bugger make a mistake."

"Jesus, that's sick," Quayle said.

"Think about it, Mr Quayle. Could normal police take you? Not in a month of Sundays. They don't have the skills. They're not trained to deal with people like us."

"What's your point?" asked Quayle, knowing the answer already.

"I think you have a Metro order on you. Why else is Geneva involved?"

"Then why weren't these two working on Rome's orders?"

"A Metro is all stops pulled out. These two were probably on the Swiss payroll."

"But for what reason? They have dead men, but that's their own bloody fault."

"You retired on... medical grounds. I think that would be sufficient to bring in the others."

Quayle didn't reply to that but drove onward, thinking hard. Eventually he turned and looked at Pope. "If that's so, then we'll have to split up to cross the frontier. Every man and his dog will have our pictures..." He sat, trying to work out how many people were after them now, until at last he gave up. *Assume everyone,* he told himself.

He was trying to piece together a plan when Pope gave a dry, mirthless chuckle.

"What?" Quayle asked.

"And you were going to go out of your way to throw the scent to the wind! Dear me, Mr Quayle. I think they smelt it in your pocket!"

"It's not that funny," he said – but then, in spite of everything, he began to laugh too, the tension broken for the moment.

They ditched the stolen car in a seedy neighbourhood of Milan.

After a solid breakfast of cappuccino bread rolls and cold meat, they picked up a new hire car as soon as the Avis office opened, and were ready to cross the border into France by lunchtime. The crossing point would take them into the French town of Modan. It would be fast and busy but Quayle didn't want to take chances.

"Holly, you drive. Mr Pope will be your father." He handed them passports. "You are called Scott. I will meet you in Modan. In the old town there's a cafe called Noire Magic. Meet me there."

"How are you going to cross?" Holly asked.

"Hitch a lift on one of the juggernauts..." And he pointed out of the windscreen at the huge lumbering giants that were passing.

Watching her drive away, he rooted around on the side of the road until he found an old cardboard carton. Breaking it open, he scrawled the words: "My truck is in Modan". After that, he barely had to hold it up. In the camaraderie of the road, a huge British registered Volvo lumbered to a juddering halt.

The truck, returning empty, was waved through the border with minimal checks. In the cab, Quayle sat chatting with the customs men about AC Milan, his black beret pulled down like a cloth cap. An hour later he was dropped off in the square, the driver, an effusive Lancashire man, refusing to drop him on the fast bypass.

Holly and Pope were already there, having passed through very quickly.

"What were the checks like?" Quayle asked.

"Good," Pope said. "They are onto us."

That didn't bother Quayle. He was feeling confident. It was the second time Pope had the opportunity to try and slip away and didn't.

They were also developing the kind of routine close protections needed. When Holly wanted to go to the toilet, she looked at Pope. He looked about for a few seconds, at the other people nearby; then he nodded and walked the twenty steps, Pope's eyes on her the whole way.

"Mr Pope," Quayle said.

"Mmm?" he murmured, not taking his eyes of the ladies toilet door.

"Thanks."

Pope shrugged. He was just doing his job and keeping his word.

*

That same day, Jonno Smith arrived back from leave and, within minutes of being in the building at Milburn, he was being briefed by the man who had stood in for him.

"So we got a red one on the Greek job. I tell ya, I don't like getting Oberon out of bed."

It had been a fast brief and Jonno was still putting his thoughts in gear and looking up at the deployment board. By the look of it, things were going crazy. There were teams everywhere, and in the bottom left corner a red square. He felt a cold shiver up his spine.

"Hang on cock, what Greek job?"

"Burmeister's three. Went to pick up some tart on Serifos and got themselves shot."

"What was her name?" he asked, praying *no, please, no.*

"I dunno."

"FIND IT, you cunt!" Smith snapped angrily.

"All right, all right, don' get shirty," the other said, slightly hurt.

"Get everything on this fuck up! Right now!"

Smith turned to the computer keyboard and slid awkwardly into the chair, his twisted back hurting at the sudden move. Tapping in his access code, he went into the system and looked for his entry, advising Oberon of the off-the-board-deployment he had made. It wasn't there. He scrolled back into the history files, watching the green figures roll over before his eyes, but couldn't find it.

Oh Jesus, sweet Jesus. It's gone. Oberon never knew about Mr Pope. They sent in three snotnoses against the old man himself. No wonder they're fucking dead!

His replacement shambled back and handed over a set of hard copy documents and bulletin records. Snatching the pile, he dropped straight to the objective brief and then, slowly putting the pages down, dropped his face into his hands.

Titus Quayle. It gets worse.

"Whatsa matter, Jonno?" the other asked.

Oberon sat in his chair, listening to the tale, his face like thunder.

"When did Black ask for the job?" he ventured. He was in on his day off, but he had forgotten that already.

"A couple of days before he was hit."

"And you put it on the screen?"

"As God is my witness, I don't make mistakes like that. You know it too."

"What are you saying Jonno? That someone got at your report?"

"Yes I am," Smith replied. "And Quayle isn't your man."

"What?"

"Come one Reg, you remember Quayle! You know the stories! It was him who beat the crap out of two of the Acton instructors in the mess that night. He doesn't like guns. Doesn't need them. Count the number of times he ever used one? Twice, three times in twenty years?"

Oberon thought about that. Smith was right. The stories said that, if Quayle ever said he wanted a gun, World War Three was going to start.

"Then who did it?" he asked, fighting the logic.

"Pope did it, for fuck's sake!"

"What? Gunned his own players?"

"He wouldn't know, would he? Quayle is such a difficult prick he probably wouldn't let Pope near the girl. The old bugger was probably trying to do his job hidden in a bush or something. Three geezers turn up, things get nasty, someone pulls a shooter and it's old man Pope on the scoreboard!"

"Quayle could have done it. He's cuckoo, remember."

"That's crap. So cuckoo he's gone underground and with every player in Europe after him, and we still can't find him? He's as crazy as you and me!"

"Someone found him. A couple of freelancers in Italy came off second best in the contact…"

"Pope?"

"Nothing. He would be on the job. Wherever the girl is. Jesu, the two of them teamed up! Pope going out in blaze of glory. Butch Cassidy and the Sundance Kid."

"I rest my case," said Smith, holding up his hands.

Oberon's face was like stone, the anger solid and real and terrible. "My boys killing my boys." He paused then and looked at Smith, "If you're lying about that computer entry, I will find out and I will cut your guts out, boyo…"

"I'll cut my own out!" Smith snapped. "We've been got at, Reg, well and truly got at! You and me, the three dead boys, Pope and Mr Black, even bloody Titus Quayle…"

"Keep this schtum. Not a whisper. Get your opo in here. Anyone else know about this?"

"No."

"Keep it that way. Just us three and Sir Martin until we find out what gives. OK?"

Sir Martin Callows stood glowering, his back to the ornamental fireplace, his big craggy head lowered like a bull.

"He wasn't to become a factor in this," Burmeister said.

"I should hope not! So now we don't have a madman on the loose at all. We have a professional bodyguard and a trained intelligence agent hiding the woman we need. Bloody clever! I just hope to Christ the House doesn't get to learn of this. Those liberal idiots would hang the service out to dry."

"Quayle is still dangerous," Burmeister said. "He is unstable."

"Is he?" Callows snapped. "Is he really? What did the shrink say?

114

That he may have recovered? That he may, in fact, be one hundred percent fit for operational duties? That he may, in fact, be better than ever after you sent three hoodlums after this bloody woman?"

"They were just supposed to bring her back."

"You ballsed it up!"

"I will call the pack off," Burmeister said firmly.

"No," Callows said.

"Pardon?"

"I said no. I've been thinking about this. We may be able to redeem something from it yet, without becoming a laughing stock. Our objective was to get Morton's daughter here. Why? Because she may have her father's files, or she may know where they are."

Burmeister nodded.

"Don't call off the hounds," Callows snarled. "Blow the horn instead! Quayle was close to Morton. He's close to the girl already. If he thinks that we aren't going to let up until we have the information, then he'll shake it out of the bitch. Their lives will depend on it."

"That's very, very dangerous, Sir Martin," Burmeister said, hiding his glee at the thought.

"We are in a dangerous business! And we don't have any choice. Who else is there? We don't even know where to start. There are too many good men dead already to give up on this, and as far as I am concerned Quayle is expendable."

*

Hugh Cockburn sat uncomfortably in a narrow row of seats, wedged between a bulky General of Tanks and a Colonel from some border regiment, and tried to keep his attention on the speaker in the stuffy auditorium. Glasnost had arrived in Hungary and he was already bored witless with its inevitable familiarisation trips and cries for global peace. On the small stage, a major swung a pointer like a sabre across huge green lines on a faded map, attempting to describe to the gathered dignitaries and reporters the field exercise they were about to visit in the hastily assembled buses outside. Taking a sneaky peek at his watch, he grinned guiltily at the Colonel who saw him do it. The Colonel grinned, winked and passed him something under a mimeographed programme of the day's events.

He took the offering, carefully smiling to himself when he felt the familiar weight and shape of a full hip flask. *Things are looking up,* he thought lifting it to his lips.

He was a tall man, six foot three in his stockinged feet, with sandy blond hair with a frosting of grey above his ears. His face was lean and the lines around his green eyes were pressed in by a constant smile. He seemed to go through life laughing at its vagaries. Today he was here, ostensibly as cultural attaché. Somewhere behind him was the embassy's military man, an Air Force Group Captain, wedged between other visitors.

He burped softly and handed the flask back to the Colonel, who took a deep swig and coughed as the fiery vodka hit the back of his throat, attracting the attention of the General who glared over his substantial jowls like a walrus.

"Sorry," Cockburn whispered, covering for his dipsomaniac neighbour. There were another three hours to go and he thought he would need both the ally and his vodka on the bus.

It was nine that evening when he got back to the Embassy and, as routine, headed straight to his office to clear the cipher machine and check the days status log. As Chief of Station that was his responsibility. The message regarding a new Metro order, the first in over a year that he had seen, was flashed in with a priority clear prefix, and as he read the details he went pale. He thought he had made a mistake and decoded the message again, but the details remained constant. He sat back with his hands to his mouth in horror.

My God, Ti, he thought, *they want to kill you. What have you done?*

CHAPTER SIX

Kirov stood deep in the shadows, watching the doorway to the building until darkness settled and the orange street lights flickered on.

Occasionally people walked past, but few looked down the alley where he stood amongst the battered bins and hungry stray cats. One large brindle-coloured tom recognised another of its ilk through its one remaining eye and, forgetting its suspicion, bravely threaded its way through Kirov's legs. Looking down, Kirov smiled briefly, before his eyes flicked upward again. He had watched the building for three nights now. The old woman had visitors but, so far, none after dark. Tonight she would, and he didn't want to be disturbed – so he waited another half an hour, then crossed the street, walked into the fish and chip shop, ordered and stood politely waiting. Finally, his wrapped bundle in his hand, he walked up to the building he had been watching and swiftly picked the lock. It was done in a second and, sliding through the door, he took the stairs three at a time.

Once at her door, he did the same trick with the pick and stepped into a small hall.

"Who's there?" a fierce old voice demanded.

He walked through to a small drawing room. There the old woman sat.

"Gabriella Kreski?"

"Who are you?" she demanded, hands pushing at the seat, seemingly trying to stand. "Get out!"

"Sit down. I am not going to hurt you," Kirov said pleasantly.

"I know you're not," she replied. She hadn't be trying to stand at all. She had been reaching for something under the cushion on her seat. In her bony old hand was a small calibre automatic pistol.

Kirov smiled fleetingly.

"My name is Alexi Kirov," he said in Russian. "I am from the Fourth

Directorate of the Komitet Gergashnov Borsnavo... and I need your help. I have also brought fish and chips."

She studied him for a second speechless. In all her years in the intelligence community she had never heard a KGB officer admit his profession, but the gun didn't waver an inch.

"You had Adrian Black go out for fish and chips, didn't you? I know. I was watching him."

"Get out!"

"They got him, Gabriella. They threw acid in his face. He never had a chance. He is blind and burned."

Her eyes narrowed for a second. "If he's hurt then it was your people! Your kind don't change," she said fiercely.

"True" he said, "but I just do a job of work. I don't scar and blind men. Any more than you did. Yes, I checked on you. Your cells are subject matter in our school. Did you know that? I never listened very well so I don't remember, but the people in records do. They say you were considered a real menace for forty years. But Adrian is blinded and he was the only man with any feel for this thing. So I need your help, Gabriella – and Adrian needs your help too."

"Why Adrian?"

"Because we are looking for the same thing."

"Did he send you?"

"No."

He could see he would need to expand on his answer.

"I was following him when he was attacked. A few feet closer and perhaps I could have helped. Now he's out of the game and the English have put a desk man on it. They're licking their wounds and, all the while, the trail grows colder."

"The trail of what?" she asked. The gun was still in her hand and pointing at his belly. He thought for a second, weighing the alternatives. So far everyone who knew anything of the matter was dead or injured.

"You don't want to know that. It would be very dangerous. I just need to know why he came here, and what you told him."

"It's dangerous now," she replied caustically, her accent thickening.

"We call it Long Knives We have never worked out why it was not an MI5 job –but the MI6 file was called 'Broken Square'."

She flinched for a second but recovered quickly. That was it! The name she couldn't remember for young Mr Black.

"Why Five?"

"Because it should have been seen as an internal security problem," Kirov answered.

"By the British?" she queried firmly.

"By everyone."

She thought about that and finally lowered the gun a measure. "Are you armed?"

"Yes."

He could have come in with a gun pointed at her. That seemed to be enough.

"Sit down, Mr Kirov," she said. "It was a Six file because the man who wrote it was Six. And that is about all I can tell you."

"He is dead. You knew him?"

She nodded.

Sitting, he offered her the wrapped fish and chips but she shook her head. "I've eaten. But thank you."

"So, Gabriella Kreski. What was it that Adrian Black wanted?"

"You wonder what a working intelligence agent wants with an old retired woman?" she countered.

"Whatever it is must be from the past…"

"He came to ask me about the man who wrote the file. What he was like, how good his work would have been. That sort of thing."

"You knew him well?"

"I did."

"And?"

"He was the best."

Kirov uttered, "Everyone says that about the old men."

She sat back, her eyes blazing at his impudence, and jabbed a finger at him. "You asked, so I'm telling. If your people considered me a threat then they never knew Edward Morton. You youngsters use computers and electronics and satellites. You know nothing! Teddy could look at things with his own eyes. He could smell things! He could take talk and news clippings and snippets and stock prices and give intelligence! Don't you sit here and mock the old men. They were squaring up before others like you were even born."

Kirov laughed softly – not at her but with her. It was a friendly noise, rough and throaty. "So he was good, then – but surely the department has files on ex staff. Why come to you?"

"They have files on staff. But the problem was the file itself."

Kirov pitched forward in his seat. "The Broken Square file? What about it?"

"You don't know?"

"No."

"Ask your mole..."

"Ask who?"

"Your agent in place."

"I'm not sure if there is one. If there was, I wouldn't be here."

"Don't treat me like a fool, young man!"

"We had someone. A woman. Your counter people picked her up and then she was killed. By the same people who did the other killings and attacked Adrian Black." He paused, letting that sink in. "So what about the file?"

"It's gone. Your agent saw to that. Try your masters," she said with forced politeness.

"What are you saying?"

"Adrian Black was here because the file has gone. It no longer exists. Your agent purged it from the system."

Kirov had turns suddenly pale. "You are sure. The file is gone?"

"Adrian told me. The reason he needed to know about Teddy Morton was to work out a way to try and reconstruct it."

"Then we have a problem, me and Adrian Black," he said softly. "Tell me, a kill order has gone out on a retired British agent. A man called Quayle. Did you or Morton know him?"

She looked up sharply. "A kill order?"

"He has gone sour, so they say."

"Sour? No. I don't believe a word of it!" she said defiantly. "He was one of Teddy's boys."

After that, the conversation turned to other things – but Kirov would never forget the way she had hardened, triumphantly, on hearing Quayle's name. When, at last, Kirov stood to leave, he looked down with newfound respect at the woman in the chair. "Be careful now, Gabriella Kreski. I found you. Others might." Then, in a lighter tone and smiling in his awkward way, he said, "There is a cat across the road. He reminds me of you. He is old and tough. If you don't mind, I will take the fish..."

*

Vehicle lights from the highway threw occasional shafts up the dark walls of the hotel room as Quayle lay back on the bed and smoked. It was a characterless room, renovated in the American style, with two double beds and a third foldout sofa. Pope slept the sleep of the dead in the adjoining room and, every now and then, Quayle crossed to the window and stared out into the car park, taking his turn to stay awake seriously in spite of the fact they were now hundreds of miles from the border.

Holly lay curled beneath the blankets, her breathing steady but shallow – too shallow, Quayle knew, for sleep.

"How long?" she whispered finally.

"For what?" he whispered, crossing to her and sitting on the bed.

"You know."

"We'll have a better idea soon. It's been two days since Venice. Things will have died down a bit. Tomorrow I go to see a man."

"Here in Sollonge?"

"Geneva," he said.

"A friend?"

He shrugged, non committal. "He was once. Now? I don't know."

The running was over for the moment. Now he would have to go on the offensive to establish if Pope's Metro theory was true. If it was, then he would have no friends amongst the players, and no way of finding out who in Geneva had issued the kill orders to the freelancers.

"Can't we just go to New Zealand or something?" she asked in a little voice.

"They'd find us there eventually. I have got to find out what the situation is. Tomorrow night we will know."

"But it's foolish showing ourselves. Ti, we've only just got away..."

Quayle shrugged. "There's only so much you can do that is reactive. Then you must take the initiative."

"That is macho bullshit!" she replied, sitting up.

Smiling at her, he did a credible John Wayne impression. "A man's gotta do what a man's gotta do."

It seemed to do the trick. Returning his smile, she pulled him back into the bed and there they lay in silence, Quayle's hand running through her hair.

"It's me, isn't it?" Holly finally said. "It's me they want. You'll have to find out what they want me for."

"They started with you, but now it's me too."

She sat up. "But what have we got in common? It's not as if we are witnesses or something..." She thought about it for a second or two, and then put her hand to her mouth in realisation. "It's Dad," she said softly. "My God, it's something to do with Dad."

Quayle nodded in the dark beside her.

Just before ten the next morning, they stopped and Quayle made his way off the petrol station forecourt to a public phone. There he dialled the number from memory, let it ring three times and hung up, then dialled again a second time. This time, it was answered on the fourth ring.

"I want to order some peaches please," Quayle said

There was a pause before a woman's voice spoke. "I'm sorry, we haven't had those in stock for some time – but if you will hold for a second..." Quayle could hear the flurry in the background. The peaches trigger obviously hadn't been used in a while, but the woman certainly knew about it. She would be trying for instructions from someone. At last, she came on the line again. "Sorry about that. Could I ask a representative to call on you?"

"I'm afraid not," Quayle answered. "Tell your sales manager I shall call again in an hour." He hung up and walked back to the car.

He'd done what he needed to do. Now, there would a mad dash to find the man they called Jack Herman, to tell him that one of his people had surfaced. Only seven or eight people had ever had the peaches trigger – and, if nothing else, Quayle knew that it guaranteed them a clean line later.

He smiled as he climbed back into the car. Jack Herman, Head Of Station in Switzerland, never knew that anyone other than him knew about the Prague cell's reporting codes.

But then there was a lot that Jack Herman didn't know.

At that exact moment, Jack Herman was eyeing up the legs of one of the three girls in the Consular and Trade typing pool. She was the rather ordinary looking daughter of a British businessman resident in Geneva and worked in the passport section. Knowing that Mr Herman was something *hush hush*, she found him terribly exciting and enjoyed his flirting over coffee – so, when the phone call came through from his office, she was disappointed to see him hurtle from the room.

"Is that the sales manager?" Quayle asked, on the other end of the line.

"It is. Can I help you?" Herman answered.

"Can we get together?"

"Who is this?" Herman asked. It certainly didn't sound like one of his people. The accent was familiar but all wrong.

"I got you out of jail in Berlin one night. You and an Egyptian dancer."

There was a stunned silence on the end of the line for several seconds.

"Jesus Christ...you! What... what a pleasant surprise," he said smoothly.

"Cut the social pleasantries, Jack. I just need to know what's going on."

"I see. Where?"

"Parc de la Grange. The Stadium entrance and round the path on the right."

"I know it... Let's meet after lunch, say two?"

Quayle agreed, a thin smile on his lips, and hung up.

Back in the car, Pope was gazing frostily out of the windscreen, unhappy with the developments. His gun was out, sitting in his lap under his hat.

Holly smiled uneasily at him as Quayle climbed into the driver's seat. After he had told them what he had organised, Pope snapped his verdict.

"You've given him three hours to line up some players. You'll be a sitting duck."

"That's if there is this Metro thing," Quayle argued. "I'm yet to be convinced."

"But why not somewhere crowded? Why pick a park? It's a killing ground!"

"Because I can see them," Quayle replied.

When they reached the destination, he looked down at his watch. If they were going to try and take him then they would be arriving soon, wanting to be in place well before he arrived. Pope had insisted he take a few precautions and, delving into his small hold-all, had produced a rolled bundle the size of a small towel. "Wear this," he had said. "It's Kevlar weave. It will stop anything but Titanium."

He dug into the bag again and produced a Browning Hi-Power pistol, its heavy rubber combat grip matt black against his hand. "It's heavy but you can handle it."

Quayle shook his head and took the armoured vest, if only to humour him. The other preparations had taken the best part of forty minutes and now he waited in the warm sunshine of the path, Pope's vest chafing his neck.

Herman stood on the path, trying to maintain his cool urbane composure. Inside, he was a maelstrom of conflicting emotions and feelings. He had reported the contact as standing orders said – and suddenly the situation had been ripped from under him. He hadn't really believed the rumours about Titus Quayle and, when the Metro order had come through in the daily coded material, he had read it with disbelief.

Quayle certainly didn't sound crazy on the phone – but then, they said, the madmen never did. Besides, now it was out of his control. The heavy mob were getting stuck in, with the senior Fairy on station talking directly to London, enjoying his brief moment of power over the head of Station. The chances of something drastic happening were very good indeed. If the Fairies got a shot at Quayle, they would take it, guns and everything. That would be all they needed, to have the humourless Swiss police involved and a public spectacle.

He watched a woman walk past pushing a little girl in a stroller, and a kid on roller skates doing lazy figure of eights while licking an ice-cream. A park worker with a stiff leg was pushing a wheelbarrow full of grass cuttings and an elderly couple were out strolling together, the man hatted and scarved even in the warm Autumn sun.

Herman was pleased that the senior Fairy knew what Quayle looked like because that might absolve him the responsibility of pointing him out. It was bad enough standing here like a Judas goat, he thought. Then he thought again. Such a bad choice of phrase. *Judas.* Bloody Quayle! *What have you done, you stupid bastard? You saved me more than once and here I stand, drawing you into a trap. What a shitty fucking world this is!*

There were eight Fairies scattered about: four full timers and four that they had found somewhere else. They blended with the public quite well, Herman noticed, but not well enough to fool Quayle. *Keep your eyes open sport.* He looked at his watch. It was three minutes to two. Quayle was never late. It was rule number one. Late is a signal to get the hell out.

I'm so sorry Titus, that it had to end this way. Maybe you are crazy. Maybe that's good because maybe you'll never know what happened.

He took a cigarette from a silver case and lit it, something he rarely did. A young man on a racing bike freewheeled past, his wheels humming softly on the wide path. The man with the wheelbarrow had dumped his grass and was walking back, a harsh cough rattling in his throat. Two children giggled, chasing a ball, and a man pushed a wheeled Bratwurst stand slowly along the path towards the stadium exit, its striped canopy bright and cheerful in the sunlight.

The day Titus Quayle was meant to die.

Quayle had been watching him for the last twenty minutes.

Herman stood tall and alone on the path, smoking a cigarette nervously, like a man waiting for his new lover. *You were never very good under stress, Jack. When you smoke, it's a bad sign.*

He thought he had flagged three possible players amongst the people walking the path and lounging on the grass. *If Jack's smoking,* he thought, *there are more and, if there are more, then it's no welcome home parade.* There on the grass two men lounged on their backs, a portable cassette playing rock music. There would be a mirror somewhere, so they could see the path, maybe in the cassette window. The figure on the bench reading a paper was too obvious, but the man pushing the Bratwurst stand was a possible. The two walking the dog were a certainty; one even had his hand up to his ear to listen in on his earpiece radio. Somewhere there was a controller, someone with a handheld radio. He would be the boss. There was a man painting at an easel further down and another man of similar age walking the path with a woman, talking into a portable phone. Clever, Quayle thought. Never look at the obvious.

Then he recognised one of them and he smiled bleakly to himself. The game was on.

It was time to disappear. Allowing a direct confrontation at a place of your opponents choosing was only for amateurs. They would have the exits covered to some extent and his picture would have done the rounds of silent men. He took the cigarette from his mouth, coughed loudly, took the wheel barrow and limped away toward the main administration area and the staff entrance.

Holly sat in the car, picking listlessly at a small cardboard tub of French fries. Her chicken, cold and claggy, lay uneaten on the dashboard. Beside her, Pope had finished his without comment and now wiped his hands on a paper napkin.

"Can't we go back now?" she asked. "Please, Mr Pope?"

"No. We'll just be in his way. We are to wait."

"But what if something happens?" she argued, turning to face him and pushing her hair back up off her face.

"That's precisely why you're not there," he replied, his eyes scanning the parked cars and the walkers around the lake shore.

Pope didn't notice the man with the motorcycle who had just thrown a drink carton into a rubbish bin or the quizzical look on his face as he re-mounted his machine. He was a junior attachment to the Geneva station and had been left out of the Park duty. The face of which he had just caught sight – he had seen it recently, and now he scrabbled to place it. Whatever it was, it was important. He wracked his memory, trying to place the image, while he busied himself fiddling with his helmet. He wasn't going anywhere until his current lady friend arrived, but he suddenly felt very conspicuous, so when he had done everything he could to his helmet, he walked back to the window at the restaurant and bought a cup of coffee, still trying to remember the face. He had decided to walk closer to the car and get a better look – and suddenly it hit him. The face had been in an operations report. She was missing and wanted by London, linked with the killings on Greece. He altered direction slightly and headed towards the phones, his coffee forgotten in his hand.

The office were surprisingly unhelpful. Mr Herman was still at the park with the others, but they would try and get a message to him. In the end he gave up and said that he would phone in later. He was about to hang up when the operator, who rather liked the young Englishman, offered to put him through to Major Phillips, the Military Attaché who was visiting from Bern. He had met the Major on two or three occasions and remembered him as a gruff, greying individual who ran ten miles every day.

Better than nothing, he thought, and said thanks.

"Phillips here."

"Hello Major. My name is Rogers, sir..."

"You're one of Herman's people aren't you?"

"Yes. I have a problem, sir."

"Speak," Phillips snapped.

"I'm calling from a cafe by the lake. I think I've just seen a woman that my people in London are very interested in interviewing. They want her very badly... if you know what I mean."

"Don't dither boy," Phillips growled. "Give me the full sitrep."

"Major, Jack Herman is out. So are the rest of the team. I need instructions and help." He quickly told the Major where he was calling from.

"Right. Is she in the cafe?"

"No, sir. She's in a car."

"On her own?"

"No, sir, she's with a man," he replied, adding as an afterthought, "An oldish type."

"Got the make, year and reg number of the vehicle?"

Rogers turned in horror and looked at it across the car park. He saw it was still there and his heart started beating again. *Christ, how bloody stupid!* he thought. *Any bloody school boy knows to do that!*

"Yes, sir," he lied. "If they leave should I follow them?"

"On your own? Don't think Herman would like that. Just try and anticipate their direction. Leave the rest to him. Understand?"

"Yes, sir"

"Rogers?"

"Sir"

"That's all you do. Nothing heroic, understood? Stay there and I'll get someone over to you as soon as they're back in."

Phillips hung up and walked back to his motorcycle trying to seem nonchalant, committing the registration number to memory as he did so.

Twenty minutes later, he saw a third person arrive and get into the car. He recognised the man's face instantly from the photographs at the lunch time briefing.

"Oh shit," he said out loud, and then breathed a sigh of relief as he recognised another car that drew into the car park.

It was one of the vehicles used by the Fairies.

Quayle sat in the driver's seat, quickly rubbing the make-up off his face with a tissue. Stopping only to take three or four of the cold French fries and popping them into his mouth, he wiped again with the tissue as he spoke.

"You were right. The place was crawling with them. Three or four Fairies and a few local hires. Jack Herman's twitchy, very twitchy indeed. At one stage I was only fifteen feet from him." He grinned quickly. This was the old Titus Quayle, the buckets of pure nerve still there. "He's losing his edge."

Rolling and throwing the last tissue on the floor, he turned and winked at Holly, who was now in the back seat. She made a sad little smile, pleased he was back but unhappy with the news.

Starting the engine, he took another handful of the French fries and pulled out onto the road. There was silence for three or four minutes before Holly spoke.

"There's a piece of chicken there if you want it, and some napkins in the glove box."

Quayle didn't reply but gently eased the speed up. As the road widened around the lake, his eye flickered to the mirror every three or four seconds.

Pope sensed the change instantly. Glancing at Quayle, he pulled his gun clear and onto his lap. He was too professional to look rearward.

"What have we got?" he asked conversationally.

"White Audi, four back. Looks like three people inside. It hasn't overtaken the car pulling the boat."

"How long?"

"Since the restaurant."

As he said, it Quayle was quickly working the odds. The rules said that, if you were with the smaller or disadvantaged force, you should always to engage first. Pull the initiative back with an offensive action. If there was one car to the rear then there could be another, and there could be yet another to the front. The further they travelled, the more time they gave their opponents to muster strength and plan their deaths.

Quayle had never liked the rules – he always found a way around them – but this road was a trap, the lake on one side and the mountains on the other. There was no leaving it, except for the short steep turnings up its side valleys. On his own, he could have simply disappeared. But not with Holly or Pope.

"We have to take them," he said to Pope. "Soon. Do you..."

Pope nodded, pulled the magazine clear, flicked eight solid nose bullets out into his lap, and rapidly replaced them alternating with Teflon rounds. Then he reached into his breast pocket and took a small roll of Elastoplast. Tearing two strips off, he carefully taped his spectacles hard to the skin behind each ear. Lastly, he scooped the spare four bullets into his pocket, took a roll of peppermints out and slipped one between his dry lips.

"I'm ready," he said.

"I'll take the next turn off," Quayle said softly.

"Go round a bend. Pull up fast. I'll be out on my side. You keep moving about twenty yards. I want them stopped under my sights." He turned to Holly. "Miss Morton, in my bag beside you there is an armoured vest. Put it on. When we stop, you drop onto the floor. Then you stay there till we are moving again. You don't get up and you don't look up until I tell you it's safe. Understand?"

She nodded quickly, her face pale against the rich brown of her hair.

Pope looked to the front and sucked his peppermint.

The driver of the tag car was a Dutch freelancer. His talents – the result of six years on the Amsterdam Police Force's armed offenders reaction team – were for hire and had been since he was thrown out of the police for consistently using unnecessary force. He was not a brutal man. He simply saw violence as an effective means to an end, and these days he was paid handsomely for his skills. The man beside him was German, as was one of the two in the back seat. They were brothers who had cut their teeth in the red-light district of Hamburg, protecting their stable of prostitutes against intruders. Both had been recruited by the Dutchman when they needed to leave Hamburg in a hurry after a multiple shotgun killing of five drug dealers who fancied themselves as pimps as well. The killings had been a gross misjudgement, but emotions had been strong. The brothers' little sister had died after injecting heroin cut with a caustic drain cleaner. They hated drug dealers.

The last man was a Corsican mute. His tongue had been cut from his mouth during an interrogation – when, as a Legionnaire, he had been captured by Algerian nationalists. At fifty-two he was the oldest in the group and a superb marksman.

Until now, the day had been largely wasted. They were not paid to attend, but to act – and, so far, the whole exercise in doing the job on the Englishman had been fruitless. Hanging around the park waiting for a man who was never going to come had left them all frustrated. The attitude of the other Englishman in Geneva was also an irritation. He seemed sickened by the whole thing.

The Dutchman had no respect for that sort of unproductive hypocrisy. After all, Quayle was their problem. He drove at a steady pace, keeping three or four cars between his and the target vehicle. God, that had been a stroke of luck, the sighting at the lake. They might just redeem something from the day yet. The other two people in the car were an easily dealt with problem. Guilt by association, and then who would associate with a madman anyway? The girl would not be a problem – but he did wonder briefly who the other older man was.

He eased forward as a big Audi moved up to overtake and, as it pulled back to the right, he saw the target Mercedes take a right turn up a side road. He swore loudly. This was not in his scenario. He wanted to follow them all the way to wherever they were going and do the job after dark. Now, with this turning, he would not have the cover of other vehicles –

and it was still broad daylight. The consolation was that the road looked very quiet. They might be able to do it undisturbed. Turning fast without indicating, he didn't slow his pace at all. He was committed now.

The sharp bend came up quickly and, as he braked to go round the Corsican – possibly with some old Foreign Legion ambush experience flashing back into his memory, possibly with instincts honed over the years, possibly with a sixth sense, or possibly all three – he made an urgent animal moan and bashed on the front seat with his fist, reaching for a gun on the seat beside him. The car took the bend, the Dutchman trying for control on the narrow road, the mute banging on the seat, the two German youngsters trying to make out what he was saying – and there in front of them was a car stopped in the middle of the road.

He hit the brakes hard, instinctively trying to correct the slide at the same second as he realised it was the target car. This was an ambush, and this was what the Corsican was trying to say.

He snatched up his gun, a Heckler and Koch, and pulled the door handle. "Out!" he shouted – and died as a hard-nosed nine millimetre took him in the temple.

His body was knocked across to the passenger seat by the second round, and the third took the German beside him high in the neck, a bright fountain of crimson blood arcing out onto the dashboard as he tried to scrabble away from the killing ground of the car.

Pope stood, then and fired four rounds into the back seat through the still-closed back door, the mute screaming soundlessly as his fingers scrabbled for the lock. Then Pope dropped back behind the rock from which he had fired the first shots. Hidden there, he counted to sixty – time for the terrible shock to have worn off and for anyone still with fight left to try to get clear. All was silent except for the ticking of the hot engine.

Carefully, he moved forward. Quayle was already back in the Mercedes, revving the engine and beginning to turn their car on the narrow road. Pope checked the tag car quickly, looked carefully at the

Dutchman, pulled papers from his pocket – and, seeing no further threat, ran to the Mercedes as Quayle finished the last of his manoeuvres.

With spinning wheels, they headed back for the lake. They never saw the man who managed to pull his motorbike off the road before they passed – or the fact that he remounted and began to follow at a safe distance.

"It's finished," Pope said, looking over his shoulder into the back. "You can sit up now."

Holly was still on the floor, her hands over her ears. As she pulled herself up, she fought the waves of fear, her hands white and trembling, unable to believe that four people had died in the brief hail of gunfire. Pope sat in the front seat, still sucking his peppermint, refilling his magazine, his hands moving with economic, fluid gestures practised a thousand times.

He completed the task wordlessly and then, dropping the gun into his lap, picked up the wad of documents he had scooped from the Dutchman's pocket.

"Thought I recognised him," he said, thinking out loud.

"Who?" Quayle asked, concentrating on the road.

"The driver. Name's Hoogstad. I saw him work once in Bremen. Freelancer. He was good."

"Not that good," Quayle qualified.

"He made a mistake," Pope said, almost with respect. "It only takes one. He was first team."

"What? You all know each other?" Holly asked, appalled.

"We know *of* each other," Pope corrected.

"And what? Have drinks, do you? Talk about your kills like fighter pilots?" She was angry now, the tension breaking out as aggression, tears in her eyes.

Pope let her rant on for a minute or two, until she fell silent. Then he turned in his seat. "The last time I saw him, he was crawling up a sewer in his underpants, lying in the shit with the rats. He had a knife in his mouth and a handgun in the hand he wasn't pulling with. He crawled into a room with four real nutters! Three Red Brigade and an Arab. They had the twelve year old daughter of a Greek banker, and they'd already cut one of her nipples off. He went in and did the job he was paid to do... Sometimes we have our place, and for the sensitive people like you it never makes the papers. Now, I didn't like him, but I hand loaded his rounds that time. If he hadn't been on this job, I may well have had him load for me one day. You don't have to like what I do. That's your privilege. Just be glad that you're alive to do it."

He turned back to face the front and, as her anger cooled, she studied him with new respect, feeling a little foolish for her outburst.

*

The Director General of MI6 was routinely chauffeured in an expensive black Jaguar, but tonight he waited in a fully licensed and registered taxi, perfect in every detail – except that the driver had been hand-picked by Scotland Yard. He had previously driven senior naval officers and was given to nautical expressions, but now he sat in silence, staring straight ahead. In the back Sir Gordon Tansey-Williams sat back, his coat wrapped tightly around his knees.

Morris, the driver, half turned his head. "That's him, Sir Gordon," he said.

"You're sure?" Sir Gordon lifted his head to stare out into the dark.

"Aye, sir."

"Ask him to join us, will you, Mr Morris?"

Stepping from the car, he pulled his jacket closer and ran across the wet street to intercept the man.

Knowing something of the background to tonight's meeting, he decided it was prudent to approach from the front and slowly.

"Jonno Smith?"

The man had a curious gait, his back twisted so that one shoulder rode higher than the other. He peered at Morris from under a tangle of wet curly hair. "Who wants to know?"

134

"I'm from Century. My governor would like a word." Morris nodded across the street.

"Then phone me at the office," Smith answered.

Morris stepped forward, his hands raised in a friendly manner. "Look..."

"Take another step and I'll break your fucking arms," Smith snarled.

Morris stopped dead. He knew the crippled man was quite capable of carrying out his threat.

"They said you were an aggressive little prick," he laughed nervously. "Look, just cross the street. Look into the cab. If you don't recognise the man inside then keep walking and he'll phone you tomorrow. On your direct line – which is the blue phone on the corner of your desk below the pin-up. The red head with the big tits."

Smith studied him for a minute. The information was correct. "You stay here," he said.

"That's never going to happen, son. He's my responsibility."

Smith nodded slowly. Any other answer would have been suspect. All official drivers doubled as routine bodyguards for the senior people they chauffeured.

As he got closer, the door opened and the interior light flashed on. Smith recognised the occupant immediately and, shaking the rain from his tired old coat, he climbed into the back.

"Sorry, sir."

Sir Gordon made conciliatory noises as Morris nosed the cab into the evening traffic. Then he came directly to the point. "A little birdie tells me that you think that you've been 'got at'. I'd like to hear about that..." He looked at Smith through eyes that gazed lovingly at his grandchildren at weekends and terrified Cabinet members during the week. "*All* about that if you will."

Two hours later, the taxi stopped up the street from Smith's flat and, dropping him off, headed immediately to Upton Manor where it stopped outside a small terraced house with a pocket handkerchief garden. Sir Gordon knocked at the door and, as he did so, a dark closed van that had been outside most of the evening pulled away. He waited a few seconds and the door was opened by a short chubby black girl in a dressing gown.

"Good evening, Miss Bowie. We haven't met but my name is Tansey-Williams. I believe you are alone. May I come in?"

She looked at him for a second.

"Hang on. *The* Tansey-Williams?" she asked, hand on substantial hip.

He nodded and she swung the door open, her bright eyes quizzical. Soon, she had made him a cup of tea and, assuming he hadn't eaten, quickly made him a bacon sandwich as well. Finally, she sat at his feet in front of a small gas heater and listened to what he had to say.

*

Quayle pulled into the parking building just as it was opening for business, the Munich streets beginning to get crowded. They had driven most of the night using back roads, stopping frequently and doubling back to check on followers. They had changed vehicles twice in that time, stealing a delivery van in one small Austrian town and deserting it miles away, before taking the train on to Innsbruck where they hired a VW Kombi. From there they crossed into Germany, dropping the Kombi off near Dachau, and hiring a new Audi from one of the proliferation of small agencies nearer the city.

Quayle stopped the engine and sat, grainy eyed and tired, easing the ache in his shoulder. It still ached when it was damp and raining. He was confidant they had not been followed. He had seen the figure on the motorbike, but not since the outskirts of Sion; that was back in Switzerland and felt like a century ago.

"We leave the car here and walk. There's a small hotel round the corner. Der Leibling. It sells rooms by the hour. No questions. It will do us for the moment."

Holly didn't care. All she wanted was a bath and then a bed.

They checked in, Quayle playing the hick country boy in perfect coarse southern German while Pope and Holly waited in the lounge. He paid extra for clean sheets, smiling like a fool as if it were normal and then, carrying them over his arm, he trudged up the stairs after his new bride and her father who went everywhere with her.

Behind them, the clerk sniggered to himself, pocketing the money. That afternoon, as they slept, he handed over the shift to his replacement and went to drink Schnapps and play cards with his friends and he related the story of the stupid ploughboy.

One of his friends was a sometime pimp, sometime thief and full-time informer. He had been asked by his owner to look out for three strangers: two men, one older than the other, and a girl. The owner wasn't Federal Police or even City of Munich Police. He was something to do with the Bundesnachrichtendienst, the BND, Germany's Secret Service, and he paid well in street currency for information. Cocaine could be very profitable indeed. He smiled and drank, played cards, and bought his rounds, feeling up the whores like a rich man. Only then did he convince his friend, the hotel clerk, to point out the ploughboy, promising him a cash reward. Together they walked back to the hotel and sat in a bar opposite until eventually they were rewarded. Quayle walked across the street to a Turkish take-away and, twenty minutes later, walked back into the hotel carrying his food.

Later that night, the informer phoned his contact. The man was away, he was told, but would be back the next morning. And so, driving his dilapidated old car round to the man's apartment, he slept in the back seat, waking whenever he heard a car arrive to see who climbed out.

Just before five, by which time his back was truly aching, he saw his contact step out of a taxi and ran to join him, hoping that the three hadn't left the Die Leibling yet. This information, he thought, had to be worth ten grams at least.

After the security service man had listened to his gabbled story, he took the lift up to his apartment and returned immediately with an envelope of photos. These he laid out beside a vase of wilting flowers on the doorman's desk and asked the informer to point out the man he had seen. He'd shown them seven times that day to informers all over Southern Germany and was surprised when the man went unhesitatingly to Quayle's picture.

"You're sure?"

"Ja. That was him. What's it worth? Fifteen, eh?"

"If it is him, and if they are all there, then maybe five," the BND man said with some distaste.

"Five! Nien!"

They began to haggle and, finally settling on eight grams of the drug, the BND man got onto the phone, trying to rustle up some help. Fifteen minutes later, a three man team picked him up on the street and, as they drove, they loaded guns on the back seat. There was no talk. The English bodyguard who had disappeared was now confirmed as being with them. He was rated as number three in Europe and, two days ago, he had killed the number two like he had been an amateur. There was no doubt about it: they were scared of the English Mr Pope.

Quayle pulled his sweater over his shirt, combed his hair quickly and picked up his jacket. Holly was in the small bathroom still brushing her teeth, and he looked across at Pope who stood ready by the door.

"I'll get the car, bring it round the back in the alley. I'll pick up some rolls and cheese too. Be about ten minutes."

Pope just nodded. He didn't ordinarily eat in the mornings. All he wanted was a cup of tea and that was always a problem in Europe. They only drank tea when they were ill. After last night he felt good, well rested, even in spite of the arguing whores and drunken singing that sporadically shattered the peacefulness through which he'd slept.

Locking the rickety door behind Quayle, he waited patiently for Holly to finish. He knew her routines now. After the toothbrush, she did her hair, long sweeping strokes of the brush that reminded him of his boyhood in London, watching his mother sitting at her dresser. While he waited, he crossed to the window and, careful not to reveal himself, looked out upon the Munich street. A van making early deliveries was unloading sacks of potatoes and a young boy was stacking beer barrels outside a bar. Men in working clothes walked the pavements in twos and threes towards a small factory somewhere nearby and a lone taxi prowled for a fare. He had wanted to be away by now – but the garage where they had left the car didn't open until 5.45.

Holly stepped from the bathroom, clutching a toilet bag. "Sorry," she said cheerfully. "Ready at last! I'll just bung this in here..." She bent over her hold all and, unzipping it, pushed the toilet bag down inside.

Pope smiled at her and looked at his watch. His room was across the hall, overlooking the alley at the back.

"I'll see if he's there," he said, his tone telling her that, if he wasn't, they were staying put.

Unlocking the door, he crossed the hall, went through the open door of his own room and looked down into the alley. There, turning in at the other end, was Quayle.

He turned back in time to see Holly stepping, bag in hand, into the hall. At the same split second he heard the heavy footsteps on the landing – and he knew.

He took the distance between them in two strides, the adrenaline rising, pulling his gun clear of its holster. Holly felt his shoulder hit her. In her peripheral vision she saw the gun rising, his body turning, the beginnings of a shouted warning, his broad back obscuring her vision as the first deafening shots blasted down the corridor. She slid down the end wall, Pope's bulk a barrier between her and whoever was at the other end, as he began to shoot back.

There were four of them, two armed with Heckler and Koch automatic assault weapons. They were on the landing and moving fast, and a third man behind them had already fired his shotgun.

Pope shot the man on the right first. Two bullets in the face and he swung the gun left for the second man, squeezing his trigger.

The bullets slammed into Pope's chest in an almost perfect grouping, punching him back against the wall. Holly fell beneath him as he fired again, the man stumbling and falling, the stubby barrelled gun tight in his fingers. The shotgun roared again and Pope felt his legs go like a sledge hammer had taken him – but, firing again, he watched the man fall. He knew he had been hit, but somehow he staggered to his knees, one hand on the wall for support, his breath coarse and foamy, blood running from his mouth, his hard grey eyes looking for the fourth assailant. They always had four, the Krauts, the bastards...

There was movement on the landing below. The figure snatched a look, but he couldn't react quickly enough; in the next instant, the landing was splattered in blood and a twitching corpse plunged to the ground.

The girl was screaming beneath his shattered legs. He fired twice, the gun kicking back in his weakening grip and the dead man's face fell away in pieces. Then, as he fell back again, he heard the pounding on the stairs – and Quayle's voice, through the misty cold pain, screaming her name.

"She's OK," he tried to say. "Quayle, she's OK..."

"Oh Jesus!" And suddenly Quayle was pulling her out from under him and holding his head in his hands.

"They're all down," he said, "all four of them. Quayle, she's OK."

The blood tasted salty and metallic on his tongue.

"Hang on," Quayle was saying. "I'll get you to a doctor..."

Pope raised his head and looked down his body. The blood was everywhere now. He felt the warmth between his legs and he knew he was evacuating his bowels. The shotgun. His chest hurt. They had Teflon rounds. Right through his armour. Jesus it hurt. He didn't want to shit himself, not in front of a woman.

"No Titus, I'm done for. Femoral artery..." He looked across at Holly who sat huddled and in shock against the wall, her face spotted in his blood "Sorry about the mess," he said. *God it's cold,* he thought. *So this is what it's like to die.*

"Hold on, Jerry. Hold on!" Quayle pleaded.

Pope looked up at Quayle and smiled weakly. He was shivering now, his body going into deep shock. "No-one ever called me that before. Tell Mr Black... that I wasn't ready... for the trains. Go now... Take my gun! Even you will need it..." He tried to smile, but it was too late; he'd already lapsed into unconsciousness.

Quayle stuffed his handkerchief into the leg wound and, pulling Pope's belt from his waist, he bound it quickly and expertly.

140

There was no time left to lose. Quayle pulled Holly to her feet, roughly wiping the blood from her face and hands, snatched up her bag and pulled her along into Pope's room. From here they scrambled down the rusting iron fire escape. Dropped the last ten feet alone, he held up his hands for her and she let go of the railing, a picture of silent hysteria, her pupils dilated, thick wet clotting blood in her hair and eyebrows and bright smears down her neck

Quayle returned the car and collected his deposit as normally as he could, knowing that anything out of the ordinary would show them up to a city about to conduct a massive manhunt. The evidence was there that Pope had been the gunman, but the hotel would give them their details. Together, they took a taxi back into town. Holly – now in clean clothes and washed, after a stop at a public toilet – sat beside him silently while he chatted with the driver, careful now to emphasise a northern accent, a pair of thick spectacles on his nose and his cheeks padded with tissue that both disguised his voice and made him look fuller in the face. Once in town, they headed for the airport where Quayle took a single room on a day use basis, presenting an Icelandic passport at the desk. Holly wandered up past security and, once in, he locked her there and disappeared, arriving back an hour later with a pair of loaded shopping bags. He produced wash-in hair dyes, a blonde wig, various items from a haberdashery and other bits and pieces.

Four hours later, a heavy overly made-up French blonde in her mid-thirties paid cash for two tickets to Frankfurt, asking about any senior citizen discount for her father who stood at the edge of the queue, tired and looking slightly bewildered by the bustle of the airport, leaning heavily on two canes.

The check-in girl immediately ordered him a wheel chair and he was taken through a 'routine security alert' by airport handling staff, then seated on an electric trolley for the long ride to the departure gate. An hour and a half later, they checked into the Frankfurt Hilton as delegates attending the Medical Convention, the canes and breast padding now in suitcases, and all their other items in a rubbish skip outside the loading area at the rear of a department store.

Quayle passed Holly a large brandy.

"You're doing fine," he said. "Here, drink this."

She took the drink and sat with her legs folded under her on the room's small sofa. He was concerned about her silence. If she was going to get over the events of the morning. he wanted her to talk about it, and soon. The longer she remained silent, the more difficult it would become.

"This morning you went through an experience that hardened professionals fear. You saw five men die in the most horrible circumstances, one of them a friend who died saving you. It's tough..." He put his hand out to stroke her cheek. "Not for nothing is it called 'baptism of fire' by soldiers. In the old days, people spoke of seeing the elephant. That means they saw death, they saw fear, real fear, gut-wrenching, puking fear – and they say that you're never the same again. It's a humbling experience, one that takes some men to God and some to a bottle." He tilted her head up to look into her big hazel eyes in time to see the first tear beginning. "So don't bottle it up now. Cry. Cry for your lost innocence. Cry for Mr Pope. Cry for everything, and remember that I love you and that I will always be here."

An hour later, he made her take two sleeping pills, tucked her up, kissed her cheek – and then, redressing in his old man outfit and carrying his canes, let himself out of the room, moving straight down to the lobby and hailing a cab.

He sat in the dark in a big leather chair and waited. The lock had been easy, almost too easy, but then the man who owned the apartment had always been casual about that kind of thing, making up the difference with small signs that would reveal he had been broken into: a hair in the door that would drop, deliberately dusty surfaces that would show finger marks, a match that would be misplaced by an opened drawer. Quayle had searched well and found them all; now all that was left to do was sit and wait for the man to come home.

It was after midnight when he heard the tinkle of a woman's laughter in the corridor and the deeper murmurs of her companion.

The key was harsh in the lock. The pause told Quayle that the homeowner was looking for the hair he'd left in the door, and this made him smile. On the other side of the door, the woman gave a giggled plea to hurry up and get inside, and moments later there was the flick of a switch and the lights went bright in the hall.

There was silence. He must have seen the note, thought Quayle, the five franc note folded under the edge of the vase. It wouldn't be long now.

Quayle watched as he pushed the giggling woman into the bedroom, closed the door and entered the lounge. He was tall and blonde, sharp featured and undeniably Aryan, with crisp blue eyes and clear youthful skin.

"Hello Kurt," Quayle said. "Still bringing them home, I see."

"God! You... you have more nerve than a bad tooth. Half of Europe is hunting you, my friend."

"Really?" Quayle said sarcastically. "I wouldn't have known."

Kurt Eicheman looked at him and his brows softened. "I will get rid of the girl. Then we can talk."

They had known of each other a long time, contemporaries when Quayle arrived in Romania to find and bring out a dissident. In the following days, he and Eicheman had competed for the prize and had finally joined forces when Quayle had broken Eicheman out of a Securitate holding facility, along with the man they we both looking for. Eicheman had been larger than life, a drinking, carousing, whoring buccaneer of a man who found something to laugh about in every situation. The pair had nearly driven Hugh Cockburn insane with their competitive efforts and their friendship had endured even after Quayle left Romania with more traded information than was normal between the BND and MI6.

In the apartment, Quayle heard the girl's complaints and she was ushered without ceremony to the door. Moments later, Eicheman was back with two full brandy balloons.

"So, my friend, every player in Europe after you and the girl. The word is you are a homicidal maniac. Are you?"

"When did the word go out?" Quayle asked.

"After the incident on Serifos, as best we can tell. We didn't get involved until two nights ago."

"Who's in Bonn who would have put a couple of freelancers onto me in Venice before that?"

Eicheman was surprised. "Before? You are sure?"

Quayle nodded, the brandy untouched on the table beside him.

"No-one. These requests are rare and treated with sufficient authority. I saw the first notices. They were the night before last. You are positive of the facts?"

"I am," Quayle replied.

"Then it wasn't BND," Eicheman replied with fervor. "This morning was, however. Your man was very good. He killed three of the better talents around... and a loyal service man."

"They came up the fucking stairs, shooting at my woman! If Pope hadn't killed them I would have. Your loyal service man is dead. So is Jerry Pope. We are quits!" he snarled, daring Eicheman to bring the topic up again.

The other nodded quickly. The fact that Quayle was personally involved with the woman explained so much.

"How did they get onto us?" he asked.

"You should know that your man is still alive. Barely, of course. The doctors say he won't make it." Eicheman paused. "You were seen buying food across the street last night. The receptionist had a friend who is on our payroll."

Quayle nodded. He had thought as much and cursed his own stupidity. He hadn't taken them seriously enough. "So, who is in Bonn who hires guns? Who has that kind of money and those kinds of contacts?"

Eicheman held up his hands in a rather Italian gesture. "What else have you got to go on?"

"Not much. A man. From Bonn. Square ring."

144

"What?"

"A ring. A square ring on his finger."

"That's all?"

Quayle nodded.

"It's not much," Eicheman said. "What's going on, Quayle? You're not a maniac. A kill order, for Christ's sake? Now this Bonn thing. Two teams after you?"

"You tell me," Quayle replied without sarcasm.

He looked at Quayle's hands. Even in the soft light the round scars were apparent. "They do that in that Libyan prison?"

Quayle nodded again.

"Jesus. They are animals, those people. I wanted to help. They owe us favours." He paused awkwardly, feeling inadequate. "But I was unable to... Look, let me see what I can get on Bonn."

Quayle stood and began to button his coat. "I'll be in touch in a couple of days. Thanks Kurt, and be discreet. You are being watched. There's a man down on the street. They've obviously gone through the files."

Kurt didn't doubt Quayle for a second, but even so he went white in the face. Then he tapped his ear and pointed a finger at the walls.

Quayle shook his head. "Not yet, anyway. I checked."

"Jesus, who are these people?" Eicheman said in awe, standing up. "I am head of station in Frankfurt. *Verschtun?* They are powerful enough to put me under suspicion with my own organisation. That means orders from..."

Quayle pointed upward with one extended forefinger. "The bloody top."

CHAPTER SEVEN

Black sat in the back of the hospital car, his face and hands still heavily bandaged, the overnight case of pyjamas, toilet articles and the clothing he had arrived in beside him on the seat. They had thrown away the shirt and overcoat, the acid having eaten right through the collars on both, but had cheerfully explained that the laundry had managed to save the blazer as if it mattered. The nurses had carefully ignored all of his questions about his eyes, and the specialist had mumbled how the eye was a wonderful thing and not to worry unduly – but the brutal truth was that, until they managed to clear away the burnt flesh that were his eyelids, they wouldn't know a thing.

For now, he was blind.

The thought terrified him. He tried to beat it with positive thoughts about returning to work, but even that was a joke. Everything he did was visual and he had never even realised it. Every file was on paper or a screen. Photographs needed looking at. Even walking across a room required eyes.

The department psychologist had called round to see him and, during their tense but supposedly informal chat, he had asked him how he had felt. Black had been surprised at his own anger and told the man to take his pity and fuck off.

The car was slowly coming to a stop. This weekend at home was a treat, the sister had said, before they started the surgery next week. At least he thought they hadn't tried to bullshit him about that. He had a friend once who had been burnt after a fall from his motorbike, and the plastic surgeons had gone to him with the knife. Black had visited him when his life had devolved down to a succession of drugged periods between skin grafts, but the drugs were never enough. That was what his life was going to be like now.

He felt in his pocket for the small metal object that the strange visitor had given him, and ran his finger around the edge for the hundredth time. He hadn't shown it to anyone because he had understood, even through the drugged haze, that his visitor should not have been there. He still couldn't place the accent and the voice. He had had other visitors from the office – Callows' secretary and even Burmeister had stood awkwardly over his bed – but this one had been different. Somehow, he knew that he was involved with Long Knives.

His wife was waiting when he got home. She was a tall, black haired, quietly efficient woman who had firmly, but kindly, told the district nurse that she could manage and shown her the door. Now she stood at the front gate of their small house, ready to help and support her man with whatever it took. She had always known this could happen and had been steeling herself for this day ever since he had first walked out in the uniform of the Metropolitan Police, very like the young man who now waited outside the house, their protection.

"We don't know how long you are going to be bashing into things, so I've moved them about a bit." She pushed the dog down and took his arm. "Get down, Wellie!" she said fondly to the big Labrador as he lunged at Black again, his pink tongue lolling happily.

Early that evening, as Black sat at the kitchen table with his wife washing dishes, he thought for the thousandth time about the missing files and the shadowy figures with the acid spray. Gently, he touched his bandaged face, his anger complete and cold and terrible.

Sir Gordon Tansey-Williams called the next day, gruffly wishing him his best. As Mrs Black seated him in the lounge opposite her husband, she warned him with a look.

He came straight to the point.

"Your heart still in it lad?" he asked. "Because we need to talk. Say so now and I'll understand if it's no..."

Mrs Black stood glaring at him. "It's time you left. How dare you..."

Black raised one bandaged hand, turning his unseeing face turned toward her. "How about a cup of tea?" he said. "I'm sure Sir Gordon would like one." His voice was low and measured, and he turned to face Tansey-Williams. "You'll have to forgive me. I will be using a straw. Can't hold a cup, I'm afraid."

He listened to her walk into the kitchen.

"So," he said, as soon as she was gone. "Start talking."

They talked until the tea was cold, Tansey-Williams firing questions and Black listening silently as the Director General told him of Quayle's run with Morton's daughter and Pope's involvement.

"It's not Quayle," Black said.

"You seem pretty positive of that."

"He only became a factor because Burmeister went after Morton's daughter. Hardly surprising with three Fairies turning up."

"And Pope?"

"Like Jonno told you. He was doing his job. So you're back to square one. Except that there's a man hunt on for the wrong bloody man. Christ! This is elementary police work. Where was Quayle when the killings took place? What does his doctor say? Has he an alibi?" He was shouting it now, the anger and frustration bursting out. "What the hell has been going on for the last week?" He swung his hand and knocked his children's beaker off the small table, its bright red straw rolling across the floor, tea gurgling out onto the carpet as Mrs Black stepped quickly through from the kitchen.

He cooled just as quickly and took a breath.

"Sorry about that," he said.

"I think you should leave now," Mrs Black said to Tansey-Williams, her expression saying it was not a negotiable issue.

"Of course," he said standing. Then he looked down at Adrian Black and thought for a second. "I'd like a friend of mine to have a look at you. He's the best in the country and I need you back at the office. In the meantime, I'll send something over for you to get your teeth into – and a pair of eyes to be at your beck and call."

"Long Knives?" Black asked, his voice husky.

"You want it?"

148

"That's like asking me if I want to see again."

Across the small room, his wife gave a look that verged on despair.

It was just after four the following morning, his second night lying awake at home, that he heard the noise. He lay absolutely still, listening to his own heart beat, as he tried to fathom it. A scrape, a squeak perhaps. He tried to think where the young policeman would be, walking a lonely beat around the house. Maybe it was him. Then he heard another noise and the hair on the back of his neck rose. So did the impulse to tear the bandages of his eyes. He checked himself and sat up, then dropped bare feet to the floor, reaching for the bedside drawer and the gun that was always there. *I have no sight,* he said to himself, justifying the action, *but I am familiar with the house. I know which stair squeaks and which door creaks. It's my house.*

He was easing the drawer shut when his wife woke, instantly aware that something was wrong.

He turned his head her way and put one bandaged finger to his lips.

"What?" she whispered. Then, seeing the dark glint of the gun in his hand, she continued, "Oh Ades, no, please..."

"Stay here," he whispered, the gun heavy and painful in his light grip. "I'll be all right."

"Darling, please don't go. There's a policeman somewhere. Let him! Please, he can see..."

But Black's mind was made up. "Stay here," he said with a dreaded finality, 'until I'm back."

Making his way to the open bedroom door, he sliding one foot ahead of the other, pleased when his hand found the banister rail exactly where it should have been. *I should have a shotgun for this,* he thought. *Mustn't fall over the dog!*

He moved down three steps very quietly and raised his hand to where he knew the electricity junction board was, feeling for the mains switch and easing it into the off position. He had become good at picking the source of sounds in the last week and, as he moved downward, he hoped there was no moon to shine in the kitchen windows. The gun was in his hand, his forefinger bandaged and tight on the trigger guard.

He stopped to listen every few feet, his heart beating loud as he strained to hear. *This time I have a gun, bastard,* he was thinking. *I have a gun and it should be as black as pitch.* Ears straining, he moved onward until his left hand hit the rounded end of the banister. Keeping low, he eased around it, the gun pointing down to where he knew the passage was.

It was quiet, too quiet.

There was a draught now, cool air moving. He had listened to Mary lock up before they had gone to bed. She was the wife of a security man. She didn't leave windows open.

He moved down the passage and into the living room, dropping down on his knees and swinging the gun back and forth as he turned his head, listening for movement. A smell now. Rich and warm, almost sweet. Familiar but not. He slid forward. Still too quiet. *Come on, you bastard,* he pleaded silently. *A window's open. Make a sound, just a little sound...* He waited for a full thirty seconds, rock steady, and then – beginning to doubt his senses – he crawled forward again.

The smell was stronger.

His heart was thumping.

His knee hit something wet.

He reached out with his left hand palm upward, to allow the exposed skin on the back of his hand to do the feeling for him. Whatever this was, it was wet, warm and slippery, bristly and hairy. The smell was now pungent in his nostrils.

Oh Jesus, oh Christ, oh no, please, you fucking bastards. Oh Jesus no, not the dog, not Wellie...

Then his hand felt the note in the blood, and he retched with the smell of guts and blood and intestines, giving a full blooded roar of hate and anger and frustration and pain.

The door crashed open and he turned, the gun coming up.

By some strange fortune, the young policeman shouted out in time, his big torch hitting the floor with a thump.

"Police! Mr Black, it's me! Don't shoot! You OK? What's happened?"

Black stayed on his knees, the young constable trying the lights and talking into a handheld radio.

"Junction box," Black said, his voice flat. "On the stairs."

At last, the constable pulled Black gently to his feet and eased him toward a chair. Then, looking down at the bloody remains on the floor, he walked quickly to the under stairs cupboard, took an old raincoat out and covered the dog's body.

"Ask my wife to remain upstairs if you would," Black said. "I don't want her to see Wellie like this."

When he came down, Black handed him the note that had been pinned to the dog's liver. "Read it."

The constable took the blood stained note and held it gingerly.

"It says 'Naughty naughty. Stay out of it. Or it's Mary'."

He never saw her standing in the doorway, only heard her choked sob as she looked down at the pathetic bundle on the floor.

*

Holly Morton moved easily through the people, sunglasses balanced on her head so that she looked like one of the gaggle of Dutch tourists at the immigration point in Palma Airport. Twelve feet behind her, chatting amicably with a pair in their sixties like a doting son, Quayle followed her toward the sleepy officials. Here she slowed down to offer her documents to a bored officer and, without a second glance, he waved her through, his eyes zeroing in on a couple behind her.

Holly wandered through into the baggage hall and waited for her suitcase. She had very little to put in it, but Quayle had been shopping again, returning with a variety of things, some second hand, some obviously new, saying that tourists never travelled with just an overnight bag, and never travelled with everything new.

Collecting her grey Samsonite, she tried to look excited as she walked to the customs men near the exit, passed through and waited for Quayle. They had driven from Frankfurt to Amsterdam and stayed there for two days while he had procured a set of seaman's papers and new passports, this time with full back-up papers like driving licences, theatre tickets, old letters, library cards – and, in one instance, a rate demand from a London borough.

Though she had managed to force Pope from her mind, delighted that he had survived, she was still getting used to not having his constant presence. Sometimes she forgot that he was no longer there and looked around for him, waiting for his imperceptible nod to move. Now, outside the terminal, she tried desperately to look like a tourist who did this sort of thing all the time, smiling at people who walked past.

Finally, Quayle walked past too. She followed him at a distance towards a hire car park, pleased to be up close again. As he started up, she climbed into the nondescript blue sedan and together again they drove out onto the main Palma road.

Only once they were free of the airport did she give an audible sigh and begin to relax.

"Have you been here before?" she asked, pulling the band from her hair and shaking it loose.

"Once or twice," he said, lighting a cigarette.

"Isn't it full of sunburnt drunken Brits, vomiting, fighting and singing 'you'll never walk alone'?"

He gave a dry chuckle. "Bits of it – Palma Nova, Magaluf, Pagera – but most if it's quiet and old and sleepy. We're going near to a place called Valldemosa. You'll like it..."

"Can't I come with you?" she suddenly asked, looking out of the windscreen as they began to head inland.

"No."

"But why, Titus?"

"It's safer here. You'll stay with a friend. Milburn don't know about him."

"What's he like?" she asked resignedly.

"His name's Marco. He has a big twirly moustache, a heart like a lion – and a thick-walled old bodega. He likes carpets, good wines and old boats. He also likes promiscuous women and dogs, and he cooks pasta just like mama used to do…"

She laughed, delighted at the rich description. "Sounds interesting," she said with a wry smile.

"Oh he is that," he replied.

Marco was exactly as Quayle had described. As they drove up his long driveway, he was standing shirtless, lean and brown, with waves of greying hair atop a regal head, a garden hose in his hand as he watered a tub of his precious flowers. Two Staffordshire bull terriers muscled around his bare legs, walking in escort as dropped the hose and approached the car.

With a huge smile painted across his lined face, he took Quayle into a huge bear hug, laughing and shaking him like a child before turning to Holly.

"Bellissima!" he said, kissing his fingertips in an extravagant gallant gesture. "Titus, she is magnificent! How can you trust me with her?" He bent to take a bag. "Come! As the natives here say, my house is your house."

The interior was surprisingly cool after the hot glare of the sun outside, the thick stone walls and flagstone floors having been built to achieve that three hundred years before. The ceiling was high, cantilevered with thick oak beams that he explained had been taken from a ship that had foundered on the rocks below Deia.

Like the house on Serifos, this one had its share of Oriental carpets thrown about the stone floors. A powerful painting of an Andalusian fighting bull stood above a huge hearth surrounded with leather club chairs. The whole effect was brightened up with bowls of fresh flowers and brightly painted wooden shutters. When Holly looked up, she could see all the way to the terracotta roof tiles.

The bedroom Marco showed her to was an odd shape, with one half of the perimeter wall circular in shape. The hand-carved peasant bed was covered in a bright patchwork quilt. She put down her bags, brushed her hair, and wandered out through the kitchen to find Quayle.

Just outside the house, the branch of an ancient olive tree formed one edge of a pergola supporting grape vines, and an old tom cat – scarred by many battles – slept on one of several white cane chairs scattered beneath the leafy canopy. There Quayle sat with Marco, an open bottle of wine between them on an old cable drum table. As she approached, Marco held up a glass.

"My God Marco, it's absolutely beautiful!" she said, waving her hand around her.

"Thank you," he said, genuinely pleased, "I like it very much. My retreat. Come take a glass with us."

"You don't live here all the time then?" she asked, taking the glass and settling into one of the chairs, near enough to rest a hand on Quayle's knee.

"Unfortunately no. I have business interests in Barcelona. I come here to rest, to think, to live like one should live!"

Quayle gave a dry laugh. "And very occasionally when a friend asks him to..."

"Paa!" Marco dismissed the very idea with a regal wave of his hand, but looked at Quayle with a half smile. "This man is like a brother," he said to Holly, explaining as best he could. "He wants my heart, I rip it out and give it to him!"

Quayle left just after dark, Marco escorting him to the gates because there were Rottweiler guard dogs loose in the grounds, their armed handlers having arrived the hour before. "A Mallorcan man. He owes me a debt of honour," Marco said indicating the armed men. "She will be safe. Now go and do what you have to do."

Quayle took the dark road back to Palma and caught the midnight flight to Lisbon.

*

She was a fifty thousand ton French-registered general freighter, bound on the midnight tide for Newcastle with a load of tinned sardines, wine and machinery parts. The dock worker said he could find the mate in a café nearby, and that he was a man one could deal with. Quayle thanked him, pulling his filthy reefer jacket about his shoulders, and went to find the man he would need to get him aboard the ship.

He was pleased. With airport surveillance systems and logging cameras, the classic way of entering Britain was becoming more difficult. But the smaller ports were still simple, and that would mean he could save the other full identities for another time.

He found the café by following the rock and roll music which flooded out onto the street. Pushing his way past a group at the door, he moved to the small bar where a woman was heating a small jug of milk under a steam jet. She ignored him for a while, until a flustered waitress took the milk, and then smiled at him.

"Expresso and cognac por favor."

She took a pre-poured glass of the brandy from under the counter and handed it to him.

"The mate from the Mariella. He is here?" he asked in bad Spanish. She pushed his coffee toward him and pointed to a table directly behind him.

"That big Dutchman in the red jacket. It is he."

Quayle thanked her and, carrying his coffee and brandy in one hand, approached the table where the man sat with two others.

Without being invited, he took a seat and looked across at the man. "I'm looking for a berth," he said in French, pushing his papers across. Then he gulped the brandy in one mouthful, following it with a sip of the black coffee.

"Sorry," the man replied. "We are full. Now if you..."

"One trip only, if you know what I mean," Quayle said with exaggerated emphasis. "My wife mustn't know I am back or *poof*... into the court I go."

"Not my problem," the Dutchman replied, turning to his friend to pick up the conversation. "Now fuck off, will you?"

"What's it worth?" Quayle asked.

"What?"

"Don't fuck about. What's it worth? Sign me on for one trip, tonight

My papers are in order. I want to get back and see my son. It's worth money to me and no risk to you. How much?"

The mate looked at him. The other two had fallen silent.

"A thousand. American," he answered softly.

"Three hundred now, and another three hundred at Newcastle," Quayle countered. "There are other ships."

The man looked at him, picked up the papers for a second, studied them and then nodded. "OK. Be aboard by ten." And he held out his hand for the money. The Captain normally got half – but this was double the normal rate, and the Captain never needed to know.

Quayle paid and left immediately, walking back to the first restaurant and slinging his bag on the floor. Here he ordered his first meal in two days. He ate hungrily, the oily fish and potatoes satisfying, then eventually looked at his watch and moved back down to the docks and the rusty hulk of the Mariella. Once aboard, he was shown to a bunk in a smelly, cramped – but thankfully empty –crew cabin by a smiling young seaman, who gleefully pointed out the pin-ups stuck to the bottom of the upper bunk by the previous occupant. *Just what I need,* Quayle thought dryly.

*

Sir Gordon Tansey-Williams occupied a corner office suite on the third floor of Century House. The building appeared from the outside to be merely another pre-war edifice. There were no splendid columns or lobbies or atriums. That was for their new building, planned for the riverside location. This was a simple five floor brick and concrete building that looked as if it should house an ageing and suitably dusty insurance company. Callers to the front door were met by a polite but firm porter, who declined entrance to any unauthorised people. Behind him the real security began, with high tensile steel card access doors, cameras and surveillance systems. The walls and basement had been strengthened to blast standards and all the windows were made with one-way armoured glass, coated in an emulsion that prevented electronic eavesdropping by computer wizards. In the basement was a complicated electronic scrambler that increased the difficulties of listening in. Also in the basement was the tunnel that took those needing covert access directly into Euston Station's labyrinth of underground tunnels full of buskers, commuters and tourists.

Tansey-Williams' offices were swept by the counter electronic people every three days, from the original Constable over the antique dresser to the plaster-of-Paris dog his granddaughter had made which had pride of place on the solid oak desk. He enjoyed a substantial private income and was old fashioned enough not to expect the service to pay for that kind of thing, so he took up the cost personally. He also supplemented the civil service salary his secretary was paid with a handsome stipend that meant he could demand nothing but the best.

The bed-sized surface of the desk had three chairs placed along the front, and each position enjoyed ample space to spread out papers. Tansey-Williams was a workaholic and was often there in the office ten hours a day – and would frequently conduct meetings simultaneously in adjoining rooms. Today he sat alone, one yellow grade one file on the desk before him and a single bone china cup off to one side, when his secretary put her head round the door.

"Sir Gordon, Sir Martin Callows is here now."

"Send him in," he growled.

Tansey-Williams was everything Callows wasn't. His family had direct links to Royalty and still owned huge estates in the south of England. Lloyds' names were maintained more for tradition than need, and the family's trust portfolio kept a small team busy at the Credit Suisse in Zurich. Well over six feet in height and always impeccably dressed, he radiated a charisma that swept others along, and tempered it by understating his actual power wherever possible. He was a product of Repton, Eton and Oxford. A Royalist and politically conservative, he did his job because he liked it.

Callows, meanwhile, was the opposite: a brilliant red brick scholar, he was the son of a Midlands' shoe merchant who was driven by personal ambition. Although only ten years separated their ages, and both held knighthoods, Tansey-Williams was considered by many to be Callows' mentor and protector in the minefields of Whitehall.

Tansey-Williams looked down his long nose as Callows entered and jabbed a finger at a chair.

"Martin. Nice of you to come over."

Callows wasn't fooled by the bonhomie. He had known Tansey-Williams too long, and he knew what this was all about.

He sat and they made small talk, until the secretary had poured fresh coffee for Tansey-Williams and brought a cup for Callows. Then, finally, rain running in small rivulets down the tinted windows, Tansey-Williams held up the yellow file that had been on his desk.

"Right. What the hell is going on?"

"Presumably you're talking about…"

"Don't presume! Know!" Tansey-Williams snapped.

"That's the problem. We don't know enough."

"You know enough to put a kill order on a man we once valued, a man to whom we pay a pension, a man disabled in the line of duty!"

"The end justifies the means," Callows rumbled back, his great leonine head lowered and his eyes glaring.

"What end? You don't have an end do you?"

"Good men are dead! Maimed! We don't know why. Someone who was close to Morton knows something that we don't. That's his daughter. We go to pick her up and three men are dead…"

"Shot, very skilfully I might add, by one of your own bodyguards…"

"We didn't know that. The fact is, we still aren't sure. Quayle is not only technically capable of having killed them; he was also close to Morton – and could well have been involved from day one. In everything!"

"I would like you to tell me about… everything," Tansey-Williams said icily, his long manicured fingers drumming on the file.

"You gave me carte blanche to get this resolved. Now, if…"

"I did not give you carte blanche to drag the name of the service through the mud. Which is precisely what is going to happen. You have people at Milburn who think they've been 'got at', a spate of murders, a blinded man who's now fearful for his wife's safety... and rightfully so! For God's sake, man. They gutted his dog on the living room floor. Who are these people? How close are we? What are they hiding? I'm not concerned with your carte blanche, nor the authority of any of my senior men. I am concerned with the defence of the nation, and by God, I will ask any question I like, of whom I like, where I like and when I like. Understood?"

Callows nodded just once.

"Let's hear it. A full brief. Then we can consider what else needs to be done."

Callows talked for a full hour, Tansey-Williams occasionally stopping him with a question, and then letting the brief go on. Finally, he sat back in the big leather chair and fingers steepled together.

"So, after you realised that Quayle hadn't done the killing, you still didn't lift the Metro order."

"No. I thought that, if I left enough pressure on him, he might just bring in the bacon anyway, even if only to get us to leave him alone."

"Her."

"Sorry?"

"Her." Tansey-Williams repeated. "It would work if you positioned the threat at Morton's daughter. He's not frightened of you. But," he said firmly, "we are not the Americans. Call it off."

"Sir Gordon, we think he's now out of Germany after that cock-up in Munich. The job is done. Let me leave it alone for another couple of days. Whatever he's doing, it's not lying idle. He'll be looking for whatever it is that's behind all this, and if he thinks the pressure is off, he'll go back to his bloody shack on the beach. He might just turn up something, and soon!"

"Just hope it's not you," Tansey-Williams said dryly.

Callows gave a dry smile but, deep in his heart, there was a flicker of fear at the thought.

"All right. Forty eight hours longer. Then call in the pack. And then I want to run him."

"You what?" Callows asked stunned.

"Run him. Like you should have done when you realised how close he was to Morton."

"You mean get him back on service? Sir, he's mentally unstable!"

"Not according to the doctor he isn't. And you were trying to use him anyway."

"At a distance," Callows qualified.

"Run him," Tansey-Williams said with finality.

At last, Callows relented. "I'll make John Burmeister his controller."

"Not Burmeister. Look in the files. There's no love lost between 'em. Berlin in '81."

"I know about Berlin," Callows said protectively. "But everyone gets one mistake, surely?"

"Not with Quayle, it seems. I will be recalling Hugh Cockburn from Prague. He and Quayle go way back. Anyone gets him onside again, it will be Cockburn..."

*

Quayle had watched the policemen round the house for half a day now, and the pattern seemed set. One constable in the garden walking an irregular patrol round the rear of the small garden shed and back up the narrow driveway around Black's car. There was a Panda parked up the street with two others, but they hadn't moved all morning, sitting in the car, allowing a second passing patrol car to drop them sandwiches just before noon. A tall dark-haired woman had stepped from the front door and walked up the street midmorning, one of the pair in the car stepping out and escorting her up to the grocery store on the corner. What Quayle noticed was that he hadn't been carrying her bag back. His hands had been in the jacket pockets.

Armed police were still a rarity in Britain, and those walking with their hands close to their guns even rarer. Something must have happened since the first hit. He watched for another hour, then climbed back out over the roof of the empty house and walked down to the public house on the main road where he had left the car.

Visiting hours at the hospital were varied, but few visitors were admitted after eight at night. He would wait until then. Driving down to the high street, he left the car in a commercial car park and walked until he found a stationer's shop. There, in amongst the cards and magazines and road maps, he found a lined pad, two different coloured pens, and a small pad of yellow sticky Post It notes. Stopping in a another small shop that had pre-wrapped sandwiches and pies in a warmer, he bought the least offensive looking plastic offering and a can of something that claimed to be real orange juice. He then sat in the car, and began to jot notes on the lined page of the pad, then similar references on the Post It notes, which he stuck above and below a centre line with dates, rather like a critical path analysis. Every now and then he stopped jotting, to lift up the can and drink, the sandwich dry and deserted on the seat beside him.

He worked until he needed the interior light to see, positioning the pieces of the puzzle as best he could – both on the paper and in his mind – and then, finally grunting in frustration, he put the pad face down on the seat and rubbed his eyes tiredly. Twenty minutes later, he was in the car park of the hospital, and soon he was walking through the front door, his new identity in his pocket. He took the lift, smiling dryly at the staff as they entered, and exited on the fifth floor, his tired looking overcoat and sensible black shoes identifying him as a policeman to anyone who bothered to look.

Down the corridor, sitting outside a door trying to look alert, was a real police officer, a second chair beside him unoccupied. Quayle ambled down toward him, pulling a warrant card from his pocket. He had had it for some years, but the design hadn't changed that much and he knew it would work.

Acting bored, he held it up to the seated officer, who was rising putting his cap on.

"Go get a cuppa, son. I'll be inside for half an hour or so."

The officer looked puzzled.

"No visitors was what I was told."

"I'm not a bloody visitor. I'm Special Branch. Now, be a good boy and go get a cuppa or something. I don't want to be disturbed. Call your nick if you like…" Quayle pushed past him, knowing, like a confidence man, that the permission to call his station would be enough to prevent him doing it.

"No, that should be OK, sir," the constable said.

Quayle just grunted and pushed the door open, silently closing it behind him.

Inside, Black sat up in the bed, his face still heavily bandaged.

"That you, nurse?" he asked. Staff usually announced who they were on entering. There were even some whose footsteps he already recognised.

"No," Quayle said, "it's not."

The voice made every muscle in Black's body turn rigid. "Who are you? How did you get in here?" he asked, pulling himself up awkwardly.

"Don't shout out," Quayle began. "Mr Pope asked me to give you a message."

"Pope? He's… Oh, my God! Quayle, you're Titus Quayle!"

"I am. How are the eyes?"

Black was taken aback by the question. "No news is good news. What do you want?"

"Half of Europe is after me. I don't like it much. I want to know what you know about it. I need your help."

"Just like that?"

"Yes," Quayle countered. "Just like that."

"I told 'em you didn't do it," Black said. "Quayle, I'm out of it now."

"I didn't figure you for a loser. Not the way Pope spoke of you…"

"Fuck you! Want to know the problem? Try taking my dog for a walk. Be a bit messy, Quayle! Dragging his guts around outside his body and with a cut throat. They said my wife's next. And I don't have any fucking eyes, so I can't fucking see 'em coming. OK?"

"No," said Quayle, understanding the police presence round Black's home. "But I can. I was at your house today. You wife is better protected than the PM."

"I know she is," Black snapped.

"So help me. No-one will know."

"Why?"

"Someone threw acid in your face. That's tough, but stop lying there feeling sorry for yourself. You know more about this whole thing than anyone. Help me and I will help you."

"How?" Black asked angrily.

"I'll get the bastards who did your eyes. I'll get the bastards who killed your dog. I'll get the bastards who won't let your wife walk up to the corner without a diplomatic protection squad officer walking with her. I'll get the bastards who are fucking up my life."

"You won't," Black said bitterly. "From what I can see, they're way too big, way too far up. Untouchables."

Quayle's eyes narrowed and he leant forward, over Black's bed.

"Bullshit. No-one is untouchable. No-one!" He paused to let that sink in. "So?"

Black sat in silence for several seconds, the only sound the clock ticking on the wall.

"This is a breach of the Official Secrets Act. It's everything I swore to defend," he said miserably.

Quayle shrugged, as if Black could see him.

"You can't use the law. You're outside it already."

"Who said I would use the law?" Quayle said innocently.

Black gave a short hard laugh, but his demeanour changed almost immediately. He turned his sightless, bandaged head at Quayle. "If I tell you what I know... they will try and kill you. They will do anything to prevent any further investigation."

It was Quayle's turn to laugh. "What's new?"

At last, Black was weakening.

"Who is running the job now?"

"John Burmeister," Black answered.

"That cretin?" Quayle shot back. Things were falling into place. "What am I supposed to have that they all want?"

"It began with Morton's Daughter. The old man was working on a file before he retired. It's been lifted. All our copies. Computer purged. Even the Russians are interested. A low grade defector came over. He knew we had a man on it back in '80-whatever. Immediately he mentioned it, people began to die. We never knew its significance. Every effort to establish what the hell it was all about ended up with people dying. It's big Quayle, very big. I thought that Morton's daughter might know where he would have left a hard copy. It wasn't complete, you see – and, from what I know of Teddy Morton, he would never have left it unfinished. So somewhere out there is the file. Whatever is in it is worth killing for. I sent Pope out to cover the girl. I knew that they would get to her soon. They knew I would too."

"What's the file about?" Quayle asked.

"We don't know. Gabriella Kreski. Morton visited her before going to Australia. He said something to her. Led her to believe it was dangerous. But that's all he said. The Russians call it 'Long Knives'."

"And Teddy left his hard copy somewhere?"

"Not just a hard copy, possibly a file nearly complete. Don't forget he was down in Australia two years before he died. He wasn't just teaching kids German and History, I don't think. That wasn't Teddy."

"Lots of time to put it together," Quayle agreed aloud. "It must detail the group that's trying to keep it quiet."

"Correct." Black paused there, thinking quickly. Then, as if coming to a decision, he said, "I had a visitor recently. The day after I was admitted."

"Who?"

"Dunno. I was pretty groggy. Came in very quietly. Said something. Guttural accent. Left something near my hand..." He held it up to Quayle. "What is it?"

Quayle took the small metal disc, tarnished by time, and held it to the light from the bathroom. He had seen one before.

"It's Soviet. A medal. The ribbon's long gone, as has the mounting, but the rest is still there. It's old. Someone valued this."

"What medal?" Black asked, intrigued. "Can you tell?"

"It's a 'Hero of the Soviet Union',"

"Shit! That's like a Victoria Cross, isn't it?"

164

"They don't come any higher in Russia."

"So my visitor was a Soviet?"

"Yes, I would say so. If you figure out what he wanted, let me know. Thanks for your input." Quayle looked at his watch. "Where can I find Gabriella Kreski?"

Black told him the address, then asked, "What was the message?"

"What?"

"The message from Pope."

"Oh yes. He said he was sorry. He wasn't ready for the trains."

"Sorry for what?"

"Not coming back when he realised he'd shot three Fairies."

"I sent him down to protect Holly Morton. He had no orders to return or to stop doing just that."

"Wherever he is, he'll be pleased you said that," Quayle said.

Quayle was already at the door when Black spoke again, his hands up to his bandaged eyes in frustrated fury.

"Quayle, fuck the law! Take these people down. If you need help, I can give it – it's yours! You hear me?"

"I hear you," Quayle smiled.

*

Hugh Cockburn's recall orders gave him twenty four hours to clear his desk and return to London. Frustrated by the heavy bookings on the direct commercial flights, he ended up flying to Berlin and cadging a lift on a Royal Air Force transport. He had packed enough clothing for an extended attachment and left most of his other possessions for the Embassy relocation people to forward when he knew where he was going. He had been following the communications surrounding the hunt for Titus Quayle and, in his heart, he knew that his recall to London was to involve him in the search.

He'd known Titus better than anyone in the Service, and in their convoluted thinking they had probably decided that he could help. He remembered the last time they had gotten drunk together, Quayle mellowed by at least three bottles of Hungarian red wine, quoting great English poets and filthy limericks in the same breath, a blowsy French Embassy secretary running her hand up his leg and trying to whisper into his ear. It had been a freezing cold night outside and the fire in the cafe was glowing so warm. But, as always, the Hungarian Secret Police were pacing the pavement outside.

Cockburn remembered it well. Quayle had lurched to his feet, dumping the French girl on her bottom, and walked outside, accosted their tail and dragged him to sit with them and drink. The man had shrugged with typical mid-European nonchalance and agreed. Well, it was colder than a witch's tit outside.

On the plane, he crossed one leg over another and shifted his weight on the canvas seat. He could not imagine Quayle being involved in anything that could warrant a Metro order – and he would need solid evidence of that before he helped anyone. Holly Morton, who was also mentioned in the updates, was even more of an unlikely villain in the plot. He remembered her before she had flown to Greece: soft and feminine, a very attractive mid-thirties widow, Holly had been loaded with intelligence, sex appeal and a sense of humour. Teddy Morton's daughter, for Christ sake! Unthinkable that she could be anything other than who she was.

A crewman twenty feet up the fuselage made a drinking motion to him and he nodded.

A moment or two later, the corporal threaded his way back, gingerly holding a Styrofoam cup that steamed invitingly. Cockburn took the cup and smiled his thanks, spilt some, swore and sat sucking a burnt finger, hating the RAF, the service and Titus bloody Quayle – who, he felt sure, had gotten him dragged into this mess.

The big jet landed at RAF Brize Norton just after dark, and a service driver was waiting to drive him to London.

The terracotta tile roof of the Valldemosa house was wreathed in the soft smoke from the barbecue as Marco, resplendent in a white chef's hat, grilled fresh fish and huge local prawns, the soft strains of Mozart filtering through from the living room stereo. Holly sat in one of the deck chairs beneath the vine canopy and watched the show, suppressing a giggle as fat dropped into the fire and flames shot upward, threatening both Marco's moustache and his reputation as a chef. He was determined to make her enforced stay as pleasant as possible, and had been a charming host, taking her for long walks up through the vineyards and olive groves, the armed men never far behind. There he regaled her with the history of the Islands, the people, and his love for his own native Italy.

"But why are you here, if you love Italy so much?" she had asked. "Wait, don't tell me. You love Italy, but Italy doesn't love you!"

"Alas, Italy loves me so much they want me to return," he grinned like some loveable buccaneer. "A small matter of some unpaid taxes!"

They sat at the table, the big cat sleepily opening an eye at the smells, and ate the fish, their plates piled high with salads and fresh bread from the bakery in the village.

"God, I hope Titus is alright," she finally said.

"You love him," Marco said. It was a statement, not a question.

She nodded.

"And you really know nothing of him?"

She nodded again.

"Then it's time you did. Maybe then you will fear for him less and fear for them more, eh?" Marco began to laugh, a rich, bass, larger than life sound. "Fill your glass and I will tell you a tale of high adventure, of heroes and dragons in another land and in another time..."

She smiled and sat back in her chair.

"I met Titus in Jebel Muhkta prison in Libya." All of a sudden the atmosphere had changed. He was deadly serious now, the laughing pirate gone and another deeper harder man manifesting in his place. "I had done a deal with them. Milk powder. They wouldn't pay – so I sent two of my people in to try and collect the cheque. They threw them in jail in Tripoli. I went to get them out, paid some people – as is the way there – but realised too late that I'd paid the wrong people. I had made powerful enemies. My men got away – but, as for me, I ended up in the Jebel Muhkta." Marco paused and slugged back his wine, as if to try and clear a taste from his mouth. "If there's a hell on this earth, then it is that place. High dry concrete walls surround a baking square and a rancid well. Above, like a rocky shrine to the dead, stands the Jebel, the hill. Every day we would go up the hill and smash rocks with our bare hands. If someone fell, they lay there until they died. At night, if we were lucky, we were marched back to eat chicken and rice. If we were not, it was Arabic bread, stale with water from the well. We had to pray to Allah and attend prayers five times a day, and if we got the words wrong we were beaten. The guards beat men with sticks and hoses and, at night, you could hear the screams.

"No-one ever leaves the Jebel. If it's not the beating, it's dysentery or beriberi or one of a hundred nutritional complaints. I'd been there two weeks when Titus arrived. They'd beaten him on the truck and threw him off the back like he was dead already, laughing and joking with one another. But he stood and walked to solitary. Only the tough ones go straight into solitary."

He stopped and took up the wine bottle, offering to fill her glass – but she shook her head, too horrified at the story to want more. He filled his own glass and carried on.

"About a week later, he joined the main population. I was one of only three other Europeans in there, so we took him with us to our room, the one we shared with seventy others. Quickly we began to learn things from him. He seemed to know when the guards were coming, when to steal something, when to speak. There was another Italian. A man called Morretti. We would pool our food, the four of us. Nurse each other when sick. Morretti was a small wizened chap, an agnostic gambler turned Christian. He had a Bible. God knows where he got it from. One day they found it. There was the usual screaming and ranting – but they found something new this time. They nailed up a cross in the square.

"Morretti wasn't strong. He would have died the first day. So Titus said that the Bible was his. That afternoon, in front of the whole population, they gave him the choice. Acknowledge Allah as the one

God and Mohammed as his prophet – or be crucified. He refused. They began to beat him, on his knees in the dust like an animal, five or six of them with long staves. He refused again so they nailed him up. They thought it a great joke, give a Christian a real Christian death." He sipped at his wine and ran the glass round his forehead, cooling his brow. "The pictures you see of Christ on the cross? They cannot convey the pain or the despair that crucifixion brings. When your knees are bent up, your chest hanging down over, you cannot breathe. For hour after hour, you can only take short shallow breaths, each one a stabbing pain because the lungs are collapsing. And, all the time, your entire weight is hanging on the nails through your hands. The pain is excruciating, enough to make strong men beg for death. Christ was young and strong and they hurried him along on the third day with a spear thrust. It is a long lingering death.

"Titus became a symbol for us. Every day he lived up there, every day he spat back at them, every time he managed a curse of his parched tongue, we rejoiced in his spirit. A dignitary was to arrive on his fourth day, so at nightfall we were allowed to cut him down. Men came from all over the prison, Muslim men, Hindu, Christian, even a few Buddhists. They gave their hoarded food and bits of medicines they had stolen and secreted around the place. More than that, they gave their prayers. He was no longer just a man. He was everything we wanted to be. He was strong, he was proud, his dignity and his spirit were intact – and his will to live was astonishing. We nursed him back to health as best we could. Eventually, he was back breaking rocks with the others, but the guards gave him a wide berth from then on. They believed he was something unnatural.

"Well, one day he told me he was going over the wall. I begged him to take me. He agreed. We broke out that night. Even weak, after two years of eating shit, he was formidable. He killed two guards with his bare hands. We took a truck, rolled it down the slope towards the main road, starting the engine a mile from the prison. From there we headed east towards Cairo, out into the desert. He saved my life more than once along the way. When we were found, we had actually crossed into

Egypt, and someone contacted my Embassy. In all that time, we never knew his job. I suspected, of course. But he was bitter at being left behind. That much was plain."

He sipped his wine again and smiled at Holly across the table top.

"So fear not for his safety. Fear more for his soul. He has seen too much for one man. Now he needs peace and laughter and family around him." He paused. "And fear for those he hunts. If I were they, knowing him as I do, I would just kill myself and be done with it." He laughed again – and then the old Marco was back. "Come, you have yet to taste my expresso!"

The car took the bend fast and Cockburn put his hand up to steady himself. The traffic was light, considering the proximity to London, and the driver was giving no quarter.

"Slow down!" Cockburn said. "Whatever it is can wait."

The man eased off the speed and studiously ignored his look in the mirror, a funny half-smile on his face. Eventually, the car drew to a halt outside a small mews house in Belgravia.

"I thought you were taking me to Century House," Cockburn said. He was tired and all the cloak and dagger nonsense was beginning to bore him.

"Orders," the driver said. "I'll wait here for you."

"You do that," Cockburn replied dryly, stepping from the car.

As he did so, the door to the house opened, and a well-groomed woman in her fifties smiled welcomingly. "Mr Cockburn?" she said. "Do come in."

Further up the mews, a black London taxi stood in the darkness.

Quayle pulled himself up the last few feet of the down pipe and swung himself across onto the window sill of Gabriella Kreski's living room. He peered in, not expecting to see much at two in the morning, but more to confirm that the room was empty before he did the job on the door. Then he climbed down, hand over hand, until he felt the ground beneath his feet. Moving back round the front, he picked the lock on the street door and moved up the stairs three at a time, barely pausing at the top to pick the old Chubb like a professional thief.

He slipped into the room and swore softly. Inside it had the unmistakable air of a house not lived in. Quickly, he checked the bathroom and bedroom. All of the toiletries were gone, as were two suitcases, the dust silhouette on the shelf proof of their recent occupation.

He was already too late.

Letting himself out, he drove back onto the main Brighton to Horsham road, then cut north to Godalming, taking the back roads. When he arrived just before dawn, he broke into the offices of a local solicitor, bypassing the basic Telecom alarm system, and crawled into the attic storage area. There he carefully moved boxes until he found the one he was after. It sat above a box of old crampons, harness, ice axes and other assorted mountaineering paraphernalia. The paraphernalia of his climbing days. Carefully sliding the masking tape off one of the boxes, he began to work through the contents with a torch held in his mouth. Half an hour later, he replaced the boxes as he had found them and was on his way back to London.

Once there, he checked into a small West Kensington hotel, one he knew had direct dial telephones in the rooms, and stood under a hot shower, the fine jets pelting his tired body. As he dried himself, he looked at his watch. There were still two hours until he could make the call. He had remembered Teddy Morton talking about Gabriella Kreski, and the fact that she wrote articles for an obscure subscription-only Chess magazine under a pen name. Now that he had an old copy of the magazine from his personal effects, he had their address and phone number as well.

At 9am, he dialled the number and spoke to a Dickensian sounding character who began to quiz him.

"What do you want her for?" he asked in a shaky old voice.

"I'm an old friend from Poland," Quayle replied, thickening his accent "She said that, if ever I was here, I was to call and we could play. She was rather insistent..."

"Well," the old man said, seemingly pleased with Quayle's credentials. "I'm afraid you shan't be able to play her. She is abroad, you see."

"Not visiting her brother again, is she?" he tried. Morton had once told him that her brother was a lecturer at Trinity College, a gifted violinist by anyone's standard.

"Oh you know him then? Jolly good. Yes she is, but we aren't supposed to know that – only, he phoned to say that her article wouldn't be coming this month. We only have a week to the deadline, you see, and a big hole on page four. So if you see her, would you..."

My God, Quayle thought, Kreski must have been getting old to have allowed her brother to make that call.

"Yes, of course," he said. "I'll ask her for you."

"She's rather good on Queens challenge, you see," the old man explained as if he wouldn't ask if she were a mere defensive player.

If she's run, thought Quayle, *then she's scared – and if I've found her, then others can too.*

CHAPTER EIGHT

At precisely the same moment that Titus Quayle was booking himself onto a noon Air Lingus flight to Dublin, Hugh Cockburn walked up the stairs into Milburn House and showed his identification to the porter at the desk.

"Sir Martin is expecting you," the porter said, his thumb jerking at the narrow dingy flight of stairs.

Moments later, Cockburn was ushered into Sir Martin Callows' office. The Deputy Director General sat behind his desk, one huge hand holding a golden pen and writing noiselessly on a white pad.

"Took your time getting here," he muttered.

"It was late when I got in," Cockburn answered. "Everyone had gone home."

Callows gave a porcine grunt and leant forward to speak into his intercom. "Get Burmeister in here," he said, and his secretary's voice buzzed back with a metallic reply that neither man could understand. "You been following the search for Quayle?" he asked, putting his pen down.

"In so much as reading the station updates, yes I have."

"How much do you know about him? You worked together enough times?"

"Enough to know that you won't find him and take him if he doesn't want to come."

"You rate him that highly?"

"He's good. As good as any man we ever fielded. But it's not that I rate him so high, he couldn't be caught. Everyone can be found sooner or later." He paused there for a second. "I just don't rate the people who are looking for him."

Callows raised an eyebrow.

"And don't ask me to take on the job or assist," Cockburn added. "I'm yet to be convinced that he's done anything that warrants this kind of extreme action."

"Don't take that tone of voice with me, lad!" Callows warned.

"With due respect, Sir Martin, I have over twenty years in the service. My judgement is what I'm paid for. My judgement and my experience. Within my service conditions there are riders that allow me to use that experience and refuse to become involved in any venture that I consider to be either foolhardy, ill-conceived, or lacking in any rational objective."

"I know!" Callows interrupted. "I wrote them!" His head turned angrily as the door swung open and John Burmeister walked in. "You two know each other I presume," he muttered. "John has been running the file since the attack on Adrian Black. He can bring you up to date."

"Why am I here?" Cockburn asked. "If it's to help find..."

"Relax," Callows said, raising a hand and his eyes to the ceiling. "You aren't going to be asked to help take him out. To the contrary in fact..."

"We need your help, Cockburn," Burmeister spoke for the first time.

Cockburn looked at them both, the realisation dawning. "My God! You want me to run him! After all you've put him through, you want me to try to bring him on service again..."

"Not try. Succeed," Callows replied harshly. "He's the only one who knew enough about Morton, the man who wrote the files."

"What do you think?" Burmeister asked, leaning forward.

Cockburn just shook his head slowly, as if unable to believe them.

"Well?" Callows snapped.

"Well what?"

"What do you think?"

"I think you're a first class prick," Cockburn replied pronouncing every word clearly and standing up.

Burmeister winced but Callows threw back his head and laughed.

"I am that," he crowed. "Now get on with it!"

Dublin is a small old weathered city and one that Quayle knew well. Over successive visits he had marvelled at the destruction of the city's

174

character by its modern day planners, its vitality and soul gouged out by demolition men, the great wounds filled over with ugly blocks of flats and office buildings. At least Trinity University remained protected by history, for this was the very heart of old Dublin.

Quayle walked the cloisters looking for the administration section, pleasant memories of his own time at Cambridge flooding back. Eventually he was guided there by a student and stood, wearing an old coat and cap, before a bespectacled young woman. He knew his local accent wasn't up to the test, so instead he adopted the broader harsh tones of Ulster.

"I'm needing the address of the Polish fella that teaches the violin..."

"You mean Professor Lomza. Stefan Lomza?" she queried, looking him up and down. "What on earth for?"

"Got a delivery," Quayle replied.

"Well, we don't give out faculty addresses."

"Suit yourself darling, I'll dump it in front there." he indicated the immaculate lawns in the main square.

"Dump what?" She rose up another inch, ready to defend her beloved Trinity to the death.

"Two tons of manure," Quayle replied.

"What?"

"Horse shit," he replied loudly, like she was deaf.

"You will not! Wait here. I'll get his address. Dump it there!"

"Make up your mind woman," he said wearily.

Now, with the chill of the evening settling down over the city, he made his way up towards Rathgar, pulling the coat up over his aching shoulder. Another month and he knew Dublin's ancient stone streets would be shrouded in damp fog, laden with petrol fumes and smog. Walking slowly up Grafton Street amongst the last minute shoppers, he realised he was too early. He wanted to be at the Rathgar address after dark, so he settled himself into a pub near Stephens Green and nursed a glass of Guinness. He'd taken a room at a small hotel near the old railway station and, as he sat and sipped his drink, he wished he'd taken the time to sleep. He hadn't had a decent rest since the passage

175

to Newcastle – and he knew, only too well, that fatigue was the cause of most covert operational problems. Tired men make mistakes.

Then he mused, with some bitterness, that he hadn't slept so well in the last few years anyway, not until Holly came along: wonderful warm Holly, her smell on the pillow and her body curled into his back, her soft murmurs as she dreamed beside him.

Look after her Marco, my friend, for without her I have nothing.

Finishing the drink, he returned to the road, the street lights bright in the night. Taking a bus as far as Rathgar Road, he got out and walked up to the turning he wanted, then moved way from the traffic and along the narrower residential street.

The address was half way up on the right, a solid Georgian building with columned portico. The street was devoid of movement and he moved round the back. Still making sure that he was unobserved, he took up position to watch the windows. He had never met Gabriella Kreski, but knew her age and her background and was pleased to notice that every curtain in the house was drawn. While it meant that he couldn't see in, it was a good sign. It meant she was probably there – and, what's more, was observing some basic security procedures.

After half an hour had passed, he used a pool of darkness to climb the back wall until he was on the first floor. Then, pulling a small battery-operated audio enhancer from his pocket, he placed it on the glass of a window and began to listen. He was rewarded on the fourth window with a woman's voice, old but strong, and speaking fast Polish. The other voice was a man's and, as they argued about the merits of some obscure composer, he used her name. 'Gabriella...' Quayle smiled to himself and eased back down to the ground. Then he made his way back to the hotel.

Tomorrow he would make contact.

He slept lightly, the cough of the man next door harsh and grating through the thin old walls, and he was back watching the Georgian House by seven the next morning. It was almost ten by the time Gabriella Kreski stepped onto the road, a sensible green coat over her shoulder and a string shopping bag in her hand. Three hundred feet away, Quayle watched her from the back of a hired van and was about to get out and follow when he noticed two men in a parked car, one climbing out onto the pavement as son as Gabriella appeared.

He had seen the car arrive just before eight and had thought nothing of it. Now, however, everything had changed. He swore silently to himself, thinking fast. They were here when Lomza left for work, so they knew she may well have been alone in the house. If they were going to take her it should have been then. So perhaps they did not know she was alone? They may have just arrived and been incredibly lucky to get a live sighting within a couple of hours of finding a potential hidey-hole.

Quayle watched her walk a few paces. Then blue exhaust fumes rose from up behind the watcher's car. He switched his gaze to the walking tag and saw him put his hand up to his ear.

Ear piece receiver. That meant the tag car could follow or give instructions. They might well be calling in help. If they knew Kreski's background, they would know she would spot a lone walking watcher very quickly.

She would be taking the bus, that much he knew. Starting the van, he drove in the other direction to take the first right turn then right again, doubling back on himself to end up back on Rathgar Road, hopefully in sight of the bus stop. She must have had a timetable because, almost immediately, a big orange double decker pulled into the stop and she climbed on board with several other people.

He tagged at a distance most of the day, following her from the supermarket to the post office and finally the library, where she sat for three hours. The watchers were still there, joined now by two others. All day long they switched positions, the walker following her into buildings and then re-appearing, changing his coat often or wearing a hat.

Finally, when she walked up to Bewleys in Grafton Road, Quayle saw his chance. He didn't know who they were – and, until he did, it was difficult to establish what threat they meant. He would try and get to Gabriella and at least warn her. Now, with a bigger team, she was less likely to realise she was being watched.

The pavement was crowded and the old coffee shop was busy. As soon as the current walker was momentarily separated from his vehicle, Quayle moved into the shop.

He scanned the room quickly but could not see her. He waited for a few minutes outside the ladies, aware he was losing valuable time, and when she finally appeared he breathed a slow sigh of relief. He was about to move forward when the driver of the watcher car walked through the doors. They had changed roles. Swearing to himself, a bitter little curse, he waited until a woman with a baby and some shopping was moving his way and quickly jumped in to offer to help. Relieved, the lady agreed. He took two of her packages and, as they brushed past Gabriella's table, the woman with the baby thanked him and said the car wasn't far. Quayle smiled easily. It was the normality of appearance he wanted. He would have to try again later.

As they pushed their way through the front door, he glanced back and took a good look at the man who had driven the watcher car all day. As Quayle looked, the man raised his hand to his face to scratch at something and he fixed the image in his memory.

From opposite the coffee shop, he watched through the windows of a store. The watchers were all out on the pavement – waiting for something to happen. *Come on, Gabriella,* he thought. *Do something soon. Go home, go to a friend's, do bloody something! You're an old lady now. You must be tired. Go home. Please. I'm getting exposed here...*

The field craft lecturers would have marked him as blown within a hour of starting, even changing his jacket and cap as he did. One watcher – tag, tail whatever you wanted to call them – was only good for an hour, and then only if they were very talented, changing the way they walked with heel lifts or introducing a change in the gait or even a limp. Quayle had never been one of the best watchers ever passed out of Norfolk – he was to big to melt into crowds – but at least he was competent. MI5 had the real experts who could watch a party for weeks and never be suspected. The danger was that he had been on the job now for over five hours. The other team were obviously not expecting to be watched themselves, or he would have been blown hours ago.

He trailed Gabriella and her fan club for another three hours, the old woman calling on her brother at the University, and finally visiting a friend. Nightfall was rapidly approaching when she stepped back out of her friend's door to begin what Quayle hoped was her way home. There were still four watchers in the other group and, since they hadn't seen him by now, he was gaining confidence. The dark would be his ally. As she moved off up the street, he moved up closer, eventually overtaking on a parallel road to work from the front.

They had moved only three hundred yards when Quayle, moving catlike through the trees just inside Stephens Green, noticed the change of pattern. There were now two watchers walking and, up ahead, a car began to move. He watched it pull over further up the road and the last man and the driver get out – supposedly to look under the bonnet. They were boxing her in, Quayle realised. They were going to snatch her.

Gabriella had noticed it too, stiffening and slowing in her walk. She was onto them at last.

Cross over, he willed her. *Cross over the road, come to me Gabriella!* In all her training sessions she had stressed the tried and tested method of breaking out of a box. Two front and two back, no flankers. Break to one side and see which group reacts first, see who leads them, see who hesitates. She turned ultra cool now, watched the traffic and stepped onto the road to cross over onto the park side. *Good girl,* he said softly, *keep coming. You won't want to because the park will make it easier for them.*

The watchers had looked up and the trailing pair hesitated for a second. Gabriella was half way over now and, as a big bus roared past behind her, Quayle called low but loud enough to be heard over the noise from the bus. "Keep moving Gabby, keep coming!"

It was the name Teddy Morton had always used for her.

He saw her look for a second, half fearful as she heard the call. Then resolution set in and she stepped onto the pavement. To her credit, not once did she look into the dark of the trees from where the voice had come from. Instead, she just walked purposefully about her business.

The two tail watchers were only thirty feet behind her now, almost abreast of Quayle in the trees. One of the other pair had left the driver closing the car bonnet. Soon, he too had crossed – but was now directly to her left.

Unless someone began to run, she had broken the box, moving two halves of the threat into one area, just like the lectures always said to do. But suddenly there were two new men further up. *Jesus,* Quayle thought, *now six. They are serious.*

One of the tail men dropped his hand into his coat pocket and Quayle moved.

He came out of the tree line onto the leafy pavement like a shadow, only feet behind the trailing pair, and took the man on the right first. Putting a full contact punch into the base of the man's neck and as he began to fall, Quayle flicked his hand over sideways and followed the blow round onto the second walker, crashing into his collar bone. As he turned, his face creasing as the pain hit, Quayle's second blow took him hard on the temple and he sank like a stone.

He bundled both men into the bushes as a car's headlights flashed over them, then ran back into the trees, moving parallel to the road at a steady pace. So far he hadn't been seen by the front group – but he only had seconds remaining. He broke clear of the pools of darkness under the trees beside Gabriella, as the man who had left the car grabbed her arm. Her other hand was coming clear of the handbag. Quayle saw the small silver gun coming up in her hand and he swung his leg up, his foot flashing out. The man grunted and fell to his knees, his hand letting go of her arm. Quayle's foot flashed up again smashing into his face with a solid meaty thump, the man dropping down onto the pavement, his kidneys ruptured and his jaw broken.

Quayle grabbed her arm. "Quick, Gabby. The trees!"

Propelling her towards the dark, he turned to the last of the watchers, the two in front. One had dropped into a marksman's crouch, complete surprise on his face, a bulbous nosed gun coming clear of his coat.

Quayle thought better of it and he too darted into the dark, pushing the old woman in front of him. Stumbling over a tree root, the string bag still in one hand, the little silver gun in the other, she plunged forward. Quayle scooped her up as the first shot was fired, a dull muffled thud through the silencer on the man's gun. She tried to turn, her old face angry, to bring her gun to bear – but Quayle pushed it down.

"No! Keep moving. Go, go!"

"I've run enough, young Quayle!" she snapped her old voice furious. He didn't ask how she knew it was him, just pushed her further into the tree line. She made to talk as they stopped, but he put a hand to his lips. "Shhhh!" Then he pushed her down onto the knees in the dark of a tree trunk.

There were now three silhouettes moving slowly towards them, two in front and a third one further up the road. All had guns drawn. *Where are the Garda when you need them?* he thought. *If they all have silencers, they can blast away all night and no-one will be the wiser.*

The third man dropped from view. Quayle knew where he was going. He was moving round the back. He didn't like that at all. Standing silently, his back to the tree trunk, he watched them approach for a second, one leading the other, their heads turning as they swept the darkness with increasingly good night vision. He pirouetted silently, until at last he faced the broad trunk of the tree, and slid around its base to see if he could locate the third man. Nothing.

Moving back around, he dropped into a crouch beside Gabriella.

He moved until his lips were at her ear.

"Stay very still," he whispered. "I'll draw them away."

Thirty yards away, he made his first deliberate noise – and earned the uneasy feeling of immediate success when a bullet *thunked* into a tree a few feet away, bits of bark flying off into the dark damp grass under his feet. He moved another twenty feet away – and there he dropped into in the darkness beneath a large shrub, saying his mantra over and over again, controlling his breathing for the attack.

Come on, you bastard. Come into my bit of the darkness. I'll be like your worst fucking nightmare come true.

They were very close now, the pair of them moving at a quick pace, thinking that their quarry had kept moving. Soon they came abreast of the bush under which Quayle lay. In the same moment that they appeared, he launched up like a pouncing panther, absolutely silent, a black shape in a black night.

One of the men was fast. Quayle felt the muzzle blast tug at his sleeve as his elbow snapped up beneath the man's chin, the satisfying feeling of the strike masking the fear of the gun. Then he turned on one foot like a dancer, low and perfectly balanced, coming out of the move like a coiled snake, fluid and black and unbelievably fast. A second shot up very close – the silencer ineffective now after two rounds had gone through it – and the bone of the man's cranium crunching under his fist.

NO! There is another! his brain screamed at him. *Not a silenced gun, but a small one, close, very close...* and he rolled down as another shot snapped off, tugging at his jacket.

A man began to scream in the dark of Stephens Green.

"Quayle, hurry! We must go!"

Rolling to his left, he spun around, looking for a silhouette. *A trick. It had all been a trick. They knew it was me.* Somewhere out here was another man with a big gun.

The screaming went on. *Knee or stomach wound,* thought Quayle. *Shit, where is he? Shot one of his own men. He'll be angry now.*

"Quayle!" the voice called. "Don't fight me. I am with you!"

He took the man from behind, the neck hold millimetres from the pressure points.

"Who are you, bastard?" Quayle's voice rasped in his ear.

"Kirov. Major. KGB," came back the strangled reply. "Alexi Kirov. I'm with you..."

"Bullshit!"

"Black... medal..."

Quayle released the pressure an iota. "What did you say?"

"I gave Black... medal..."

"What medal?"

"Let me go first."

Kirov was getting tired of the pain in his neck and shoulders, so Quayle released more of the pressure.

"What fucking medal?"

"My father's. A 1944 Hero," the wiry little Russian replied.

"Why?" Quayle snapped, letting go. The man's gun lay on the ground.

"Not now. The Garda will be coming. We must go!" He bent to pick up the gun, a big automatic, and brushed the damp grass of it, then holstered it in one fluid move.

"They will now," Quayle said acidly, pointing to the man who had stopped screaming and now just moaned and sobbed.

"It's noisy but effective," Kirov replied. "Come on. Kreski is by the tree where you left her."

"I want the driver. I want to know who they are."

"That's him." Kirov pointed to the man on the ground. In the distance the sirens had started and were getting closer. "Come on!"

Quayle crossed to the man and bent over. Something he had seen earlier in the day was worrying him. He grabbed the man's right hand and lifted it.

On the little finger was a ring.

He pulled it off and rolled it in his hand.

It was square.

*

Hugh Cockburn had spent two days reading the files in central registry and, now up to date, he was ready to begin.

Throwing his coat on one of the hard steel chairs in the cheerless little room he'd been allotted, he took a look around. Except for the computer terminal, nothing had changed in here since the '60s; he half-expected to see a camp bed somewhere and a map on the wall with one lonely little pin where some man was trying to stay alive. *John Le Carré, eat your heart out,* he thought. There was a neat stack of jotter pads and six sharpened pencils lined up side by side on one desk and, on the other, an old black bakelite telephone sat in obsolete solitude. On the wall was a photocopied request from accounts to record the number and time duration of all international calls, and a notice about a change in the canteen hours. The small window was grimy and sad little trickles of rain obscured the street lights outside. He shook his head. *Home again, home again, jiggedy jig. Fucking magic.*

The door burst back open – and there, solid like a rock, black face smiling cheerfully and a hot coffee steaming in her hand, was a person he hadn't seen before.

"Hi! You must be Mr Cockburn. Milk and no sugar. Right?"

He looked at the cup in her hand.

"Who are you?"

"I'm your dogsbody and bottle washer," she said, holding out her other hand, "Chloe Bowie. Your assistant."

"Ah," he said dryly. "I didn't know I had an assistant."

"Well you have. Welcome back to Disneyland. I'm looking forward to working with you."

"Oh? Why?" Falling back into his chair, he crossed one leg over the other.

"You have a bit of a reputation. Fun to work for, I suppose."

Cockburn smiled grimly. "Not on this job I won't be."

In return, she smiled bravely at him. "It won't be too bad. You know him well, don't you? The elusive Mr Quayle. From what I've heard, I think I'd like him."

Cockburn threw back his head and laughed.

"What's funny?" Chloe asked.

"It's like liking a Spanish fighting bull. Admire them from a distance, preferably from behind a big concrete wall..." He paused. "No, I'm being unfair. Ti's OK. His problem is he gets involved. Allows things to become a crusade. Good and evil, it's all simple to him."

"And not to you?" she asked, intuitively.

"No. Not to me," he replied, sipping gingerly at the coffee.

"And you don't get involved. Become a crusader?"

"Rule number one."

She studied him for a second. This was the other half of the reputation. Hugh Cockburn was the original ice-man on a job. As a controller he was flawless, his planning was immaculate – and, the worse it got, the cooler he became. Unflappable was the word used by one of the women up in travel.

"I like crusaders," she said.

"You like the romance. Not the reality. They marched three thousand miles, some of them in bare feet, they starved, they perished from diseases – and, when they arrived in the Holy Land, two or three years later, they took their swords and slew the foe. Blood ran in the streets and the bodies piled up. They were driven by something deep inside them and men like that are dangerous. They don't lie down and die, they don't give up. They just keep going."

"Is Titus Quayle like that?" she asked.

He nodded, sipping the coffee.

"Do you like him?"

He looked at her and smiled, "That's the bugger of it. Yes, yes I do. Come on. I'll buy you a drink."

*

"How long had you been onto me?" Quayle demanded.

They had gathered in a small rented cottage that Kirov had found two days before. The furniture was old but functional and a small coal fire burned in the hearth.

"I was not onto you. I knew you would turn up sooner or later at Kreski's. Once I knew where she was, it was easy. I was following the second group that had tagged her yesterday. Coming across you at the park was a stroke of luck. For them too. It was you they were after. They knew you would come."

"How did you know I saw Adrian Black?"

"Because I would have. We are not so different, you and I."

Quayle smiled at that. "You're not the run of the mill Kilo man. Not at all."

"I joined late," Kirov said, as if it explained everything.

"Militia?"

"*Nyet.* Army."

"If you wanted intelligence, why not GRU?"

Kirov tapped his head with his finger, as if to say they were crazy.

"Really? Or did you fail the selection?"

Kirov gave a short dry laugh. "I was Spetznatz!"

Quayle shrugged as if unimpressed, but viewing the little Russian with a new respect. A special forces officer who crossed over the great divide. Army to KGB. The antipathy was legendary and they spent as much time watching each other as they did genuine enemies of the state. That made him a real maverick.

"OK," Quayle said. "Start at the beginning. What's the KGB interest in this shit fight?"

"It began," Kirov said, "with the killing at your safe house in Sussex of a man your people called Yuri Simonov and the team of people from MI6."

"What do you mean *called*?" Quayle asked.

Kirov bent over the embers in the hearth and prodded them with a poker. "Its been going on a while now. Your Morton knew it, long before we did. Yuri Simonov was not a KGB analyst. KGB yes, but operations from Directorate Four. I never met him, but he was good. Hand picked for this job..."

"What was the mission objective?"

"He was to try and stir up your end. We were aware that Morton had done some work on a group he'd found. Extreme right wing, we think – but thinkers, conservatives, not neo-Nazis. We had people working also. Then we began hitting walls. Every time our people followed a channel, it was blocked for them. Our mistake was one of priorities. We didn't put sufficient resources on the problem at the time. By the time we realised the importance of the issue it was too late. We needed to see if we could trigger a reaction from your people, and maybe move Long Knives up on your priorities. A case of: if they have, maybe we should have..."

"There are other ways of getting other teams interested," Quayle rebuffed. "Seems very convoluted."

"What is this word?"

"Long and twisting."

"Ah yes, the feeling in Centre was one of... how should I say this?" He thought about it, then said, "Too little too late. It was playing an ace. We knew that, if your people thought they'd extracted something significant, it would be given the right treatment."

"It set off a witch-hunt," Quayle said dryly.

"We thought that, once they had the girl, the investigation would swing to the other factor. The file. Long Knives. Credibility feeds on itself, yes?"

"So what is Long Knives?"

Kirov squatted, staring into the embers, the soft warm light flickering of his face. He pondered his answer for a second or two, and at that moment Gabriella came in from the small kitchen with a tray of sandwiches.

"Our name for a file. A group. Big. Powerful. Everywhere. Very wealthy, very influential. Extreme. That's all I can tell you."

"It's not much."

"It's all we have."

"I thought you said that you had an investigation running?"

"We did."

"And?"

"We have a problem. The same as your people..."

Quayle was getting irritated. "What are you saying, man?"

"Both investigators died. Mysteriously. Our files have gone too."

"From Moscow Centre?" Quayle's eyes opened fractionally wider. "Jesus! The place is supposedly impregnable!"

"That's what we thought. So... we were hoping Morton's work was intact somewhere."

"It will be," Gabriella said firmly. "It will be." Settling into the armchair, she held out a plate, offering him a sandwich.

"And they think I have it," Quayle said, the words tinged with bitterness.

"Or Holly," Gabriella corrected.

"Not Holly," Quayle said firmly. "No way."

"She may know without realising it," Kirov suggested

"Unlikely. Teddy completely divorced his service life from his personal. Even more so with a thing like this. He would have known, back at the start, that he'd uncovered something very nasty. So you can go back and tell your masters that I don't have the file and know nothing of it. Neither does Teddy Morton's daughter."

"I'm not going back until all this is over."

"It is over," Quayle uttered.

"Not for me. Not until the files are recovered. Either ours or Morton's. It's not over until we find out who's killing our people. And it's not over for you either. You wouldn't walk away from this. It's them and us, Quayle. MI6 and KGB, if you like."

"Six? No thanks, I'm retired."

"OK then. You and me."

"Why?" he asked. "Even if I go for it, I don't need you."

"You were close to Morton. You knew the way he thought, the way he planned. If anyone can work out where he left his files. It's you. Now, you may be good. But so am I, and I have the resources of Centre. That's not a bad package."

For a time there was silence in the room.

"Listen to me," Kirov snapped. "The people who are after you are not the players any more. That order was rescinded last night. These people took out a safe house in Sussex and they took out an entire office in Moscow. There are about thirty people dead to date. They have resources and they have talent. They are dangerous. They are good. They are after you and the girl. You are the last links with the last hard evidence. Do you think they will stop? Eh? Because you want to be left alone? No," he smiled warily, "you're not giving in on this one, you just don't want me getting in the way. Sorry, Tovarich. I'm on the job. Either with you or not, but I'm there. Now, you can muddy my water, or I can muddy yours. I say we'd be better together."

Quayle gave up on the soft retired stance. "You're sure about that? The metro order has been rescinded?"

"Yes."

"Thanks for small mercies. The bastards. I'm going to find the files. You just stay out of my way."

"And when you get them?"

"I'll decide what is to be done with them."

"We need access, Quayle. It's a problem for your government and mine, maybe the Poles, the Americans... Everyone!"

"I'll decide," Quayle repeated.

"There's a man in Moscow who knows more than me. If he can convince you, will you co-operate?"

"Who is it?"

"My boss. General in charge of the Fourth Directorate."

"Bullshit. You're a major. You report through to a section Colonel"

"Not any more. Head of Directorate. That's how important this thing is. I have no controller. I'm free to do what I think best. Quayle, I think you should meet him."

"How much does he know?"

"More than you and me," he laughed, "but that's not difficult."

Quayle turned to Gabriella. It was time, he decided, to accomplish the very thing he'd first come to Ireland to do. "Tell me about Teddy before he went to Australia. Did you see him at all?"

"Yes. He came down to my flat twice the month before he left. We sat and talked about old times, but his mind was elsewhere."

"How do you mean?"

"We played chess and he lost twice in a row. Unthinkable that he should do that! In all the years we played, I only ever beat him four times – and each victory was rich and well-earned. He was a master, as you know. Well, that night, it felt hollow. Hollow because his mind was on something else and not on the game. I rebuked him. Him the original clear thinker! He was thinking clearly, I know now, but about something else entirely..." She waved her hand theatrically, seeming to enjoy the contribution she was able to make, but then her demeanour changed and a flash of something clouded her eyes. With his long experience of people under pressure, Quayle knew it to be not uncertainty, but fear. "He would tell me little. By then, I was retired and need-to-know is still a good policy. But I could tell that he had found something. Something evil."

"Why evil?"

"What do you mean?"

"Why that word?" Quayle asked. Teddy Morton was not a dramatic man. He was a scholar and a pragmatist. If he had used the word himself then it would be significant.

"It was not a thing one could pin point. But he was uneasy. Normally he found his work for the service a challenge. Stimulating. A battle of wits with worthy opponents." She smiled at Alexi Kirov. "But not this time. This time, he was disturbed. He was worried to the point where he wasn't interested in winning a game of chess. That, for Edward Morton, was tantamount to a priest doubting his beliefs."

"Did he say anything about it at all?"

"No, just a reference that may have been the file name."

"Which was?"

"Broken Square." She paused, taking them both in. "He finished the visit very depressed but trying not to show it, quoting 'Drake's Drum'. 'And drum them up the channel like we drummed them long ago...' " At last she shrugged. "It's strange, but I never really did understand his passion for lesser English poets."

*

Cockburn arrived, bleary eyed, at seven the following morning – and was pleasantly surprised to find Chloe there already, her notes piled across the desk and a sheaf of file requests for him to sign. The canteen was yet to open, so he got himself a cup of coffee from a machine on the floor above and sat down at his empty desk, pushing the old telephone off to one side.

"So where do we start?" Chloe asked.

Cockburn lit a cigarette and looked at her.

"This is a no smoking area," she said, with a raised eyebrow looking at the door.

190

"Fuck 'em," was his reply. His head ached and he wasn't feeling well.

She laughed delightedly. "Big night?" she asked innocently, knowing the answer only too well. She had dragged him round half the trendy wine bars in Soho.

He shook his head, regretting ever going out with her, and even more trying to keep pace. "Put a big piece of paper on the wall. One of those flip chart things."

A couple of minutes later, she was back with a pad and a couple of marker pens.

"Right, let's start at the beginning. Our man spends twenty odd good years in the service. Very talented, very handy chap all in all. Learns fast, thinks on his feet. Is forced into retirement on medical grounds. What have we got?"

She thought for a moment. "Experience, anger, enough knowledge to be a real handful?"

"Good, write that up. Now, experience... Let's list the things that he can use that for. Start with the basics. What does an experienced field man have that he can use?"

"How do you mean?"

"Well, do you buy your veggies at Sainsbury's?"

"Hell no! I have a mate with a..." She paused, as realisation hit her. "Contacts!" she exclaimed.

"Right! Mark it with a tick. We want all the file references on every job in the last ten years where he reported a local name or a new source..." He paused, and returned to his analogy. "What do you pay your mate with?"

"Money?"

"Bank accounts. Every field man worth his salt has about a hundred all over the place. Check on all the personas issued by passports, then match the names against accounts on the continent where there have been withdrawals in excess of ten thousand sterling in cash."

"How the hell do I do that?"

"Interpol. Channel the request through liaison at the Yard. Code it with a Charlie X-Ray. That means it's a job for Number Ten. You'll be surprised at the speed of response..."

"This is fun!" she said, lighting a cigarette herself.

By 4pm that afternoon, they had filled up nine pages of notes and had seventeen people of various disciplines working to provide information. Even so, Cockburn knew he was only covering ground that others had done before. He wrote out a short message and asked Chloe to walk down to the offices of the Telegraph and the Times and insert it in the personal columns for one week. The message read 'T. Phone home. All is forgiven. Love Hugh.'

"It's worth a go," he said to a sceptical looking Cloe. "When you've done those two, get on the phone, do La Monde, The Herald Tribune, and one of the big German dailies."

"Doesn't seem very original," she said.

"Nothing that's good ever is. It's all been done before..." He looked up quickly. "Titus has a lawyer here in this country. Check his file, get the man's name. See if he's been in touch or anything. Then get onto the Tate Gallery and Sotheby's. Find out where someone would dump a collection of religious icons if they needed to..."

"What?"

"Titus. He restores icons. His collection was substantial some years ago. He may want to realise some cash."

"I thought he was what is termed comfortable?" she asked.

"Very, but as with most of these family things, it's largely tied up. He couldn't access much of it in a hurry. Having said that, talk to the bank. His family have used Coutts for years. If they give you the run around – which is quite likely – talk to the Five counter people. They must have records." He stood up and took his coat from the steel peg behind the door "Then talk to travel. Get me a ticket to fly to Frankfurt tomorrow."

"Where are you going?"

"Adrian Black is coming out of hospital again tonight."

"New angle? He's been interviewed by everyone except News at Ten..."

"Dunno," he replied, "but I have a feeling we only have half the story."

"How do you mean?"

"The file story on the art dealer in Venice. That was a friends of Ti's. Well, two bodies turned up a couple of days later."

"We knew that," she said.

"Well, it turns out they weren't players, and they weren't freelancers on the King's or Kaiser's shilling either."

"Sorry," Chloe said, shaking her head. "You've lost me."

"Two heavies have a go at Ti's friends. They turn up dead in a canal out by the glass factory. But they weren't ours, and they weren't put in by the Surete or the other players. These guys were outsiders. So who the hell were they?"

"Are we sure he did them?" she asked, incredulous. "Seems a bit extreme."

"Let me tell you a story. Did you do the martial arts course at Lincoln?"

"Sort of," she admitted.

"Then you know the rituals. The bows, the protocol of the bout?"

"Yeah."

"A few years ago, some idiot administrator at Century was looking at Ti's records and saw that he hadn't done a recent competency test on the mat. Believe it or not, he was recalled from Romania to do it. Anyway, he arrived back, pissed off as you can imagine, only to find the instructors endorsed the order. So he goes up to the Oxford place. That's where the really nasty bits go on. Instead of waiting in the dojo, he walks into the changing room where the instructors are waiting, fully dressed in his street clothes, and beats the three of them then and there. No bow, no protocol, no niceties." Cockburn shook his head, half appalled, half impressed. "He must be a fourth dan by now. He would have taken out those two in Venice without a murmur after what they did."

*

Quayle placed a message to Kurt Eicheman from Orly airport and, as he stood in the booth waiting for the Bremen housewife on the other end of the line to get a pencil, he watched the arrivals area behind him. He was confident he had shaken Alexi Kirov at Heathrow and was checking more from habit than anything else. Soon, the woman came back on the line, and as he spoke she took it down verbatim. Once Kurt received it he would know where to meet Quayle.

Putting the phone down, he walked direct from the phones to his departure gate for a flight to Oslo where he would buy a third ticket under a third name and enter Germany from the north. If all went to plan, he would be in Frankfurt that night – and, by then, he hoped that the German BND man had been able to find out something about the Geneva connection.

By 8pm that evening, he had room in a city centre hotel – and, taking a bag of recent purchases into the bathroom, he went to work. An hour later, his short grey hair was blond and he leant over the dressing table to look into the mirror as he dropped the green contact lenses into his eyes. Satisfied, he pulled on a pair of shoes that he had altered to change his walk and, grabbing an old coat, he walked out into the busy streets.

The rendezvous was a dingy porn theatre. Twenty minutes before the contact time, he slid his money under the glass window to a bored middle-aged woman and pushed through the grubby double doors. Inside there were seventeen rows of seats and, in the flickering light from the screen, he could see men scattered in the rows. Taking a seat up in the back – from which he could see both the entrance and the exits – he settled back to wait. Up on the screen, in vivid colour, a busty brunette was entertaining two black men. The sound was out of synch with her movements, mouths moving soundlessly, only to be followed a full second later by what the producers had hoped would be a lusty groan. A few rows in front, a transvestite moved seats and sat next to a balding man and they exchanged whispers, the blond wigged head then dropping into the other man's lap.

Moments later, the door swung back and a figure entered, sliding into a seat with a coat folded in its lap. Cigarette smoke drifted up from somewhere down front and, to Quayle's right, a man began fondling his partner, her head thrown back as his hand worked between her thighs.

Turning her head toward Quayle, she smiled invitingly. On her outstretched hand, he could see the glint of a wedding ring. One large white breast was now out of her blouse and a man in the row in front leant over and began to join in, his erection jutting clear of his trousers.

Up on the screen, the scene had changed. Now a girl dressed in a school uniform walked down a street and stopped to talk to an old man in a Mercedes.

The theatre doors eased back again and another figure entered, paused to allow his eyes to adjust to the light, and then moved up toward the back rows. It was the BND man. Quayle lifted his hand in recognition and Kurt dropped into the seat beside him.

"Nice spot," he whispered.

"Thought you'd like it," Quayle replied. "Anything for me?"

The woman down the row groaned as someone did something to her that she liked. In the dark the pale shapes of her legs were reaching upwards, toes pointed to the ceiling, as one of the men thrust into her.

"Ja. Maybe." He held out a piece of folded paper. "This man is a sometime right wing academic, sometime critic. Nasty little shit, but a good thinker. He was involved in something a few years ago and we got some photos. In one he wore a square ring. I'm told he's been low key in the last few years – so he may be out of favour and prepared to talk. Who knows?"

"Thanks Kurt. What about Geneva?"

"Nothing. This is it. But I'm still being watched. The kill order is off, so by whom eh?"

"Be careful," Quayle warned.

"Always!" he chuckled, the buccaneer still there. "I'm going to pull them in. Get them rousted by the police in the morning. Then we see who gets them out, and maybe get a link that way. Call tomorrow afternoon. Say you're looking for Annie. If Bremen says 'lemon' try the post restante at Fredrichstrasse. There will be a couple of leads for you. What name?"

"Collins," Quayle replied. Eicheman nodded and smiled, then stood and moved back down towards the doors.

Quayle gave him twenty minutes and then left by the fire exit, its old worn crash bar unlocked as he knew it would be. The Federal

Government might have put up with filthy porn theatres, but they were very strict on fire precautions.

On the street he moved carefully for a mile, then took a taxi back to the hotel.

The man he would need to visit lived in Goch, about an hour's drive away towards the Dutch border – so, the following morning, he checked out of the hotel, hired a car and took the main autobahn north-west. By 9am, he had reached the village.

Steiner's home was a solid old farmhouse outside the village, tucked into a stand of evergreen trees, remnants of the huge forest where Hitler's SS had once hidden an entire Panzer division before the push into the lowlands.

Parts of the Goch area were often off-limits to NATO personnel from nearby RAF Larbruch because of strong ties to the SS that dated back to the war, and some evenings the strains of the Horst Wessel anthem could be heard from the cellar bars as old grey-haired men remembered another time.

Remaining hidden, Quayle watched for an hour, but the late model Opel remained in the driveway and their were no visitors. A pair of Wellington boots stood by the kitchen door and smoke drifted lazily up from a chimney towards the front of the house.

Finally, he left the car behind and, having walked the last few yards to the front door, knocked loudly.

It was opened by a surprised, portly individual of around Quayle's height.

"Ja?"

"Herr Steiner?" Quayle asked, using his northern accent.

The man paused for a second, as if considering the question.

"Ja. But who are you?"

"We have mutual friends. May I come in?"

The florid-faced man looked at Quayle suspiciously and finally swung the door back to allow him to enter. Inside, the hall was dominated by a large Jacobean dresser and a coat rack festooned in jackets and scarves. Quayle followed the man into a large living room where a fire burned brightly in the hearth, dark smoke pluming up the chimney. A bright rug was spread between two large chairs and, on the floor beneath the dining table, a big antique Qashqai carpet gave the room a warm tone. The table itself was covered in papers, and shelves of books took up one entire wall. A stag in a hunting print gazed balefully down of another.

"Nice Shiraz Qashqai," Quayle said, pointing to the big red carpet under the dining table.

"Yes it is. So what can I do for you?"

"You can tell me where Herr Steiner is for starters," Quayle said, smiling nicely.

"What?" he replied indignantly. "I am Steiner. I own this house!"

"Bullshit. That carpet is very valuable. It's a real Qashqai, not a shiraz. No owner, however modest, would let me malign it. You are a big man. The boots and the coats are all small. And the fire burns brightly because you're burning paper. Paper that isn't yours..." Quayle swung his arm at the dining table. "You're not Steiner. So where is he? I won't ask again – and, if you're co-operative, you may just walk away from here. Vershtun?"

The man looked into Quayle's eyes, the contact lenses giving him a slightly crazed look.

"He has gone. I was looking for him also."

"Why are you burning his stuff?"

"We are partners on many projects. I don't want any material falling into the wrong hands. Publishing is very competitive," he said, raising his hands defensively.

"Where do you think he is?"

"I think, I think he may be dead..." The man stopped. "It's the cat. He didn't feed the cat for three days or more. He used to phone me and ask me to come over to do it if he was going away. He was always sticking his nose into things that were dangerous. Well, this time he stuck it in too far. Where do I think he is? I think he is dead! Some partner! Stupid little fool. Now I am making sure that nothing he has here will bring them to me!"

"Bring who?"

"Whoever it was that did for him..."

"Who might that be?" Quayle asked, his voice low and laced with menace.

"I don't know and I don't want to know," he answered childishly.

Quayle dug into his pocket. "Did he ever wear a ring like this?" He held it up for the other man to see.

"No."

This man was lying and Quayle knew it. He reached forward, took a hold of the man's cheek between two fingers and squeezed.

"Yes, yes, he did!" the man squealed. "Let go please, please..."

"When?"

Quayle let go and the man rubbed the red spot on his cheek with three fingers. "He stopped about a year ago. But he wore it often for three or four years before that."

"What was its significance?"

"I don't know. I asked once and he laughed. He said they would feel the might again."

"Who would?"

"Liberals, greenies, communists, the anti-nuclear people. He hated the lot of them, he said they were weak. A cancer. Then he stopped wearing the ring. He was bitter, angry. His work was also affected. He was like a boy who had his toys taken from him. Sulky."

So, thought Quayle, he got thrown out of whatever it was. *They obviously thought him a liability, and now they've iced him.*

"Did he travel at all? Anywhere regular? Over the period he wore the ring?"

"Regular? No. He went lots of places. Work."

"What work was that?"

"Critic. Theatre, ballet, films, art. I do food. Together we used to produce a package for the magazines."

"What were you looking for really?"

"What do you mean?"

"Don't fuck me about! Food and art is hardly competitive stuff. What was it that he was working on that you wanted?"

The man seemed to give in then, deflating before Quayle's eyes. As he sagged, he sat down in one of the chairs.

"The manuscript. He said he was doing an exposé. He had that look in his eye. It would be good. When he put his mind to something, he was quite talented. Better than me..."

"Did you find it?"

"No," he replied miserably. "It's gone."

"Where would he take it? Did he have an agent or a publisher?"

"No agent. He was too mean for that. He spoke of a publisher in Berlin. Melchun and something." He brightened up then. "They may have, it I suppose."

*

Cockburn sat opposite Black, who lay back in bed. The bandages were off his hands now and ugly weals of new pink skin and scar tissue criss-crossed the unburnt areas like a child had done it with a paint brush. His eyes were still covered, but the bandages had been taken off the rest of his face – and the deep pitted burns across his cheeks were horrific. Fresh dressings covered the places where the plastic surgeons had gone with the knife.

"I told you everything I could yesterday," he said to Cockburn.

"I'm not a copper, Adrian," Cockburn said. "I'm the poor bastard trying to find Titus Quayle."

"Well he's not under my bed."

"You're not helping, are you?"

Black sat up, angrily. "Why the fuck should I? Tell me! That poor bugger was hunted by every bastard with a gun because some fucking idiot in London fancied himself as a great detective! He had nothing to do with the missing file or the killings. The whole thing was an unmitigated disaster in the true traditions of the service. So why the fuck should I help you? So you can kiss and make up?" He leant back, his anger spent for the moment.

Cockburn looked at him and stood up. He had had enough. "He's an old friend of mine – that's why. I was pulled out of my station to come and find him. The hunt's over and the DG needs him back. Now, I personally don't give a shit if he tells Tansey-Williams to stuff it. In fact, I'd rather like to be there when he does. But someone else is after him. I think it's the same bunch that got the files. So you can lie here in your own self pity – I don't like losers anyway – but find him I will, and help him I will, with you or without you. "

With the final words ringing in Blacks' ears, he marched towards the door.

To Black, it was only too familiar.

"Cockburn? You on the level? You really trying to help?"

"Yes, I am."

"If you're lying to me, I'll get you for it. You know that."

"Yes," he replied softly. "I think you probably would."

"He was here. The night you flew back in. Walked in, bold as brass, past the police outside. Sent them off for a cuppa." He smiled at the thought.

Cockburn walked back to the bed. "What did he want?"

"Same as you. What did I know about the Long Knives affair."

"How was he?"

"Never knew him before. But he was all there, if you know what I mean. Scary."

"That's him," Cockburn said, pleased. "Where did he go from here?"

"Dunno. He had his own leads. He wants to get to whoever's after the girl. But I had another visitor..." And he told Cockburn about the strange man who had left the medal.

"What's your feel?"

"If he's on the Kilo payroll, then they're as concerned as we are. Quayle knows about him too."

"If you were to find him, where would you look?"

Black thought for a second or two.

"That stupid manhunt would have chased any normal operative underground, back into his own channels, back into his contacts of long ago."

200

"That's the intention," Cockburn said dryly.

"Not this one," Black said. "Quayle's way too smart for that. He'll avoid the old haunts like the plague. Try the opposite. I'd look where he has a life the service doesn't know about, at more recent contacts."

"I never thought of that," Cockburn admitted.

"It's my job, son. Been finding people who didn't want to be found for years."

Cockburn thought for a minute, walked to the phone by Black's bed and dialled the office. *You know how to find people and I know Quayle,* he thought.

"Chloe? My friend spent some time in the Middle East. Yes. When he left, he travelled with a friend. I'd like his name, if you would."

That was all he could say over an open line, but he knew she would get the message.

CHAPTER NINE

Quayle had stopped at an autobahn service area and, through the noise of the manoeuvering juggernauts, he telephoned the conduit in Bremen, using the lemon code. It was affirmative and, smiling broadly, he ran back to the car. The post restante at the main post office closed at four. There were names waiting there for him. Something concrete at last. He silently blessed Kurt and, wheels spinning, headed back onto the autobahn and Frankfurt.

An hour later, he sat in a commercial parking building and split open the envelope. Two eight-by-ten inch black and white photographs dropped onto his lap. One was a grainy, badly lit shot, obviously from a surveillance camera. Three men sat round a desk in a crowded office, the two facing the camera circled in red pen. The police station, thought Quayle. The second was a better shot of the two men walking towards a car, obviously after release.

There was a note paper in the envelope too. He opened it now.

'Two watchers circled. False names no doubt. The thin one was called Gasser, Swiss, and the other, Duboir, is a French national. Definitely not playing on any national team. So who for? Release organised by Herr D.G.Schuter – lawyer of dubious background, but recent links put him as an occasional subcontracted advocate for Munchen Dag AG, a Bavarian holding company, and the Geneva law firm of Wald Dressen. Address in the phone book. The watchers dropped at the tower of executive apartments on Feldstrasse. Lift went to the seventh floor. Two apartments only. Clean up crew on the number on the back. Ask for Pauli. Call Bremen tonight.'

Geneva! The name leapt out of the page at him. He tried to place the name of the law firm but couldn't. *They'll be representing clients anyway,* he thought. *Maybe even Munchen Dag.* He started the car, then drove back onto the street to find a shop that sold maps of the city. He wanted the Feldstrasse. The two watchers would be pulled out quickly, now they were blown – but more would arrive. *Be there when the change over happens,* he thought. *Nice to have a little chat with one first.*

He stopped at a magazine stand, bought a map, and then crossed the street to a quick printing shop where he could borrow phone book. Schuters' name and address were there, just as Kurt had promised. He copied it down and handed the book back to the girl behind the counter with a smile, then walked back to the car map in hand. Now he wanted a list of the directors of both the holding company in Bavaria and the Swiss law firm, and he would ask Kurt for one more favour. Driving into the city, he found yet another friendly shopkeeper, who looked up enquiry agents on his behalf.

Twenty minutes later, he sat opposite a jowly ex-policeman in a shabby Formica and plastic office suite.

"My clients in England have been recommended a law firm in Geneva. It is their custom to check these things carefully. I want a full list of directors and senior partners, established clients and a feel for their reputation. Any hint of, shall we say anything untoward, would be most prejudicial to my clients interests."

"I understand, Herr..?"

"Collins."

"And the firm recommended?"

"Wald Dressen."

The man sat back in his chair, disappointment on his face. He was essentially an honest man and he felt bad about taking a client's money for nothing.

"Herr Collins, Wald Dressen is a very reputable well-established firm. They also have offices in Munich and Berlin. As a law firm they are above reproach. I would be stealing your money to do a search on them."

"Nevertheless, I have my brief from my client. Are you prepared to take the commission? If so, what is your fee structure?"

"If you insist. Of course. What currency?"

"US Dollars. Cash."

"Five hundred a day plus expenses. That buys you my expertise and some people on the ground."

"Here's fours days in advance. I have a second commission, same brief on a company called Munchen Dag AG in Bavaria. I don't have their address..."

"We'll find it."

Quayle stood. "I'll be in touch in forty-eight hours. Please have the task complete. For five hundred a day in cash – which we both know will never be put through the books for the Federal Government to tax – I expect confidentiality. Total and complete confidentiality. Do I make myself understood?"

The big man smiled. "Mr Collins, I forgot you were even here."

Quayle drove straight to the short stay executive apartments and parked the car up on a side street nearby. Slinging his bag in the boot and rubbing his tired eyes, he walked round to the front and entered the building.

The management office was on the ground floor and a bespectacled young man was delighted to show him a vacant apartment on the tenth floor.

"You have nothing lower?" Quayle asked.

"I'm sorry sir, only one on the eighth floor. The remainder are occupied until the end of the month at the earliest."

"Well," Quayle smiled, "the eighth floor should be fine. Same layout?"

"All identical, sir, other than the penthouse up on twelve. That's larger and has a sunken bath."

"Good. I shall pay you a month's deposit now, and take the keys with me."

As they turned towards the door, Quayle silently dropped his car keys onto the thick carpet.

A few minutes later, as they sat in the office, the young manager filling out the registration forms and receipt, Quayle's eyes swept the small room, the desk top and the wall planner. Finally, he saw what he was looking for. It wasn't on the wall at all. It was on the small computer screen. The house list and reservations diary.

He patted his pockets meaningfully.

"Oh dear," he said, "I seem to have dropped my keys. Must have been up in the apartment we looked at."

"If you would wait here sir, I could go up and get them?"

The manager was pleased. This booking put him on ninety per cent occupancy –and that was his trigger level for bonus from the company.

"That would be very kind," Quayle said – and, as the man left the office, he stepped behind the desk and sat down at the keyboard.

The menu was easy and simply asked him for the room number, or date requirement. He tapped in 701 and a name flashed back at him. Morse. Nationality English. He came out and went in again, this time entering 702. The name Keppler came back at him, but the address was familiar. He pulled out his jotted notes. It was the same as Schuter, the lawyer. Must be close to home. They were being careless. He smiled grimly, came out and tapped in 801. Another name came back, so he tried 802. Vacant. It must have been the apartment he had just taken. That meant he was in luck. He was directly overhead. 'Captain art though sleeping down below,' suddenly flashed though his mind. It was part of Drake's Drum, the poem quoted by Teddy Morton on his last visit to Gabriella Kreski. He came back to the menu, walked round to the front of the desk and sat down again. 'And we will drum them up the channel as we drummed them long ago.' The warning of the Armada. Full stretched canvas, salt and spray and heavy guns – and a man, legend said, playing bowls on Plymouth Ho. Henry Newbolt's particular style of patriotism.

Then it came in a flash. The warning. Quayle's eyes glittered for a second. Then he smiled as the manager re-entered the office, holding a sets of keys aloft.

"Ah. Thank you. That was very careless of me."

Soon, Quayle left with the keys, collected his bag and made his way up to the apartment. Rolling the carpet back from one corner of the wall, he leant down and attached a sucker cup device to the thin concrete floor. Then, taking the trailing wire, he plugged it into a small micro recorder and listened for a few moments.

Voices and a television in the background. He rolled the enhancer dial a fraction and the sound became clearer. The set was state of the art technology four years ago and had been given to Quayle by a grateful CIA man.

They were in, settled by the sound of it. He listened for half an hour longer, until finally he heard one of them phone out for food and talk about the evening television movie. Satisfied they weren't going anywhere, he dropped the earphones and turned the battery pack off. Then he showered and decided to try for some sleep. He hadn't slept properly in days, and now he had a few hours to kill.

He rolled between the clean starched sheets – but with the sleep came the demons, angry and malevolent, and he sat up, sweating and shaking, within an hour of lying down. It was the first time since leaving Serifos. He thought about Holly with Marco in Valldemosa.

It seemed like an omen, so with a shaking hand he reached for the phone – but somehow he found the discipline to be able to put it down again. He could have been traced this far already. Unlikely, but possible.

Getting up, he walked into the shower and stood beneath the pelting hot water.

*

"That's it then," Cockburn said, leaning over her shoulder. The microfiche reader was big and cumbersome so they had walked down into registry to read it there.

"I believe so," Chloe said. "The date's right. Italian business-man escapes Libyan Prison. How many could there be?"

"Bugger all from Jebel Muhkta, that's for sure..."

The news story was from page seventeen of the Times, and rated only four paragraphs, but the man's name was there.

"OK. Get onto Rome station. Ask them to get a recent address on this individual. Assume they'll have something by tomorrow. I'll put together a team from Milburn. Be ready to move in the morning."

"Milburn? Is that necessary? I rather liked it without them," she muttered.

"We aren't the only people looking for them, remember. I don't like the rough stuff."

That night, the Station Chief in Rome met a friend for a drink in a cafe after work. The man was in the anti-terrorist section of the police and owed MI6 a favour after they had handed over information about a Red Brigade member who was transiting through Italy. He left almost immediately and, by 8pm, had accessed the police computers, then hauled out operators for both immigration and the expatriate division of the tax department.

By 9pm, he was able to supply not only the man's Madrid address, but the name of a Spanish journalist who had recently finished an article on eccentric millionaires, a distinction that he felt included Marco Gambini. He handed over a sheaf of photos. The quality was good and the station chief was pleased. They would transmit well. Century would be happy and he could get an early night.

Chloe then raised the station chief in Madrid and asked him to pay a call on the journalist. "We need to know where this Marco character is now. Any hidey holes round the place, weekend retreats, boats, that sort of thing..." She paused to allow the voice scrambler to unravel things and spoke again, "I'll wait here for you to call back, shall I?"

"Who wants it?"

"Hugh Cockburn," Chloe answered

"Oh. Coming up in the world, are we?" He paused there but she didn't rise to the bait so he continued, "Don't wait. I'll get onto it tomorrow."

"Sorry. This is a grade one request," she said firmly.

The man was in the middle of a dinner party and his wife was not going to be impressed when he made excuses and walked out.

"It always is," he replied miserably and hung up.

Quayle crossed back to the listening device and bent down, lifting the headphones to his ears. He could hear television noise in the background and someone doing something in the small kitchen. Crossing back to the bedroom, he pulled on a dark blue track suit, running shoes and a wool balaclava, the face piece of which he rolled up over his eyebrows. He had no heavy knife, so made do with a small paring knife from the apartment's kitchen. He didn't need a weapon, but the psychological effect of its presence was crucial.

Pulling the apartment window open, he climbed out onto the balcony. The drop to the next floor was absolutely silent, and once there, he paused, listened and moved up to the window. It was open, draughts of warm air shifting the curtain in a soft wavy flow like seaweed. Swiftly, he moved along the balcony to the bedroom window. It too was open and he silently slid the window back and climbed in, the warm air stuffy and soporific after the freshness of the night outside.

In the living room, the television blared. From the hall, he could hear someone talking on the phone in angry fast French. *Duboir,* he thought. *If your masters aren't pleased, they'll be even less so after tonight.* He waited until the telephone was angrily slammed down, the tension and noise at their maximum. Then he stepped from the darkness of the bedroom.

The Frenchman looked, unable to believe what he was seeing. His consternation did not deter Quayle. He simply kept moving, his hand rising to strike low beneath the man's left ear; then, catching the falling dead-weight, he lowered him silently onto the grey carpet. Then, listening for a second, he moved smiling into the living room like a welcome visitor.

"Hello," he said. "It's me!"

The Swiss man was faster, standing and reaching for something in his jacket pocket – but Quayle was already there, gripping the other man's forearm with astonishing strength, the vicelike grip forcing him back down into the seat. The smile was still there, but Quayle's eyes were hard like granite as he looked down and saw the square ring on the man's finger.

He reached down into the man's pocket and pulled a small automatic clear, throwing it across the room.

"Sorry," he said in French. "Bedroom window was open! You really should be more careful. Never know who is about these days."

The man looked up, his eyes betraying the pain in his arm. "Who are you?"

"Titus Quayle. The one you're all looking for. Remember?" The man's eyes widened at the sound of the name, but he covered it quickly. "It's time we had a little talk, don't you think?"

"I don't know what you're talking about. I'm an engineer."

"Engineers don't have guns in their pockets. Engineers don't follow people. Engineers don't have cute little rings..." Quayle took the man's hand and squeezed the fingers together, crushing them against the ring. "Your friend Duboir. He is out in the hall. Can't tell me much for the moment, so you'll have to. I will ask a question and you will answer. No more, no less. Understand?"

The man spat an oath.

Quayle squeezed harder. "We can do this as long as you like," he said in a conversational tone. "What will happen is that you will have irreparable damage to the tendons in your fingers, and maybe break a bone or two."

As the man gave a gasp of pain, Quayle leant forward and spoke in a comfortable whisper, almost like an old friend might. "Then we can progress to some other part of your body. Don't get me wrong. I feel nothing. You're not protected by the law, or by anyone else. You have no rights whatsoever. There is just me and you. I want information and I will do anything to get it. That makes me a particularly nasty proposition. Take the line of least resistance. Tell me what I want to know."

"Fuck you," the man sneered through the pain.

"Oh well," Quayle said. "Into each life a little rain must fall." He smiled like a madman and took the small knife from his pants. "*Sabatier*. French. Not very sharp, but the point is quite good. Look!"

He stabbed the knife down into the man's thigh, the point tearing through his trousers and entering the muscle with a meaty thump.

The man groaned, his breath exploding from his lips in a saurian hiss of pain.

"Oops! Sorry. I can be so careless sometimes." Quayle smiled sweetly. Then he leant forward, his face inches from the other's, his right hand still holding the Swiss's left across his stomach. "Like I said. We can go on all night. You're frightened of the people you work for. I can understand that. It is all very well them expecting your silence. But then they aren't here and you are. You're the one with a veggie knife four inches from your pecker. Who knows where it will go next? You're the one who may be needing a blood transfusion before midnight because all yours is on the carpet, with your manhood. So, honour and all that aside –" He twisted the knife a sixteenth of an inch and the man snapped his head back, stifling a scream. "– who are you working for?"

"Schuter!" he gasped.

"Not good enough. He may be your boss, but who pays the money? Who calls the tune?"

"He does!"

"I'm not stupid."

"You will die for this..." he hissed.

"Maybe." Quayle shrugged, reaching for the knife handle. "But I don't give a fuck."

The Swiss man blanched.

"NO! Jesus no! I'm just a soldier! I don't know anyone senior. People are coming up soon. Day after tomorrow to see Schuter..."

"Who?"

"I'm to pick them up at the airport. Sikon. An American, and a Chinese."

"Coming from America?"

"From London."

"What flight?"

The man remained silent, so Quayle reached for the knife handle again.

"British Airways! In at 8.30pm. The American, he will be wearing a black coat and a checked hat!"

"Why were you following the BND man?"

"We thought you might come to see him."

"What have I got that your masters want?"

"We were to find you..."

"And?"

"Kill you. Nothing personal. I just follow orders."

He was frightened now, all his bluster gone – but Quayle knew that he had heard all he was going to hear from the Swiss. Time, he decided, to put them on ice.

Walking to the phone, he dialled the number Kurt had given him for the clean up crew.

*

It was in the pitch black darkness just before the dawn when the two cars coasted silently round the hill, engines and lights off. As they reached the boundaries of the property they slowed to a halt and remained there, just off the road. There were seven men and, as they climbed clear of the doors, they carried with them light packs of equipment and webbing rather like a soldier might. All were heavily armed. As soon as they had disembarked, they moved off into the trees, one group to go into the house and the other to secure the grounds. They would need to move fast. It would be light in an hour and they wanted to be well away by then, the job done.

The first group arrived at the high barbed wire fence and the leader dropped to his knees, pulling out a small pair of insulated bolt cutters and a small meter. Lifting the small crocodile clips up to the wire, he tested each strand for current. Satisfied that he knew which were live, he began cutting through the remaining strands. Finally finished, he pulled a gas mask over his thick curly hair and, looking to make sure the others had followed suit, he crawled under the wire and moved forward, a small gun in his right hand and a canister in his left.

It was only a minute or two later that the first dog came upon them. The leader dropped to his knee again, fighting his fear as the huge animal bounded at him, silent and fast. Lifting the spray can, he pointed it at the animal. Then, as soon as it leapt, he pressed the nozzle, directing the fine mixed spray of cyanide and CS gas into the great slavering jaws and eyes.

The hundred-and-thirty pound weight of the dog hit him full in the chest, and they both hit the ground with a thump. But the dog was already blind and dying, its great lungs having drawn in a fatal dose of the spray. With legs scrabbling, it rolled off him, huge blind eyes streaming as it rolled in its death throes, trying to understand what had happened to its strength and balance.

The man watched, pleased for a second, and then moved forward, the rest of the team hard behind him, the last man walking past the still twitching corpse three seconds later.

Two more dogs died in the next four minutes, the last near enough to be touched by his handler – except that the man was dead too, killed by the same lethal mixture.

Carlo Benitez was twenty four years old that day and had spent the morning in the village with his brother, drinking coffee and watching the village girls, and just enjoying being of the estate. He liked the work. God knows, he thought, few men in Espania pay wages like the Italian – but it was nice to be off for a few hours. He worked his way round the wire in the dark, his shotgun over his shoulder, its sawn-off barrel stubby and menacing. He had developed a fondness for it in the army, where in the elite unit he was proud to be part of, they were encouraged to innovate and show individual style. They had even guarded King Juan Carlos one summer when the Basques had threatened the unbelievable, but the drugs scandal had put paid to that career. Seventeen of them had been thrown out for the crimes of three.

Afterwards, the Italian had been there – or his people had – with offers of employment for all. At first he refused, deciding to return to his home on Majorca – but he remembered the offer when times got hard. Now here he was with six months pay guaranteed for what could be a shorter job. He had two other men with him trailing behind and to the left. There was another group somewhere opposite. The system of challenges worked well enough. He moved at a steady pace looking for the turnaround point and almost fell over the body of the dog by the wire.

He didn't pause for more than a second. Pulling the gun from his shoulder, he snapped a command at his men and began to run for the house, pumping a cartridge into the breach as he ran, feeling the adrenaline begin to course through his blood. The excitement was hot, like the matador in the ring before the horns of the bull. This was his honour and he was young and a man.

The guard at the heavy oak bodega doors saw the intruders seconds too late and took a full dose from the spray can in the face. He fell, a muffled rattle coming from his lips, his leg muscles beginning to convulse before he hit the ground. The intruders were pleased. They were at the doors and not a shot had been fired. Now there was time to take the locks the silent way. One of the group moved forward and pulled from his baggy pocket a set of master keys, keys that would open any lock made outside of the Iron Curtain. All had been purloined from their makers. The fifth key, a Chubb, turned the levers and they were in.

Confident that the other team would secure the grounds behind them, they broke into two pairs and began to move through the building, its circular shapes, turrets and solid walls unfamiliar, flashing powerful torches with hooded beams as they went. While the first pair moved all the way through to the kitchen, the second pushed through their third door and found Holly Morton curled up beneath a peasant quilt in bed. A powerful gloved hand covered her mouth and a dark shadow leant over her as she struggled.

"Come quietly puta, or you are dead like the rest!" one of them hissed. The accent was local, and thick with garlic. As the hand lifted up, a wide strip of white surgical tape was plastered across her mouth, and a second strip bound her hands. Then she was pulled from the bed with one mighty tug.

By now, the small procession was re-entering the living room, the man carrying the wide-eyed and terrified woman following the leader's hooded torch beam. Moments later, Marco Gambini appeared at the top of the steep stone stairs, a gun in his hand.

The leader turned, dropping into a crouch, and snapped away two rounds from his silenced gun. Marco staggered and fell back onto the landing, and they moved on, the two from the kitchen waiting at the door.

All hell seemed to break loose.

One of the waiting men seemed to be lifted by a flash of blue orange flame, flung backwards into the stone walls as the second man, turning too late, took the second deafening blast from Carlos Benitez's pump action shotgun at a range of three feet. The charge blew a great gaping hole the size of a bread plate out of his back, splattering gore on the carved doors and white painted walls.

The leader dropped to the floor and rolled behind one of the club chairs. While he scrabbled for safety, the man who was holding Holly dropped against the wall, reaching for his own gun.

As he did so, a vicious fire-fight developed out in the dark, the chattering slides of the silenced automatic weapons drowned out by the full throated roar of shotguns, and the berserker screams of bloodlust and pain. By now, the two groups were close enough to touch in the dark, close enough to be confused and die by a comrade's hand. Blue yellow muzzle flashes illuminating the dark.

All in all, it lasted less than a minute.

After it was done, the leader moved carefully back. Then, hurrying through the kitchen door, he ran around the side of the building to view the scene from a safe vantage. Nothing moved except for a man, one of his by the look of the pack, who tried to crawl somewhere.

He moved forward, called out to his comrade, who lifted Holly back on to his shoulder and came out of the main doors.

The leader walked toward the wounded man, the one crawling and bent down.

"Sorry," he said – and, putting the gun to his head, pulled the trigger.

He did it for each of the three wounded, and the last, Carlos Benitez, proud and Latin to the end, spat in his face as he did so, the saliva laced with pink frothy blood.

Flies were buzzing and settling on something inside the wire and the Fairy, an experienced man in his forties, lifted the binoculars to his eyes to try and get a better look. It was mid-morning and he was sweating in his heavy tweed jacket. *Sod these rush jobs,* he thought. *Going home for a pint at the local and suddenly we're all on a bloody blue job special flight of to sunny Palma. Could have given us time to get a change of clobber at least.* Focusing the lenses, he looked across the fence.

Oh fuck. Oh fuck. It's on!

"Get Cockburn. Quick!" he snapped to his partner.

"What?"

"Dead dog. Rottweiler or something. This place has been hit. We're going in..."

Bending down and speaking quickly into his radio, he scooped up his firearm from the seat of the car, slid over into the driver's seat and started the engine.

Cockburn and Chloe Bowie sat with a Milburn driver in a maroon sedan a hundred yards up the road. A third car, this one with a team of three Fairies and a borrowed medic, had pulled in behind them.

Cockburn saw the man running back toward them and heard the crackle of the radio in the team vehicle at their rear, its wheels spinning as it tore around them, throwing gravel in the air.

"What's happening?" he asked quickly

"Dunno. Frank's called the troops. He's going in. Do you want to follow?"

"Of course I bloody do!" Cockburn snapped as the runner arrived. "Well?"

"Dead guard dogs, sir. The governor reckons the place has been hit already."

Oh Christ, not when we're so close, please. If they tried to take him, there'll be many dead around – and, if he survived, he'll have gone back underground, deep underground.

"MOVE IT!" he thundered, and the runner bailed into the back seat with Chloe. Moments later, the driver gunned the engine and chased the other two cars down the long access road to the gates. Up ahead, the team leader hadn't stopped; he'd driven straight through them, his bonnet buckled from the impact, and kept on going.

"One of ours, is it, sir?" the driver asked. They didn't usually go in like the cavalry. Not damaging cars and things. That meant reports and claims and the admin men getting involved.

"I hope not. I hope he got away," Cockburn replied. Flies rose from the body of the dog as they roared past. "But catch up if you can!" he shouted over the engine noise. "If he's there, then he may think we're trying to hit him."

The big converted stone winery came up very quickly. As the driver pulled on the handbrake to slew the car sideways on the drive, blocking the road as he had been taught, Cockburn could see the two other team members running to a trellised rockery by the front doors, one stopping and the other going round the side of the house. As he threw open his door, he could hear them shouting Quayle's name, calling out that they were friendlies.

"Over here Mr Cockburn!" one called from the rockery.

Cockburn ran over to him, certain already, from the man's expression, what he'd found. Shouting for Chloe to stay where she was, he walked round the carnage.

"Any of these your man?"

"Jesus, what happened here?" he asked appalled.

The Fairy, a Falklands veteran shrugged. "Firefight. Two teams up close. The one lot locals by the look of the weaponry. They were probably guards. The others? Silenced Ingrams... Uniforms."

The man who had run around the house appeared back again, shaking his head.

Shit, Cockburn thought. *We've missed him.*

He thought for a minute, then turned to the pair. "Any of these people killed by hand, up close?"

The man looked back down at the bodies, big blue flies hovering over terrible wounds now dried and darkened in the morning sun.

"Not so far. All GSWs, but this one here had his last up close."

"What are you saying?" Cockburn asked.

"Someone went round and finished them off," the Fairy replied. "Your man perhaps?"

"Not his style," Cockburn replied.

Someone called something from the house and the young Royal Marines Medical Officer that Cockburn had borrowed grabbed his bag and ran inside.

"Live one!" the Fairy said. Then, flicking a look at the last man who had searched around the house, he called out, "Stay here!" and he too ran for the door.

Cockburn was hard on his heels, Chloe running from the car where she had waited. When they arrived, the medic was bending over a big barrel-chested man dressed only in shorts, who was lying at the head of the stairs. Blood had dried on a head wound but it had begun bleeding again, and he had a gun shot wound in his shoulder.

The doctor was flashing a torch into his eyes.

"Well?" Cockburn asked.

"Difficult to say with head wounds. Looks like a crease, certainly concussed. Involuntary reflexes seem alright but I want to do some X-Rays. The shoulder looks nasty enough but the entry is way over. Nothing vital in there except the bullet." He stopped talking, pulling a saline drip from his bag, stripped the feed needle clear and pushed it firmly into Marco's arm, handing the bag up to one of the Fairies to hold above the patient.

"Is this him?" the team leader asked.

"No. This is Marco Gambini. The owner of the house. I wonder why didn't they finish him off..."

"Angle of attack is from below. Two rounds would have knocked him on his back, then the punch-up starts outside. They probably thought he was dead already."

"I want a hospital," the doctor said.

"Not yet," Cockburn said. "I want to talk to him first."

"This is not negotiable," the doctor replied firmly.

"I said no."

"I don't take orders from you. I take my orders from the Officer Commanding Medical Services for the Corps of Royal Marines, and even then my first duty is to my patient. In this case, one who may die. Head wounds are tricky."

"How soon can I talk to him?"

"When he comes round."

"OK," Cockburn said, "I need a phone."

Fifty minutes later, a Spanish Air Force helicopter settled like a large insect onto the grass lawn and Marco Gambini was transferred to a military hospital outside Palma. Cockburn and the doctor travelled with him, while Chloe was left to liaise with the Spanish Intelligence operatives who would precede the arrival of the local police. She had been sick when she brushed past the dried gore on the wall, and almost fell over a body in the hall, one that seemed to have no chest left at all – but, for now, she was coping as well as she'd hopes.

Marco faded in and out of lucid thought throughout most of the day, sometimes rambling, sometimes just staring at the ceiling. It wasn't until nearly 5pm that Cockburn was able to talk to him when he suddenly tried to sit up, holding his bandaged shoulder with one hand and his head with the other, remembering the attack in vivid flashes.

"Holly. Where is she? Is she alright?"

Cockburn sat forward in his seat. "She was with you?"

Marco eyed him suspiciously. "Who the hell are you?" he thundered, then winced and held his head in his hands.

"My name is Hugh Cockburn. I am a friend of Titus. Was Titus with you?"

"He wasn't there," he answered, "but the girl was. Is she alright?"

"She wasn't there, Marco..."

"They got her then. Bastards! I saw them carrying her when I was shot..." Suddenly, he remembered his guards. "My people?"

"I'm sorry Marco," Cockburn replied, shaking his head.

"All of them?"

Cockburn nodded.

"My God..."

"Where is Titus, Marco? I must find him. He needs help."

The Italian fixed him with a look. Then, in perfect English, he delivered the only two words fit for the situation.

"Fuck off," he seethed.

An hour later, with the doctor signalling him from the hall, Cockburn was still trying to bring Marco around.

"Look, Marco. You're a friend of his. So am I. There are people after him. The same ones that took Holly. He can't fight them on his own. Sooner or later, they'll corner him somewhere."

"They better hope they don't. I know who I'm betting on."

"I still need to talk to him. He must have indicated where he was going."

"He didn't. He just said he had things to do and left me his most valued possession. Which I have lost..." he finished sadly.

"How will you tell him?" Cockburn tried.

"My public relations team will do that for me. I'll have the story of my home under attack in every paper in Europe. He'll know by tomorrow morning."

"And then?"

"He'll find them and take her back."

"And if she's dead?"

The Italian looked at him for a second, the bull strength and will faltering for a second.

"Then he is dead too. Inside."

Cockburn nodded, understanding it all perfectly now.

"Do me a favour?"

Marco nodded.

"Have your people write me into the story. Try and get Ti to phone me. Call me..." He dredged through his memories, all the way back to the last job they had done together. What had his cover been back then? He had been an engineering lecturer. "Call me Mr Spokes," he said. Some wag in travel had dreamed that one up and it had stuck for the entire mission.

"He spoke of you once in the Muhkta. He liked you. You and the German."

"The German..."

A look like revelation flickered across Cockburn's face. *I'm a bloody fool,* he thought, *a stupid incompetent arsehole. The German – of course!* "Kurt Eicheman!" he shouted triumphantly to himself. *If there's anyone, it's Kurt!*

He ran from the room, in time to be stopped in the hall by Cloe. They had been recalled to London.

*

Quayle looked at the small group of men sitting round the edges of the room. He would have preferred a mixed team – some women, some old, some young – but the cast-offs and the retired and the invalids was the best he could do. Kurt had risen to the occasion magnificently, giving the names of nine ex-BND and Customs men who could use the extra money and who would, he thought, be itching for a return to the harness. Of the nine, five had agreed. Now they sat around the briefing table in various types of dress, one with a suspiciously shaped bulge in his pocket. They knew they were working for an Englishman, but they also knew he was clean and that payment would be in cash. The job was simple. A full tag and follow operation. No watching, other than final destination, and then call him in. Their new paymaster evidently was not short of cash, so three cars and a motorbike sat waiting for them down in the basement parking area. One of the cars was even a taxi. He had Motorola handheld radios and the cars all had cell net phones. Full two-ways would have been better, they thought, but no way could they get permission and installations in the two hours they had left. Three of the five had been together in the BND in the days when they followed Russians all over the city; not only did they use the same jargon, they knew the street layouts like professionals. The other two were ex-Customs investigators, one in his 40s with only a stump where his right arm should have been, and the other breathing with a rasp, his lungs seared after a drum of chemicals had spilled over his face during a raid on a warehouse.

"These people use guns?" the one BND man asked.

"Yes," Quayle answered. "Do not become compromised, or you may find yourself in the shit. There'll be no police or back-up on this job, but it's one time only, so..."

"No problem," the man said, "I just like to know."

"What about decoys?" another asked.

"Unlikely, but bunch up at the start, and then be ready to split up if you have to. These people are very confident, but I think they're also so close to home that they're careless."

"Just like the Ivans," the oldest said.

Quayle looked at him and smiled. He hadn't heard that expression since Lincoln and the instructors, all wartime operatives.

The old man caught his look. "Don't worry about me, sonny. I was following men in these streets before you were born."

The others ragged him for a few seconds before Quayle spoke again. "Right, you have your radio call-signs. Heine will be here at this phone, in case your handhelds give out or you lose contact. Help me find where this man goes and you know what it's worth. I'll be in the taxi with Klaus. I'll tag the target in the terminal, and we'll take the first few kilometres. After that, wait for orders."

As they stood, Quayle moved forward to one of the BND, the one with the bulge in his pocket. Quayle tapped the object and the man's hand covered it defensively.

"Out with it."

The man shrugged and pulled an ageing Walther P38 from the pocket of his windbreaker.

221

"I know how to use it... and when to," he said firmly, in response to Quayle's look.

"Be sure you do. If you frighten my man off, no-one gets paid."

The others all glared at him. "Alright, alright," he conceded, lifting his hands dramatically. And the gun was given to Heine, the one-armed customs man, to hold with their other kit until the job was finished.

An hour later, Quayle – bearded, blonde, green-eyed and dressed in the uniform of a chauffeur – was holding up a fictitious name on a hand panel in the arrivals area of the terminal, hoping that his hastily assembled team of watchers could do the job. He had his doubts. The best teams had worked together for years and could almost anticipate each other's thoughts and actions, the drills and procedures – the fallbacks, the overlaps – worked and reworked a hundred times.

His taxi was out the front now, and the first relay car was only a mile away in case the target took the autobahn south and not north. Schuter lived to the north of the airport. *Come on then,* he thought, *let's be having you.* Quayle was almost sorry the man was an American. He liked them as a rule, the romantic in him finding their naivety appealing, their faith in justice and their leaders childlike. He was always disappointed when one turned out to be sour. Like a vintner with bad grapes from good vines and good soil. Teddy Morton had once described it that way, saying the soil of the American dream was no longer what it was, leached dry by the greedy and overworked by its own success.

He had been ignoring the possibility that the man wouldn't show all day – take another flight, fly into another airport or simply abandon the visit after the two men had disappeared – but he hoped that they were so confident that they would stick to their plans. Kurt's clean-up crew would have packed bags, toilet articles and enough to suggest a deliberate move. The two men had turned up as casualties in a road accident, unidentified until this morning, drugged to the extent that the last few hours would be fuzzy, the residual effect lasting some months. It was the only solution that allowed them to live, without

222

compromising the mission, one insisted on by Kurt. Quayle didn't care one way or another and conceded to Kurt's wish immediately, knowing that he needed the German's help in the coming hours if not days.

He looked down at his watch, thinking the arrival process through. American passport meant the non-EEC line and the usual delays of checking Turk and Sri-Lankan visas. *Give it twenty minutes,* he thought, *another twenty wondering if his suitcase had gone to Antigua or something. Any minute now.*

He left the position he was in, put the name board down, trying to look disappointed and walked back towards the exit doors. He wanted to see who the man left with when he did. He hung around another ten minutes before spotting his target. The description was accurate. A big heavily-jowled man, his hair grey and spiky: real middle America, complete with plaid shirt, loafers and striped trousers, the overcoat incongruously formal. Quayle watched as he shook hands with a man he hadn't seen before, noting the ring on the finger. A few stiff Germanic nods later, the stranger took the man's bags.

A moment later, another man appeared. Oriental in appearance, he came from behind, stepping forward for the introductions. Quayle looked at the men doing the pick-up. *These two are another calibre from the pair last night,* he thought. His eyes scouted around. *Probably, there was a fourth man in the car.* As they walked past him, he half turned away, already slipping the brocade buttons on his tunic. Then, once he was certain he had not been sighted, he followed them through the doors, a man and his wife between them. Pulling an overcoat on, the cap folded up and thrust into one of its voluminous pockets, he watched as a big cream coloured Mercedes Benz pulled up. Soon, the three Caucasian men were arguing good-naturedly about who would sit where, the Chinese watching and saying nothing.

Quayle dodged cars across the wide road, arriving at the waiting cab. There he slid into the seat.

The driver lifted the Motorola handheld to his mouth. "Cream 500 Mercedes, five men, licence as follows: Lima Seven Three Three Five. All acknowledge please."

The engine gunned into life and the taxicab darted out into the flow of traffic. Soon, they had taken up a position four cars behind the Mercedes.

"On the main road half kilometre from the first exit, fifty kilometres an hour, inside lane behind a red trailer. Did you get that, Two?"

Two came back with a snapped "Ja, rolling", and moved off the verge where he had been sitting with his bonnet up, looking miserable in the rain for the last half hour.

The driver looked across at Quayle, thoroughly enjoying himself. "Don't worry English. We won't lose him."

*

There was a car waiting at Gatwick Airport for Cockburn and Chloe, the same driver who had picked up Cockburn the night he had flown in to the RAF base only days before.

"The office doesn't know you're back, sir. Sir Gordon requests no contact until you've met with him."

"Same as last time?"

"No, sir. We're staying in Sussex." And, with that, the glass panel slid across, leaving the back seat in privacy.

Chloe looked at Cockburn, who shrugged and sat back in the deep seats. For a time they sat in silence, while the big car eased its way westwards through Crawley, the light drizzle softening the hard yellow street lights.

"You seem pretty sure about what's-his-name," she said softly.

"Eicheman?" He shrugged to himself. "Yes I am. I'm a bloody idiot. I should have thought of him before. He and Titus go way back. Career BND man, bloody good at his job. If Ti's convinced anyone to help, it will be Kurt. And if anyone will be willing to help, it will be Kurt. He owes Ti favours. Eicheman's a man who respects that type of thing."

"The old school," she said.

"No. Just another disobedient, stubborn, innovative, loyal bastard."

"Oh!" she said, chuckling. "You like him too then!"

"Don't remind me! Those two have given more controllers grey hair in both services than the rest put together. Kurt is now quite senior. Station Chief Frankfurt was his last move."

It was close to ten o'clock when the car pulled into a long gravel driveway a few miles outside Godalming. The house was a large red brick affair with roses growing in careful columns out front and a large barn along the garden's south aspect. Bright lights gave the whole area a showy staged look.

They were ushered into the drawing room by a uniformed maid, who closed the big double doors behind them. There, in front of the fire, stood Tansey-Williams. Behind him, a pair of long crossed legs protruded from a high-backed Queen Anne chair.

Tansey-Williams raised a hand in welcome.

"Come in, Hugh. You too, Miss Bowie. Sorry to drag you back like this – but things have been happening. First, I would like you to meet someone..."

The figure in the chair rose. The first thing Chloe saw was the eye patch on a lean hard face and, as her eyes dropped, taking him in, she saw the right arm hanging down, its hand in a glove. He smiled at her, a raffish confident smile – and, if only for a second, she went weak at the knees.

"My God," Cockburn said, "General Borshin."

He had studied pictures of the man a thousand times, the man responsible for all Soviet external operations. Here he was, in the same room as his arch-rival the Head of MI6, drinking brandy and chatting by the fire.

His thunder stolen for a second, Tansey-Williams glowered at Cockburn and then turned to Chloe. "May I introduce KGB General Nikolai Borshin, Head of Directorate Four in Moscow?"

She put out her hand, her mouth dropping open at the mention of the name.

"How do you do?" she said

He took her hand and nodded formally, then turned to Cockburn. "You are Hugh Cockburn?"

"I am."

"Interesting career. Prague, Berlin, Bucharest amongst your tally. Never Moscow?" Borshin was trying to score points.

Cockburn smiled. "Several times, but your people never knew. I took a photo of you the day you got the Directorate."

"Touché," he replied gallantly.

"Just as our people will never know he has been here today," Tansey-Williams said, stepping forward. "Sit down everyone. Let's get our cards on the table. Hugh, what news of Quayle?"

"He wasn't at the villa. But they got Holly Morton alive. He was never there. Just dropped her off."

"Dead end?"

"Not quite. I have another lead. I am also hoping that Quayle himself will be getting in touch when he hears about the kidnapping. But of his whereabouts? We have no idea."

"It would seem we have had more luck," Borshin said.

Cockburn leant forward in the firelight, his face a mask of disbelief. "What?"

" I have had a man here for a while. He met Quayle in Ireland, offered him help."

Cockburn allowed himself a wry smile. "Your man gets about. He also saw Adrian Black, didn't he?"

Borshin nodded.

"I wish he would stay the hell out of the way," Cockburn said bitterly. The comment was unfounded and he knew it. He was just frustrated that the Russian had beaten him to it twice in a row.

Tansey-Williams looked up sharply, but the KGB man waved him back.

"If it's any consolation, Quayle told him the same thing," Borshin chuckled out loud.

"Perhaps some background here?" Tansey-Williams said. Clipping the end off a cigar and taking a taper from the mantle, he dipped it into the fire and held the flame up to the cigar, puffing strongly. Finally satisfied, he looked at Chloe and Cockburn. "General Borshin inherited

226

a small team of people on a file they called Long Knives. We had Teddy Morton working on the same project without realising it. One day, the team is dead and the file is gone. Directorate Four put a man in as a defector. A top flight agent we had at the Midhurst House. He tempts us with a little titbit and ends up dead, the first in a string – and our files are gone too. Both teams at a dead end, except for Adrian Black's enquiry. General Borshin puts a new man in to try and watch our progress. He thinks, maybe, we'll stumble on something at our end…"

Cockburn interrupted, "Sorry, Sir Gordon, we are sure we're after the same thing?"

"Little doubt of that," Borshin said firmly.

"Then you've lost me. What has this to do with me?"

"Titus Quayle – who we inadvertently dragged back into this – is being hunted by the same group that we're after. But Titus is Titus, and now he's turning the tables on them. He came across three of them in Ireland and took out two more last night in Frankfurt. For the first time, there's someone getting close and staying alive."

Cockburn looked at Chloe with a raised eyebrow. "Kurt Eicheman," she mimed.

He nodded and she rolled her eyes to the ceiling as Tansey-Williams kept on speaking.

"So you're back here to fully understand the gravity of the situation. General Borshin is here with the approval, and on the suggestion of, Premier Gorbov – and was talking on the telephone this evening with Number 10. You are to team up with Alexi Kirov, the KGB man who found Quayle in Dublin, and work this one together. Find Quayle. See it finished as one."

"Resources?" Cockburn asked.

"Just what you've got for now. You will understand why later."

"I want a chap out of the BND, if you can swing it?"

"Reasons valid?"

"Very."

"Who?" Tansey-Williams asked

"Kurt Eicheman. He's Station Chief Frankfurt."

Tansey-Williams harrumphed a bit. He hadn't missed the significance of the city. "Keep it lean until you need muscle – then shout and I'll get you the Royal Marines if you want 'em…"

Borshin interrupted there with a dry smile, "I'll go one better. I'll get you a Spetznatz unit."

Tansey-Williams glared at him with hooded eyes for a second and then continued, "Get straight out again. Stay away from any mainstream contact. Come straight through to me. Quicker that way."

"Alexi Kirov is in Germany. Following your Mr Quayle," Borshin said. "He's waiting for you there."

"One last question," Cockburn said, leaning forward. "What the hell are we up against here?"

So Borshin began to speak.

*

"Move up three. Left, left on the roundabout…"

Up ahead, Quayle could see a motorcycle's rear lights in the rain. The car, number three, would be coming up to take over from the bike who had shadowed now for six or seven kilometres. So far, so good. They were now on a much smaller provincial road – still two lanes each side, but with a preponderance of farm vehicles, trucks with produce heading into the towns and cities. Quayle thought they must be somewhere near Kitzingen or Ansbach but was unsure, so kept his eyes peeled for a road sign. He was now confident that his motley old team could tag the target all the way. They hadn't put a foot wrong since the airport in Frankfurt two hours ago.

Up ahead, something was happening. The driver touched the brakes and, as he did so, the radio crackled into life. "Right turn right turn after the petrol station bottom of the hill. I'm overshooting…" As he said it, the car crossed the brow and began to descend.

Quayle looked across at the driver. "That must be a small access road."

"Ja."

"Right, let's move up. Take over."

The man's foot hit the accelerator. Quayle looked into the back seat, where the taxi sign and wiring sat. They had pulled over for a minute, thirty kilometres back, and ripped the frame off the roof. Now, they were using a second configuration of lights – so that, from the front at night, it would look like a fresh car. He groped for and found the map, pulling it onto his lap.

"Where are we?" Quayle asked the driver.

"Mittelfranken. Ansbach is maybe six or seven kilometres that way," he replied, jerking a thumb to the left.

The car began to slow. Up on the right, the petrol station lights appeared.

They took the bend fast.

"Don't lose him," Quayle warned as he looked back down at the map. He hated not knowing where they were.

Thirty seconds later, the driver cut his lights and brought the car to a halt on the road side in the dark.

"What?"

"There. Ahead. The turning with the sign. They went in there..."

Quayle threw the map on the floor, all thoughts geographical gone in an instant.

"Wait here. Lift the bonnet and mess around in the engine in case we're being watched. Tell the others to wait up by the road. Don't bunch up. I'll be ten minutes. If I'm not back then take off. Leave someone at the petrol station to bring me back."

"Ja."

Quayle slid out of his door and doubled over, dropping into the deep ditch at the roadside. From here he began moving back up the road to find somewhere to cross, somewhere where he hoped whatever cameras were hidden out there would have a blind spot.

He waited two minutes for a passing truck to rattle by and, in its wake, darted across the road and into the trees. There he stopped. Taking his overcoat off and dropping it over a stump, he began to move down toward the gate, dressed only in a blue tracksuit and woolly hat.

This was the bit he had always liked because here he was good, better than anyone he had ever seen. He moved fast and lightly on his feet like a forest animal.

Four minutes later, he was at the gate. Up in the trees he could see a small platform with three mounted cameras, one overlooking the gate and the other two aimed at the ten foot hurricane fencing that headed off in both directions. Crawling a few feet closer, he stopped below the big signboard and looked up. There was a company name he didn't recognise, but down the bottom there was one he did. The small black letters said the company was part of the Munchen Dag AG Groupen.

Retracing his steps for forty yards, he moved back into the darkness of the trees, searching for a place to cross the fence. From its structure it didn't look electrified – but there was enough trace wiring to suggest touch alarms. He was watching one sector when something moved in the trees above him and he saw the familiar shape of a squirrel scrabbling noisily in the branches. He smiled. If there was one, there were more – and that meant the alarms were constantly being set off.

He crossed a grassy strip, very close to the limit of what he thought was the cameras' focus distance – and, praying that whoever manned the security monitors was asleep, he quickly but carefully climbed the fence and dropped onto the inside. Then he moved straight into the trees to meet the road a few hundred yards in.

The complex sat half a kilometre back from the main road. In the security lights it looked like a converted farm, with some newer prefabricated structures off to one side. As he watched, a four-wheel-drive with three men arrived at what was once the main house. From his hiding, Quayle saw them walk within, every last one of them dressed in the uniforms of security officers, with high peaked caps, side arms in holsters and big torches in their hands.

He moved closer.

There it was: the thing he'd come here for.

Alongside the main building, standing stark against the darkness, was the cream coloured Mercedes.

CHAPTER TEN

Quayle pulled the front of the balaclava down over his face and, still lying on the cold ground, began to shuffle forward on his elbows towards the side of the building. Muted strains of laughter carried across the gravel parking area from one of the low buildings and a bright shaft of light swept a short rectangular beam from an opened door. He paused, waiting for a set of crunching footsteps to pass on, and moved forward to the wall. Above him was a window. As he slid his left hand up, he could feel the dampness of the old bricks and the moss in the cracks.

Standing up slowly, he looked through the dirt streaked window.

Inside, a figure was walking down a hallway of some kind, carrying a huge tray on which sat covered dishes and bottles of beer. Quayle tried the window. It was locked. Moving backward, he looked toward the upper floor and the roof eaves above. There, a little further along, one of the windows was hanging open.

Like a burglar, he moved towards a drainpipe and began to climb. This was too good an opportunity to miss. The window opened into what had once been a bedroom, but was now being used to store boxes. After hauling himself through the window, he threaded his way to the door and stood listening for a full minute. The floor seemed quiet enough. Walking back toward the window, he undid the screws around the lock before closing it and then moving back toward the door.

Outside was a passage narrower than the hall below, the stairs at its far end. He slipped the small pack from his back and delved into it, producing a coil of what looked, on first impression, to be black rubber hose. Stretching it out, he lay it on the floor. It was a modified fibre optical device normally used for obstetric examinations by doctors, but intelligence operators had long ago discovered that it had other uses. Coupled to a re-chargeable battery pack, it threw full colour pictures onto a tiny two inch monitor. He connected the battery pack and plugged in both the endoscope and the listening device he had used in the apartment complex in Frankfurt, then moved back toward the door. Here he settled on his knees, the microphone on the floor, to listen to whatever was taking place below.

It was quiet, so he picked up the gear and moved carefully out into the corridor, the thick carpet soft beneath his feet. Bypassing the first door, holding the microphone out towards the second and hearing only silence in return, he slipped through the door of an office. Inside, a newish desk dominated the centre of the room and, against one wall, there was a second work station with a computer screen.

Quayle didn't know much about computers – but he knew this was part of a bigger system. Somewhere on the complex was the hardware. What could they need a machine like this for? he wondered. Scooping up a sheaf of papers from the desk, and walking to the window to get the best out of the carpark lights below, he held them up. All that he saw were rows of figures and some business German about pork prices. Commodity by the kilo. Maybe this place really did produce pigs.

But pigs weren't guarded by uniformed armed security.

Dropping the papers back where he had found them, he crossed to the wall, where the floor was bare, and once again went on his knees to listen. This time he heard voices. Pressing the record button, he put the system down and crossed to the door with the endoscope, pushing the fine head under the door so that he could see the comings and goings in the passage. When things went quiet, he would move downstairs.

He looked at his watch. It was just after 1am. He thought momentarily about his team of watchers waiting at the petrol station. For what he was paying them, they could wait. Settling back behind the desk, the headphones on his head, he listened carefully, occasionally adjusting the enhancer dial, his eyes narrowing as he tried to focus on what was being said.

It was just after three when he moved, cat like, down the short steep staircase and into the main room. He now knew what he was looking for.

By 4.30, he was back at the petrol station. As the taxi tag car pulled away for the return run into Frankfurt, a delivery truck pulled into the station and threw several bundles of newspapers towards the office door. Across the bottom of the front page, below the stories of East German policy changes – 'Panzer Perestroika' as one column called it – coal miner strikes in the Ukraine, and the resignation of the Bulgarian Party Chief, was a story about an armed assault and kidnap at a millionaire's hide-away villa in Mallorca.

*

Kurt Eicheman was at his desk early that morning, sitting back reading the reports of a surveillance exercise on a small group of extreme left-wingers. This group was of interest because two of them were suspected of having links with the old Bader Meinhof group. Yet, try as he might, his mind was not on the file, and when the phone rang he snatched it up.

"Ja?"

"Kurt?" The voice was English.

"Who is this?" he asked. Very few people had his private number.

"Hugh Cockburn."

Eicheman sat forward, putting the report down and creasing his brow. "Hugh! I have been expecting your call."

"We need to meet."

"I know. As a matter of fact, I had a call this morning..."

"I'm at the Hilton. Room 617."

"I'll be twenty minutes."

The call had come at 4am, from Helmut Blucher himself. At the mention of his name, Kurt was wide awake in milliseconds. Blucher was Head of the BND, a measured stern old man, and often took his orders direct from the Chancellor's office. He, in turn, ordered Kurt to hand over Frankfurt Station to his assistant until further notice, and lend all possible aid to the MI6 people without – *repeat, without* –

233

involving unapproved BND resources. He was to consider himself on secondment.

Picking up his coat, Eicheman moved toward the door, looking at his watch. Quayle was due to contact the Bremen conduit between 8 and 9pm, so he had another hour at least. Things must have gone well because there were no reports coming through from the civilian police that could be linked. Two people dead after a domestic quarrel and a body in a foundry pond was the sum total of the night's police activity, and as yet there had been no calls for a clean-up crew. *But things could get tricky now,* he thought. *With Hugh here, there's every chance it's Titus he's after.*

He stopped in the lobby of the hotel, bought a paper and walked straight to the lifts, ignoring the front desk.

Hugh Cockburn answered the door.

"Hello, Kurt. Come in." He pointed across the room to a stocky black girl sitting on one of the chairs by the television. "This is Chloe. She works for me."

On the table beside her was what the services called a bug-alarm. It was a box of sophisticated electronics the size of a small portable Walkman that would sound an alarm if there was an audio bug within one hundred feet. They were extremely sensitive and the little red operational light shone reassuringly.

"Hello," he said to Chloe. Then he turned back to Cockburn. "I believe you have something for me?"

"I do." Cockburn handed over a sealed envelope. Eicheman slipped it open, quickly scanned the contents, and then slid it into his breast pocket. They were the confirmation of his orders. "Do you know why you're here?" Cockburn asked.

Eicheman shook his head. "Not really."

"Kurt, I have to find Titus Quayle, and find him fast. Now, I think you know where he is or how we can contact him..."

"What makes you think that?"

"Everything. You're good friends. He would have contacted you, and you couldn't possibly have said no."

They looked at each other for a few seconds, each knowing better than to lie to the other.

"Look," Kurt said, "just leave him to finish it. These people have had their own way long enough. They just tried it on the wrong man this time."

"Do you know who these people are?"

"That's the problem," Kurt replied. "No-one does."

"Except Titus."

"Not yet," Kurt said firmly, "but he's getting close."

"Can you contact him?"

"Can't you leave it alone, Hugh? Let him take these bastards. They've tried to kill him and his woman. Enough is enough."

"They got her," Cockburn said. "Here, look at this."

He threw a paper across to Kurt – who began to read the story. Once he was finished, he dropped the paper Hugh had given him and took up the one he had bought in the lobby. The same story was there but on page two.

"We mean him no harm. You have my word of honour on that. Quite the contrary. I need his skills. I want these people as well, Kurt. That's the job. Find Titus, get him back on service and take this organisation down."

Kurt walked to the window and looked out over the grey damp city, shrouded in rain. It was quiet for a full minute before he spoke, his mind in a turmoil. For years he had protected sources: his cells, both guilty and innocent. Never. in all his time as an intelligence agent. had he ever betrayed a confidence.

But now the time had come.

"He's here," he said sadly. "In Germany."

"Great!" Cockburn stepped forward eagerly. "Where? Can we contact him?"

Kurt turned and looked him in the eye. "He uses a conduit. All I can do is ask him to see you. The choice is his... and the way he's been treated, I don't like your chances."

"How soon can we get word to him?"

"He's due to phone in any minute."

Cockburn brooded, inwardly. "Tell him there's been a problem. In Mallorca. Tell him we're on his side. Tell him... tell him to get a newspaper."

Kurt bent and picked up the paper he had bought in the lobby, re-reading the story again. "She better be alright. Bastards," he said bitterly. "I hope he kills the lot of them."

There was a knock at the door.

"That will be the KGB," said Chloe dryly, rising to her feet. "One big happy family."

That night, they stood amongst goods wagons, silent steel giants in the falling rain, the signal lights flickering as big diesel locomotives shunted wagons somewhere across the thirty acre yard. Quayle had insisted on a covert meeting. They had waited for two hours for him to phone the hotel after getting the message to the Bremen conduit, and Kurt had told him outright about Holly. After that, there'd been absolute silence down the line. Then it went dead. They'd had to wait another three hours for him to call back, listening for strength in his voice, hoping that his will was still there and strong and still fighting. Cockburn had taken the phone from Kurt, pleading with him to meet with them. "Don't just go to war," he'd begged. "Don't just melt away. Think it through. Don't go back underground Titus, let us work together. You have your reasons, we have ours, but the result is the same. Twenty years Titus, twenty years we've trusted each other."

Now, they could only hope it had done the trick.

Chloe stood alongside Cockburn, wrapped in a huge coat, the empty freight wagon behind them shiny and wet. Kurt Eicheman stood a few feet away and miraculously managed to keep a cigarette alight, the brim of his fashionable hat pulled down over his face. Alexi Kirov waited back at the hotel in case of a fall back plan, settled in by the phone with a thermos of soup, a new Time magazine, and a feeling of resentment at being left behind.

Above them, the floodlights spluttered for a second and then went out. Full darkness settled over the yard.

Kurt smiled to himself and took another drag on his cigarette.

"Is this it?" Chloe asked Cockburn in a whisper.

"Could be a short or something."

"It's him," Kurt said firmly.

"Will he have a gun?" Chloe asked. "I mean, what if he decides we're the enemy or something?"

Neither man ventured an answer to that. They just stood in the darkness, the rain falling gently, the wind buffeting and tugging at their coat tails.

Suddenly a figure appeared. There he stood, a few yards away, his head uncovered, his short hair dripping water down his face. He wore no coat, just a lightweight shirt that stuck to his skin. As he stepped closer, Chloe recognised him from his pictures. Already she could see the exhaustion in his face. The eyes she had studied were real; they burned and glittered with an intensity, an anger that she could not describe. He seemed thinner and tired but the aura was still there. *He's down,* she thought, *but by God he's not beaten.*

"Hello Titus," Cockburn said.

The eyes narrowed for a second and then he spoke, his voice laden with fatigue.

"What happened?"

"We got there a couple of hours too late. Marco's OK. He saw them carry her out. Alive."

"You couldn't leave it alone, could you?" Titus seethed.

"We..."

"You had to try to find us."

"We knew we weren't the only people looking." Cockburn replied.

"But you found her," Quayle said bitterly. "Thanks Hugh."

"What the hell..."

"You don't understand, do you? You stupid cunt!"

"Oh Jesus," Chloe said, realizing suddenly what he meant. "We led them in..."

"Yes," breathed Quayle, "and you didn't even know it."

"Impossible," Cockburn said quickly

"YOU SHOWED THEM WHERE TO LOOK!"

"Oh my God," he said, his brain reeling at the thought. "But that would mean they're in..."

"Sussed it have you?" he threw back sarcastically. "The master spy. You were always a good controller, Hugh, but you slipped up this time. You're dangerous. Why couldn't you stay out of it?"

"I'm sorry, Titus," Cockburn said, understanding immediately Tansey-Williams' reluctance to involve any further personnel. Somewhere inside Six, somewhere inside Century, was one of the people they were looking for.

"So am I," Quayle replied – and, with his head bowed and his clothes soaking wet, he began to walk away.

Cockburn tried to follow, but Kurt caught his arm, shaking his head.

"Send the girl," he advised. Slipping his overcoat off, he threw it to her.

Chloe looked at Cockburn, and only when he nodded did she hurry after the figure who walked slowly away into the dark, like someone with nowhere in particular to go.

She caught up to him and tried to match his pace over the granite stones.

"What do you want?" he asked.

"Only to help..."

"I think you people have helped enough."

"At least put this coat on," she said.

"Why?"

"So you don't catch pneumonia," she dryly replied.

"Piss off."

"No I won't piss off," she replied testily. "Look, you're supposedly shit-hot. I've seen your record and heard the chat in the canteen. I even had a case officer who would shift nervously in his chair whenever your name was mentioned. But even the great Titus Quayle can't take this mob on his own..."

"What do you know?" Viciously, he turned on her. "Tell me what realms of experience you draw upon? What are you, a grade three? Fresh out of Lincoln and the FO French course?"

"Yes I am!" she retorted. "But I'm something else. I'm a fan, and outside those two men back there, you don't have many of those. I sat in front of my gas fire in a miserable little north London terrace house and listened to Tansey-Williams tell me the story of a man who paints like a dream, who can recite Shakespeare, a man who read history in the finest university in the world and gave twenty years to the service being hunted like an animal. I learnt to like him. I also learned of a girl called Holly who sounds a lot like my big sister. I wanted to help, but now we need help too…"

Quayle turned and walked away – but Chloe continued after him, and this time he didn't try to send her away.

When she slung the coat over his shoulders, he left it there.

Cockburn and Eicheman drove back to the hotel and picked listlessly at a room service breakfast while Kirov powered his way through a huge bowl of fruit salad, then sat back and began to strip and clean his weapon. The juxtaposition of silver foiled butter portions and a single carnation, and the stripped blued parts of his big gun, was both ridiculous and poignant.

"I think we better round up that surveillance team he used. Find out where they went to ground and pick up the threads from there," the Russian said.

"He'll be here," Eicheman said in German. "He would have told all of us to get stuffed, but the woman's touch will work with him."

"He's close to something. That much is certain."

"How do you know?" Eicheman asked. He hadn't briefed Kirov like he had Cockburn.

"I just feel it," the Russian answered honestly, easing the slide home and giving the barrel a final rub with a rag.

Neither of the other two men found that odd. Both had been running agents long enough to respect their instincts without too many questions.

Moments later, they watched him get up and walk to the phone.

"Who are you calling?" Cockburn asked.

"Borshin," the Russian replied.

"May I ask why?"

"If he joins in, then we're close. Close enough to want some backup close too."

"Look, I don't want half of Moscow's hoods roaming round Frankfurt," Cockburn said wearily.

Kirov laughed and kept on dialling. "Not KGB. Don't worry."

"What then?"

"You call yours the hooligans from Hereford. Ours have more respect."

"Spetznatz? Here in Frankfurt?" Eicheman snapped. "Jesus! That's all we need!"

"We may do, and if we do, there is nothing quite like them..."

Cockburn sat back and let the two argue it out, wondering how Cloe was getting along. As far as he was concerned, Eicheman was right. If there was a way to bring Titus in it was with a woman. His old fashioned values would work against him there, even one as young and different as Chloe.

She returned three hours later, let herself in with her own key and begged off a de-brief until she'd showered and changed her clothes. But this wasn't good enough for Cockburn. Too impatient to wait, he stood outside the bathroom door, asking her questions while she dried herself off.

"And?"

"I left him at a bratwurst stand about two miles from the station. Or rather he told me to go home, and I wasn't going to argue. My feet are killing me..."

"Go home?"

"Yeah. Nicely, you know, like go home and get warm and I'll see you later sort of thing."

"Will we?"

"What?" she asked.

"Oh for Christ's sake!" he said, exasperated. "Will we see him later? Is he going to come in?"

She slid the door back, her bright face beaming at him. "I think so. He has things to do first."

"What things?"

"I don't know. I don't ask you and I didn't ask him. I just know he has things to finish. He'll come looking for a deal, I think."

"What sort of deal?"

"Not sure... but the flame of altruism has waned, I'm afraid. The Metro order saw to that. I think he became rather fond of Mr Pope, so don't try Queen and country on him. He won't laugh, he'll just walk out. He believes we need him more than he needs us. And he's probably right."

"What's his frame of mind?"

"Resolute. Strong. He's tired, no doubt about it, but he's going to take down this 'Broken Square' group with us or without us."

Cockburn hesitated. "Broken Square?"

"That was Teddy Morton's file name."

"What did he say exactly?"

"That he was going to blow it back in their faces."

"Titus getting personally involved again," he mused out loud.

"Can't blame him. He's in love with her."

"Did he say that?"

"No. But I could tell."

Cockburn sounded sceptical.

"Women can," she added.

"And if she's dead already?"

Chloe thought about that for a second or two, then shook her head. "He doesn't think she is."

Cockburn breathed deeply, trying to imagine what Titus Quayle in love might look and sound like – and what, in the name of all that is holy, that might mean if Holly was dead.

"Let's hope not," he sighed.

He arrived unannounced just before 7pm that evening and didn't seem surprised to see Alexi Kirov in the room with his classic rivals.

"The band's all here, I see," he said dryly.

"Now it is," Cockburn said, smiling and very pleased to see him.

"Not yet," Quayle replied. "I'm here to talk. That's all."

"You're not a talker, Titus. That's what I do. You are here to do it."

"Not this time, Hugh."

Chloe watched them squaring off, trying to countenance Cockburn's stand, understanding his need to control the meeting, to stamp his authority on it, because without that he would never be able to control his agent later. All controllers had their own style. With some it was paternal, with others it was fear. For others a respectful distance was the key. They usually had themselves being called Mister, because with the formality and the positioning came obedience. The last group were those who treated their agents as full equals, sometimes even superiors, servicing their needs rather like a secretary or a personal assistant, massaging their vanities and jabbing at their weaknesses while supplying logistical support and running interference for their men on the ground.

Cockburn was trying to be agreeable but strong, but Chloe wasn't certain how successful he was being.

"Why not? We both want the same thing. You do what you're good at and so will I..."

"You want an operator. Use Dirty Harry here." Quayle jerked a thumb at Kirov. "He's quite good. Better than the wankers at Milburn. Or get Phillips. He's still alive, is he? Or did someone decide he was better out of the way too?"

"That was a mistake, Titus. Someone fucked up."

"Some fuck-up. Tell Jerry Pope that."

Cockburn said nothing. He knew there was more to come.

"You probably never met Jerry," Quayle continued. "Funny old guy, but a good bodyguard. They hit him with Teflon rounds and took his legs out with a shotgun. He was embarrassed because Holly was there. Imagine being embarrassed to die. What dignity did he have? None. We have none. None of us. I'm as bad as the rest. If I was a better man, I'd walk away." He shrugged as if it didn't matter. "But I'm going to get

242

Holly back and take these fuckers out – and you won't be running me when I do it. This is personal."

"Pope is alive."

"Yeah. With a rubber bag to shit into for the rest of his life."

"Holly," Cockburn ventured. "What if she's already…"

"She isn't," Quayle replied, his eyes glittering like wet slate, his voice so loaded with conviction and strength that it came like a force from within.

The tension was palpable and Kirov broke it by coming to his feet, taking an apple from the bowl and biting into it. Then he turned to them both and talked with his mouth full. "I'll come too. I'm still young and foolish!"

Quayle couldn't help the dry smile that crept across his face.

Cockburn piped up, "OK. I won't try and run you, but you have to agree that we can work better on this together…"

"There's only one way we're going to work together at all."

"Go on…"

Kirov bit noisily into his apple and Cockburn shot him a look that could kill.

"I go alone until I'm ready for support," said Quayle. "My decision all the way. I'll tell you people what I need and you supply it. Nothing at all until I say the word. You throw nothing at this that I haven't asked for, and when I do, you give me the best you have."

"That's some demand," said Cockburn. "What do I get in return?"

"Broken Square."

"The whole group?"

"Enough to work with," Quayle confirmed.

"The people responsible for the Midhurst killings, for Henry Arnold…"

"Sorry Hugh. No promises there."

"Why?"

"I told you, this is personal."

As they faced each other, Chloe realised the meaning of what Quayle had just said. He was going to finish it himself. She had just heard a death warrant.

"Alright. You have a deal," Cockburn finally said. Solemnly, her turned to the others in the room. "Let's come up to speed and see where we go from here…"

Some time later, they gathered around the table together.

"OK Ti," Cockburn began, "what have you got from your last few days?"

"A little. Got a couple of names from Kurt and followed them up. I had an enquiry agent sniff about a bit. Not much on the surface. Have had several contacts with group members. Some of them wear a ring like this…" He threw one onto the table. "But they're very tight and very security conscious. Anyway, I found out they were going to have a visitor so we picked them up at the airport and followed them down to a farm a few hours outside the city."

"Do they know you're onto them?"

"Not yet, but they'll be expecting me to retaliate any moment now, try to find where they have Holly. That's why they took her She's the bait." He rubbed his eyes tiredly.

"They still want you," Cockburn said. It wasn't a question. It was a statement. "Any demand yet?"

"It's not me they want, Hugh. It's the file."

"So other than the ring, and a cell located here in Germany, we don't have much else."

"It's more than a cell. Could be dozens of them in this country. This is a big organisation. Big resources."

"Any idea who they are?" Chloe asked. "What they want?"

Quayle picked up one of the many newspapers and threw it to her. "What's all over the front and international pages?" he asked.

She looked at the page.

She scanned the page quickly. "Reform… the Brandenburg gate open… Peace Marches… East Germans shopping in the West…"

"That's it," he said, biting hungrily into a bread roll.

"What?"

"Think about the last year or so. Hungary. Last year Jano Kadas out.

Honecker in the East out. Solidarity in power in Poland. Riots in Czechoslovakia, even that prick Ceausescu six feet under. In Bulgaria, Zhivkov is out and Mladenov in, but for how long? In the Soviet Union –" he gestured towards Kirov, "– localised nationalism like never before. The entire fabric is changing. That worries some people."

"That makes Broken Square extreme left wing."

"Or extreme right," Cockburn suggested.

"Or both," said Quayle. "A bunch of the old guard in the Soviet Union watching their power dwindle, their cronies in the Warsaw Pact, and their equals in the West. Men who liked the shape of the bear. Big and understood and stable. Men who don't want thirty little states bickering and fighting amongst themselves. Men who liked the way it was. It wasn't perfect, but at least everyone understood where the lines were drawn."

"Who in the West would want the Soviet union that powerful?" Chloe argued.

"Men who have shares in Northrop or Lockheed or a hundred other defence contractors. Men who remember Mongols on the streets of Berlin liked the Warsaw Pact-NATO stand-off because it kept them in Mongolia. Men who hold power now. Men who are frightened for the future. Men who are shit scared at the thought of a united Germany again..." Quayle paused. "Do you want me to go on?"

"So you're saying that someone has welded these factions together," Cockburn ventured.

"It fits."

"But there's more, isn't there?"

"The rest will cost," he replied.

"Why?"

"*Pro patria mori*..." he quoted.

"I'm surprised at you, Quayle. You're one of the few honourable people I know."

"Oh my honour is intact, Hugh. It's yours that is suspect. Or should I say that of your masters... This has all been a bit one sided. My risk, my money, my life. Now Six wants in on the spoils – Six, who only days ago, was gleefully trying to kill me."

"What do you want?"

"A letter. Signed by Tansey-Williams. It's to state that there was a Metro order on me and the reasons for that. A full explanation if you will. When this is over, I want some peace of mind – and that letter sitting in a vault will help explain to the hostile back benchers the nature of the beast... should I suffer an early demise."

"Titus," Cockburn began, "you have my word..."

"You word is worthless at Milburn and you know it. No-one's word is worth a pinch of shit except the Director General's – and then only in writing. The world, Hugh, is full of ambitious men, and you are as expedient as I am. That's the deal. Get it and get it soon. What I have won't wait for ever."

"And then?"

"And then I get Holly back and we take these people down."

Cockburn got wearily to his feet. "Titus," he said, "I'll get it now."

He was away for twenty minutes. While he was gone, Kirov called room service for more coffee and Kurt stood in silence, watching from the window. No-one spoke. Chloe, who found the silence unsettling, got up and started to pace.

At long last, Cockburn returned.

"He doesn't like it," he said, "but it will be here tomorrow."

Quayle stood up and gave a dry laugh. "So will I."

They watched him leave in silence, and only after the door had closed behind him did Cockburn shake his head quizzically.

"What?" Chloe asked.

"I don't think he has any intention of helping us take them down. The moment Holly is safe..."

"Then why did he come at all?" she argued. "He needs us."

"No," said Cockburn. "He can use us, and it's easier to have us in sight than blundering around his penetration. But he doesn't *need* us. Gentlemen," he said, looking around the room, "we're playing this game according to Titus Quayle's rules now."

Quayle returned at ten the following morning, rested and clean-shaven, and gave Chloe half a smile as she opened the door to him. Eicheman and Cockburn were already here waiting, but Alexi Kirov had been gone for hours, settling in his reaction team who had arrived at dawn.

"Do you have the letter?" Quayle asked Cockburn.

Cockburn held up a buff envelope. "It's got your name on it. I guess this is it."

Quayle took it, slit it open and pulled a single closely typed page from the envelope. Reading it, he smiled bleakly.

"Well?" Cockburn asked.

Quayle nodded.

"So we can start?"

"We can," Quayle said. Walking to the table, he lifted the coffee pot. "Munchen Dag AG are a company registered in Munich, but they have a Bonn office and a farm outside Frankfurt. They're in the thick of this scene somewhere." He threw another envelope on the table. "This is my investigator's report on them. You'll also find a report on a Bonn law firm who have had a stringer doing work for this outfit." He paused. "We need to push the investigation from within. Kurt will be able to find us some BND computer time after hours and an operator. Let's see what shit we can dredge up." He began to pour coffee into a cup that someone had already used. "Then we want a safe house and a tame shrink. Someone with experience and access to interrogative drugs."

"Why?" Cockburn asked.

"I'm going to snatch two men tonight. Wring them dry and deliver them back none the wiser. We'll need a linguist as well. Someone who speaks Cantonese."

"Not the Chinese," Cockburn said. "That's all we need."

"No, it's not just them. Its the other side too."

"Taiwan?"

"Hong Kong. The billionaires, the triads, maybe both. They're the third piece of the puzzle. Destabilise perestroika. Create suspicion. I think they're funding the bulk of it..."

"For what?" Kurt asked.

"My guess is for an extension of the lease on the island and territory."

"Say again?" Cockburn said softly.

"I think they've done a deal with Beijing. If they put a halt to the reform process in Europe, they get another lease period on Hong Kong Island, Kowloon and the new Territories."

"Jesus Christ. That's incredible!"

"And profitable for everyone. This is a meeting of some great financial minds and some huge resources." He sipped his coffee. "If I'm right, then it's also the single largest conspiracy in history."

"But why would they want to give up Hong Kong?" Chloe asked

"They never had it in the first place," Cockburn cut in, immediately understanding Quayle's theory. "Secondly, when they get it, they wouldn't know what to do with it – turn it back into China proper under the regime? Allow it free port status? How to reconcile that with the new clamp down? All they really know is that they have a powerful bargaining chip with the right quarters."

"Why not offer it back to Britain?" she asked

"The Brits don't want it. They've been shaking off the colonies for years, and still suffering the effects. The last thing they want is to extend one of them. Boat people, nationalism, the passport issue. They can all be addressed now, once and for all. If they extended the lease, they'd extend the problems and give them time to magnify later... No," Cockburn went on, "the Foreign office is adamant about this one. Get rid of the bloody place and make it someone else's problem."

"Then why not allow it independence?" she countered.

"Under Brit control the Chinese have been content that the subversive elements are at least kept in check. They just wouldn't grant independence to a section of their powerbase anymore than to Canton or any other place. No, I'm quite certain Ti is right. They'll hand over to a select few, with certain guarantees. The big business interests, the powerful families. But not for nothing. They want the world's interest away from Tiananmen. They don't want to be the last bastion of a system they believe works. They're Communists remember, in the only place it ever worked."

Chloe looked at Quayle, who nodded and swilled around the contents of his cup.

"How are they going to do this?" Kurt asked him.

"Perestroika has its internal enemies, men ready to revert to the old ways, to take the seats of power. The Generals, the old party hard liners. All it needs is the..."

"Removal of the existing reformers," Cockburn interrupted.

"And Alexander wept, for there were no more worlds to conquer," Quayle misquoted softly.

"You're saying..."

"They're going to kill Gorbov, Walensa, Mladenov and the others at the Warsaw Pact Summit in Prague."

There was silence in the room.

Then:

"Oh my God," uttered Cockburn. "That gives us less than two weeks!"

*

Quayle and Kirov lay in the pitch darkness beneath the trees and waited.

It was before midnight and lights still burned in the upstairs rooms of the farmhouse. Kirov had convinced Quayle that they should have support nearby. They would enter and take the subjects, but Kirov felt they should have backup. "Remember Spain," he had said, and reluctantly Quayle had agreed. Now, deployed out in the dark behind them were two four man sections of the Red Army's elite special forces, the Spetznatz. Dressed in black lightweight overalls and armed for night vision assault, they were better than the Fairies could ever hope to be for work like this – but Quayle still thought of it as inviting failure. Alone and without close support, you didn't make mistakes because you couldn't afford to. The mere knowledge of support often dulled an operative's cutting edge, and he agreed only because he would rather know where they were and then put them from his mind.

Up above, the last light went off in the house. *Give it an hour,* he thought, *and the dogs another sweep*. Kurt Eicheman and Cockburn waited at a house not ten minutes away with a clinical psychiatrist from the Hagne Institute, a man who owed Eicheman favours. According to Eicheman, he was close to developments in the clinical treatment of the mentally disturbed and the latest drugs, some of which had interesting side effects. Effects like making the subject talk about anything and everything without being able to remember later. Ethics aside, Eicheman had arranged for the man's niece to cross the Berlin Wall three years before, and tonight the debt was being called in.

The time had come.

Quayle got to his feet like a dark shadow rising and began to move forward, so that he could see the dogs pass. Behind him, he could feel something moving up to take his position. The Spetznatz. On his right, Kirov was up and moving too. They didn't have long to wait. A guard with a big silver coloured dog moved along the damp concrete path between them and the house, the dog not sniffing at the air and the ground but bored with the patrol and lagging behind his handler. Quayle was pleased. They had made the classic mistake with a dog and left it too long on the job. The handler jerked the leash and muttered a muffled curse at his canine charge, then kept moving. Quayle watched them push onward another twenty yards, then crossed the few yards to the wall fast and silent, Kirov on his heels. As soon as they were there, he began to climb the drainpipe hand over hand, his strength incredible. Fifteen seconds later, he eased open the window he had tampered with the last time and dropped through into the store room, Kirov dropping in behind him. As he reached the door, he began delving into his pack for his endoscope and microphones. The doctor had delivered instructions on the correct dosage of the clear fluid in the hypodermics he was carrying. Their instructions were simple: they had to be back with him for the second dosage within forty minutes of administering the first. From that point on, they would have just over an hour for the 'therapy'.

They found the American in the second bedroom they tried. A hooded red torch beam picked out his features on the pillow: his hook nose, bushy eyebrows and close cropped hair. He was breathing deeply when Kirov gave him a sniff of the gas and his eyelids fluttered briefly as he dropped from sleep into unconsciousness. Quayle pulled him upright and placed a wide band of surgical tape over his mouth, then pulled plastic restraints from his pocket and cuffed the man's hands in front of his chest. Nodding to Kirov – who eased back into the passage with the endoscope and microphone to find the Chinese – he picked up the inert form of the American and carried him to the store room window where he lay him down.

Part One complete.

As soon as that was done, he went back into the passage and found Kirov at the last door, listening on his knees listening. Soon, Quayle had eased the door open and was crossing into the darkness, headed towards the bed, the gas canister in one hand and the little red torch in the other. Thirty seconds later, he was carrying the smaller man up the passage to the store room where Kirov was busy laying out a climber's safety harness. Sliding the man into the thick nylon straps, they worked together to ease him onto the windowsill where Quayle tied a fast knot in some nylon rope and guided him over the edge, Kirov moving out after him and sliding down the pipe.

The American was heavier and his pyjamas got caught in the straps. Quayle took his time getting it right. The dog wasn't due for another eight minutes and, when he was on the ground, he clambered back up the pipe to close the window before dropping down and carrying the unconscious man back into the dark of the trees.

They had been in, done the snatch, and were out in fourteen-and-a-half minutes, not one word spoken and not one mistake made.

The doctor, a small bespectacled man with tufts of hair sprouting from his ears, stripped the gag tapes off with some distaste and arranged the two subjects in separate rooms, both devoid of anything but the chairs they sat in.

"I don't approve," he said to Eicheman, who just shrugged.

"I don't care," Quayle replied. "Just give him the rest of the drug and let's start."

The doctor took a small metal case from his bag and extracted a hypodermic syringe and two phials.

"Does he have any allergies?" he asked.

"Assume not."

"What if he does? He may..."

"Then we go to Plan B," Quayle said dryly. "Just do it."

The doctor looked at his watch and raised an eyebrow at Eicheman who nodded. Then, rolling the man's pyjama sleeve up, he pushed the sharp needle into the arm and pressed the plunger down steadily.

"Two or three minutes and you can start. Shall I do the other now?"

"No," Quayle replied. "Give me twenty minutes here first." Then, finding another chair, he sat down at the side of the American and began lightly slapping his wrist. "Hi there," he said with a West Coast accent. "My name is Eddie and I am your friend."

The man mumbled something and shook his head. Behind them, Eicheman looked at Cockburn with a raised eyebrow. He hadn't known that Quayle was an interrogator. Alongside them was a young bearded man in dirty jeans, the Cantonese interpreter.

"Don't you remember me? I'm your friend Eddie," he said soothingly. "We always have lots of fun talking and things... Let's talk now, shall we?"

The man mumbled again – but this time the enunciation of the sounds was clearer.

"So Don, how are things?"

"Not... Don..." he said, slowly lifting his big head, eyes still closed. "Leonard. Leonard Kavics."

"Sure," Quayle said. "Sorry Leonard. My mistakes! So how's things? Pretty good?"

"Yeah."

"Where are we keeping the girl. Leonard?"

"Which girl?" One eye opened a fraction.

"The one we grabbed in Spain."

"The limey bitch? Oh sure..." The voice was slurred. "They gave her to the gooks. They should sell her ass on the streets..."

"What gooks?" Quayle asked, keeping his anger in check. "The slopes? The ones in Hong Kong?"

"Yeah. Fung Wa's boys. They got her tight waiting for the man."

"What man Leonard?"

"The Brit pinko."

"Quayle?" Quayle asked.

"Yeah."

"What's our group called, Leonard?" In the next room, two tape machines faithfully recorded every word, a technician leaning over them to adjust audio record levels and enhance them wherever he could.

"Our group? Why don' you know what we're called? Everyone knows what we are called" His answer had a childish tone.

"You know me, Leonard. Had a few beers. What can I say. I forgot! So tell me again Leonard..."

"Minutemen."

"We're called Minutemen. Everywhere?"

"Just in the old U S of A. Here it's something else."

"What's it called here?"

"Can't say it. Kraut something. Night guard."

"Nachtwatch?"

"Yeah that's it," he said, smiling awkwardly, one eye open like a drunk.

"Why are you here Leonard?"

"I'm a Spec," he said proudly through his haze. "Mission specialist."

"Wow. An expert!" Quayle said admiringly.

"Yes, sir!"

"An expert at what?"

"Things that float through the air. I'm an expert aerosol," he giggled.

"What things?" Quayle asked, his spine going cold.

He put one finger to his lips. "Shsss... bugs. C.D.T.B.As."

"What does that mean Leonard?"

"Tactical Bacterial Agents... command dispensed." He held up a hand like he was holding a spray can. "Yessiree. Twenty-two years at Fort Dixon."

"We gonna get some lefties Leonard?"

"They ain't telling me, but I tell you this. You don't use faox ATs for fruit flies."

"What's faox?"

"Fast oxidising. Two minutes later, three at most, you can breathe deep and live long." The drugged speech had a drowsy monotone quality and Quayle tried to match it as best he could, like a bad amateur actor reading lines.

"Getcha ha ha... breathe deep live long, ha ha. ATs?"

"Alpha grade is sci-fi stuff. A thimble sized toxic nightmare for the baddies. Whole companies... poof!"

"Gee Leonard, that kind of stuff must be hard to come by. Where did we find it? Tell our friend John here. John likes sci-fi. Tell us all about the alpha grade." He signalled with his hand for Cockburn to move forward.

Quayle stood up and looked at Eicheman, indicating he was going next door to start on the Chinese and that the interpreter should join him.

As they reached the corridor, the young German breathed out loudly, relieving his tension.

"My God, they must be mad!"

"Did you here my tone in there?" Quayle asked when the interpreter arrived. "Soft, like to a child..."

"Yes. You want that style?"

"Must have. Will it work in Cantonese?"

"Mandarin would be easier, but yes. I've done unconscious interrogations before," he replied in English.

"Good. We want to know where they have a girl called Holly Morton. They're holding her somewhere in Hong Kong. But where exactly? And who is this Fung Wa character? Get all the names you can. Locations, contacts, any clues to finding them quickly. Got that?"

"Yes," he said, suddenly all business, "but we must record this. Cantonese and Mandarin are tonal languages. In a drugged state the tones might be out. That could give different meanings. I'll need to listen again and again to some words he'll use, to fix the context correctly. Also if he was an accent or a dialect." He paused. "If they sent him here, he'll speak English, surely?"

"He may remember using English later. Also his English isn't that good. Use Chinese. Just do your best. We are recording. I want Holly back. That's first. I don't care what Kurt has told you. We get the information on Holly first. Then you move onto anything else. That clear?" His eyes glittered for a second, the force of will flowing from him like heat from a brazier.

The young man nodded and pushed open the door into the second room.

*

The team arrived at Hong Kong's Kai Tak airport within an hour of each other, using four different airlines.

Quayle had travelled alone. In the men's rooms at the airport he changed into the uniform of a Qantas flight steward and, watching the time, emerged half an hour later in time for the Qantas flight in from Melbourne and the reciprocal flight eastbound. That would give him a group of upwards of twenty men in similar garb to become lost in, and each crew would think him part of the other. After waiting until he heard the landing announcement, he gave it another twenty minutes and then walked onto the crowded concourse, his cabin bag in his hand, his blonde hair hanging wild over the fake tan he had applied. As he arrived at the crew immigration counter, he saw that others in the familiar blue jackets with orange cuffs had arrived and dropped in behind them. The ruse worked, as he had known that it would. The checks were minimal and, soon, he was waved through. As he approached the baggage carousel, he shrugged off his jacket, slipped a lightweight coat over his shoulders and walked past the real crew members, out through customs.

Taking a look at the waiting hotel men, he randomly selected one that he knew was over on Hong Kong island. Apologising that he had no reservation, he flashed the attendant a hundred dollar bill and was soon being whisked away to a liveried driver in an awaiting limousine, with assurances that there were rooms available.

The hotel was new: a massive towering glass structure on the other side of the Hong Kong convention centre, between Causeway Bay and the central business district. As soon as Quayle had taken his room, he stood at the window and gazed out upon the city below. The location was perfect; Wanchai, the old red light quarter, the famous world of Suzie Wong, sprawled like an old slut out behind the complex. And there, in amongst the food stalls and girlie bars, the street traders and massage parlours, the noise and spitting and exhaust fumes, was the small flat that Steve Chung had found.

Steve Chung was a moon-faced laughing little man who seemed perpetually pushing his glasses up his nose, and had over the years provided Quayle with what he lacked on the streets: language, contacts, access to the black market, forged documents and information. He was a curious individual, one who claimed to do nothing for free and anything for money, but consistently broke his own rules by being loyal to his friends. That night he would meet Quayle at the flat in Wanchai while Cockburn and the others waited at the MI6 safe house overlooking Aberdeen Harbour. The first meeting here in the hotel was with a dour Scots Hong Kong Police Special Branch officer and, later, his MI6 counterpart.

Quayle welcomed the first into his room, a big beefy solid square block of a man called Jamie McReady, and they got right into it.

"You what?" he growled.

"You heard me. It's the only way," Quayle replied looking him straight in the eye.

"I have sworn to uphold the law," the Scot replied. "I will countenance no such thing!"

"Crap. You're SB. You spend more time breaking the law than upholding it. Anyway, the law is a mockery here and you know it. These people are untouchables. Too big, too rich, too powerful for you to get at. We do this my way."

"Nevertheless," he countered, "it's the law. We may bend it a little to make a case, but never like this."

"That's shit, McReady. Besides, I don't want to charge them in court. I want to get Holly Morton back. All you have to do is make sure I'm not compromised by one of your more zealous types. I'll tell you when and I'll tell you where. You file an SB operation blue sheet on the area and keep the uniform people the hell out of the way."

"I don't like it." The rough burr rolled off his tongue.

"You don't have to. Just do it," Quayle snapped. Then, softening, he offered McRerady a bonus. "I'll get him for you. Signed sealed and delivered. He'll be your grass forever."

"For Christ's sake man, Fung Wa dines out with half the board of Jardines. He's a consultant to the Swires! He's one of the most respected business men in the colony. You can't just deliver men like that..." He waved a ham sized fist out over Kowloon.

"Business set up on filthy money. He's also in with the drugs dealers, with the extortion racketeers and, without a doubt, is a kidnapper. Twenty years ago he would have been a Triad warlord!"

"None of it provable in any court in the world," McReady said. "Look, if he's kidnapped someone, then give it to the Serious Crimes Squad. Let them deal with it."

"No. I want this over in the next forty-eight hours."

"There's more to this than just a kidnapping, isn't there?" he said. It wasn't truly a question. "Level with me Quayle. What's going down here? If this is political or subversives I want in. This is my patch."

But Quayle just looked him straight in the eye.

"Just keep your people clear."

As darkness fell, the MI6 man was given a list of instructions to take back to Cockburn at the safe-house and Quayle, slipping into jeans and a sweatshirt, disappeared into the throngs of people emerging from the conference centre and began to walk into bustle and noise of the Wanchai. His method was established. Now all that remained was the plan and its execution.

Quayle used the walk to come closer to the streets and the people that had made Fung Wa what he was. Fifteen minutes later, he pushed through a doorway. There, an old man in a tattered blue jacket squatted on thin haunches, stirring noodles on a primus stove. He barely glanced up. This was a place where many men came and went. Quayle stepped past him and took the filthy stairs upwards, the only light the garish red reflection of a neon sign outside, and the smell of urine strong.

The rooms were on the third floor. He paused on the landing to read the number on a door. An old metal '5' hung at an angle from a screw held in place by peeling blistered paint. From the other side of the door came the smells of cooking, the coarse laughter of a woman – and, somewhere, the cry of a baby.

Moving down the passage to the place where the silhouette of a long-gone number '7' glared down, Quayle pushed against the door. When it swung back, he paused in the darkness of the hall and allowed his instincts to roam ahead. Finally, he felt for the light switch and flicked it on.

A tired old forty watt bulb that someone had forgotten to steal illuminated the tatty room. An old packing case stood in one corner and upon it sat a plastic bowl that someone had placed there to catch the drips coming from the ceiling. If they had meant to return, they had forgotten; it had gone green and overflowed some time ago, and the case beneath it was sodden and mildewed. Cracked linoleum peeled up at the edges of the walls and, where the four legs of a bed had once stood, it was worn through – no doubt, Quayle thought, due to the hard work of the occupant.

Crossing to the door, he looked into the second room, a smaller dirtier version of the first. In the corner was a pile of dried crusted faeces. Whoever had felt the need had pulled one of the magazine pictures that adorned the wall to wipe themselves. He looked at his watch. Two minutes.

He crossed back to the front door, swung it shut and switched the light off, then leant against the wall to wait. No sooner was he in position, he heard light footsteps in the hall, followed by a soft knock at the door.

Quayle remained where he was and eventually the door swung back.

Steve Chung moved through, his posture suggesting he was confused and slightly lost as it always did.

"Ah little bird. Long time no see!" He beamed at Quayle as he turned on the light. "How the fuck are you?"

Quayle crossed to him to take the offered hand. "Hi Steve. I'm fine. How's the family?"

"Two more since you were here last. They eat me out of home and house!"

Quayle smiled at the thought. Steve Chung had six children on his last visit.

"So you like this shithole I find for you? Very desirable for whore but not for you. Let me find something else. This place seen more cock than Madame Chang Kai Chek..."

"No, it's fine," Quayle replied. "You want work?"

"Always!"

"It's close to home and it's big. You may say no."

"I say yes! You just pay plenty!" he roared with laughter, slapping his thigh.

"Fung Wa," Quayle said.

The smile dropped from Steve's face. "I know you crazy. But you not that crazy, little bird. Fung Wa is bad."

"I heard he is a respectable businessman."

"To some. He runs for government this year. He has two halves like a dragon that has two heads. To others he is powerful gang boss!"

"His joss just ran out," Quayle said softly. "He's taken something of mine."

"Something of value?"

Quayle nodded. He handed Steve a photo of Holly.

"This is what I want."

When he had finished, Steve shook his head like he had heard something insane.

"He is not normal Joe. He has many men. He pays big money for things to go right. This is going into the mouth of the storm..."

259

"It will work," Quayle said firmly. "Fung Wa has forgotten the taste of fear. He has been above it. He thinks he is invulnerable. He thinks he is safe. Now it will all come home to roost."

"Maybe," Steve said, shrugging. "Fung Choi."

Quayle know those words.

Fate.

CHAPTER ELEVEN

It was seven hours before Steve contacted Quayle, who had gone to ground in a flat overlooking Happy Valley Road. He thought he had been tailed going back to the hotel. If it was a big team then he would never see all of them and, not willing to try and confirm it, he simply did what agents do who want to shake a tail.

One minute he was there; the next he had disappeared.

In fact, he had climbed into the back of a police car and flashed a Hong Kong Special Branch warrant card, one of his collection. The Chinese constable almost saluted at the sight of it but caught himself as Quayle slid down in the seat and asked to be dropped at the first quiet spot. The policeman – who had seen this kind of thing before –gave an imperceptible nod and, looking straight ahead, meandered round to the back of one of the hotels on Causeway Bay, where Quayle slid from the rear door as it was still moving. With money and papers, he could move indefinitely – so he phoned the Aberdeen Harbour safe-house and nonchalantly asked them find someone to go over and pick up his laundry.

Cockburn understood immediately and asked him to call back in an hour, then immediately dropped into business as a field controller. His agent on the ground needed support; this was how he had earned his money before the dizzy heights of the Head of Stations desk.

Chloe sat back to watch. He phoned the embassy, roused the local man and sent him down for a list of any British who had left the island in the last two days on home leave. Someone who lived near the city on the island. Forty minutes later, he had several names jotted down, amongst them the address of a homosexual gold trader who had a flat above the Happy Valley Road. Cockburn picked it straight away because people would be used to strange men arriving unannounced.

"Will you go over and water Rupert's plants for me?" he asked when Quayle called back.

"I've forgotten his address," Quayle came back.

"Oh you silly! Here I'll read it out to you!" Cockburn really turned it on. "We haven't got the key but I'm sure you'll think of something. Not sure if the houseboy is coming in, so just in case..."

Great, Quayle thought when he hung up. *I've got to break into this man's place. I hope he doesn't have a big dog.*

In the end, he got through the locks inside a minute, pushing through into a spacious hall jammed with rare brasses and a huge delicious monster in a tub. On the wall was a small Qom rug and, for a second, Serifos flooded back into his memory, the smell of scones baking and Holly covered in flour, trying to read a Greek recipe. Afternoon lovemaking and the warm breeze of the sea swirling the curtains. An image of all that was good for him. *Soon, Teddy. Soon we will have Holly back.* He stepped down one shallow step into the living room. He was expecting it to be overdone in Laura Ashley cushions and matching photograph frames but was pleasantly surprised at the two hefty club chairs either side of a carved teak chest. It felt right.

He was hungry but checked the remainder of the rooms before heading for the fridge, hoping that Rupert had left something in the freezer. He had, complete with a note to himself not to binge, saying *fat fat fat!* Quayle smiled and helped himself to what looked like a TV lasagne. Only the microwave would know. Rupert wasn't a fussy eater by the look of things.

Settling back in of the chairs, he wondered how Steve was getting on. Anyone who had made it like Fung Wa had made enemies along the way. Steve would have to find them, find people who would talk. Find men who had waited years for the opportunity to play some small part in his downfall. He considered the watchers. They had only had him for five minutes along one of the busy Wanchai streets. They could not have confirmed his identity in that time, even working from photographs. It was pure bad luck. There was a time, long ago, that he would have let them follow, drawing them in, leaving them secure that they weren't blown, waiting for their move. But that was for networks and teams, not a man on his own, not a man who was the target. With a little luck, they wouldn't even report the incident, mindful of their masters' wrath. If they did, then Fung Wa's machine would begin to turn and security would be tightened immediately. They would know he was coming to take back what was his, to come for the bait. Fung Wa would be worried. He would have made commitments to others, he would have made assurances that he could deal with the problem, assurances to Broken Square. Together they would keep it from the Chinese. There was too much to risk in allowing shy paranoid xenophobic Beijing know that there was a loose cannon on the deck. Fung Wa couldn't afford a battle on the streets, not with Beijing watching so closely, not with a political career in the offing, not having spent years going legitimate in preparation for the handover of the colony to the Peoples Republic of China. Fung Wa was risking everything on one magnificent gamble. The tightrope walk between Broken Square and the Chinese could bear staggering fortunes.

Quayle walked to the windows, gazing down over the layers of light that was Happy Valley at night. It was still too simple. Broken Square, whoever they were, was big. So big as to include the minutemen and nachtwatch and exert some control over even Fung Wa's organisation and all he could muster. So why become the hired gun, even if it achieved their own ends? He toyed with the words for a minute, looking for a relationship between Tiananmen Square and Teddy Morton's file name, but it was all hollow. Teddy was dead long before the massacre in Tiananmen signalled the end of reform on the mainland, long before the old party hard-line Marxists crushed their own bright future beneath the tracks of their tanks.

Had Teddy foreseen it? Was that his warning, woven through the words of Newbolt? No, Quayle thought. His warning was not the broad screech of the tabloid press crying yellow peril. It was something more esoteric and infinitely more evil. It was deeper and closer and with more at stake than the possession of an island half a world away.

Through Fung Wa, Beijing had made an offer with ironic timing, like offering a nymphomaniac a million dollars to go to bed with a super stud. The minutemen and the nachtwatch were going to do it anyway;

Beijing had simply offered a convenient scapegoat, and Fung Wa and his associates a substantial war chest.

If they put up any less than a billion dollars for the expenses they had gotten away lightly. Somewhere out there was the real threat. If Nachtwatch and the minutemen provided the soldiers and the infrastructure, then someone else had provided the strategy. Who? *Talk to me Teddy. You either knew or you were close. Close enough that you lost at chess. Cclose enough that they could peer over your shoulder...*

The phone rang, a cricket warble loud across his thoughts. It stopped after one ring, then rang again and stopped after two.

Cockburn.

Quayle crossed the floor in three strides and picked it up on the first ring of the next attempt.

"Got someone who wants a word with you here," Cockburn said dryly.

"Put him on." Quayle said pleased. Only Steve could have gotten Cockburn irritated so fast.

"Little bird?"

"Mmmm."

"Remember where we met and ate noodles last time?"

"Yes... you wanted a Budweiser."

"Correct. One hour. OK?"

"One hour," Quayle confirmed.

Almost as soon as he hung up, he was on the move. The noodle place Steve had mentioned was over in Kowloon. He quickly scrounged through the wardrobes in the master bedroom until he found a jacket that fit. Pulling it on, he went straight to lifts. Once outside, he walked four blocks before hailing a cab and had it take him across the harbour in the tunnel, then drop him at the cultural centre. From here he walked up to the Regency Hotel and took a limousine to the airport, and from there a another taxi to the rendezvous.

It was a cheap eating house with Formica-topped tables, neon lights and incongruous calendar prints of the European Alps upon the walls. Sitting just inside the kitchen was Steve Chung. He nodded to Quayle and stepped out, leading him directly through the back door into the alley where a car waited.

"My brother's son," Steve said, pointing to the driver.

They drove through busy streets for a few minutes before the car pulled over and drew to a halt. Steve looked up an alley.

"Come, we go."

Two floors up, over a seedy photographer's studio, was a dingy little office complete with overhead fan, wooden desk and old metal filing trays.

"A guy is coming in half an hour. He can help. But it will cost more than money."

"What does he want?"

"Other than money? What everyone want. A passport. A real one," he finished wistfully.

Quayle thought about that. It was possible. "Who is he?"

"Driver," Steve said seriously, miming steering with his hands. He had never mastered the art and was in constant admiration of anyone who had.

"Why is he prepared to betray his master?"

"Family. His older brother was killed some years ago in a gang fight. Fung Wa's people did it. He only find out when his father die six weeks ago. He want revenge."

"Do you believe him?"

"If it was money only, no, I think not. But the passport show he thinking about running anyway. I know the family. It all fit. But we take precautions. He betray us and his cousin's sister never get over the wire. She in a boat people camp now, pretending she a Vietnamese. I said you could help there too."

Quayle nodded. This might be the break they were looking for.

"Whose driver is he?"

Steve smiled. It was a leery triumphant thing that said he had hit paydirt. "Fung Wa family!" he said gleefully.

"Jesus!" said Quayle, almost disbelieving. "That is a stroke of luck."

"Fung choi," Steve said happily. Fate was on their side.

Half an hour later, fate arrived.

They sat with the man for five hours, grilling him first on the motives for his act and then – when convinced he was genuine – on the routines and habits of the family: the time Fung Wa travelled to the office, and left for home, the security systems, the staff in the household, where the family ate, where the staff ate, everything they could think of, Quayle promoting Steve and keeping the two Chinese men to a rigid chronological pattern for a typical day. Now immersed in the concept, Steve would suddenly stop to offer Quayle good used Thompson machine guns or a bulk rate on tear gas by the crate, but Quayle tactfully refused each offer and brought them back onto the subject.

The size of the task was becoming clear. Fung Wa had a low visibility security machine that was based round a few talented well-trained people, rather than hordes of men and fences. The triad wars over for some years, his security was residual and seemingly routine for an Asian millionaire: personal bodyguards for all members of the family supported by electronic measures – and the entire show overseen by supervisors from a security company that Fung Wa owned.

The last servant of his gang days seemed to be his choice of major domo in the house, an old retainer who had a bulge under his armpit and frightened the servants. Aside from that, Fung Wa had shed the remainder of the old network to two trusted captains and now enjoyed the benefits of the rackets at a distance, while publicly deploring their existence.

But Fung Wa had one other weakness...

One of the privileges that he regularly indulged in was a call girl called Fay Ling. Fay was one of the ultra high priced string that the organisation ran and she made regular appearances at the office in the lunch hour, taking the private elevator to Fung Wa's thirty-eighth floor office. Her speciality was anal sex and she sometimes brought other very young girls with her. The driver Quayle sat with had twice been asked to pick them up from the plush Peak apartment where she lived. He felt a sudden flash of fear for Holly. *If they have touched you, just one hair on your head*, he promised to himself, *I will kill them all.*

Fay Ling was due in the office at 1pm, and that meant that Fung Wa would be lunching at his desk. With a plan formulated, Quayle gave Steve a list of things to do and headed back to the safe-house at Aberdeen Harbour. It would be after 8am by the time he got there. He needed a meeting with Cockburn and Alexi Kirov. There was much to do.

They were in place by 10.40, Kirov and Quayle down near the big Causeway Bay department store, waiting in the back of a delivery truck parked away from the shop fronts. Sogo, the Japanese-owned shop, was forty meters down the street on a busy corner and Steve – who sat in the front of the truck – could see the main doors that led into the designer goods section on the ground floor. Here, Gucci and Dunhill vied for space with Louis Vitton and the perfume houses of France – and it was here that they would do the job. Cockburn was with McReady the Special Branch man, ready to run interference and Kurt Eicheman was supervising the fifty-eight foot pleasure boat as they moved it from its berth up to the typhoon barrier and the walkway. The crew who normally operated the charter vessel had been told to take the day off and now two of Kirov's Spetznazt boat section men were aboard, one massaging the big twin throttles in the wheelhouse as the thrusters nudged the sharp bows round to the wall and the fuel pumps. Lastly, Quayle's demonstration would be completed by three of the Spetznatz team, already on a boat and moving towards their target. It had all taken just two and a half hours.

It was only seven hundred yards from Sogo's to the marina, but driving meant risking the one way system and getting round the entrance to the harbour tunnel, so it would take five or six minutes. Quayle stretched in the back of the truck and looked across at Kirov. The Russian was altering his shoulder harness so that the big gun hung grip down, its barrel suspended by a thin piece of rubber. It was designed for one use only and, if it saw action today, it would be as a last resort. His prime weapon would be the nasty little KGB number wrapped round his fist: a reinforced Kevlar glove with a tiny CS canister in the grip that released a fine spray into the victim's face as the punch connected. It would completely incapacitate the victim until their eyes were washed in a special solution by the casualty department of a hospital.

For now, all they could do was wait. The 600 series stretch Mercedes would stop directly outside the doors as it always did – and Quayle wanted to move then, rather than wait until they came out laden with parcels and possibly separated.

"The car comes," Steve called through the small window to the back.

"We're on," Quayle said to Kirov. "Ready?"

The Russian nodded and together they jumped down from the truck, moving straight round to the front and onto the sidewalk as Steve's brother eased the truck out onto the road in front of the traffic. They could already see the Mercedes, royal blue with tinted windows. Just four cars down, it had stopped short of Sogo's doors.

Kirov stepped off the pavement and tapped arrogantly on the passenger window. Knowing that the person couldn't see the impatient gesture he was making, the bodyguard in the front seat slid the electric window down to tell him in no uncertain terms not to tap on his car, muttering in Cantonese about stupid pink-skinned tourists.

As the window lowered, the driver – eagerly awaiting his chance of revenge on Fung Wa – slid his hand across the electric controls and unlocked all the doors. In that same instant, Kirov bent to look through the window at the thin faced Chinese in the front seat, then jabbed out with a punch that would have floored a professional, even without the CS spray.

At that precise moment, Quayle came through the back right-hand door with a burst of power, the other bodyguard twisting to see what was happening in front. His hand reached for his weapon, but he was too late; Quayle delivered a sharp two-fingered jab at a point below his ear, and he collapsed across one of his charges, a stunning Eurasian woman in her late thirties. Bodies were bundled onto floors and, in three seconds, Quayle and Kirov were in the vehicle, guiding it forward as the truck across the street finally got on its way.

Sitting where the guard had sat on the small fold-down seat against the front wall of the passenger compartment, Quayle put his foot on the bodyguard's head and looked at the three people sitting stunned across the wide back seat. On the right was a young girl in her early teens, very like the Eurasian. The daughter, Quayle thought. The third was a woman in her forties, pretty but dressed plainly with her hair up in a bun and wide frightened eyes. Unknown. It had happened so fast that none of them had really understood what had taken place.

It was time that he told them.

"You are the wife of Fung Wa?" he asked the woman the bodyguard had fallen against.

She nodded her head fiercely. "I am and you will not get away with this."

"I can and I will. I do apologise, but your husband has something of mine. We will swap within the next few hours. Until then, just co-operate and no harm will come to any of you."

"Why are you doing this?" the girl asked.

"Ask your dad when you are a bit bigger," Quayle answered with a reassuring smile.

The mother put her hand across the girl's lap and glared at Quayle.

"And who are you?" he asked the third.

"She speaks no English," Mrs Wa replied. "She is my maid."

"I don't think so." He turned and tapped on the glass. "Who is she?" he demanded of the driver.

"Wife big man from Canton. Communist," he said.

"So..." He turned back to face them. "A little shopping for a few capitalist luxuries. Very nice too. Tell her not to worry. She'll be OK. What is her name?"

"Noi Seng," Mrs Wa replied, glaring at the back of the driver's head. "Her husband is meeting my husband for lunch today. Top level discussions!"

I'll bet, Quayle thought. *Like who's going to give it to Fay first.* He tapped on the glass again. "Let me out here," he said – and, as the car pulled over, he fished in the bodyguard's pocket, took the gun out and handed it through to Kirov.

"Just do as you're told and you'll be home for dinner. But first: give me your purse."

She glared at him like he was a common thief but noticed, for the first time, the resolute determination in his tired eyes. There was nothing else to do. Believing him when he said that they would come to no harm, she felt the first thrust of real fear – not for herself, but for her husband. Producing her purse, she thrust it out to him with one long elegantly bejewelled hand, her eyes now betraying her thoughts. "Please..." she began.

"There is nothing you can do," he replied. "It's up to him."

He had two hours until Fay was due to arrive at the man's office. He could either give the boat an hour to clear the harbour and go straight in and get it over with, or wait and catch Fung Wa literally with his pants down. The initiative would be his. Choosing the latter, he made his way down the street past the hotel he was still checked into, towards the new towers that graced the waterfront. The private elevator could only be entered in the basement.

Security would be a problem if he tried to penetrate in daylight, so the only viable course of action was to take the direct option. Striding brazenly through the front doors of the building, he began to peruse the tenants board. By the look of it, Fung Wa's companies had the entire building and, already, he could feel the cameras on him. Somewhere in a control room people were watching him.

Sauntering to the lifts with Fung Wa's wife's purse in his hands, he waited for a car to arrive, whistling a sad little tune to himself like a man bored with nowhere else to go. Above him, somewhere, he knew they would be scurrying like rats. This was the last place they would have expected him to walk in so boldly.

A bell pinged in the roofing tiles above him and a little arrow began to flash over one of the lift doors.

He stepped towards it and, as he did so, Teddy Morton's beloved Newbolt flashed into his mind again, this time lines from Clifton Chapel: 'to honour when you strike him down, the foe that comes with fearless

270

eyes'. Quayle couldn't stop himself smiling at the irony as he remembered words that came later in the same piece: 'Qui procul hinc, the legends writ, the frontiers grave is far away, Qui ante deim perit, Sed miles sed pro patria'. *My eyes don't feel fearless,* he thought, *and I won't die for my country. So will you Fung Wa? Will you die for yours?*

Stepping into the lift, he pressed the button for the thirty-eighth floor. The doors hissed shut and the car began to move, the floor numbers lighting up above the doors as the car rocketed upwards.

When the doors opened, he had a reception committee.

There, evenly spaced across the wine coloured carpet and silhouetted against the floor to ceiling glass of the windows, four men in identical grey suits waited. Reptilian eyes set in expressionless faces awaited an order from somewhere. Behind them, at a huge reception desk, a pretty Chinese girl sat in fear, her face pale. The silence was palpable and lasted for three or four seconds before one of a pair of matched carved doors swung back and a man walked through. Tall and dressed elegantly in an expensive charcoal grey cashmere suit, his hair was combed back above a wide intelligent forehead and the tortoiseshell glasses gave him the look of a young banker. Nevertheless, the streaks of grey in his hair betrayed his age – and the eyes behind the lenses were not those of a banker. They were the eyes of a predator.

As he walked closer, Quayle could feel the power and the energy in the man. He oozed confidence like a man used to winning, like a man who thinks he has just won again. Fung Wa. It had to be.

"Mr Quayle. How considerate of you to visit us. You have saved me the trouble of finding you."

"For you the trouble has just begun. Tell your gorillas to back off." Quayle's voice was loaded with menace.

Fung Wa laughed softly. "How amusing! You walk into my offices and make demands? And what if I don't?" Putting his hands behind his back, he nodded to one of the four suits and the man stepped forward with a wolfish grin.

Quayle shook his head at the arrogance. You never knew who you

271

were dealing with. Without taking his eyes of Fung Wa for more than a millisecond, his foot flashed up and took the approaching individual hard under the chin, his head snapping back viciously. It was a full contact blow and the man fell to the floor, his neck broken.

The others dropped into various stances, two drawing firearms, bulbous nosed silencers pointed at Quayle.

"We don't get to talk and it's bye bye to mummy Fung and baby Fung," Quayle answered, his eyes glittering, holding up the purse, "and the wife of your visitor. Now, call off the fucking dogs."

Fung Wa's voice snapped a command but his tone was hesitant. He was thinking. Calculating the odds.

Quayle pushed his advantage. "Blue stretch Merc. I took them myself an hour ago outside Sogo's. Your daughter is wearing jade green silk." He paused. "Make your mind up! Do we deal or do you just let your mainland visitor give Fay Ling a quickie up the arse while you think about it?"

That threw Fung Wa. His eyes narrowed and he snapped another instruction in Cantonese. The three remaining men came up out of their stances, the two with the pistols slowly holstering their guns.

"My office is this way," he said in English.

Quayle followed him through the big carved doors, the three remaining bodyguards between him and their master, the fourth left lying on the rug where he fell.

The office was big. Teak cabinets dominated one wall, the alcoves filled with prized pieces of carved jade. An antique table was surrounded by Louis XIV chairs and the remaining pieces of furniture were from the same period. The only evidence of the Twentieth Century was the bank of five telephones and the matched pair of facsimile machines beside a computer terminal on a smaller table.

"So, what is your proposition?"

"Easy. You give me back Holly Morton, unharmed, and you get your people back."

Fung Wa studied him for a moment. "How naive you are. Do you really think it that simple?"

272

Quayle stepped forward a pace, his eyes narrowing.

"It's people like you who complicate it. Now watch my lips. You have taken something of mine. I want it back. If I don't get it back, your wife, and daughter and the woman from Canton, will just be the start. Your world, as you know it, will cease to exist." His voice dropped lower until it was barely a whisper. "And you will die as sure as the sun will rise tomorrow. Understand me now."

Fung Wa studied him for a moment. He was a man who respected courage.

"Come now. Let's discuss this. I have a large organisation and I always have room for a... consultant like yourself. What do they pay you? Is it the woman? Come and work for me. You can have her back..." He waved his hand as if it were of no consequence.

"I am not employed by any government. I have no rules but my own. Just return to me what is mine."

"Think about it. You can become part of something spectacular."

"Who the hell do you think you are?" Quayle asked him, wearied. "Some Ghengis Khan? You're no more than a petty hoodlum turned politician who thinks he can pervert the course of history. Now, you may not give a fuck about your wife and kid – but I will bet you need the safe return of the other woman. You wouldn't want a senior man from the Peoples Republic pissed of at you now, would you?"

Fung Wa's eyes widened.

"Yes, I know about that. So do my associates. If I don't get Holly back, your deal with Beijing is over. You will have no family, no business, no future. But that won't matter because I will get you too. Believe me. Do you understand what I'm saying to you, Fung Wa? This is not a negotiable issue."

Quayle stepped back a pace without, giving the Chinese tycoon time to think, and took a pointed look at his watch.

"Have Holly ready to hand over to me by 5pm today. I will tell you where at 2pm." Quayle walked to the big plate glass windows. "Nice view of the harbour. You went public a couple of years ago, didn't you? Shares nice and stable? That's one of your ships, isn't it? I believe you insure your own vessels. Well, come and have a look. I've arranged a little demonstration. That bulk carrier down there? Nice boat. A cargo of rice from Shezou, I believe. What's it worth? A couple of million? Maybe three?" He paused. "Say bye bye, Fung Wa. It's about to sink. Just like your stocks. Things have only just begun."

He turned and walked to the doors. "5pm... or you're fucked."

After Quayle was gone, Fung Wa walked back to the window and watched in white seething anger as his ship began visibly settling in the water right before his eyes, the work boats and barges backing away, the sea boiling under their transoms as propellers thrashed to gain purchase and a police launch turned towards her, the thin wail of her siren reaching upward.

Quayle spent the next fifteen minutes making sure he wasn't being followed, then took a cab across to Kowloon. The boat he had waiting was a noisy twenty-five footer with two berths tucked away in a lower cabin. It was here that he found Cockburn, sitting in one of the bunks with a large duffel on the seat beside him. As Quayle dropped down through the tiny companionway, he dropped his feet off the other bunk.

"How'd it go?"

"He'll play. He's a prick but he's shit scared. That other woman did the trick."

"I should hope so. Do you know who you kidnapped?" Cockburn asked.

"I don't care, as long as it works."

"I would think the daughter of one of central committee will work wonders," he said dryly. "London are having kittens."

"If London did their jobs in the first place, we wouldn't be here." The remark was pointed at Cockburn but he let it ride as Quayle continued, "Anyway, it's my scene. They want to pull you out, fine... What the fuck was she doing here without the diplomatic protection people watching her?"

"Little shopping trip while her husband does the deal, by all accounts." Cockburn raised his voice as the engine revs picked up and beneath them the hull began to plane over the water. "Where do you want to do the swap?"

Before Quayle could reply, a young Chinese man called over to them and pointed off to the left. Out on the water, a gaggle of boats was surrounding an oil slick that shimmered with creamy grey light. Police craft shuttled back and forth and a harbour authority vessel was hove to, its crew looking down into the water and talking and pointing.

"Shame," Cockburn said, "looks like something sunk." He looked at Quayle. "And we've just added piracy to the list of this morning's crimes..."

"I want an aircraft to get us out of here tonight. Can you line up seats on an RAF flight or something?" Quayle lit a cigarette and inhaled deeply, enjoying the wind in his face. It was his first for days. "If it means getting back onto the mainstream mission, yes I can."

"Do it."

"What if it's not over?"

Quayle's face hardened. "It will be. One way or the other."

"And the exchange?"

"Five o'clock. Nice and busy with lots of ferries about. We'll do the swap on the water directly outside the port police facility."

"Do you think that will stop him doing anything hostile?"

"No," admitted Quayle. "He has too much to lose. He'll try something. Did you get the stuff I asked for?"

"Below in the bag. McReady is bitching about laser sights and things."

"Wait until you tell him I want a man on the Port police building roof."

Quayle laughed then, a sharp dry chuckle.

They were in place at exactly ten minutes to five. Above the fourth floor on the roof of the Port Police building, two of Kirov's Spetznazt men were in position. One was a wiry twenty-six year old sergeant, whose commanding officer claimed was in amongst the six best rifle shots alive. He cradled his own rifle, a customized Dragunov. Four inches had been added to the barrel length, and the butt had been reworked to improve the balance. Chambered for five millimetre magnum rounds and sporting a big American telescopic sight, the young Soviet could put ten out of ten bullets into a football at twelve hundred yards. Today the range would be nearer four hundred, but he was concerned with the windage and its effect on his light ultra fast bullets. A puff of wind, he thought, and he would blow a hole in the Englishman. That was why he had a second rifle at his side. This was a standard Parker Hale 270 that delivered a bigger slower round. With the variable Bushnell scope, it would become his choice if the breeze began to blow. On his head he wore industrial earmuffs that contained a small radio receiver, through which he could receive instructions from the boat. Watching the water below, he mused at how rapidly things were changing. Here he was, with the full knowledge of the local police in a British Crown Colony, reporting to a KGB officer. He had never had much time for the GRU, the Red Army Intelligence section and Spetznazt's nominal parent regiment, but he thought that the KGB were even bigger wankers and he normally avoided any association with them. The hatred the two held for each other was legendary. They were the opposition. Although Kirov was OK. He'd been through the hell of Ryazan himself.

To his left, and lying on his side, was his partner, an older Afghanistan veteran, sometimes morose, sometimes laughing – but always there, watching his back. He would operate the laser sight. Normally mounted on a rifle, today he would simply point it at the target. In the failing light it would do its job. On the surface of the roof beside his hand was an electronic detonator that would set of a chain of fire crackers in the street below. No-one would hear the sharp whiplash crack of the Dragunov on the roof.

Below them, on the water, Quayle stood alone on the flying bridge. It was warm but, in spite of that, he wore a long-sleeved T-shirt and a pair of baggy track suit pants. His feet were bare and, although he hadn't trained for some time, the layers of hard skin around the edges of his feet were still thick. He lifted a cigarette to his lips, inhaling deeply. Below him, in the main wheel house behind the tinted windows, Kirov sat behind an array of weaponry that included a flare gun, his own pistol – now with a silencer affixed – and the queen of any infantry battle, an M60 machine gun. One of the Spetznatz men loaded a belt into it and cocked the action. If it came to that, then they were in trouble. No amount of fire crackers or police blind eyes would help then. But then, if it came to that, as Quayle had said, who cared anyway?

The three hostages were below in the main saloon, guarded by one of the Soviets, and the final pair of Kirov's men were suited up and waiting, breathing through snorkels to conserve their tanked air at the bathing platform. They carried light waterproof arms and powerheads and, if necessary, would board Fung Wa's boat from the rear.

Quayle took another puff and inhaled deeply. Given the timeframes, they had taken all the precautions possible for a counter strike by the Chinese. Now all they could do was wait. He looked across the harbour and, smiling, picked up a pair of big Ziess glasses. *Come to me, my darling.*

At the wheel of the boat, Cockburn sat in a big leather chair and wished the Royal Navy were tied up alongside them, not the little ski-boat. As he muttered curses to himself, Chloe appeared and handed him one of the cups of coffee she was carrying. He took it wordlessly and she began to climb the steep stairs to the flying bridge.

"Chloe," he said. "Leave it now." Lifting a finger, he pointed out the big opaque wheel house windows. There, across the harbor, moving towards them, was a big modernistic boat with a cathedral hull and square ports. Behind it moved a second smaller boat. She felt a flicker of fear move up her spine.

Quayle dropped cat-like through the hatch from the flying bridge. Smiling at Chloe, he took the cup from her hand.

"Alexi – your two divers. The second boat. That's the back-up. The marksmen stay on the big job. They're to wait for your signal, unless something breaks that we can't see. And tell 'em not to bloody shoot me or Holly. OK," he said, his eyes lighting up. "Let's get the women up now and into the fizz boat."

"How long has he known about this place, here on the water?"

"Three hours," Quayle answered. "Why?"

"Long enough to get his own divers," Kirov replied pointedly.

Quayle swore softly. He had missed that possibility. He looked at Kirov. "Suggestion?"

"Da." The Soviet turned and spoke rapidly to the two men waiting in wetsuits on the bathing platform. "We will watch the fish finder. If he sees something, he can alert one diver. The other will cross to the other boat."

"One enough?" Quayle asked.

The expression on Kirov's face told him the question was stupid.

"Good. Let's do it."

Kirov nodded and, taking his gun from the shelf, he picked up the radio, dropped it into his pocket and put the slim-line headset on.

The other boat hove to two hundred yards from Quayle's. As he watched the last of the women clamber into the runabout, he wondered how many people were watching the switch from offices and hotel rooms.

Kirov started the motor, then dropped down below into the tiny cabin with the hostages. Quayle took the wheel and eased the bows round. Then, with the engine barely above an idle, he headed for the midpoint between the two bigger boats. Ahead he could see a small tender leaving Fung Wa's boat and he resisted the temptation to pick up the binoculars. Kirov, however, had no such compunction. Scooping them up, he poked his head above the gunwale and trained them on the tender.

"Three I can see." He paused for a second. "But there may be more below..."

"Did you see a woman? Dark hair?"

"She'll be down in the bows, just like ours. Don't worry, Titus. We'll know soon enough."

Please God, he prayed, *let her be safe and well. She is just too good and too decent to be a victim of this. She deserves better. I swear to you, you whom she believes in, her God, that if anything has happened to her, then I will put it to rights. With you or without you. An eye for an eye.*

Easing back on the power, he let the boat settle in the water.

They were almost half way. In another minute, the diver would be under the hull of Fung Wa's boat.

The other boat was close now. Here it came, idling towards them. Quayle no longer needed the binoculars to clearly see Fung Wa standing at the wheel, the man beside him openly holding a small automatic weapon.

Meanwhile, up on the roof of the port police building, the sniper zeroed in on the man while his partner took a last look at the photo and peered through the laser sight his finger on the trigger. The spot would appear dead centre on Fung Wa's chest.

The two boats were now in hailing distance. Quayle turned his boat beam on.

"Let's see her!" he called.

"All in good time, Mr Quayle," Fung Wa called back. His voice had lost its resonant quality and was filled with tension.

No doubt about it: he was up to something.

Quayle tapped his foot once and Kirov spoke into the tiny microphone. A second later, a tiny red spot danced across Fung Wa's chest as Quayle said a silent prayer of thanks for calm waters.

"Don't misunderstand me," he called, his eyes glittering. "Take a look at your front. That red spot is a laser sight. One funny move that my man doesn't like and someone dies. Now bring her up!"

Fung Wa looked down quickly and then hurriedly stepped to one side, pushing the armed man – who was sweeping air with his gun, looking for the threat – aside. But no sooner had he moved, the spot reappeared on his breast. His anger flowing, he snapped out an order and, as the guard lifted his weapon, Quayle heard the meaty thump of a high calibre bullet hit flesh and bone. In that same instant, the guard slammed back and downward onto the transom. His body twitched for two seconds. Then it relaxed.

He was stone dead.

Several seconds later, the faint crackle of fireworks carried over the water.

Kirov bent into his earpiece to listen, and quickly turned to look to the rear. Quayle resisted the temptation and kept his eyes firmly on Fung Wa. There in the water, bobbing on the surface thirty metres behind their boat, were the bodies of two divers. The first's buoyancy jacket was inflated and the water around what remained of his head was pink. The second was also dead – but this time seemingly intact. The powerhead blast, it seemed, had taken him in the back.

Kirov turned, his gun resting on the gunwales, aimed at Fung Wa. Below them, in the small cabin, someone began to sob and another voice spoke in rapid, almost hysterical Cantonese.

"Temper temper!" Quayle cried out. "Next time, you say good-bye to Noi and the China deal. Now bring her up!"

Fung Wa looked back at Quayle, trying to believe what had happened to his men, trying to understand where the shot had come from. For the first time, it seemed, he was realising that he had been out thought. He snarled down at the helmsman who still lay prone on the deck between the seats. The man stood and ducked forward into the bow section, reappearing a moment later, pushing a figure.

She seemed smaller, bowed over, a hood masking her features. Her hands were bound behind her, pulling her arms back cruelly – but Quayle had no doubt it was Holly. Her foot hit something on the floor of the boat and she tripped forward, smashing into the deck.

Quayle's anger and frustration peaked. As he cried out, Kirov's hand shot out and took his shoulder, standing up, his gun aimed rock steady at the Chinese.

"Cut her free, you bastard, or they'll be scraping your fucking brains off the deck!"

The helmsman didn't wait for Fung Wa to tell him. He pulled a small knife from his pocket and rapidly cut away the bonds.

"Now the hood, you fucker of your own mother!"

Kirov had a mad look in his eyes, the Cossack blood of his forefathers bubbling up inside him.

Fung Wa glanced down. There, on his breast, the red dot still danced.

Fung Wa's helmsman pulled the hood pulled clear and, at last, Quayle saw her: her tousled rich brown hair, her eyes wide and frightened, her red-rimmed mouth covered by tape.

"Hands up!" Kirov shouted. "Both of you. Very high. We will come alongside. Exchange."

Fung Wa stood back, a look of complete defeat across his face. In front of him, the helmsman lifted his hands high over his head – but Kirov wasn't satisfied with the speed of response. Bent in the classic marksman's crouch, he squeezed the trigger. The big gun gave a silent cough and the perspex windscreen beside Fung Wa's head shattered and split into a spider's web of opaque cracks. Recoiling instinctively, the surge of fear bought him back to reality. His hands came up. The faint crackle of fireworks reached them again and, as Quayle eased the throttles forward and manoeuvred the boat around, keeping the tender between them and the big cathedral hull, he knew that someone on the big boat had done something stupid and had died. His face was a mask of anger, his grey eyes glittering and his jaw set. It was taking all his self control to allow Kirov command. It was right and he knew it. He was too close, too emotionally involved.

In the other boat, Holly was coming to her feet. Quayle watched with immense pride as, with shaking hands, she pulled the tape from her mouth, squaring her shoulders and holding everything back, determined not to give Fung Wa the pleasure of seeing her break down.

The boats nudged and Quayle crossed from one to the other like a big cat. Now it was his time. Up close enough to use his hands and feet.

Fung Wa must have remembered, because he was already backing away to the far gunwale, his confidence gone and his eyes full of defeat.

Quayle paused before Holly and ran a finger down her nose. Then he looked around. The boat held no other threat. Scooping up the bodyguard's gun, he threw it over the side and finally faced Fung Wa.

"You've killed four people in two minutes with your stupidity. Lie on the floor. Face down, palms upward. Do not look up until I tell you. If you do, you'll be the fifth. Do you understand me?"

The man nodded impassively and dropped slowly to his knees, then forward onto his front, holding his face up out of the blood of his bodyguard. Holly began to cry then, slow deep sobs of relief, her shoulders heaving with each breath. Quayle turned and, in one fluid motion, picked her up and crossed back into the other boat, where he put her down on the rear seat.

"OK Alexi. Bring 'em up," he said without taking his eyes of Holly. "Be brave a few minutes longer, my love. Then we're away and safe." She didn't acknowledge him with more than a tiny nod, but he wiped a tear from her cheek – and, fighting the desire to hold her close and cuddle her and make the world go away, he stood and watched the tender as the first of Fung Wa's women came up from the cabin. Then he pointed to the tender alongside. "Thank you for your co-operation, ladies. There is your ride home."

Fung Wa's wife glared at Quayle and, ignoring the sight of the bloody body stepped, across the gunwales inelegantly, swearing coarsely in Cantonese.

On the other side, she was about to say something to her husband when he silenced her with a look that could wither gorse. Instead, she remained in silence and waited until her daughter and the wife of the mainland official had clambered over.

"You women sit in the bows," Quayle said. "Fung Wa, you stand and move to the back of the boat, sit on the engine. Now!"

After they had done what he demanded, Quayle nodded to Kirov, who spoke into his microphone. Moments later, the red dot danced back across Fung Wa's chest, now blending with the bodyguards blood down the front of his shirt.

"When the dot goes, you go. Understand?"

Fung Wa nodded imperceptibly. Realising he was going to be allowed to liv,e his eyes had lost their fear and were full of hate.

Kirov took the wheel.

*

282

"I'm so sorry Holly."

They were sitting below in the master stateroom, Quayle holding her close as the big boat thundered her way round to Aberdeen Harbour. The tears had stopped and she gave him a last strong squeeze.

"It's OK," she said, her face snuggled into is chest. "I'm here now."

"No it's not. I promised you and I failed."

"No you didn't," she told him. "You got me back." Sitting up, she wiped the last tear from her eye and tried a brave smile. "I knew you would. How is Marco?"

Quayle smiled. How like her to ask. "Strong as a bull when I spoke to him. He'll be fine."

Smiling, she looked him in the eye. "When will this be over, Ti?"

"Soon, my love."

"Can't you hand over to Hugh now? Let them do it. They aren't after us any more are they?" She had seen Cockburn on the bridge as they came aboard. "Or have you corrupted him too?"

"No. He's here on the job. But there are a couple of things to tie up first..."

"Like what?"

"I have to finish it," he said, looking away as he searched for the right words, wondering if he should tell her.

"I know," she said.

No you don't, he thought.

Two hours later, in the house overlooking the bright lights of Aberdeen Harbour, the men sat round the table in the kitchen.

"OK," said Quayle. "You people head out to the airport. I'll meet you there."

Cockburn looked up. He had arranged for a helicopter to drop them on the air-side to avoid making targets of themselves on the trip out. "Where are you going?" he asked.

"I'll see you there," Quayle repeated, then turned to Kirov. "I'm going to leave Holly in your care, Alexi. Please..."

"Of course," the Soviet interrupted, waving a hand like it was of no consequence.

Right now, Holly was with Chloe in one of the bedrooms of the safehouse, looking for something to wear. After she was bathed and ready, Quayle walked through to tell her he would see her later. She nodded, understanding.

As Quayle left the house, Kirov signalled to two of his men. Standing wordlessly, they followed him. At the window, she watched him leave. All she had seen of him recently and all Marco's stories of his invincibility could not help her completely forget her fears, and she was pleased to see the pair of men follow.

*

The high white walls of the house stood back from the road and the main gates – wrought iron, heavy and gloss black in the moonlight – were recessed back a further ten feet. Quayle went over the top of the wall where the corners met, fifty yards from the gates and the security guard's hut which seemed ominously quiet.

Stopping below the wall, he waited in the darkness, a half a smile on his lips.

Fifty seconds later, the two men thudded to the ground beside him and grinned ruefully, like two small boys caught out.

Quayle raised an eyebrow and one of them shrugged as if to say 'Orders, what to do?'

Quayle shook his head. At least Kirov himself hadn't followed. He was more use where he was now, looking after Holly. Indicating that they should follow, he set off across the silent lawns to the house, his new companions close behind.

The house was in darkness, all except for a dim light that crept from a curtained window further round. Quayle didn't like that. The place ought to have been alive with servants and noises and the routines that households have. Turning to one of the Soviets as they arrived at the base of the wall, he pointed to the gates.

"It's too quiet..." He spoke little Russian but knew that all Soviet special forces spoke good German and used that language. "Check the gates."

The man nodded and, pulling an automatic from his pocket, disappeared into the night. Quayle and the other stood together and began to move round the wall to the service doors at the rear of the house.

One minute later, they were in. The back door to the kitchen was open. Moving into the house carefully, they checking room by room, moving methodically towards the room where the lights were on.

It turned out to be a small crowded bedroom, probably used by a servant. Someone had cleared out recently and quickly. There was still cigarette smoke on the air, and drawers had been hurriedly emptied as the occupant moved out. Satisfied that there was nothing more to see, they moved back into the main section of the house, down corridors kept dark by heavy drapes.

They first bodyguard was slumped back against a wall, dead. He had been killed with one shot. The second, who had suffered a similar fate, was sprawled face down on the hall carpet. Quayle's Soviet ally picked up his firearm and sniffed the barrel, shaking his head. He hadn't even got one shot away.

It was then the Spetznatz man heard it. A shuffle or a scrape on the carpet behind a door, followed by a liquidy moan.

Quayle moved up from the door he was at and listened. Then, taking the initiative, he pushed to door open, the Soviet, with his firearm drawn, moving close behind.

They heard it again. Quayle felt for the lights and, finding the switch, turned them on.

"Oh fuck," the Soviet said in English.

There, tied in a chair in the middle of the room was a something – a person, still alive, blood everywhere on the cream thick shag pile carpet. Through the blood and the pain and the tortured features, Quayle recognised Fung Wa. His legs were spread and tied back to the chair legs and his groin was black with blood that had dried, its central area still bright red and fresh. His face was contorted in pain and his mouth seemed to be gagged.

As they moved closer. Quayle saw that the gag wasn't cloth. Whoever had castrated him had taken the penis as well as his testicles, pushing the whole bloody piece of his manhood into his mouth.

The Soviet dropped to his knees and produced a battle medic pack from the voluminous pockets in his jacket, then swiftly produced an ampoule of morphine. He looked at Quayle who nodded.

"Keep him conscious," he warned softly. "I want him to talk."

The special forces man nodded and pushed the hypodermic straight into the Fung Wa's thigh. Pressing the plunger, he forced the drug into his bloodstream. Then, taking a large battle dressing, he forced it over the gaping hole in Fung Wa's trousers, his hand applying the necessary pressure to halt the blood flow, his other hand pulling out a mini disposable saline drip and tossing it to Quayle.

Quayle knew what to do. Stripping the paper off the needle, he pushed it through Fung Wa's shirt sleeve into his arm. Then, draping the bag over the wounded man's shoulder, he watched as gravity began to feed the solution into Fung Wa's arm.

Soon, the morphine was taking effect. Fung Wa's breathing turned from the ragged sharp shallow breaths of a man in extreme pain to a deeper, measured normality. Quayle reached up and gently pulled the bloody mass of gristle, skin and tissues from his mouth.

"Who did this?" he asked. "Beijing? Fung Wa, you're dying. You're going to meet you ancestors. They have killed you! You owe them nothing. Nothing!"

The Chinese eyes flickered open. The life force had gone. They were flat and glazed.

"Was this Beijing or Geneva? Was this Geneva?"

Fung Wa nodded, blood weakly dripping down his front.

Geneva. Jesus Christ! Two hours was all they had. They got in did the job and were gone. They're close, thought Quayle. *They are very close indeed.*

"Who in Geneva?" Quayle demanded.

"Not... not..." The man's voice was a rasping whisper, and Quayle lent forward to hear. "Not Geneva. Chamon... Chamon... Gira."

"Chamongira. A name?"

"Name.. is.. Girad... French.." Each word was tortured, produced by the last reserves of Fung Wa's strength.

"Girard?"

He nodded weakly. French, not Geneva. Quayle's mind raced. Somewhere near Chamon?

"Chamonix?"

Fung Wa nodded again, his head dropping forward. Quayle pulled it up. Not fucking Geneva at all. Just the nearest airport and big city. Chamonix. He knew the valley. The Arve and above it Mont Blanc, the Aigulle Du Midi and the Brevent. He had climbed there years before. It was big. Too big to find one Frenchman called Girard.

"Where in Chamonix can I find him? I will kill him for you. I will spit in his face with your name on my lips, Fung Wa. Don't die yet. Where? Tell me where!"

The thought of Quayle after them as he had been after him, seemed to give Fung Wa renewed strength.

"Albert... Albert Hotel..."

"They stay there?"

"No Chalet. Big Chalet. Guards good table at Albert."

Quayle knew the Albert. The old hotel was the favourite of the visiting Americans and its food was good, rated in the Michelin guide.

Fung Wa's head dropped forward again. Quayle looked at the Soviet – but he just shook his head and gestured at all the blood on the floor. In front of their eyes, Fung Wa began to shiver, and Quayle knew that this was the last stage of massive blood loss, the remaining blood unable to keep the body warm, the heart pumping still trying to keep blood going to the brain and vital organs. It was a cold and lonely way to die.

At that moment, the second soldier entered through the door. He didn't seem surprised at what he saw.

"Guards dead," he reported. "Two cars gone. No staff anywhere. No sign of the wife and kid."

287

"Let's go," Quayle said. There was no saving the man in the chair and he gestured to the kneeling Soviet to administer the rest of the morphine. At least, that way, there would be no pain.

CHAPTER TWELVE

As soon as Quayle put in the call, Kurt Eicheman went to work. For this, there was only one man he would trust. In turn, he put in a call to his local network leader, in the south east of France, who dropped everything to run down the man called Girard in Chamonix.

Quayle, Holly and Eicheman, along with Kirov and his team, would be flying in directly while Cockburn had been recalled to London to re-brief Tansey-Williams. The plan was to enter through Frankfurt and then Geneva on four different flights, and soon all but Quayle and Kirov were fast asleep. It seemed days since they had last slept, and all except the pair had taken one of the sedatives offered by the Spetznatz medic.

Quayle stretched back in the aisle seat, Holly next to the window, and took the opportunity to think through the last twenty four hours. Kirov, the tireless wiry little KGB man, sat on the other side of the aisle, headphones on as he watched a movie. It was a period production set before the Great War, young men in baggy flannels watching a cricket match. The next shot showed a slow bowler pacing his run and the cheery youthful grin of the schoolboy batsman, tea and sandwiches being served at the pavilion somewhere behind.

Quayle watched the silent images through a wreath of his own cigarette smoke, his eyes occasionally flickering to look at Holly. Up on the screen, people clapped mutely and the batsman walked back to the pavilion, his disappointment hidden in a mask of good sportsmanship. *Jolly good stuff,* Quayle thought cynically. *It's not who wins that counts but the game and all that.*

Stirring beside him, Holly looked at the screen and smiled. "Play up play up and play the game," she said sleepily. And Quayle smiled back, thinking how like her father she was at times, quoting Newbolt.

As she snuggled down again, he thought about what she had said, and Henry Newbolt's words flashed back to his mind.

'There's a breathless hush on the close tonight,
ten to make and the match to win,
a bumping pitch and a blinding light,
an hour to play and the last man in,
and it's not for the sake of a ribboned coat
or the selfish hope of a season's fame,
but his captain's hand on his shoulder smote,
Play up! Play up! and play the game!'

As he repeated the verse to himself, he thought about old Teddy Morton. The poem was a favourite of his and he could conjure vivid images as he read, the rich tones of his voice filling the room with Vitae Lampada. The glory of courage that only poets ever found.

'The sand of the desert is sodden red,
red with the wreck of a square that broke,
The Gatling's jammed and the Colonel's dead,
and the regiment blind with the dust and smoke,
the river of death has brimmed its banks,
and England's far and honour a name,
but the voice of a schoolboy that rallies the ranks,
Play up! Play up! and play the game.'

Suddenly, there in the half dark, the movie flickering on the small screen and a hostess tucking in a sleeping passenger, his eyes narrowed. The sudden realisation was clear and strong. *Teddy, you tricky, clever, wonderful old bugger. The pack was close. You knew where to put it so that only I would know. You knew, sooner or later, I would find it. Red with the wreck of a square that broke. Broken Square. You knew they would come for you. So you named the file as a clue, knowing that I and only I would find it...*

The BND ground operator had been busy. By the time the team arrived in Chamonix, he had found a large well-equipped chalet for them to

290

move into and also had news on the Frenchman. As people threw bags into the warm wood-panelled bedrooms, Quayle and Eicheman moved through into the dining area and pulled the concertina door across behind them. The central heating had kicked in, and outside the air had a crisp alpine sharpness. In the window, the massif of Mont Blanc rose above the trees, the slopes crisp and white and smooth like a wedding cake. The beauty was deceptive, the ice cliffs and avalanches, the sub zero temperatures and the sheer hostility muted by distance.

Nearer, and starkly more impressive, stood the Augille du Midi, a towering narrow spire at the crest of a ridge. It reached towards the heavens like the devil's accusing finger, its last few hundred metres sheer walls of rock and blue ice. Atop the spire stood a cable car station and observation deck. A warm restaurant served coffees and chocolate and light meals, but outside the temperature, even in summer, was below zero, and the air at twelve-and-a-half-thousand feet thin.

Quayle looked up. He had been up the Augille many times, twice the hard way. With crampons and rope, up the great columns of rock and ice chutes with Pierre Lacoste, a respected guide in the valley.

"Your man, Girard," the BND man began. "Your information was correct. He eats at the Albert three or four times some weeks. I saw him there last night. He leaves there and sometimes calls in at the Shuker bar, or the Blue Note. But he's rarely alone. Usually he's with two or three others. Same age. Mid thirties, early forties. He lives in a chalet complex up the road towards Argentierre. Three chalets set together in the trees. Security is very good. Fences. Patrols. I think he is not... how do you say? Top Dog?"

Quayle nodded and he continued.

"I watched him go into one of the smaller chalets. The larger is occupied by others. I spoke to a man in the village at Le Lavancher. He delivers things there. Has done for a few years. They climb every year here, this group."

"It's late for that," Quayle said. The true climbing season ended in the Autumn. Light alpine climbing was a summer pastime, when the weather was more predictable.

"This year they climb ice," the man replied, his gesture saying that he thought anyone who did such a thing was not all there in the head.

"Who's in the big chalet?" Quayle asked.

The man flicked open a note book, rather like a country policeman. "A politician type from Paris, and an industrialist and his party. I think the industrialist owns the place, but I won't know for a few days. Girard is apparently respectful of these two."

Quayle thought for a second or two. Girard could be the front Man. The negotiator. What he wanted was to be able to run the names through the computers and see what was dredged up, but with the network they seemed to have in place they might well know they were being searched before it was even completed.

"Same people all the time?"

"No. The residents change. Usually all from Paris, but sometimes others. He said he doesn't talk to them. Just sees them about."

The location was ideal, Quayle thought. Remote and yet, with a constantly changing population, they could hide themselves up here in the valley and disappear into the hordes of visitors, winter or summer. Guests could come and go, meetings could be held, plans laid behind the veneer of the alpine resort's attractions.

Quayle turned to Eicheman. "This is what I want to do. Let's try and get a look inside the complex. I have a feeling this is the European headquarters of this thing. Nachwatch, Minutemen, whatever they call themselves in France. Fung Wa would have been dealing with the big boys and not just some cell. If that's the case, then getting in will be tough and we risk not having enough time to see it done. It would be better to separate our targets. That may be easiest while they're climbing."

"The security is tight inside the complex. Why not outside too?" Eicheman asked sensibly.

"It may be, but this is home ground for them. People get over confident and sloppy this close to home. They might just take a few heavies and rely on the fact that, this late in the season, they'll be the only party about."

292

Eicheman shrugged. "I wouldn't know. I hate the mountains. Let's do it at ground level anyway."

Quayle smiled but shook his head. "Let's have a look tonight. Plan A is the complex. Alexi can have a look with one of his people. If it's a no go, then we see where they're climbing and look at Plan B."

"Ah," the other BND man said, "I think I have something there. One of my sources is in the Bureau de Guide. These people don't use the Bureau, you understand, but one of them was in there only yesterday asking about..." He pulled his notebook out. "...the Refuge de Leschaux."

Quayle looked up. "You're sure? Refuge de Leschaux?"

The man nodded.

"You know it?" Eicheman asked.

"I know it," Quayle said. *You proud, unforgiving, merciless bitch. You nearly killed me once before. This may be your chance again.* "It's the starting point for a number of climbs. A hut. But if these guys are serious and looking for ice and a challenging climb..." He pictured the steep flaky walls and chutes, the falling stones that could kill. "Grand Jorasses. They'll try and climb the Grand Jorasses." He thought further. "That's the ice they want. It might just be cold enough to freeze the stones on the chute. But dangerous, very dangerous..."

"It is bad?" Eicheman asked, already hating this mountain more than the rest.

"The interesting bits of the north face, off the Walker Spur that is, were only really cracked in '76. Not as big or as demanding as the north face of the Eiger. It's all loose stone and ice. Bonnington called it an elegant climb. And it is. On a good day, it's a sheer delight. But on the bad days she is formidable. She has killed good men." Quayle walked to the window and looked at the sky. The weather killed and injured as many as stonefall or a missed handhold. It might just be cold enough for them to try Macintyre and Colton's '76 winter route.

"I have a couple of calls to make," he finally said. "But let's get together with Alexi for an hour first. Then I'll be away for a few days."

The first call he made was to Pierre Lacoste, the guide who had taught him to ski and climb. Pierre was one of the old school, of piton and hammer, and he and Quayle had argued many an evening over the merits of the new techniques, the wedges and cramming devices. Pierre, his black curly hair framing almost black Gaelic eyes over a proud hooked nose, would jab his finger to make his point, incessantly smoking crumpled Gauloise from his back pocket. He felt as if the Alps had lost something in fast light ascents and saw it as the end of an era.

Pierre was nearing sixty now and had officially retired, but was delighted to get Quayle's call. They had last seen each other four years before and done a fast ascent of one of the Augilles on a Saturday, Quayle using the new clean style. Even he, Pierre Lacoste, guide and mountain man, had to admit that it worked well.

On the evening Quayle called, Pierre had guests – his daughter and her children were staying, so he couldn't begin preparations straight away. But, in the morning, he would bundle them off to the town and begin. A noisy game had developed between the girls and, with Quayle's request on his mind, he walked to the open windows and looked up at the darkening sky. The weather had been unpredictable recently. It had snowed this early in the valley before but he had never known it quite so cold so early in the season. They could use snow this year, he thought. Three bad seasons in a row and the talk was now about everyone going to America to ski. He pulled the windows shut. It would be good to prepare a trip again, to sharpen crampons, choose rope and wax the randonee skis, even if he wouldn't be going and he wasn't to talk of it to anyone.

*

The flight into Melbourne, Australia, touched down early in the morning.

Quayle had asked Kirov for a pair of eyes and a fast hand to keep an eye on Holly, and the young Soviet trailed her as he had been trained. A man had flown down from the Soviet Embassy in Canberra and handed over a firearm in the toilets without seeing Quayle and Holly, and within an hour they were driving towards Geelong and the school where Teddy Morton had spent his last days.

Holly was quiet as they drove, seemingly uncomfortable with the prospect of visiting the place where her father died. The windows were down and the dry warm air was blowing her hair back. Quayle's one concession to security was allowing her to sit in the front while her bodyguard sat in the back.

The school was built facing the bay at Corio, the main facility built of red brick with creepers growing up the walls and a quadrangle that was surrounded in as much history as the young country could offer. On either side, buildings stretched along a clean swept road that separated the main school from the sports fields. The grounds sprawled with contempt for land values along the shoreline and back into what was once farm land, with wide streets of staff housing, annexes, old halls and a sanatorium. Quayle stopped at a crossroads to get his bearings before turning left, slowing down to let a group of boys lugging bags of books cross the road in front of them.

"Why here, Ti?" Holly asked. "I mean, of all the places he could have put it?"

A short fat boy bounced across after the main group and, as someone shouted at him to hurry up, he gleefully extended two fingers at the group. Then, suddenly realizing that perhaps the car contained somebody's parents, he grinned at Quayle, hoping that he was eminently forgettable.

"He was still working on it. When he began the file he probably knew he was coming here, and he knew he would finish it here. That's why he chose to take the name from Vitae Lampada. Broken Square. The school. Play up and all that. He left a teaser with Gabriella Kreski. Drake's Drum. He knew."

"What now?" she asked softly.

"The house," he said. "But... you don't have to come."

"No," she said softly. "I'll come."

Quayle wound down the window and hooked a finger at the boy.

Realising he was caught, the lad trudged miserably across as his friends guffawed from the pavement.

"What's your name?" Quayle asked.

"Phillips, sir. John Phillips, sir. Sir, I didn't mean it. I just.."

"Relax, John Phillips Sir," Quayle said. "I just need directions."

"Oh!" He brightened up immediately, pushing his glasses up his nose and dropping his books to pull up his socks. "Where to, sir?"

"The administrators' office."

"Back down the road to the first left, past the Head's house and round to the left again. Then you'll have the main field on your right. Scroggy's's office..." He grinned again and, when Holly did too, he thought he may have gotten away with it. "Sorry, I mean Mr Mortimer's office is in the main Quadrangle. You'll know it by the clock tower. Cars aren't usually allowed. Well, except for parents..." he trailed off seriously.

"I suspect we shall be alright," Quayle said equally seriously. "Thanks."

"You're welcome," the boy said. He bent to pick up his books as Quayle edged round and drove back the way they had come.

Three minutes later, they were parked in front of the main quadrangle.

"Not here please," the young Soviet said in German. "The wall is too close. I want a clear area."

You want a killing field, Quayle thought, *but that's what you're here for.* So he moved the car to the playing field side of the road.

As he clambered out, he looked back at the man and caught his eye. He had a light coat over his lap. Quayle knew that beneath it was his firearm and, as he stepped clear of the car, the soldier nodded just once. *Go and do what you have to do,* he seemed to be saying. *She is safe.*

The office was down one of the long airy edges of the quad, and Quayle pushed back the old heavy door. As it swung back noiselessly, a woman looked up over her horn rimmed glasses from her desk.

"I'd like to see Scroggy," Quayle said, unable to remember the name the boy had given him.

The woman laughed delightedly and pointed to a second door. "Mr Mortimer is in, please go through."

Inside, a tall owlish individual stood behind a desk that was covered in neat stacks of papers, with a personal computer dead centre.

"Come in, come in. I'm Mortimer. Welcome. Are you a parent?"

Reaching for a pipe in amongst the clutter, he began patting his pockets, looking for his tobacco. "Damn and blast, where is the wretched thing? Ah there, yes, jolly good!"

He began filling the pipe and looked up again smiling. "What can we do for you?"

Quayle smiled too. Teddy would have loved it here. Tousled academia, bright minds unconcerned with trivia, classrooms filled with chalk dust and hope, history and heritage.

"My name is Arnold," he lied. "Have you been here long?"

"Fifteen years. Seems like yesterday that I arrived." He lit a match, held it to the pipe and began to draw the flame in, great gouts of smoke puffing up.

"I knew Edward Morton rather well," Quayle said. Mortimer looked up then, his eyes serious for a second or two, and Quayle continued, "I'm travelling with his daughter, in fact. We were wondering if we could see the house and wander round a bit."

"Yes, of course," Mortimer replied, shaking the match out, the pipe clenched firmly in his teeth. "I rather liked Teddy myself. Wasn't with us long, but made an indelible stamp on everyone he came across, even the little tikes we're trying to turn into ladies and gentlemen. It isn't far away. I'll walk over with you. Need a breath of air anyway."

Mortimer greeted Holly warmly and, after Quayle introduced the soldier as a friend, they walked past the chapel towards the lines of trees that gave the staff houses some privacy from the main school.

"Not much left, of course, after the blaze. Tell you the truth, we haven't got round to rebuilding yet, so the site is pretty bare."

It was. The only evidence of a fire were scorched branches in the upper levels of the big tree that stood sentinel on the plot. Mortimer stopped on the edge of the site, as if unwilling to cross onto the ground where

Edward Morton had died. Only Holly moved forward, stepping slowly over the rough ground, fighting the tears that were welling up inside her.

"We packed up what bits were about," Mortimer said gruffly. "Things in his desk and what have you. They were returned to England. Not much else, I'm afraid."

"Did he ever watch the boys play cricket?" Quayle asked.

"He did, as a matter of fact. Used to sit beneath the trees over by the scoreboards –" He turned and pointed past the trees towards the main field "– and if the weather turned he would stay and move into the old pavilion. Had a spot there he rather liked. Became his, sort of. Gone now of course."

"Sorry?" Quayle asked

"It's gone. We took it down last year. We broke ground with the new one only last month. The old boys have been very generous, and this new one will be just the job. Of course, as you know, the real money came from Teddy. It was a very handsome endowment."

"I didn't know that," Quayle said, "but it doesn't surprise me."

"Even so, we're a little bit short. But I dare say we'll muddle through."

Quayle felt the first fingers of concern. The house was all gone, the pavilion gone. Anywhere that Teddy spent time and may have left something was reduced to rubble and memories.

"Do you have a chess club for the boys?"

"Certainly do. Teddy was a stalwart there. It's over above the tuck shop, opposite the middle school dining hall. Nine o'clock from my office outside the quad. Now, that hasn't changed since he was last there. Even the furniture is the same." He gave a short brittle laugh.

Holly was moving back towards them, head down and arms crossed, lost in her thoughts.

"Thanks for your help," Quayle said. "We'll just have a bit of a wander around, if you don't mind?"

"Not at all," Mortimer said. "If there's anything I can do, let me know." And, with that, he smiled a goodbye at Holly and strode off towards his office. his tweed sports coat flapping as he took long ungainly strides.

Half an hour later they were walking through a set of cloisters that ran between the chapel and the main quadrangle, groups of boys and girls parting to allow them through.

"Daddy would have loved it here," Holly said. "It's like Eton moved somewhere warm and friendly."

Quayle smiled across at her. He was directing them towards the chess club. He had to begin somewhere and it seemed as good a place as any.

The building was wood, one side of which had once been the science labs, its exterior made up of white clapboard walls and heavy sash windows. The door was open and, inside, a flight of worn stairs climbed past a notice board full of upcoming events for the members. At the top, windows overlooked a grassy square and the modern low slung building that was the middle school dining hall. Beyond that, four desks took up the central floor area of the small room and two boys sat at a chessboard, arguing heatedly about the legality of a move that the black player had completed.

"That's absolute bull crap! You took your hand off the bloody piece and that's the move over! You can't just move the fucking thing again!"

"Says who? Anyway, my hand was still on it shithead! Checkmate!"

The other boy shook his head, as if he was forever committed to playing with morons.

"Hi," Quayle said.

They both turned to see the figures in the door. They hadn't heard a thing. Usually the stairs creaked signalling arrivals, particularly masters. But not this time.

Quayle walked over and took a quick look at the board. "Not over yet. King to knight four will also put him into trouble."

The boy grinned and pounced. "Thanks, sir!" Then looked round to sneak a frank and appraising look at Holly.

"Mind if I have a look around?" Quayle asked them. He had seen it already. Up on the wall. A photograph. A group of boys, six or seven smiling faces, and in the middle of them, holding the trophy, was Teddy Morton. The likeness was good; the camera had caught the twinkle in his eyes, the proud smile. His boys had cleaned up.

"Please do, sir." Then he turned to Holly. "Would you like a game?"

She smiled, shaking her head – and, as Quayle pointed to the picture, she moved across to join him. The silence was palpable as she ran her fingers gently over the image.

The boys stood uncomfortably now, not understanding what was happening. She felt it and turned to them.

"My dad," she said.

One of the boys understood instantly. He had played in this room as in his eighth year and remembered Mr Morton well. He also remembered the fire.

"We better be going," he said, and shot a look at the other that said 'let's leave her to it.' Then, they quickly reset the pieces on their board and took the stairs three at a time.

After they were gone, Quayle stepped up beside Holly and studied the picture. It was mounted on a piece of yellow card and pinned up on the board with copper drawing pins. Taking a coin from his pocket, he levered the pins out, slipped out the picture and took it to the desk the boys had used. *Talk to me, Teddy. I'm here now. Tell me where to look.* The background was unclear. The boys along the back stood proudly over the seated row in front, Teddy in the middle holding the trophy. Quayle looked for anything in the way the hands held the statuette, anything unnatural. But, at first glance, there was nothing.

Be difficult to contrive on the spot, he thought. *Easier to come back to.*

With this thought in mind, he turned the card over. A message was there to an individual called Robby. 'One on the board for the blues!' it read, with a familiar neat signature underneath. There had obviously been a print for each boy and Teddy had signed each. Beneath that, two other signatures had been haphazardly scrawled. Robby obviously hadn't gotten round to collecting the entire team's autographs.

Talk to me, Teddy!

It was Holly, looking over the front of the print, who saw the faint oblique slash through the 'o' on the word 'board'. Quayle had missed a clue that was there, plain for the eye to see. The letter 'o' was an upside down 'Q'.

300

She pointed it out to him and, turning the card over, he saw it himself and grinned. "Right. Let's start," he said, standing.

"Start what?" she asked.

"Searching. It must be in here somewhere."

Quayle took the walk-in book room and Holly started on the shelves along the far wall.

"What am I looking for?" she asked.

"A file. A sheaf of papers, wrapped in something dustproof. Possibly a key to a safe deposit box, possibly another lead. You knew him better than me..."

Pierre Lacoste sat at his kitchen table with Alexi Kirov, going over the list of equipment they were going to need. The foray over the wire into the chalet complex had given them little and nearly compromised their mission. The security, once inside, was formidable – and, although the team could have destroyed the compound with firepower any day of the week, it would not have met the objective, that of taking Girard and the two or three senior men quickly and quietly and having a little chat. A snatch was also out of the question as they had yet to travel together. Time was becoming critical and they could no longer wait for a new option. Kirov had been assured by General Borshin that the Warsaw Pact meeting would be postponed at the last second if necessary, but he would deem that a failure. Perestroika would not be held back by fanatics, and the effective re-unification of Germany was top of the agenda.

Eicheman, meanwhile, had returned to Bonn to re-brief his people and would be back that night. Quayle didn't really seem to care one way or the other. Something else was driving him.

They were down to four days now and that meant that they would need to take the men up in the snow, up on the Glacier de Leschaux or on the awesome north wall of the Grand Jorrasses itself.

"So you will all have randonee boots, oui?" Pierre asked.

"Yes. They will be ours. We will also have smocks and personal clothing. We'll need skis, poles and rope, all prepared. The usual stuff for touring. One of my men will come with you to choose extra gear." He paused. "We'll need a workshop as well."

"If the boots are good then it will be easy," Pierre said.

The boots are good, Alexi thought. American. There would be other gear coming for the Spetznatz team, winter bivouacs and survival kit, but Soviet skis were shit and he wanted them bought here.

"They will be. Titus is due back in tomorrow night. His gear is ready?"

"Of course." Pierre had spent a whole day on that alone. He had found an excellent pair of K2 205 touring skis and had mounted the race bindings himself. Quayle's Scott boots would fit like a glove. The rest of the gear was loaded into a new pack and the parapente Quayle had asked for had been unrolled and checked three times. There was a lot of gear, too much for one man to carry in or out. But that was what he had asked for.

"Have you seen the weather report?" Pierre asked.

"Yes," Alexi replied, looking up from the list.

"It will snow tonight."

"Didn't say that..."

The Frenchman shrugged. "It will snow tonight," he said confidently.

That would be bad, Kirov knew. Without a base to settle on, and some nice cold weather to keep it stable, it would be like marbles on a billiard table.

Kirov left, and soon Lacoste went back down to the basement to finish packing Quayle's gear. Much had only been collected an hour before from the Patagonia shop in the village. There was expedition thermal underwear and the familiar alpine synchilla snap t-neck sweaters and pants. He had also bought a guide jacket with the American manufacturer's version of Gore-Tex lining, and a goose down jacket and pants. Even with a sleeping bag it was cold at altitude and, without a tent or cover, the wind chill factor would kill in hours.

But, if the clothing was American, the climbing equipment was as French as could be, all of it made down the valley at the Simond works in Les Houche. It was arguably the finest climbing gear in the world and had supported every major expedition since Hillary had conquered

Everest. A small gunny bag was filled with a selection of stoppers, cramming devices, pitons and pegs – in case Quayle's clean climbing style gave way to safety – ice screws, figure eights, three ice axes and a multi-purpose thigh harness. Lacoste had selected good Chouinard eleven millimetre guide rope. Other Chouinard gear he selected included the skins for the skis, probe poles with self-arresting grips for the entire team, and headlamps rather like those used by miners. He hoped they simply planned a night ski and not Titus thinking he could climb the Macintyre route on his own after dark. That would be madness. Tomorrow he would pick up the ice axes. Old-fashioned, with long handles, they were ideal for ski touring and the Glacier de Leschaux was no place to be after early snow without sensible equipment. Fashionable with cute pink handles, they weren't. Save lives, they would.

He walked to the window. The snow had begun.

"I wonder how many he left?" Holly asked.

"Enough to know that one would make it," Quayle replied. They were walking around the path towards the bottom end of the main field. A group of girls in tracksuits were wandering back from the swimming pool, hair wet and eyes red from the chlorine. It was mid-afternoon and the warmth was soporific. Holly trailed her jacket over her shoulder and Sergi, the bodyguard, had his unzipped all the way as usual. He didn't seem to notice the temperature.

"Do you think it's there? After all... all the killing. In the scoreboard. Just sitting there?"

"Why not?" he replied, thinking it better be, because I am running out of ideas.

The search of the chess club had been fruitless. Every book had been opened and shaken out, every box or cupboard emptied, wall units shifted. They had found two half full packets of cigarettes, a small pile of mildly pornographic magazines, a long empty sherry bottle, numerous sweet wrappers, newspapers dating back to 1969 – and, behind one cupboard unit, an ancient fountain pen. But that was all.

Short of ripping up the floorboards, and that wasn't Teddy Morton's style, they had done the job well. Quayle had even climbed up into the ceiling through an inspection hatch and searched the dark corners of the roof, reciting the word 'board' and applying it wherever possible. Chess board, chopping board, milk board, black board... scoreboard, scoreboard! *Stupid prick,* he cursed himself, *the fucking scoreboard! He used to sit there. Scoreboard for the cricket. Play up, play up and play the game. One on the board for the blues!*

Five minutes later they were almost there.

"That's it," he said, pointing to the edge of the field.

The board's display area was raised above ground level with a small scorer's shelter behind it. Taking the four steps at the rear, they pushed their way through the rickety lock on the old wooden door. Inside it smelt of dust and dryness, and two old chairs sat empty before the closed up viewing ports. In here, it was dark, the only light coming in through chinks in the walls. Quayle looked around until he saw the shuttered window at the rear and the skylight hatch. When open they would provide ample light for the scorers, who would sit bent over their pads with sharpened pencils in hand, calling to the runner who would change the scores on the display itself. Lifting the shutter over the window, he propped it open with a length of broomstick and light streamed in, a golden shaft that highlighted the dust in the still air. The wall's interior surface was bare timber, the skeleton showing the clap-boarding on the exterior. The other two walls were panelled, one containing a soft-board notice area. On its surface was a stern message to keep the place tidy, and a list of the season's fixtures. A series of photocopied pages from a rulebook took up the remaining space.

Shrugging, he began running his hands over the high edges of the frame.

"Sergi, have a look on top will you?" he asked.

The soldier nodded and, taking a jump, pushed the top hatch open and hauled himself up onto the roof.

It was Quayle who found it. He had worked his way around the walls until he was at the noticeboard, and there he saw that a screw had been loosened. The others were countersunk all the way in, but this one had been unscrewed and then replaced. *Some bored kid with a Swiss army knife could have done it,* he thought to himself. *Better have a look anyway.*

Sergi popped his head through the hatch.

"A teacher's coming," he said.

Quayle looked at Holly. "Do you have a nail file in your bag?"

"No," she said, immediately beginning to rummage about in it, "but I have a bottle opener on a key ring. Will that help?"

"Let's have it," he replied, "it may do."

She handed him the key ring but, as he put its edge to the screw, a man appeared in the doorway.

"Can I help you?" he asked frostily. He was wearing a track suit and fingering the whistle around his neck like he was about to blow it for a foul.

"No thanks," Quayle replied, putting his weight behind the turn. "Not unless you have a screw driver."

"What?" he demanded. "Now, see here! Who are you people?" They weren't behaving like parents at all. "What do you want?"

"I'm looking for something," Quayle replied reasonably.

"What?" the fellow demanded.

"I won't know until I find it."

At that exact moment, the screw came clear. Quayle caught it in one hand and, taking the sharpened end of the opener, prised the board back. Then, risking the spiders and other things that might have been resident inside, he slipped his hand inside, thinking: *scoreboard, one on the board for the blues, notice board in the scoreboard, it's got to fucking be here...*

"I insist you stop at once and leave the grounds – or I shall inform the authorities!" The hand on the whistle was becoming agitated, but Quayle ignored him and bent awkwardly, trying to slide his arm further behind the board.

The teacher stepped forward and, as he did so Sergi, came through the hatch like a ninja, dropping to his feet inches before the startled man's eyes. "Go back and play with the children, da?"

Quayle touched something. His eyes lit up. He withdrew his hand slowly, the prize gripped gingerly between his fingers. It was flat, about six inches square and wrapped in plastic. He rubbed the dust away and, through a layer of opaque thick plastic, he could see a floppy disk.

"Did he have a PC in the last years?" he asked Holly.

She looked back from the angry teacher, who was still unsure if he should give way to the demand to leave.

"Yes..."

"Now see here!" the teacher exclaimed. "Amongst other things I teach here, I teach self reliance – and if you think I'm going to just walk away..."

"Oh, do be quiet," Quayle said. He tore the plastic open and out fell a faded envelope and the foil wrapped computer disk. Then, sliding the envelope open, he read the first line and put the contents in his pocket with a tired smile. "How short are you for the new pavilion?"

"What?" the teacher asked, amazed at the new tack the conversation had taken.

"The pavilion rebuilding fund. It's short of target. How much?"

"Ah... about sixty thousand dollars I think," he replied.

"Tell Mortimer he's got the money. But there's a caveat. It's to be called the Morton Pavilion. And this structure and the trees that shelter it are to remain standing always. Tell him my solicitor will be in touch. Of course, no-one is to know where the remaining funds came from or of my visit here today." He smiled then, the urbane benefactor.

"That is very generous," the teacher said, trying to view Quayle as a wealthy eccentric rather than a vandal.

*

Sergi drove back to Melbourne, Quayle sitting beside him and reading the letter over and over. Holly had read it until the code began, the tears coming freely along with her father's voice from the grave, his wonderful full looped handwriting so familiar.

'My Dear Titus,

If you are reading this missive, my old friend, then it means I have passed on into the great wonderful unknown. What an adventure that will be! I shall of course be sad to leave those I love and England, but the task shall not remain undone, of that I am sure. If it is not you reading this, then it matters not, as you will see.

In writing this I have placed you in some danger, but you are a competent chap and can deal with that issue as it arises. Never could abide that sort of thing myself.'

The fourth paragraph was an introduction to an access code and, although it was written for Quayle alone to understand, he grappled with it as the car powered though the miles.

'Remember well the incidents. Each is stand alone and only you can answer them. Leave no spaces, and work in capital initials only. I tried to calculate the probability of someone breaking the code by chance and stopped in the billions. I am not a mathematician, and understand code-breaking is an electronic art in these technical times, so I have built in safeguards with the help of a very bright young man who is part of this technical generation. Think it through carefully, Titus, before committing to the keys. If any part of the access is wrong then the programme will destroy itself.

The file has been updated regularly but is not complete. One question, while answered, remains to be confirmed. I leave it in your hands and am confident you will finish what I began. Opportunities to do the right thing in the face of adversity are common. Men who rise to the challenge are rare. You are one.

Give my love to England, her green fields and warm fires, and remember me to the walls of the college when next you visit.

One last favour to ask, old friend, although I realise you would never refuse a one. Keep a gunner's eye on Holly for me. She will have received, at the start of my great adventure, a modest inheritance – so will lack nothing material. But she will, like all mortals, require good measures of solid advice; and at times the warm hand of friendship. Impart of those as you see fit and it will be such a thing that money cannot buy.

I remain,

Yours Sincerely

Edward. G Morton.

He had signed with a formal flourish as was his way, the bold blue ink strokes hard across the carefully formed longhand script.

Quayle knew he should have felt things, then. Relief that he had found the file, sad at this last message from his oldest friend, elated at having found the file. But he was tired and he knew it wasn't over yet. Far from it.

The tone of the letter said much to confirm what he had suspected, and the code was yet to be broken – and he knew how lateral Teddy's thoughts could be. Once in, he knew there were things to be done, the file to be closed once and for all. He rubbed his eyes tiredly and leant back. As he did so Holly leant forward and stroked the back of his neck.

He turned to speak but she put a finger gently across his lips.

"I know," she said, her eyes still red from crying. "I know."

They bought a Compaq laptop computer at the airport and, with spare batteries and the salesman's assurances that it would run for the next four hours on that power supply, they boarded the first leg of the northbound flight back to Europe and the team waiting in Chamonix. Sergi took a look around the aircraft, decided they weren't in any danger and, on Quayles bidding, allowed himself to fall asleep.

But sleeping would have to wait for Quayle. His time had come. The Englishman lifted the top of the computer, turned it on and inserted the disc.

*

Alexi Kirov picked up Jean Girard in the Albert Hotel. There he was eating in the old dining room, sitting at a table in the corner from which he was able to see the entire room.

Kirov requested a table behind a small wood-panelled pillar that would shield him from view, but allow him to observe through the reflections in one of the dining room's gilt-edged mirrors. The fact was, he wanted to be noticed – and, if possible, to engage the Frenchman in some small conversational exchange to help him remember. That would become important in establishing his credibility.

After watching Girard eat through a mountain of local and provincial cheeses, he finished his own meal and walked to the bar that stood in the lobby. Girard would have to walk past him to get to the doors, so he ordered a cognac and watched a foursome of old Americans playing bridge in the quiet lounge, the hotel's big black dog occasionally shoving his head under one of their arms trying to get some attention.

Kirov sipped his drink and waited. Finally the Frenchman appeared, looking as satisfied with his meal as only the Gaelic can be.

"Pardon," Kirov said jovially, "would you care for a night-cap? My last night in civilisation and a shame to drink fine cognac on my own..."

Girard was tall and good looking, in his mid thirties. His tan was real and he moved like a man who was fit, but his eyes had a flatness that left Kirov uneasy. He had seen it before, in those who could kill without feeling and sometimes even enjoyed it. *If Quayle doesn't do the job on you, you cunt,* he thought, *I will.*

"Thank you but no," he answered.

"Are you sure? It's cold outside! Let me warm your way!"

Kirov lifted his glass to try to persuade him, every inch the happy drunk, but Girard would not be convinced. "No, thank you," he replied stiffly – and, taking his coat off the rack, he moved out onto the street.

Good enough, Kirov thought. *He'll remember me now.* Then, scooping up a handful of peanuts from a small china bowl on the bar, he settled on his haunches and called over for the hotel dog, who snuffled them up with clear rolling sweeps of his big pink tongue.

"Dosvidania," he said, stroking the dog's head.

Then he too walked out onto the street and the cold crisp night. It had been snowing for forty hours now, and one of his team was watching the chalet complex. As soon as they looked like moving into the mountains, they would know. There was a ski equipped aircraft chartered in Girard's name in two days' time. The pilot had talked in a bar in Sollonges. He didn't like new snow on glaciers but, for this fee, he would fly anywhere.

Everything was ready. Quayle's instructions had been followed to the letter.

*

Quayle had taken a look at the code on the screen, written the questions down verbatim on a pad, and then shut it down without touching a key. He worked better on paper and now sat for the seventh hour, considering the questions. They had passed though Singapore and were airborne again, Sergi and Holly still asleep in their seats as they had been throughout the stop – and, lighting another cigarette, he let his mind wander back twenty-five years to his days Cambridge University and the first icon he had watched Teddy Morton transform from a mildewed filthy write-off to a thing of beauty again.

"The first letters of the full name of the background colour and the last letter of the frame colour of the first Orthodox piece you ever handled in my rooms."

He remembered it like yesterday. The fine brushes dipped in turpentine and the bright smear of blue across the heavy cardboard shoe box top. What blue? Cobalt blue? Sky blue? Royal blue? It was mid-range and strong. Cobalt blue.

He wrote down CB.

The frame was easy. It was heavy and of carved timber and painted in thick gilt gold leaf. Writing a D after the CB, he moved onto the next question.

"The final move of the game of chess you won" was next. It didn't give a time or date or who the opponent was. It didn't need to. He had only ever beaten Teddy once. It was with a move that Boris Spatsky had used to advantage with Bobby Fischer the American. They had been sitting in the book-lined study in Morton's house in Cambridge, a fire in the hearth and a bottle of Russian Vodka on the small occasional table between them. Quayle was pleased to be back. He had just finished a long job in East Berlin and it was nice to unwind. Queen to King four. QTK4. He wrote that in after the D.

"The departure time of the train that you took to Lincoln for the first time. Drop the points."

Now that would have been on file at registry. The train he should have taken anyway. He had gone up the day before and spent the night with a girlfriend who lived nearby. Only Teddy knew that. She had sneaked out of work to meet him at the Station. Mid-afternoon. He had nearly missed it because of the idiots briefing them at the FO. He remembered it because it was the girlfriend's address. She lived at number 212. The 2:12.

He wrote in 212 and moved on.

"The poet whose words have brought you this far. The year of his death less the number of bicycles you owned over the years at college. Key the number in backwards."

Newbolt died in 1938. Less two bikes made 1936. He wrote down 6391 after the 212. That was it.

CBDQTK42126391.

Flipping up the top of the computer, he inserted the disk again and took a breath. *Fuck it*, he thought. *Mine is not to question why. Mine is but to do or die.*

He punched in the code slowly, careful, with his thick fingers, not to make an error.

The screen flashed a fast series of figures and finally asked him if he wished to change the code. Breathing a sigh of relief, he hit the 'N' option and, as he scrolled down the files, he lit another cigarette. For the next two hours, he read and made notes on the pad, his jaws clenching and his eyes glittering. *Bastards.*

*

Chamonix was veiled in new snow and looking crisp and serene, as peaceful as the scene on a Christmas card. It was too cold for the snow to thaw so there was none of the muddy slushiness of early winter streets. Excited children ran and played where the snow ploughs had built snow banks at the sides of the road. The roof eaves were laden and café workers shovelled snow off the sidewalks so they could put out tables for people to take coffee, or maybe a measure of rum if the sun came out. Carved wooden balconies jutted out from warm chalets, and at the cable car station the crowds bad begun to gather, forming long lines as they awaited their turn in the car that would take them up the Aiguille Du Midi.

Maintenance staff had been clearing ice from the lines since early morning and, for a few hours, Kirov was concerned that they would close the cable car down. Now they stood not in a group, but scattered amongst the others, the only difference between them and the other late season climbers and skiers that their packs were heavier. Otherwise they were dressed in brightly coloured ski jackets and hats and two were wearing traditional salapets under their jackets. Anyone would have noticed that their skis were covered, and close observers would have noticed that the boots were all randonee, for ski touring rather than simple downhill. Three of the six Spetznatz soldiers now wore light beards and one, with supreme confidence, leant indolently against a wall and chatted up two German girls.

A car number flashed up on the sign and they all began to move forward, their fifty kilogram packs seemingly light in their hands.

The easy confidence they exhibited when faced with the prospect of the coming days was testament to their training. Four of the six had done the advanced winter survival course, phase one in the Ural mountains and phase two in Siberia. They had lived off marmots and sable, pulled down reindeer and killed them with their bare hands and lived in snow caves, being hunted for weeks on end by their equally talented colleagues. One of them had lost a finger of his left hand, frostbitten during a forced march in the endless February night in the mind numbing cold above the Arctic circle. For them glacier, crevasse, snow and ice were routine conditions. They were arguably the finest winter troops in the world.

They went up in two separate cars, the second half arriving twenty minutes after the first group and joining them at the end of an ice tunnel that opened out onto the ski run and the valley blanche.

Kirov took one look and knew that they would have to get away quickly. The visibility had closed right in and the ridge line down to the ski-off area was only an expanse of loose powder, yet to be trampled down by anyone foolhardy enough to go out. It was bitterly cold and the winds added fifteen degrees of chill to the already sub-freezing temperatures. The air was thin and, as Kirov breathed in, he reminded himself that they were twelve-and-a-half-thousand feet up.

With this in mind, he watched the team donning skis and adjusting packs. The cloud swirled away for a second and, for the first time, he got a good look downward to the flat plateau at the bottom of the steep access ridge. *Jesus Christ,* he thought, *Quayle has climbed this for fun!*

As soon as the last man was clear of the tunnel and had his skis on, he lifted one of his poles to signal he was ready. A woman, one of the several people who had turned back from the prospect of walking the ridge in boots and crampons, was watching from the end of the ice tunnel, unable to believe what she was seeing. These men were going to ski the edge, diagonally off the ridge down to the plateau, and she held her breath as the first led off. If she hadn't been watching so intently, she would have heard the only word said, and may have even been able to tell by its tone it was an order. But she spoke no Russian and would not have been able to understand it anyway – and, as the last man dropped off the steep edge, she shook her head and walked back into the tunnel, knowing not to bother telling anyone because no-one would believe her anyway. One crazy hotdogger maybe, but seven men, one after another, wearing huge packs, in Randonee boots? No way!

The new loose powder was crisp and squeaky and flew upwards as they moved with precision down the slope. The cloud had closed in and Kirov – who had given up the lead to his senior NCO – watched with pleasure as he swung the team expertly round the ridge and onto the plateau. There they stopped and, without speaking, dropped their packs and began reversing their gear quickly in the cold. The inner side of each man's outer clothing was white and, as they reversed the garments and pulled them on again, they began to look like soldiers again, winter troops in snow camouflage. The last items pulled on were white gloves, white balaclavas and white thermal smocks, that covered the packs on their backs, and broke the outline. Now the only things not white were the skis, and for that they had spray paint. That could wait for tonight and their first bivouac above the Leschaux glacier opposite the refuge.

Soon they had pushed off again, down the long gentle approach to the Valley Blanche, now a line of white shrouded figures almost invisible against the snow. From here they would ski for two hours down hill and glacier, before moving up the Leschaux glacier towards the awesome, almost vertical, broken slabbed beginnings of the mighty Grand Jorasses.

Below, in the valley, the Chamonix Bureau De Guide charged with the safety of people in the mountains closed the lifts up to the Brevant and the Augille Du Midi, re-evaluated the avalanche danger, pegged it at eight, the highest level, and flew the yellow and black chequered avalanche warning flag outside the bureau offices. The other Bureaux in the valley did the same, all the way up to the Argentierre.

Half way up the valley, in the chalet complex Girard reported this to his masters – who, being men who liked risks, and being men who had been waiting to climb the Macintyre for weeks, shrugged and agreed to go anyway. It was cold enough and they were experienced climbers – and half of climbing was evaluating the risks and accepting that they were part of the challenge.

It would, they all agreed, be a fitting prelude to the events of the coming week.

CHAPTER THIRTEEN

The helicopter was fitted with a compressed air system that fed its engines, and advanced high altitude rotors. Even so, the pilot was concerned about weight and watched carefully as Quayle threw his packs into the rear door. No problem here. This job would be a breeze. One man and his kit was a lot easier on the aerodynamics of rotary wings in the thin air than six with dogs and probes and a stretcher.

As part of the Italian Mountain Rescue service, this particular job was a little odd, but the order had come from someone high up in the Ministry of Defence and had been countersigned by the correct people. The method of its delivery had been strange – arriving by uniformed courier from – but the pilot didn't care. He was paid to fly choppers in the Alps and that's what he did.

But the job wasn't just strange; it was dangerous as well. Dropping some crazy man on the top of the Grande Jorrasses meant first stealing over the border, hugging the mountain's side, hovering over the line and letting him jump from the skids. Down drafts and high winds were a problem up close to a peak that size, and time was pressing. He signalled to the man that they needed to hurry, pointing to the turbulent sky. Up there, the swirling clouds over the peaks were grey and heavy. If they left it much longer, it wouldn't matter who had signed the order. Zero visibility was zero visibility.

Quayle nodded and jumped in after his kit, thrusting a map at the pilot. He had already marked the point he wanted – and, as the helmeted flyer took the map, he nodded, raising a thumb.

Soon, the collective was being raised and the rotors began their meaty thumping, the engine revs picking up. Seconds later, they hovered a few feet over the ground; then, the nose dipped and they began to move forward, gaining speed, like a huge dragon fly over a pond.

Through the scarred perspex canopy, Quayle could see the rising massif of Mont de Rochefort and, towering above it, the south aspect of the Grand Jorasses itself. The track should take them parallel to the range; after that, it would be a slow thin air climb for the rotors, up the glacier to a point opposite the head of the Walker spur. There he would have to cross on foot back into France and over the ridge summit – and, once he got there, he would be positioned above the final towering pillars and stacks of the Macintyre route.

He had collected his gear from Lacoste, the guide having been in fine spirits the night before. 'I got myself a new job, Titus!' he'd exclaimed. 'Maybe retirement isn't for me after all!' he'd joked, with a wink. Then, wishing Pierre well and leaving Holly with Kurt, Quayle had driven through the Mont Blanc tunnel, happy with their security arrangements. Kurt had returned from Bonn with two men whose sole job was to guard Holly Morton, and they had unpacked their equipment and silently set things up as they liked. Sergi had immediately collected his gear and taken the last cable car up the Augille du Midi and planned to do a night run down the Valley Blanche to catch up with the rest of his unit. Quayle didn't even ask if he was comfortable with the thought of a lone night ski down a mountain he had never seen in his life, nor the seven hour up-glacier trek that would follow. He had supreme confidence in his abilities.

As the helicopter took flight, Quayle took the opportunity to run through his packs and re-adjust some of the weight. He had brought three, including the parapente – and, in addition, his skis and boots. The large pack would go on his back, the smaller at his waist with the parapente, and the boots on the front. For the last hundred meters, the climb was not technically demanding. Just tough on the legs.

The pilot eased the machine slowly through the billowing clouds, watching the vapour for the tell-tale signs of down drafts and eddies that, while picturesque from the ground, were sure death for light aircraft within scant feet of rock walls.

Quayle pulled on his thick warm pants, pulled his boots back on and slipped on the crampons, leaving the bright yellow plastic protective covers on to protect the floor of the helicopter. Then, tightening the spring clasp at the back, he secured the safety binding at the front and sat back.

The pilot raised a thumb at him and held up two fingers. Quayle nodded back, sliding his packs towards the door. As he did so, the helicopter began to ease its way in towards a boulder strewn shoulder, picking its way through the scudding cloud like a small boy through the couples on a dance floor.

As soon as the tips of the skids touched, Quayle was out, pulling the packs after him, the wind gusting at the machine while its rotor wash flattened the snow. As Quayle found his footing, the cold seared into his lungs. Slamming the door shut, he banged once and dropped clear, lying down across his gear as the machine backed up from the ground. Within seconds it was away, its clatter dying – and, suddenly, Quayle was alone in the mountains, with only the lonely moan of the wind to keep him company.

Shivering, he broke open the pack pulled out the guide jacket, which he pulled over his jumper. Warm again, he looked upward at the ridge line. This close, the summit was a sharp jagged jumble of rock, deep fissures eroded by wind and ice, deep enough to lose a man. *I've an hour at least,* he thought. *Better get on with it.* Loading the gear and humming out 'Knocking on Heaven's Door', he pulled his Vuarnet sunglasses from his pocket and slipped them on; up here, snow blindness was an ever-present threat, even if the glare was filtered by cloud. And so, with a long-handled ice axe in hand, he set out for the ridge line, the hundred-pound load making the pace slow over the broken rock and ice fields.

At that moment, several things were happening. Four men were converging on Chamonix from different directions. In the last miles of a journey that had begun in Moscow, KGB General Borshin drove the Saab Turbo hard up the valley. He enjoyed driving western cars and took the opportunity whenever possible, his driver sitting in terrified silence beside him. Meanwhile, Tansey-Williams had just arrived from Geneva with Kurt Eicheman's boss, the head of the BND. The last man was an American, the Deputy Director of the CIA. He was not travelling alone, but with a retinue of three aides, who were hurriedly trying to piece together exactly what it was that the Brits wanted, and why they and the West Germans – in the absence of the Director himself – had insisted he attend. Leo Gershin was not a man who liked surprises, and it looked as if they were about to be brought in on something right at the very last second.

Three hundred feet above the Leschaux glacier, Kirov's team had dug their first snow cave at the base of a rock monolith. They had chosen the site with care. Whatever the snow conditions above them, whatever avalanche risk existed, the rock had been there ten thousand years and another few days seemed likely.

There, in the deep snow, dug in and back, packing the walls and smoothing them down. Like Inuit people, they built a sleeping platform well above floor level with an air hole above them to allow the air to circulate. The cave was big enough for all of them, but would only ever have half the team inside at once. Below the main cave were two smaller two-man observation caves. These were narrow and long enough to lie in out of the wind and in relative warmth. Through a small entry hole, normally obscured by a white nylon flap, a man watched the glacier below and the refuge up on the other side through powerful binoculars.

The day's preparations were complete. Two men had crossed the glacier that morning and had worked their way up the other side, the route to the Jorrasses from the refuge. They had found the places they needed and had returned by early afternoon. The others had prepared for the specialty of these winter troops: crevasse ambush.

Five crevasses had been prepared, with ice screws and cables set four feet down the wall. On the cable, and secured by a safety line, a soldier could wait in ambush almost indefinitely, appearing as a white shadow against a white world, to wreak havoc on any advancing army and disappear seconds later.

Kirov himself was in the refuge in civilian clothing, a collection of oddly dated equipment about him, the trappings of an eccentric, waiting to play his part. As the sound of a helicopter reached the men in the cave, they tapped the transmit button on their radio and his hissed softly. Kirov himself reached over, switched it off and then concealed it out the back of the dilapidated hut in the snow. They were coming in by chopper. He had expected that. Too much powder snow for ski aircraft. The helicopter made four trips up the valley that afternoon and, by dusk, there were sixteen men at the refuge. They had quickly broken into two groups, four inside the hut and the remaining twelve outside, setting up small four man frame tents. They did so clumsily and there wasn't the sheer bulk of equipment to support four four man teams on the face. While it had all the appearances of a major expedition by modern Alpine standards, Kirov – who had his gear spread across one of the bunks in the hut – quickly classified the group's structure. The twelve outside were muscle, there to see no harm came to their masters while they indulged in their sport. They had been surprised to see anyone in the hut, but the demands of mountain etiquette kept their suspicions down and, when Girard recognised Kirov from the Albert after his ebullient greeting, he had spoken to the other three quietly and explained that he had seen the man before in Chamonix and he was harmless enough. Kirov had then welcomed them all – as one does in the mountains – and used one of his solid fuel blocks to heat water for coffee.

"Here long then?" Girard asked in French.

"Sorry," Kirov said in English. "I only speak English and Finnish."

"Ah," Girard said, pleased, repeating the question in English.

"No. Away. Later tonight. I will do a night ski down the valley. Fund raising for the Sisters of Mercy Orphanage in Helsinki," he explained, noticing Girard's raised eyebrow.

"And you? By the look of your gear, it's the Petit Jorasses."

"No," Girard corrected, stiffening. "The Grand Jorasses."

"Mister, had you noticed that winter is here?" Kirov warned him, good-naturedly. "That's no mountain to be on in the winter!"

"It needs to be winter to climb where we go," he replied arrogantly as his three companions entered the hut.

"Oh well," Kirov said, smiling like a fool. "Rather you than me, eh? I don't like that ice..."

"You have done the Jorasses... in winter?" one of the other three asked.

Kirov looked at him. He was the oldest of the group, silver hair well cut, nails manicured, a look of prosperity about him. "Yes. Some bits good, some bad. The stones..." As he spoke, he remembered the words with which Quayle had coached him, and added a Gaelic shrug for authenticity.

"Which route?" he asked.

"I tried the Macintyre two seasons ago. The weather closed in. Then last year.."

"The ice on the Macintyre?" one said, a little too eagerly. "How thick at the top of the runnel?"

"Well," Kirov said, "half a metre in places in mid-winter, but now enough for a screw." And, inwardly, he grinned. *Thanks very much, gentlemen. The Macintyre it is. Tomorrow you can discuss the ice with my friend who knows much more than me. He's looking forward to meeting you up there. If you like the thrills of climbing, you're in for the thrill of a fucking lifetime.* "Well, that's the coffee finished. I shall get my gear together and one of you can have the good bunk, eh?" Then he began packing his gear into a faded khaki coloured pack, and finally took his skis from where they stood outside in the snow. They had watched him in silence so he thought he would add some authenticity to his story. "I'm night skiing every major glacier in Europe. For a few centimes per kilometer, you can become joint sponsors. It's a good cause. The children are..."

"I serve charity through other channels," the silver haired man said. His tone was bored and his eyes gave away nothing, now that talk of the ice was forgotten.

"Oh well," Kirov said cheerfully. "Good-bye and may God go with you!" And he went around the room, shaking each man's hand, thinking: *if Titus doesn't get you, then I'll see you over my gunsight, fucker.*

320

But, as he left, there was one man whose hand he didn't shake; one man whose presence he didn't even detect, sorting equipment, down in the tent line.

Quayle sat in a narrow fissure just three feet below the crest. He had selected the spot because, from there, he could see the valley below, and by rolling three feet he could look straight down the big wall itself, the sheer face of the ice field and across to the central couloir. The drop was three thousand feet straight down, the blue ice and black rock becoming one as the light fell.

He had laid out his gear for the night bivouac and, just to be sure, had put a piton into the rock, then made a safety line through to his thigh harness. It was bitterly cold even out of the wind, but that could change in seconds and, in down pants and a heavy down jacket – and with the sleeping bag ready – he sat with his binoculars, watching the valley floor and the twinkle of light from the refuge. Some time later, he took a solid fuel cell from his pack and, setting up the tiny stove, he warmed a tin of macaroni cheese as best he could. At this altitude, nothing ever really boiled, but warm would be better than nothing. To follow it, he would drink cups of sweet tea and, later on, there was soup and high calorie iron rations in the form of chocolate and peanuts, broken up in a bag to be eaten by the handful.

Focusing the Zeiss glasses on the hut, he swung them across the valley floor, pleased when he could find nothing on the darkening western slopes of the Tacul where his support team were dug in, watching the hut like he was. They were invisible on the mountainside; they had done their job as well as he knew they would.

Putting the glasses down, he lifted the tin of food from the burner straight to his lips and hungrily sucked in the thick, cheesy mixture. Then, finally, he dug around in his gear and, finding the ice screws that Lacoste had bought, took a hack saw blade and began to cut through the tip of one. An hour later, he zipped up the down jacket tight and, taking a head lamp just in case, lowered himself off the edge into the darkness.

Below him there was nothing for almost a mile straight down.

After abseiling two hundred feet, he took his barracuda ice axes in hand and began a fast traverse across the ice wall to get hard in the runnel. The axes were specifically designed for ice waterfalls and, with the crampons and the blind faith that ice climbers need in their gear, he was up against the jutting rock shoulder in under fifteen minutes. There he paused to slip a crammer into a small crack and then, leaning back, took the ice screw he had tampered with and, taking a final check of his position relative to the wall and the remaining climb, hammered it in an inch. After he was sure it was in, he turned it, careful not to put too much tension on the weakened head.

As he worked, the wind began to pick up, taking on a more urgent force. Braced against it, he finished his work and, rubbing his hands together, took the crammer from the crack, then began to work his way back to the point he had come down, but now diagonal upward. His axes and crampons slammed into the ice as he moved upward against the frozen face, the wind snatching at his coat and the ice forming on his eyebrows. He stopped to take up the slack in his figure eight and tie off, then moved on, his breathing harsh in the bitter cold, and rolled over the lip, back into his bivouac.

He'd been away only an hour.

Breaking open another fuel cell, he began heating tea, working out the odds that they might use his ice screw in the morning. *If they come. Talk to me, Alexi. You must be away by now,* he thought.

It was another twenty minutes before the radio hissed and Kirov's voice came through.

He had followed the glacier for two miles until he was sure he was out of sight, and then ducked behind an odd shaped hummock that he had found earlier that day. Hidden here, he changed into the camouflage gear that had been left for him and moved back up the glacier. Half an hour later, he was back in the snow cave, his legs aching from the awkward uphill run. He got through to Quayle on his fourth attempt.

"Blue one blue one, weather for tomorrow is as expected over."

Quayle didn't speak, just smiled grimly and pressed his transmit button twice to signal he had heard. His eyes glittering, he stood on the ledge in the wind and, for the first time in months, began to perform his mantra, settling his mind and becoming one with his body for the dawn and whatever it would bring.

*

Tansey-Williams took the proffered drink from Borshin and stood before the big fireplace, facing the American.

"So you mean to tell me that this has been going on for some time and you only involve us now?"

"Relax," Borshin said dryly. "You're lucky you are in at all. This is a localised problem, other than your minutemen being involved..."

"It's a question of 'who is who'," Tansey-Williams said, sipping his drink noisily, then coughing and peering into his glass to see what measure the Soviet had used when pouring the Scotch. "Your people, from the Supreme Court down, could be involved."

"Bullshit, gentlemen! My people are clean!" Borshin laughed out loud and Gershin glowered at him. As a KGB General, he would know. "And I don't consider an attempt to wipe out half the heads of Eastern Europe a local problem..."

Into the silence that followed, the German spoke for the first time. "It's not a question of clean, Leo. It's a question of politics and beliefs. The company is made of extreme right wingers and conservatives. That's why you, amongst others, take them." Then, leaving that thought to dangle in the air, he stood and walked to the drinks trolley, starting to heave ice into a cut glass tumbler.

In the anteroom, the German's aides sat eating sandwiches with Chloe Bowie, who had accompanied her Director General from London. Upstairs, listening to the conversation on a speaker in one of the bedrooms, was yet another man, grey haired and drinking milk from a tall glass. Only Borshin knew he was there.

"Minutemen, you say they are called. Let me at a secure line and I'll

323

let you have what we have inside half an hour. The policies on co-operation are clear here..."

"Which means you help us when you feel like it?" Tansey-Williams said. "And bugger you Jack when you don't. Rather like ours, really." He paused. "There's a phone in the study. My communications people tell me it will patch you through London."

"They gonna listen in?"

"Certainly not!" Tansey-Williams replied stiffly.

Up in the spare room, the grey haired milk drinker turned of his speaker and sat back to think. As Director of the CIA, it was something he did a lot of.

*

A hour before midnight, Kirov took his turn at the observation hole, drawing back the nylon flap and the space blanket that shielded the cave from infrared imaging equipment. He had seen none amongst the gear the men were handling at the refuge, but that meant nothing. Behind him, the remainder of the team – with the exception of Sergi, who was out in the dark somewhere with a radio – were checking their own equipment. Two of them sat on the sleeping platform and the others gathered around the gas lamp, cleaning and oiling their weapons, waxing skis, and preparing ropes. Another sergeant crouched, stirring a pot of something thick and meaty. When they left the cave, they would not be back.

Kirov wiped some snow from his face and leant into the glasses again. Across the glacier, the glow of lamps around the refuge was warm and cheery. He looked again and saw a silhouette move across one light. *Here we go,* he thought. *Movement.* Titus had said they would leave just after midnight to give themselves enough time to cross to the foot of the mountain safely and be in place before dawn. He looked at his watch. It was near enough. Satisfied, he crawled back into the main chamber of the cave and grinned at the others.

"We go soon."

"Right, you fuckers!" the senior man said, lifting the pot from the tiny burner. "Eat and drink now. There'll be fuck all until we're back."

Kirov held the radio to his lips.

"Grepon grepon Pierre…"

Sergi came back, "Grepon allo Pierre."

"Grepon message for you, please phone Phillipe when you are in. His wife has had the baby, he is leaving now."

"Oui Pierre, I will do that."

Up on the mountain, Quayle – who was waiting for a message about a woman with a baby – turned his radio off and settled back to rest. It would be six hours before there would be enough light to begin the climb, and he pulled the sleeping bag, with its oilskin outer, on and rolled back against the ledge. The snow began to settle immediately so, drawing his balaclava down, he closed his eyes and tried to sleep. At this altitude it would be days before he could acclimatise enough to sleep properly, but he had to try.

As soon as he closed his eyes, all he saw was Holly. *Soon now my love,* he thought. *Soon all this will be over.*

For Kirov below, the problem was now how many of them were leaving to cross to the head of the glacier, and how many would stay at the hut. He had seen two telescopes. Big powerful ones that could see up the mountain at that distance. That suggested that the bulk of the team would wait at the refuge, there to support the main attempt and provide security, but going no closer unless the situation demanded it. Vague silhouettes were still moving around the lamps, fetching and carrying, figures bent and coffee cups lifted. *So how many of you will go and how many will stay?* he wondered. He had planned their deployment as best he could. Their job was to support Quayle. To take care of the base camp group if the need arose. Now much depended on just who donned packs and walked out of the refuge in the next hour. Putting the glasses down, he took a piece of chocolate from his pocket, broke off several squares and ate them, wiping his hand on his smock and then going back to the watch.

Quayle opened his eyes for the hundredth time and peeled back the layers of clothing to look at his watch. It was still dark, but he knew that to his right the sun was rising. Because the north face dropped into a glacial basin, there would be no light below for some time yet. Once they began the climb, they would be at least five hours before getting to him. He rolled to look over the edge for the last time in the relative safety of darkness, and thought briefly about what he would need to do today. All his instincts and training in the mountains, all the background and legend, the ethos and mystique, came back to one thing. Life. On a mountain, as anywhere, life was sacred. But on a mountain it seemed more precious than ever. Men risked and sometimes gave their lives for others on mountains. He had selected this place because, up here, they would be most exposed and distanced from their retinue by altitude and technique. And here, where life was more sacred than ever, he would confront them.

He flicked his lighter and held it up to the cigarette, drawing back deeply. It was light now. They would be at the base of the big wall now, and he had to resist the urge to look over and count. It made no real difference. He would just need to isolate one of the three – Girard, the industrialist or the politician – and he would have what he needed. If the others came to his aid then he would have to deal with that situation as it arose.

Kirov's men had settled in just before the dawn. One sat dug in to one side of the Glacier de Pierre Joseph, a small steep flow that was little more than a vast ice fall, ending at the wide flat bottom of the main Leschaux. The new snow was deep at the base of the glacier and, along the base of the spur, the ground was steeply sloping, ideal for what they intended.

He watched the refuge with binoculars from behind a hummock of ice and snow he had built up himself. Beneath him were two cables, one set at four feet and one at seven – where he could rest well below the surface and possible sight. He had set two other screws into the wall and rigged his thigh harness so that he could hang there indefinitely.

With water, chocolate and high energy cubes of sugar and honey, he would need no resupply. His job was to alert the remaining members the moment any of the support group left the refuge. They were spread in a line along two huge crevasses, three hundred meters further out, positioned either side of two snow bridges that were the obvious choice for a crossing.

Kirov sat down in his harness and eased the straps around his thighs. They had been in position for two hours now and they were as ready as they would ever be. He looked up at the scudding clouds. *Come on,* he thought. *Let's get it over with.*

Quayle was thinking the same thing. Perfectly camouflaged against the grey brown rock, he leant over the edge of his ledge and focused the glasses down the ice wall. Beneath him, four figures moved steadily upward, deep in the shadows of the Walker spur. First, the leader moved, then settled down to await his partner, the other two following the route on the same holds. At one stage, Quayle thought he saw the leader of the second pair point and shout – but the gesture was lost in the wind.

It was after noon when Quayle first heard the lead climber's axe heads biting and his crampons scrape. He had cleared up his bivouac, re-packed his gear and set up two other secure points further along the ridge line. He was ready. Now that he had three of the prime movers in the conspiracy separated, it was time to go to work. He sneaked a look over the edge. His position was, he knew, the only half decent flat section in the entire area. They would head for here, planning their ascent to finish here, drink some tea and rest before moving east along the ridge for the long abbess down to the Hirondelle. Even so, this late they would want to keep the rest as brief as possible.

He checked his lines one last time and then, using a small mirror, checked the position of the lead climber. A hard face, tired, dark hair, late thirties – this had to be Girard. He was scarcely ten metres below him. He heard him pause, take a breath, swing his boot against the ice, then move upward again. He moved the mirror slightly to look across the face and downward to the place where he had placed the screw last night. There was rope trailing back to that point. They had used it. Five metres. He would be looking upward any second, looking for the final stretch of ice, where the rock came through. He would need hand holds – possibly a wedge or something. He would be aware that it wasn't over yet, but the elation would be there already.

Quayle counted to twenty and, as gloved fingers scrabbled over the lip, he rolled to the edge and peered over smiling, his face just twenty inches from Girard's.

"Bonjour, dickhead! Time we had a little chat."

Girard's eyes widened in fright and surprise as Quayle grabbed the hand, pulling it back.

"No, you're not going anywhere..." Quayle seethed.

Looking down, found a hold for his other hand, and someone below shouted a question at him. "Let me up, Quayle!"

"No..."

Another question came flurrying up from below, this one more urgent.

"You're not going to do anything to me," Girard said, his boot scrabbling for another hold, his arms aching now. "So let me up and we can talk about this."

"I will do what I like," Quayle answered.

"Take a look down, you interfering bastard! That's your friend! A bit of insurance. Now let me up!"

Friend? What friend?

Quayle quickly looked over the edge, as Girard shouted, "It's Quayle!" down to his companions.

Oh Jesus, thought Quayle. There, leading the second pair, looking upward in growing confusion was Pierre Lacoste. *The job! He said he'd taken on a job!* Quayle flashed a look across at the man roped to Lacoste. He was tugging at something in his jacket. A gun was being drawn.

Quayle didn't hesitate. He swung his ice axe down hard and Girard screamed in agony as the serrated blade drove through his hand, pinning him to the mountain face like a butterfly to a display board.

"Hang around a while, you cunt! I'll be back!" Quayle snarled, then dropped off the face like an avenging angel, all mountain honour aside.

They had started it.

But he would finish it.

His abseil jump took him thirty feet, straight onto the man with the gun as it went off. His crampons pierced and skewered the grey haired man's left hand but, as he screamed, hanging in his figure eight, he turned the gun on Quayle.

Quayle was ready for it. The climber never even saw the sharpened blade of Quayle's ice axe swinging downward. The first blow took him in the neck and the second cut his rope like a cotton thread. Screaming with his final breaths, he cartwheeled down through the air, his body striking the face every few seconds, the thuds sickening to the ear.

Quayle looked across quickly. One shot had been snapped of.

"Pierre!" he called across the face, his voice echoing back. "Are you OK? Pierre?" The old guide was hanging on his line, moaning in pain, blood dripping from his sleeve. "Hold on!" Quayle cried. "I'll come for you!"

He looked back upward to the last of the three. *Your turn, bastard.*

The man looked down at him. His face was a mask of terror.

"No, please!" he cried. "It wasn't my idea! I'll tell you whatever you want to know..."

Quayle went up the rope, hand over hand like a sailor, until he swung next to the man, his eyes on fire.

"You have a gun? If I have to find it, you go too..."

"NO, NO, NO, GUN!" the man shouted quickly. He had been sick down his jacket. Suddenly, the enterprise had lost its glamour.

"Stay here," Quayle said. "Don't move!" Moving across the face, he took the rope that linked the man to Girard and tightened it, then moved back down to Lacoste who hung unconscious in his harness.

On the glacier things happened fast. The two men charged with watching events on the mountain raised the alarm simultaneously and, within seconds, men were running for skis and pulling guns from covers. Sergi watched for five seconds and then picked up his radio.

"Table, this is chair."

"Go chair," Kirov crackled back instantly.

"The movers are coming."

"Thank you."

Sergi dropped back down onto the second wire and scooped up his assault rifle. Then, in one hair raising jump five feet across the width of the crevasse, he crossed to his second set of wires to await the beginning of the action.

They passed him ten minutes later, some skiing well, others badly. In camouflage whites, he was next to invisible and, as the last man passed, he climbed up to the higher cable and calmly set up his rifle on the small pile of snow he had prepared earlier.

He would not fire unless someone broke from the main group, but would remain hidden and safe below the surface – because where he was, he was in the direct line of fire of his own team.

Kirov initiated the contact, a classic crevasse ambush. They rose from the ground like white ghosts and, with short measured bursts from silenced weapons, it was all over in under twenty seconds. Just bodies on the ice. There had been only four rounds expended by the annihilated force and, after forty seconds of wind blown silence, two of Kirov's team came up from the ice and moved amongst the bodies, checking they were all dead. Thirty seconds later, the corpses were bundled into the crevasse, and Kirov picked up his radio and spoke quickly into the mouthpiece.

They moved off fast, back towards the refuge. Three minutes later, the last man in the team – who had been sitting on the side of the Glacier Pierre Joseph – picked up his rifle and, aiming at a spot he had isolated the day before, he fired a rifle grenade.

There was a flat crack at the head of the snow line and a blasting roar

330

of wind shook the valley as two million tons of snow and ice began to slide, gathering momentum down the slope. Fifty seconds later, as the ice dust and snow settled, there was no evidence of any deaths on the glacier below. The entire scene was buried under thirty feet of snow.

The bodies would be covered for the next three hundred years.

Quayle was moving slowly upward, Lacoste over his shoulder, when he heard the solid roar and felt the wind tug at his jacket. Barely acknowledging the event, he kept moving up and past the man, still hanging frightened below Girard. Eventually, he pushed the old guide over the lip, his arms and legs aching with the effort. Then, pulling himself over with an axe in one hand and the rope in the other, he settled down to have a look at the guide's injuries. Girard had stopped trying to free his hand by now, his face just a mask of pain and shock, his eyes on the axe blade that protruded from his hand.

Ten minutes later, Quayle had dressed the single entry wound under Pierre's left armpit. There was no exit wound, and that meant that the bullet fired from a nine millimetre was still inside him. He would have to be moved soon or he would die.

Quayle settled on his knees and pulled up the rope that the last man hung on. As he reached eye level, the Englishman spoke. "Answer my questions or you both go the way your friend did."

Even Girard nodded through his pain a few times, confirming the answers of the other. When he was finished, Quayle stood back.

"You two are responsible for the deaths of many people."

"You won't do anything to us. Not defenceless as we are..." The second man was gaining courage, the tearful babbling over. But Girard's other hand was now moving now slowly towards his jacket. "You must take us in."

"So you can pull strings and get off?"

"You represent the law here. You must!"

Girard's hand still moving imperceptibly.

"I don't represent the law," Quayle said. "Just the ghosts of dead men."

"You won't let us die here. You can't!"

Quayle leant forward. "You called me a bastard. You were right." And as Girard's hand came up with the gun, Quayle jerked the axe out of his other hand "I am!"

Girard's numb bloodless fingers slipped on the ice and, as he fell, his weight on the rope pulled the other man screaming backward into nothing.

After they were gone, Quayle assembled the parapente in minutes and, gently taking Lacoste over his shoulder again, he ran ten feet down a sloping rock and, with his heart in his mouth and the feeling of the parachute filling with air behind him, he jumped from the ledge.

With warm air rising from the valley floor, he was a full twenty minutes in the air before landing one hundred yards from the refuge.

One of the Soviets took the old guide and redressed the wounds. An hour later, with a pair of randonee skis and a shovel as a stretcher, they moved onto the ice. It took all day, but they reached Chamonix by eight that evening.

The following night, Quayle broke into a Paris apartment, slid open the ageing locks on an old wall safe and took out the contents: a series of papers, and a set of diskettes.

*

The Fairies at the Milburn back door were young and bored and would not have remembered Titus Quayle from his days at Century anyway. They just looked at the pass he held up and, as he was admitted to the inner secure chamber, the others in back room – watching through the cameras – barely looked at him before the steel inner door clicked open. *Still slack,* he thought.

Quayle was tired, unshaven and wanted a shower. His iron grey hair seemed greyer somehow, powdered with the dust of the mountains. He still wore the guide jacket, stained brown with dried blood, and he looked like he belonged on a building site. But men like that did come in the back door of Milburn every now and then. It would be the talk of the canteen later.

Upstairs, the pass was waiting for him. It had a bar-code, a magnetic stripe, a hologram, a familiar logo and looked very like a bank card, just like it was intended to. Running his fingers around its edge, he took the last flight of stairs. The card wouldn't get him past the man at the top. Appointment only up here. He looked at his watch. He was on time.

"Callows," Quayle said to the Fairy.

"He's busy. Phone first."

"He will see me."

"Fuck off sunshine," he said, indolently standing up.

Quayle reached out, took the man's left nostril in his hand and squeezed, his other rising and taking a pressure point on his neck. The man groaned and fell to his knees, the pain making his eyes water.

"I'm tired. Too tired, to deal with this in a mature fashion. So take a seat over there, or you'll be going down the stairs on a fucking stretcher. Understand?"

Pushing the man backward into the chair, he opened the door.

In Sir Martin Callows' office, the faces turned to look at him: John Burmeister standing by the window, impeccable as ever in a three piece suit, Callows himself huge and leonine at his desk, Hugh Cockburn and Tansey-Williams in the chairs alongside.

"Hail, hail, the gang's all here," Quayle said, his voice barely above a whisper.

"You've got a bloody cheek walking in here," Burmeister snapped. "Who gave you a pass?"

"A blind man," Quayle answered. "We spent a few hours last night on his wife's personal computer."

He drew from his pocket the diskettes and tossed them onto the desk. As Tansey-Williams reached out, Callows' hand closed over them.

"Broken Square," Quayle said. "It's all there... the file Teddy Morton created and the stuff I took in Paris."

"Ah," Burmeister said, a trace of confidence coming into his voice. "This all of it?"

"Adrian Black has a copy, as does Alexi Kirov."

"What are you saying?" Burmeister snapped

"They earnt it"

"Why Black?"

"He's back with Five now. Didn't you know?"

"Know what?" Burmeister snapped. The others were silent, Callows watching from big brooding eyes.

"He's onto you. Teddy Morton was as well." Quayle's voice was rasping with menace. "Long before he went to Aussie. He knew. He warned me through Gabriella Kreski. Only she didn't know it..."

"Why are you doing this?"

"You killed him," Quayle said, his voice so low they had to strain to hear him. "Edward Morton was my friend. You had him burned to death. And the others. Jerry Pope seriously injured. Adrian Black. Henry Arnold. They were all your own people. It's over..."

"You're mad!"

"Take a look outside. That's the Metropolitan Police, Special Branch, Uncle Tom Cobley and all out there."

"You've been under a lot of strain. I am sure we..."

"Ah, yes! *We!* The plural." Quayle turned to Hugh Cockburn. "You're slipping, Hugh. Did you really think you could get away with it?" Cockburn sat, absolutely poker-faced. "That business in Hong Kong. Only you could have set up Fung Wa's killing so fast. Very amateur. Had Milburn written all over it. And, when you'd fucked that up, you ran home to daddy's apron strings and daddy himself had to get involved."

"It's not too late to join us, Ti," Cockburn finally said. "You don't know what you're destroying here."

"Yes I do. This went beyond just fear of reform the day you killed my friend. That day you became the beast – and I have just driven a stake into your fucking heart."

"Now see here!" Burmeister snapped, stepping forward.

"You don't learn, do you?" Quayle's fist flicked forward, the punch taking Burmeister full in the face, shattering his nose. He fell, spitting blood and teeth onto the carpet by the window.

A gun had appeared in Tansey-Williams' hand.

"And big daddy himself," Quayle said. "Henry Arnold became concerned you had him killed. Then, when Oberon called, you had to get personally involved yourself. The saviour. The gun isn't your style, Sir Gordon. Unless you want to point it at your head and do the honourable thing, put it away – or I'll take it from you, and that will be very painful."

Tansey-Williams stood up, straightening his coat.

"Think about it Quayle. What reform will really mean! Thirty bickering mini-states, most of them with nuclear weapons, pointing them at each other, threatening each other, threatening us! Selling them to Iran and Iraq, North Korea! Age old hatreds surfacing. Islamic fundamentalists. The threat is real. On top of all that: a united Germany, ready to..."

"So you and the Generals decided that it was your job to prevent it?"

"Tasks fall on the shoulders of men," Tansey-Williams said, raising his head and squaring his chin like a preacher.

"Spare me that shit," Quayle said. "You're responsible for the deaths of many. No less than the Nazis were."

"And if your proof fails?"

"Just hope it doesn't. Because then I'll take care of it myself, like the CIA have just done with Leo Gershin. He just had an accident. Believe me – you are better off in prison."

Callows stood, reached across and took the little silver gun from his Director General as Quayle turned and walked down the stairs.

*

She could feel it. He was tense and looking out of the window as they drove and she had to say something.

"I had to," she said fiercely.

"What? Lie to me?"

"I didn't lie!"

"You knew, dammit! You knew from the time you arrived."

335

"I didn't know. I suspected, that's all. It wasn't anything I could put my finger on." She began to cry silently beside him, turning to her window so that he wouldn't see.

Even so, he must have known – because his next words more gentle.

"Like what?" he asked.

"Remember I said I'd seen Hugh? He was odd. Behaving strangely. Wanted to know how I was getting along. He'd never cared before. Afterwards, I realised he had turned the flat over. There was nothing missing that I could tell, except a few files of daddy's. There was a photograph too. Not an old one. New. It had been taken only days before he went to Australia. But it was missing. Only Hugh could have taken it. I was scared, then. And I knew you were a long way away and out of it."

"What was the photo of?"

"A group of men at a 'club' dinner," she snorted, sarcastically blowing her nose. "It was Daddy, Sir Martin, Sir Gordon, and one or two others. I think it was his farewell dinner."

"How long have you been working for Martin Callows?" The question came fast and caught her off guard.

"What?" Her face was a mask of surprise.

"Answer me!" The car screeched to a halt and he turned to face her. "How long, damn you?"

"Since the flat was searched," she answered in a wiser tone of voice. "He suspected too. He suggested I come to you. That then I'd be safe. But he also said that there was a chance that you might be involved. I had to take that chance…"

"And tell him what you found?"

She nodded. Then, wiping the tears from her eyes, she abruptly opened the door, climbed from the car and walked away into the rain.

*

The round up had begun immediately in a total of seven European countries, with simultaneous arrests in the USA. Charges varying from high treason to breaches of the Official Secrets Act had been laid in Britain, with many senior people agreeing to turn Queens evidence in exchange for guarantees.

The controversy had been raging in the press for two months now, some supporting what the media had called the 'Doomsday Group', and others labelling them common criminals. In the Soviet Union, the whole scenario had been played down by an administration with its own problems – but an oblique reference in Tass had been made to the round ups in the West after some European leaders had talked of the conspiracy and its fast demise as a step along the path of trust and a move towards disarmament.

The fact that massive restructuring had taken place within the Red Army and its GRU had not escaped the notice of the West, and several senior KGB and Politburo men had dropped out of sight. The Chinese-attempted deal with the Hong Kong triads and the Broken Square group had, so far, escaped publicity – and, as Quayle expected, they had remained silent and xenophobic throughout, making no comment to the world.

He walked up from the village just before lunch, a bag of groceries in his arms and some English newspapers stuffed down his shirt front. Nico had ordered new chairs and tables for the extension to the restaurant and had insisted that Quayle view them, what with him being a partner. Quayle had nodded uncaringly and then wandered up to the small supermarket.

There had been visitors.

Martin Callows, now Director General of MI6, had arrived unannounced one day at the house on the hill and had sat, big and brooding, on one of Quayle's chairs. The visit was an effort to make the peace, and his attempt to re-recruit Quayle was turned down without consideration.

Marco had also visited and spent a week at the house, his big yacht moored in the harbour. His head had healed well and the hair was growing over the still livid red scar. That night, they got happily drunk

– but Quayle missed Holly terribly and Marco, understanding the pain, had sought to take his mind off the matter with whatever came to hand, including attempting to juggle plates one night in the taverna. He gave up after two hundred odd lay broken on the floor and a crowd of tourists had gathered to watch on the street as his last attempt put paid to sixteen at once. He paid up manfully as Nico presented his massive bill. That night, too drunk to walk the hill, they slept on the boat.

Marco had been gone for a month now and, for Quayle, the nightmares were back. Often, the lights in the house burned late into the night as he played chess with himself while Plato, the little tom cat, watched from a cushion, or worked on one of the icons that had sat waiting his loving touch in the cardboard box under the kitchen table.

Most of the weight in the bag he hefted was bottled beer and cat food and, as he took the last steps up to the house, he pulled the papers from his shirt front.

He had just dumped the lot on the veranda table when he heard it. The singing.

He walked inside and there she was, drying her hair with his big towel like she always did.

"Hello," she said. "I'm back if you'll have me."

He didn't say anything so she continued, "You need stuff for Plato, and you've run out of flour and beer, and I love you and I miss you and I want to come home..."

His kiss silenced her.

Printed in Germany
by Amazon Distribution
GmbH, Leipzig